THE STYCLAR SAGA

LAILAH

Nikki Kelly

FEIWEL AND FRIENDS
NEW YORK

A Feiwel and Friends Book
An Imprint of Macmillan

LAILAH. Copyright © 2014 by Nikki Kelly. All rights reserved. Printed in
the United States of America by R. R. Donnelley & Sons Company,
Harrisonburg, Virginia. For information, address Feiwel and Friends,
175 Fifth Avenue, New York, N.Y. 10010.

Feiwel and Friends books may be purchased for business or promotional use.
For information on bulk purchases, please contact the Macmillan Corporate
and Premium Sales Department at (800) 221-7945 x5442
or by e-mail at specialmarkets@macmillan.com.

Library of Congress Cataloging-in-Publication Data Available

ISBN: 978-1-250-05151-6 (hardcover)/978-1-250-06424-0 (ebook)

Book design by Anna Booth

Feiwel and Friends logo designed by Filomena Tuosto

First Edition: 2014

10 9 8 7 6 5 4 3 2 1

macteenbooks.com

You either die a hero, or you live long enough
to see yourself become the villain.

—District Attorney Harvey Dent,
The Dark Knight

PROLOGUE

LIGHTNING STREAKED AND FORKED INTO THREE, the thunder pounded in waves of two, and the silence fell at once.

In the stained-glass window, the lightning forks illuminated an image of the Virgin Mary holding Baby Jesus in her arms. In the vestry, the devoted clergyman desperately scrawled his panicked thoughts, pausing only to add more coal to the fire behind him. Another clap of thunder exploded and, startled, he hesitated, scraping his hand through his graying hair.

He couldn't leave, even though his wife and children would be waiting for his return.

He thought he would surely be safe here in the church until daybreak.

He scolded himself for coming here, for bringing his family. He must warn his wife and children, tell them that the Devil's brood walked among them. Though he hardly knew his congregation, he prayed that, should the evil prevail on this darkest of nights, his letter would be found and they would take heed.

As the rain lashed down, he scribbled a final apocalyptic message, signing *Reverend O'Sileabhin*. He folded and tucked the pages into his Bible.

All the sounds of the storm suddenly ceased. Silence engulfed him.

The burning candles flickered and, one by one, died out. The fire seemed to explode before it too blew out, and in an instant he was thrown into darkness.

He knew then that he had run out of time. It had come for him.

The curate felt his way to the door and cautiously passed through to the chancel, tightly clutching the cross around his neck.

On the west wall of the church, the newly installed coffered panel doors flew from their hinges, creating a crashing sound that echoed down the aisle.

Reverend O'Sileabhin stepped into the nave and froze, dumbfounded. Before him, lumps of battered wood lay strewn across the entrance, and in the doorway stood an immense figure swathed in a black cloak.

"You cannot enter the church, Demon! This is a house of God!" the curate shouted, though his words trembled as they met the air.

The figure was thirty feet away, and the clergyman considered turning and running, but he was fixed to the spot, unable to take his eyes off the shadowed silhouette.

Then, as quickly as the storm had ended, streaks of lightning cracked and the curate stumbled backwards. As he looked up at the figure, which was lit up briefly by the forks riding the night sky, it seemed to move, shifting in and out of focus.

Without warning, it was no longer outside of the church.

The creature was towering over, lifting him high above the floor while squeezing his neck, slowly suffocating him.

Reverend O'Sileabhin dared to reach inside the dark orbs of his murderer. He thought himself in a state of petrifaction, as though the creature were turning him to stone, for when his eyes locked with the Devil's, he froze.

The creature tilted its head and hissed through shiny fangs. Then it shrieked—a shrill cry that bounced off the pillars, ear-piercingly deafening. The curate almost begged for the end to come quickly. The creature's outstretched arm bulged; something seemed to be moving under its skin.

The creature snapped the curate's neck in one clean movement and dropped his body to the cold, hard floor with a thud.

Cracking its own neck from left to right, it trampled over the lifeless body, the curate's bones crunching underfoot. The creature strode through the chancel and crept inside the doorway of the vestry, where it waited.

Silence wrapped itself around the pews, and the air hung low. All became still once more. The creature drooled in anticipation. It would not be long now.

A bright white light descended through the stained-glass windows, filtering through the entrance, finally reaching and then surrounding the lifeless body.

The creature squinted and was forced to look away as the brightness filled the vast space, stepping back so the light would not spill over and touch him.

She appeared.

The creature snarled, excited that its plan had come to fruition.

She sang, and the creature shriveled at the sound as she guided the reverend's soul toward her. The Angel paused for a moment, gently closing her eyes, concentrating on the energy. The light hovered in the air and she directed it up into the glow that cascaded all around. She pushed her blond locks from across her forehead before she moved her palm over the crystal gem that beamed, set in the nape of her neck.

With her touch, the glow parted and the entrance to the first dimension opened. It sparkled in waves of silver and gold. She took a deep breath and smiled as the clergyman's energy passed across— disappearing into a blur, transferred into her world, to Styclar-Plena.

The light began to disperse and she prepared to follow, but she hesitated. The gold cross around the neck of his hollow human form caught her gaze. She edged toward it and cupped it softly. She blew on it gently and a twinkling white light swirled all around it, before finally being absorbed into the metal. Now whoever held it would experience an undeniable sense of peace.

She stared down sadly at the curate's expression and moved her fingertips to close his eyelids. She thanked him for his gift and readied herself to return.

As she floated down the long church aisle, the Angel felt once more for her gem so that she too could move across. Before she even had a chance to will it to life, she felt a searing pain as the creature's fangs tore through her chalk-white skin. She screamed in surprise and began to glow, trying to mask herself so that he couldn't see her. But it was too late. This was a Pureblood Vampire and he had already begun to fill her with his poison.

She was paralyzed. Her gifts stalled and dulled; helpless, she dropped to the floor. As he twisted over her body, his fangs bore deeper into her neck, his poison spreading through her with such speed that her veins became swollen. He moved down her, running his clawed hand over her belly, searching.

The Angel's eyes widened in horror as his fangs pierced through her skin once again, this time reaching her child. His venom was agonizing. She could already feel the darkness changing the Angel Descendant that she was carrying. Her porcelain skin was bruised and marked with crimson.

When he had finished, he dragged her across the ground by her hair and glared at her with contempt. Finally, his eyes fixed on the crystal gem. The Pureblood snorted and his uneven lips quivered as he salivated.

The Angel, still paralyzed from the Vampire's poison, could do nothing to hide the crystal from his glare. He extended his free hand. Jagged talons protruded out of his knuckles; he gouged them into the back of her neck. Effortlessly he extracted the crystal, detaching it from its rightful guardian. Satisfied with his work, he contemplated the gem, balancing it between his sharp claws.

The Angel lay with her cheek on the cold ground. From the corner of her eye she saw Azrael.

He appeared suddenly and propelled himself behind the Pureblood Vampire, swinging him into the church pillar, which fractured with the force.

The crystal, now void of any light, dropped from the creature's grasp, landing perfectly on its point.

Leaving the Pureblood dazed, Azrael turned his attention to his Pair, Aingeal. Knowing he only had moments, he scooped her limp body in his arms and parted her cold, blue lips. He blew lightly into her mouth and white light danced through her. Aingeal's eyes blinked frantically as she felt his gifts evaporate the poison that ran through her veins, but there was nothing he could do to remove the venom that now flowed through the Angel Descendant's blood.

As the Pureblood catapulted back to his feet, Azrael spun around; it was then that he saw it. The raised cicatrix between the Pureblood's orbs formed the distinguishing mark of the beast—Zherneboh.

Azrael threw up a sheet of light, keeping the evil pinned to the other side.

Turning to his Pair, their eyes met. She didn't have to explain; they both knew what the Pureblood had done.

You must leave and you must hide. I will consult with the Arch Angels and I will find you, he told her without any words being spoken. They were connected.

Keeping one hand raised in the air balancing the sheet of light, struggling, he helped lift her up. Sadness unfolded across his expression as he placed the crystal in her palm. Squeezing her skin against his, he closed her fingers tightly over the gem.

Aingeal nodded as she shined brightly, and then quickly faded—invisible now, a part of the darkness. She turned on her heel and fled the church; she knew what she must do and that it would mean never being able to return home.

But she desperately hoped Azrael would find a way to return to her.

A FEW MONTHS LATER, a baby with skin as white as porcelain was placed on the doorstep of a couple's home in the South East of England. It was covered in nothing more than cotton wrappings, but buried within the sheets a crystal gleamed and sparkled.

ONE

THE EVENING WAS DEEPLY BITTER. The night was drawing in and the sound of silence was deafening. The most perfect setting for a liaison with a Vampire.

I pushed back the blond wisps of hair crowding my eyes and remade my long ponytail, while eyeing the garbage bag that I had attempted to balance at the top of the pile, out in the backyard of the pub. I would have welcomed a moment's peace, but not out here. The darkness frightened me.

"Francesca!" Haydon's thick Welsh accent reached me, piercing through the surrounding sheet of ice, as if he were a red-hot poker.

I sighed, bolted the back door, and hurried back into the bar. I was dead on my feet. Thank goodness it was closing time. We were short-staffed, as always. Haydon's wife hadn't returned from her shopping trip in Cardiff, so I'd had to play kraken and pretend I had many hands to pull an inordinate amount of pints this evening.

Sometimes I wished I could just be normal and have a pleasant little office job and not have to deal with drunken locals. But then, with no legitimate identification, cash-paid bar work was the best I could hope for. I was grateful for employers like Haydon who sought out a willing workhorse in exchange for a little money.

"Just one more p-p-pint my love, come on, fill her up!" The middle-aged man waved his empty glass at me, and I smiled politely.

I hadn't worked here long, but it was long enough to learn that he was always the last to leave.

"Come on now, Mr. Broderick, it's closing time, you need to get back to your lovely wife." I pried the glass from his tight clutch.

"Ah, pull the other one! We both know she's anything but l-l-lovely. . . . She u-u-used to be a whore, that's why I m-m-arried her! Of course she chose to change once sh-sh-e had the r-r-ing on her finger!" He stumbled over his sentence.

"All right, Glyn, that's enough, on your way!" Haydon shouted over.

Darting my eyes in a concerned expression to Haydon, I nodded my head toward our last customer. He shrugged, so I made my way around the bar and placed my arms out, enticing a hug from Mr. Broderick.

"Ah, that's n-n-ice. Elen doesn't hold me anymore . . . or anything else for that m-m-atter. . . ."

I slipped my hand into his coat pocket and felt the smooth coldness of his car keys. Holding my breath, I retreated, placing them into my jeans' pocket. I could definitely have made a better living as a thief, but sadly that wasn't me. I had to do things the good old-fashioned hard way.

I called Mr. Broderick a taxi and began wiping down the tables, slyly sneaking him a packet of honey-roasted nuts in a bid to help sober him up a little.

Twenty minutes later, I thought the driver would likely be nearing so I signaled to Haydon, who barely noticed my gesture for help, instead flicking through channels on the television on the wall in search of sports highlights.

Sighing, I said, "Come on, you." Locking my arm into Mr. Broderick's, I balanced his weight against my petite frame.

"You're a good girl," he bumbled, patting my head as if I were a well-behaved dog who'd just brought back a stick.

Propping him against the exposed brick wall, I struggled with the locked doors. It was even harder given that I hadn't taken a fresh breath in over three minutes. "Thank you, Mr. Broderick." I exhaled.

As we reached the bottom of the slope, I halted at the curb, still maintaining Mr. Broderick's two-hundred-pound weight. Standing still was clearly too much to ask for, as he stumbled forward, taking me with him into the middle of the road. He dropped to the ground and I tried to ease his fall.

Suddenly, bright lights appeared from nowhere and the screech of tires skidding across the iced road took me by surprise. Defensively, I threw my hand up in the air. For a moment, the world seemed to stop moving. My arm outstretched, my open palm prevented the yellow headlights from blinding me. In between my fingers the glare of the vibrant yellow light flickered into a dull neon. The square shape of the old Volvo station wagon changed into a curved yellow-and-green cab, and nighttime in Creigiau gave way to dusk in New York.

As though I were staring into a crystal ball, I was presented with a memory of the end of one of my lives.

Hand raised, the yellow-and-green Checker cab hurtled into me and I slammed into the windshield, causing it to crack before rolling off its hood and lying still on the road. Onlookers rushed over, and panic ensued. A young man pushed past the crowd of bodies that had gathered, now gawking over my broken body. He was wearing a cardigan sweater, narrow suit trousers, and suede shoes; I realized that this had happened sometime in the 1950s.

He seemed to check me over before taking my hand in his own, and I noted that my knuckles had turned skeleton white as I squeezed it back. He bowed his head, his derby hat casting shadow over his expression, as I took a final breath and my arm fell limp.

Static phased in and out, and I jolted back to reality, back to the smell of burning rubber. The taxi driver skidded to a halt only several inches away from Mr. Broderick and me.

"Are you all right?" the taxi driver shouted as he rushed out of the car.

It took me a minute to acclimatize. Mr. Broderick drunkenly laughed as he hauled himself off the ground with the driver's help.

"Erm. Yes. Fine . . ." I trailed off.

"He's trouble, this one," the taxi driver nervously rambled, bundling Mr. Broderick into the backseat. "You sure you're okay?" he continued as I wobbled back to the curb.

I merely nodded.

Once they were gone, I slumped myself against the wall of the pub and took some time to gather myself before going back in to finish my shift.

I continued on with my work diligently and in silence, trying to forget the vision I had just seen—it wasn't one I cared to remember.

Eventually Haydon's TV show came to a close. "Okay, Francesca, you done with those tables?" he asked, leaning against the bar, swishing the whiskey at the bottom of his tumbler, his attention now focused on me.

"Yes, anything else you need before I go?" I asked, pulling up my V-neck top and eyeing my jacket on the coat stand.

"Nope. Go home." He paused and then, turning to my chest, his eyebrows arching slightly, he asked, "Say, you got anyone waiting for you? You could stay, have a drink with me?"

I forced a polite grin and shook my head, making my way over to my navy jacket. Sadly, I didn't have anyone waiting for me. I was alone; all alone. I wasn't able to stay anywhere long enough to make any friends, and if I did stay for some time, I found it difficult to get close to anyone. The only character I had built a meaningful relationship with, in this lifetime at least, had stripped me of any trust I might have had a few years back. And while he was now gone, the damage he had inflicted on my skin was a permanent reminder, scarring down my back.

With the thought of him inevitably came my recollection of her. The girl in shadow; yet another enigma in my life that I didn't know whether to welcome or fear. A girl who magically appeared in my times of crisis, yet I had no idea who she was.

"Francesca?" Haydon broke my train of thought with an irritated tone.

"Sorry, no, must be going, see you tomorrow."

Zipping up my down jacket—a key piece of winter wear in

Creigiau, I had learned—I hurried to the door. I put my hands inside the lined pockets and made my way down to the country lane, back to the house.

The thick forest that hugged the roadside entwined itself into the black backdrop. The branches of the bare trees twisted and married themselves together, as if they were protecting some lost castle with a city of people sleeping, placed under a spell. In the forest, time seemed to stand still, like me.

A damp smell wafted over me as I paced quickly up the steep roadside. I tended to dwell in these quiet communities; it was easier to find abandoned properties in which to take up residence than in a major town or city. Here, I had stumbled across an old, derelict shell of a building that I liked to think once provided a home for a happy family. I had imagined, on many a cold night, the children playing and laughter filling the rooms. I could picture them running through the surrounding woodland and messing around in the stream that ran alongside it.

Now the house was bare, broken, and boarded; but it was a roof over my head, until I moved on to the next place. I had to keep moving; my appearance was frozen at seventeen. With fake ID, I passed for twenty-one, but I knew I was far older than I looked. I didn't know how or why; I just knew that when I slept, I dreamed of lives gone by. And even when awake, sometimes an old memory would resurface, as it had done just a while ago. I had instincts I couldn't name almost etched into me, but the world was still a confusing, jumbled place. I had no idea who I was, or where I had come from.

Holding my head down to the concrete, I considered that, much like the road, I was far from living; I merely existed. At least the road led somewhere, it had a purpose. I certainly didn't know what mine was.

My dreams told of dark experiences, but also light: one light to be exact. It was a light so bright that it seemed to will me on, pushing me forward. One image, one face, consumed my daily thoughts. He was glorious. His smile tantalized and played with me, but he existed only in my mind. As far back as I could remember, as far back as my visions and dreams went, he was always there. And even in the present, I felt a pull toward him. Crazy as it seemed, I somehow knew he held the key to my Pandora's box.

I had to find him, his name always balancing on the tip of my memory, echoing all around me, whispered by the breeze that rushed through the trees, skimming my pale skin: *Gabriel.*

And as I began to fall into thoughts of him, there was a sharp movement to my left; then I heard the whine. It sounded almost like a fox, but one that was in agony.

I stopped dead still.

I turned my head slowly toward the woods, and I made out a figure in the darkness. The wailing became louder and more pained. I mustered my bravery and tiptoed into the thickness of my makeshift fairy-tale forest until I could see a shape. I moved in closer. The figure threw his head up and his eyes penetrated mine. Glaring at me, his face was completely cold and his skin looked as fragile as porcelain. He looked around my age, perhaps a few years older. His dark hair was ruffled and messy, but did nothing to detract from his perfect features.

I knew then that he wasn't human.

He was hunched over in a heap on the ground. My first instinct was to turn and run away as fast as I could, but he was hurt and in pain. I stopped myself from bolting, but kept my distance. Perhaps he could smell my fear.

"What do you need?" I asked. His eyes were still locked with mine.

"I need to get outta here, they're coming for me," he whimpered in response. His voice was soft, but quivering, and his accent was American—at a best guess, East Coast. He was a long way from home.

I nodded, even though I had no clue what he could be afraid of or how it was that he had come to be in a ball beside my feet.

"I won't hurt you," he said. I couldn't help but sense he was lying.

"I'm staying in a place not far from here. Can you walk if I help you?"

He snarled at me as if I had said the most ridiculous thing he'd ever heard. Searching around, I considered the possibilities. "Stay here," I said, realizing immediately he had no choice.

I raced down to the bottom of the road, looking for any cars parked by the pub.

Finally, my eyes settled on a small truck just off the main road, sitting at the corner. It was Mr. Broderick's. I tapped my jeans' pocket—I still had his keys. Making a beeline for the truck, I approached the driver's door. He hadn't even bothered to lock it. Squeezing the handle, I threw myself into the driver's seat, quickly turning the key in the ignition. It started, making a loud, angry noise as I dipped the clutch and moved away from the curb.

I ground to a halt alongside the woods and jumped out, leaving the door ajar in the rush. Dashing back to where I'd left the shadowed figure, I saw him now slumped against a tree. I could see he had barely any energy, and he seemed uncomfortable as he shifted his weight where he sat.

"Come on," I whispered as I approached.

Hesitating before I placed his arm around my shoulder, I tried to lift him. His eyes rolled toward me, a look of desire bouncing between them. A shiver ran up my spine. I instinctively pushed back.

"W-w-why are you helping me?" he stuttered as I helped him to his feet.

I thought about that for a moment as I struggled toward the vehicle. "Because sometimes we all need help, no matter what we are."

I thought for a second he hesitated, wondering perhaps if I knew that he was a Vampire. Little did he know that this was not my first encounter with one of his kind. I had been tricked by one of them before; I'd paid for it with my scarred skin.

We reached the truck and I eased him into the passenger seat and slammed the door, and as fast as I could I jumped back in. Dipping the stiff clutch into first, I sped off up the country road.

"You got a name?" he asked.

"Francesca. Do *you*?"

He sniggered. "Yeah. Jonah."

"What can I do to help you?" I asked. He didn't answer.

It didn't take long to get back to the house. I could see from his face that he wouldn't have the strength to attack me. This gave me some reassurance that I wasn't about to be drained dry, but I was starting to reconsider my decision. I didn't know how I could offer any help, not really.

The engine grumbled as it came to a stop and I flipped the headlights off. In front of us was the oversized shell of what was once someone's home. In summer it would be an incredible spot, but here, in the blackness of night, it was an eerie place full of dark secrets.

I paused and collected myself. I reconsidered my actions for a moment. Perhaps this was a ruse—there's no way someone so strong could be so powerless, could they? But, if he was genuinely in need of help, I had to try.

"Right. Let's get you inside," I said.

"We're not nearly far enough away!"

"From what?" I asked, fidgeting in the driver's seat. Silence, again. Not a talker apparently. "How far would be far enough?"

"Just drive!" The look on his face suggested this was not a debate.

Reluctantly I turned the key in the ignition once more, and as it struggled to start, my eye was drawn to the red light on the dashboard. Huffing, I rotated the key a final time.

"What are you doing?" he shouted. "I said drive!"

"No can do, it's nearly out of gas," I answered. I was beginning to feel a little less sorry for him. Who did he think he was anyway?

With some effort, I managed to get him up to the doorframe and through into the living room, where I placed him down onto my sleeping bag. His whole body was shaking and his forehead was covered in beads of sweat. He looked as though he was burning from the inside out. He wrapped the insulation loosely around himself.

"I'll just be a minute," I promised.

Gathering some wood from the kitchen, I produced a pack of matches and a fire starter from my bag. The same as every other night, I set a fire in the ancient fireplace, but for the first time since I had taken up residence in this house, I had someone to share the warmth with. Strange how suddenly, even in the most bizarre of situations, a house can feel like a home.

As the room lit up I was finally able to fully see Jonah, his figure illuminated against the flicker of flame. His dark jeans and chocolate brown half-zip sweater were torn and disheveled. His collarbone protruded prominently in the V-gap of his shirt, and I could see he was strong. His dark hair was tousled and scruffy but still looked attractively thick and shiny. My gaze traveled down to his wrists, which were bloodied. The damage continued across his hands and knuckles and I grimaced, as his fingers appeared burnt and blackened.

"What happened to you?" I asked as I tended to the small blaze.

He looked at me blankly and replied without answering my question. "You know what I am?"

"Yes. I've known your kind. You're not too difficult to spot now."

His eyes ran over my body, from the tip of my toes all the way up to my face, where his pupils rested on my own. He took some time to gather his thoughts, fixating on me as he did. I instantly felt self-conscious, though I had no idea why. I pulled my jacket down and straightened myself up.

"If you've known my kind, you really shouldn't be around to tell the tale. . . ."

"The acquaintanceship didn't end well, but here I am. I'd rather not talk about it." I shifted uncomfortably. He didn't argue.

"You got a cell?" he asked.

"Yes, it hasn't got many minutes left but enough to make a quick call I think," I answered, shuffling around in my pockets for the cheap Nokia I carried with me. "Why, who are you going to call?"

"I'm not traveling alone." He gestured for the phone. I handed it to him.

Just moving his arm seemed a real effort; he was in an unusually vulnerable position. I could tell he wasn't used to it. I couldn't help but admire him; even in this state, he was truly remarkable to look at. His cheeks were so perfectly smooth; I wished I could touch him. I shuddered, agitated by my thoughts. Of course his skin was flawless and of course his eyes were glazed with a watery sparkle. He was resplendent. But when it came down to it, he was evil. I knew evil came in the most wonderful forms. It was easier to corrupt someone that way.

Everything about him looked as though he had been carefully carved by an expert craftsman and then breathed into life. I was sure this was how they survived. Jonah's extreme beauty had given him away instantly. Thanks to the Vampire I had once ignorantly befriended, I now knew what hid beneath features like that. I was angry for allowing myself to be sucked in by his looks; they were merely a mask, disguising what he truly was—a killer.

Jonah dialed a number and spoke so rapidly I could barely catch the conversation. He hung up just as swiftly. "My friends are coming, they'll be here soon," he said.

"These friends of yours, are they like you?"

"Yeah . . . for the most part." He paused. "Thank you for your help," he said begrudgingly.

I snapped back a look that read a sarcastic "you're welcome." I was surprised he had even attempted any form of thanks. Something about the way he looked at me was chilling; I didn't dare ask any more questions.

I got up and started puttering about nervously. I could hear how difficult it was for him to breathe. Despite his arrogance, I found myself softening toward him once more. But then I'd soften even for a raging killer pit bull if it were in pain.

Reaching for my bottled water, I offered it to him. He simply snorted. I'd forgotten for a moment. Putting it down, I reached over to the sleeping bag; it had fallen away from around Jonah's body. Instinctively, I yanked it nearer to his shoulders.

Without warning, he grabbed my wrist, flinching as his injuries met my skin, and taking me by surprise. I flashed my eyes to meet his. He held me so tightly I couldn't break free. The Vampire tilted his head and pulled me in. My heart began to thud, and I froze, filling with fear.

Crap, maybe this hadn't been a smart idea after all.

Running his lips close to my neck, his breath tickling my skin, I found my insides doing strange somersaults, and suddenly I wasn't afraid anymore. His bottom lip skimmed my earlobe, sending little shock waves through me. He lingered and then whispered, "I meant . . . thank you." His words were sincere and soft—I felt my heart flutter.

He released my wrist and I hovered over him, searching his eyes. They bore into mine. I indulged myself, feeling both confused and elated, but after a few minutes, I broke the connection and slid away. I didn't want or need the distraction of Jonah, a Vampire no less, derailing my thoughts away from Gabriel. Even if sometimes it felt as though I was hopelessly searching for a ghost.

I made my way into the bare kitchen to retrieve some more logs for the fire. I was glad I'd gathered them this morning, before I went in for my shift at the pub.

Sitting on the floor, I absorbed the situation and took a few minutes to myself. I would help him however I could because if I knew anything about myself, it was that I was a good person. And perhaps in exchange he might share some insights into his world; he might have some clues about what I was, and where I belonged. It was an extremely dangerous game, but what choice did I have? I returned to the living room and added the wood to the fire. We sat for what felt like hours in silence. Eventually he broke it.

"Is this where you live?" He raised his eyebrows as he strained to take in the hollow shell around him.

"For now."

"You're not from here," he guessed. "This place isn't your home."

"Home is wherever I hang my hat. I don't exactly belong. Time just goes by, the people change, scenery changes. I don't change." I teased a little, testing his reaction.

He tilted his head to the right at my response; he was trying to figure me out. "Your eyes . . . they're older than your smile, but you're not like me," he mused aloud. "But you're not, well, human either."

"What would make you think I'm not human?" I rebutted, a little too high-pitched, feeling slightly offended. I had never considered myself unhuman.

"You have no scent. I didn't know you were coming until you were in front of me."

I considered that for a moment. As far as I was concerned, I was human, even if I apparently couldn't die—well, not in the conventional manner. "So what? Given your condition, perhaps your senses are somewhat impaired," I reasoned. I didn't want to give too much away, not yet.

"What are you exactly?" he said, dismissing my vague reply.

I pondered for a moment. "I suppose that's the million-dollar question," I said. "Oh, and by the way, I don't remember smiling at you."

That made him laugh a little and I flushed, unable to stop a grin spreading over my face.

"See? You do like me after all." He choked, shuddering, and shifted uncomfortably, seemingly trying to subdue the overwhelming agony that flowed through him.

I sat for a while, calmly weighing my next move. "You can call me Cessie, by the way."

He raised his eyebrows a little, encouraging an explanation.

"My friends called me Cessie."

"Past tense?" he asked.

"I haven't seen them for a while, but that's what they called me. I guess you can, too."

With the faintest curve of his lip he said, "Honored, I'm sure."

Hoping the olive branch had softened him to me, I tried again. "You didn't answer my question before—how can I help you? You're in a lot of pain. I can see."

He looked at me emptily. Finally, through gritted teeth, he said, "My friends will take care of that."

"Who are these friends of yours? What happened to you?"

He contemplated his reply and then offered it, albeit reluctantly. "My friends are the ones I travel with now. We came here, hoping to rescue another, well, another Vampire like me." He paused. "It didn't exactly go to plan, and the Pureblood's clan took me captive." He snarled angrily, revealing his fangs.

The sight of them caught me off guard and I took a second to collect myself. "The Pureblood's clan? I don't understand."

"Purebloods were the first Vampires to inhabit the Earth. I was human—once. But I was bitten, changed, turned—whatever term you'd prefer to coin. That makes me a Second Generation Vampire. Vampires serve the Pureblood who changed them, as part of their clan, or army, if you'd rather." He struggled on, shaking.

"If you serve one of these Purebloods, then how is it you have your freedom?"

"Vampires are evil, infected with venom; their souls become submerged in darkness from the change. Free will is not something they seek. But, sometimes, just sometimes, we might see light. Long enough to remember who we were before. My companions are Vampires like me, freed from our Pureblood Master, with some help. . . . We don't want to be slaves to them anymore."

"But you are still a Vampire," I stated.

"Yes, and I still drink blood to survive. We all do. But we're selective over our meals." Pausing before he continued, he said, "I don't want to have to kill, you know. I wasn't exactly given a choice."

I raised my eyebrows at his statement. I felt compassion for him, but I didn't believe anyone should play God when it came to who deserved to die. "What did they do when they . . . captured you?" I pushed, wanting to know more.

"I was not turned by the Pureblood of that clan. It was not the right of the Gualtiero—Eligio—to end me." He saw my confusion and answered it. "Gualtiero means the Leader, the Master. Eligio is the Pureblood's name." He inhaled sharply. "They locked me away with no . . ." He stopped, searching carefully for his next word. "Food."

He looked at me blankly as I flinched.

"Withholding my ability to feed is torture. I don't know how long I've been kept in the darkness. They had me bound in silver." He nodded to his wrists. "I managed to escape, but I've got nothing left inside me to be able to fight them if my companions don't find me first."

"Would the Pureblood have eventually ended you?" I asked.

"No. My Gualtiero was coming to end me himself," he replied.

"Is that what Eligio told you?"

"No. My Gualtiero—Emery—and I are still connected, though not so much now that I've been parted from him and the clan for some time. But I can still sense him to a degree."

I was trying to comprehend what he was telling me. It was an existence I knew nothing about.

"Eligio will know I have gone by now. It won't take him and his clan long to track me down."

A sense of alarm rang through me—would they come here? Could they track him to this house? Just as I was contemplating the notion of a Vampire ambush, the ground beneath me started to vibrate and shake. Panic began to run through me and I sprinted to the window, checking that the boards were in place, as if that would somehow help.

I turned back to Jonah, terrified.

"That's them, they're coming . . ." His eyes flashed and he snarled a deep, low growl that made the hairs on my arm stand up.

"What do we do? Where are your friends?" I said hurriedly, checking that the wooden boards covering the windows were still sturdy.

23

"They'll come, but they may be too late. You need to leave, take the truck and drive as far away as you can get," he ordered. "Then run and don't come back!"

Now he was trying to save me.

"I can't leave you here, they'll kill you. I won't let you die like that!" There was something about Jonah I was oddly drawn to. Somehow he had spared me and that was an almost impossible thing for a creature such as himself. I couldn't let him be destroyed by them. I couldn't!

He almost sniggered when he said, "I am already dead."

"You didn't answer my question: How will your friends heal you?" I demanded.

He looked at me, puzzled. "They will bring me someone to drink from." His reply was flat.

I thought about it for a few seconds. If he drank from me, just enough to make him regain his strength, he could fight them off and we could escape. Both of us in one piece, I hoped. If I didn't, his existence would be painfully ended. And they would likely kill me, too. "Drink from me."

This time I was the one giving the orders.

I frantically searched through my bag and drew out a Swiss Army knife. I rolled up the sleeve of my jacket hastily, my hand quivering as I brought it to my wrist.

"No! I won't be able to . . ." He trailed off.

"It doesn't matter!" Even if he couldn't stop, I knew he wouldn't end my existence. It was a hunch. I tried to remain calm.

Suffering death didn't have the same meaning for me as it did for a mortal; if anything I think I dreaded it more. Unlike them, it wasn't the fear of the unknown once death had taken hold, because I knew I would wake up again.

It was the waking up part that petrified me.

I could only hope that Jonah would overcome his desire in time to pull me back from death's white-knuckled grip.

Clenching my legs around him, I sat with my thighs touching either side of his waist. Taking the knife, I sliced a deep cut a few inches below my wrist, instantly drawing blood. For the briefest moment, Jonah's orbs flashed incarnadine, startling me; the blade slipped from my grasp, clanking as it hit the floor.

"No!" He moaned as loud shrieks came from the distance.

"Drink!"

Jonah shook his head violently. His bone-chilling glare told me that if he had the strength, I probably would have been thrown across the room by now.

I held my wrist slightly above his lips and, squeezing the skin together, encouraged a steady flow of blood to seep, trickling down to meet him.

I watched him struggle to resist. Luckily it didn't take long for his hunger to take over. He tasted me. Within a second, his mouth was latched around the gash and I felt the sudden sharpness of his fangs cracking into position, stabbing me.

Slowly at first, as if he were sampling a glass of wine, he swirled his tongue, nuzzling at my flesh. It was a strange sensation, and I began to realize quickly that I was the striking surface to his match. I held his stare with my own. I watched as the hazel color of his eyes changed and was replaced by red flames that burned fiercely.

It was exhilarating.

He moved his eyelids downward and began guzzling harder and quicker. It was in the loss of his sparks that it occurred to me that I was now becoming a meal to a starving Vampire.

Only a few minutes had passed and I started to feel faint. Jonah showed no sign that he was ready or able to let go. "Jonah, stop," I whimpered, feeling hazy.

I was losing all strength in my body, and my legs gave way.

TWO

THE WHOLE HOUSE SHOOK, and at the same moment what felt like an electric shock seemed to pass between the two of us. A startled look smacked across Jonah's face as he was brought back from wherever he had gone, and he withdrew and fell away from me. He put his hand behind my back to steady me and glanced at my pale skin glowing in the darkness.

I opened my eyes and was amazed to see Jonah no longer looking like a withering flower, but instead positively revived. His eyes lit up so red that it was as though Hell itself was burning inside them.

Using his free hand to move some wayward strands of hair from my eyes, I noticed his wrist was completely healed and I was left totally confused. He couldn't have looked any more superb, yet nothing could have filled me with more fear than in that moment as I watched his eyes blaze.

"Come on!" he yelled through the thunderous noises surrounding us. "This place have a back door?" His voice was rushed.

He scanned the room, alert and ready. I nodded toward the

hallway that led to the kitchen, which had a sort of back door, but I was sure by now that we were surrounded. I reached for the Swiss Army knife and flipped the blade inside before stuffing it into my jeans' pocket. I tried to stand and eventually found my feet; Jonah grabbed my hand and I felt a surge of energy run through it. He moved swiftly and we darted through and out of the house. When he saw I couldn't keep up, he tossed me over his shoulder.

Jonah raced toward the woods. I turned my head and, sure enough, I caught in my peripheral vision several figures jumping and dashing. What happened next was a blur: something landed on top of me, knocking Jonah off balance, and we plummeted with a tremendous thud. I fell away from him, grazing my arms on the grass below me.

A hand was around my throat, my head was forced backwards and I began to gag. I reached into my jeans' pocket and pulled out the Swiss Army knife that I had used to help Jonah, and as forcefully as I could with my left hand, I thrust it into my attacker's side. It simply bounced off his flesh. He growled viciously, kicking me back down to the ground, hard.

My eyes shot up to see Jonah leaping through the air like a wild animal, smashing into the offending Vampire. I couldn't block out the sounds of my attacker's choking spit, but I looked away before Jonah ended him.

I caught my breath. I saw other shadowy figures in the distance, hurtling toward us. I didn't know what to do, which way to turn, but I couldn't leave Jonah here. And I didn't stand much chance without him.

Seeing Jonah battle against the evil nature that had been bestowed upon him through no choice of his own, unwilling to accept it, I first came to appreciate that there was no such thing as good and evil; it could never be that simple. Somewhere between black and white, there were shades of gray. I wondered if, given the complexity of my own existence, perhaps I belonged somewhere among the spectrum of the in between, right next to the likes of Jonah?

I staggered back up and spun around, just in time to see Jonah a few feet away from me, shattering several fierce-looking Vampires one by one. He was possessed. With one swift movement he literally tore a limb from one, at the same time as slamming another to the ground with his free hand. It was terrifying. He was so powerful, quite a contrast from the forlorn being I had rescued a few hours ago. He no longer needed my help, not that I had anything to offer. I debated running and hiding; I was just a hindrance, distracting him from his fight. But it was like the morbid curiosity of watching an accident unfold; it was impossible to turn away.

A pair of ferocious crimson eyes caught my attention. Crouched on the ground, a couple of feet behind, was a Vampire ready to pounce on his prey: me. I drew a deep breath, closed my eyes tightly, and waited for the inevitable; there was nothing else I could do. There was no point trying to run and I wouldn't give him the satisfaction of the chase.

Nothing happened.

I forced my eyes open a moment later when I felt his breath on the tip of my nose. He stood over me, leaving barely any space between us. Staring intensely into my eyes, his own seemed to smolder for a moment into a dull brown. He was a perfect statue. Long, dirty-blond hair was tied behind his neck and he wore a white frilled shirt. Judging by his attire, it was easy to surmise that he was from another time.

To my surprise, he slowly moved his hand to my face and carefully, with the back of his fingers, he stroked me. A cold, thick gold ring grazed my skin. At his touch, for a second, I was transported into the past.

These hands had brushed my cheeks before.

I didn't have a chance to focus in on the memory; the thread was snapped as he jolted away from me. The sound of heavy footsteps careering across the field echoed through the air, cutting through this surreal moment. There were only minutes now before Jonah's friends arrived and Eligio's clan would be outnumbered, or so I hoped. As the ground shook, I stumbled a little.

When I snapped back to the Vampire, he was gone. I scanned the area but couldn't see him anywhere through the darkness of the night. I wondered if he was one of Jonah's friends who had arrived first and had let me live. But that didn't explain how I seemed to know him. I hadn't been given enough time to try and place him, and with every second that passed the thought of who he was only became cloudier in my mind.

I shifted my attention back to Jonah, who was still fighting, ending each Vampire as quickly as the last, until six remaining soldiers stood in awe of his strength. As Jonah hissed and bared his fangs to his audience, a sudden taste of smoke and ash engulfed my senses, and then I saw it. Though I was not sure what it was.

An enormous figure cloaked in black, somehow manipulating the darkness in an attempt to camouflage itself, was plunging through the sky toward Jonah's back. My gut instinct told me that whatever it was, it was powerful and moments away from ending him.

My eyes began to burn and I clawed my skin as a fury seemed to hit me from nowhere. My mind cleared of thought and my legs stretched into a sprint toward Jonah, when *she* appeared ahead of me. Shrouded in shadow, she sprang off the ground as the silhouette of the terrifyingly large figure prepared to wrap itself around Jonah's shoulders from behind him. She crashed into it first and it soared back through the air, while she landed perfectly balanced, hunkered low on the ground.

The cloaked figure had disappeared. What it was, and where it went I was unsure.

I strained to focus as I approached her; she seemed to just blend into the night. As I extended my arm to reach for hers, for the briefest second, I was distracted. A strange light seemed to flicker, illuminating the woods some distance away.

I flashed my gaze back to the girl in shadow, but she was already gone.

Though Jonah did not turn to face me—instead, keeping his focus on the Vampires that crouched all around—he knew I was behind him. A particularly young-looking boy, no more than fourteen in human years, regarded me with an astonished expression. Frothing at the mouth, he growled at Jonah and gestured for the others to retreat. He was in charge of the losing side tonight and though reluctant to concede it, he knew this fight was over. Turning his back, he vaulted into the trees hanging over the house and away into the night.

As the branch sprang back, I watched as the bare twigs drifted and fell to the ground in slow motion. Time seemed to elude me, and as the moment became extended, I heard the echo of a gunshot from some distance away. The air seemed to swell and I smelled the silver melting as it sped toward Jonah.

I couldn't stop time, but time itself seemed to become lost. It was slowing, giving me just enough precious seconds to swoop half a foot to the right, and I swung my back to the bullet and protected Jonah's chest. A sharp, scolding shot of red-hot lead fused with silver components perforated my skin. It ate its way through my flesh, finally lodging itself in my shoulder. I peeked up at Jonah's frozen face and as his eyelashes finally started to move, time seemed to catch back up with me.

My legs gave way and I fell.

Jonah threw himself underneath my body, stopping me from hitting the ground.

"Cessie! Are you hurt?" he shouted in alarm as he shifted my weight on top of his body. His muscular arms now wrapped around my back, supporting me as he sat up. He glared powerfully at my face and I grimaced in response.

"It's okay, they've gone. You're safe now. . . ." He trailed off as he removed his hand from behind me. His expression spread with confusion as my blood seeped down his hand.

I blacked out.

THE NEXT THING I WAS AWARE OF was the icy breeze skimming my cheeks as we fled into the night, my body bundled in Jonah's strong arms. The blaze from the bullet was fierce and it coursed through me; it was hard to catch my breath and even harder with the wind whipping my body. It sounded like Jonah was talking about me, but his words were all muffled and disjointed.

As we ground to a halt, a new voice sounded. "We should be safe here. I need to put pressure on the wound. We'll do the rest back at the house. Go, we'll be right behind you!"

"I can't leave you here! What if they come back? What if they've followed us? We'll wait for you, love, and we'll all leave together." Another voice, though it sounded lighter and softer, that of a woman, retaliated.

"It's too dangerous, it's an open wound. Please, leave."

I didn't hear any further complaint, and the next thing I felt was the ground underneath me as Jonah carefully placed me down. My ponytail had fallen out and my mass of blond hair was sodden in the blood sticking to my skin. I sensed Jonah was still present, but he had now moved back, and someone new was taking me in.

"Her name is Francesca," Jonah said.

Gentleness was touching my face, moving my hair from over my eyes. "You're okay. . . ." His voice was such a soothing sound, hushing the screaming pain that was vibrating inside me. "Francesca, can you hear me?" he murmured gently, his words reverberating all the way through my skin and into my bones.

I tried to sit up, but the wound in my shoulder made it impossible for me to move. So instead, I fought the urge to pass out and with all my will forced my eyes to open.

My vision was hazy at first, but with every passing second the smoke cleared until eventually I could see him. He stole what little breath I had left. There he was, right in front of me. I deliberated, unsure if he was real or whether I was no longer conscious and just dreaming this. To my surprise, his expression mirrored my confusion; though it was like he was looking into me, through me, and past me, all at once.

"Gabriel . . ." I finally stuttered through the sweet-tasting blood in between my teeth, shattering the silence between us.

In an instant he was on his feet, hovering over me on the ground.

He was so beautiful that he could not be of this world. His loose blond curls framed his perfect chiseled cheekbones and jaw; his eyes were so deep that if you fell into them, you would never be able to climb back out. Not that you would want to. He exuded an aura of light all around him, but then perhaps I was imagining things.

He turned away from me, still barely moving, standing over six feet tall, his body muscular and toned. His hands were clenched into fists, making the veins running up his arms jut out.

I tried to say his name again but this time it was harder to speak. I let out a cry, my shoulder continuing to burn. The lead and silver fusion was boiling my flesh; the pain was growing. My agony seemed to bring him back to me and he spun around immediately.

"How?" His short question was fired with such intensity, but still the words seemed to dance from his tongue.

"I know your face. . . ." I tried to answer, though I wasn't sure if his question had been directed at me.

He scanned me quickly and unzipped my jacket, tearing my top to reveal the extent of my injury. He removed his woolen sweater and with no effort tore the sleeves off. Working swiftly, he wrapped one around the top of my shoulder tightly, desperately trying to stop the blood flow, and then seemed drawn to my wrist.

Shoving the fabric out of the way, the look on his face was pained as he took in the fang marks from where Jonah had pierced my skin and fed from me. It was raw, red and ravaged, and still smeared with traces of my blood. He flinched as he wrapped part of the other sleeve around it firmly.

Gabriel glanced over his shoulder and although I couldn't see, I sensed Jonah move farther back from where I was lying, helpless.

"We need to get the bullet out before you bleed to death," he ordered.

"Okay," was all I could manage to choke out.

Gabriel lingered, and I could taste his fear. Fear for not knowing what to do next and fear for not understanding what I was. "I'm taking you back, I'll remove it myself."

Without even a moment passing, I was in Gabriel's arms, the wind hitting my body again; only this time I forced my eyes open. I didn't want to forget this.

I had to keep breathing.

I tried to recall how I had ended up with a bullet in my back. The girl in the shadow was the last image in my mind. I tried to push past it, but I couldn't. Jonah's expression as he had observed his bloodied hand was the next thing I could clearly remember. I tried to focus, to stay conscious.

It felt like forever, but eventually we made it to a house with only rolling fields, laced with frost, for company. It was deadly quiet now. The blackness of the night had long reached the doorway that I was being lifted through.

Once inside Gabriel seemed to search for his companions but was greeted only by one. Creeping in the shadows, she merely nodded in acknowledgment of our arrival. My hair had fallen once more over my eyes, and I could barely make her out; she almost seemed to blend into the emptiness.

Gabriel carried me up a winding spiral staircase and placed me down carefully onto a firm mattress. "Don't worry. I'm taking care of you," he whispered in my ear.

I wanted to say something, urgently needing to talk with him, but I couldn't speak. My body was failing me, and the burning had begun to fizzle away into a dull ache. My senses were also starting to fade. I knew him. I knew those eyes. After all this time, I had started to think that he was just a dream, a mirage that I had created from the depths of my mind. Yet when I tried to block him from my thoughts, his face only seemed to work even harder to reach me.

I tried to breathe through my nose, but I couldn't find any air. I opened my mouth and gasped, but all I could taste was blood seeping into the back of my throat, slowly choking me. My gaze was drawn to my side and though I couldn't feel him grip my hand with his, I watched him as he did.

I stared up into his eyes one last time as the thoughts whirling around my mind started to dissolve. The aching in my shoulder was no longer apparent. In fact, I could no longer feel any part of my body. My consciousness was slipping away; it was on the edge of the emptiness that I found Gabriel's face in the distance.

I remembered this dream.

I watched as he stepped toward me, as he bent down and kissed my hand so gently, greeting me. Dressed smartly in a white shirt and deep green jacket with gold buckles, it was like watching something from a very, very old film. The smile on his face, which I had witnessed so many times in my sleep, imprinted now in my memory. I remembered the love beaming from his eyes that blinded me, eclipsing my own. The eyes were deep set, and a piercing blue, like a Morpho butterfly's outstretched wings; his gaze was full of hope in that moment. Deeper and deeper into the dream I floated, at ease with everything in the haze.

Then I was falling.

I jerked as I felt my body being shaken. In the distance I could hear raised voices and panic. I shot back to reality and flipped my eyes open, taking in the scene around me. I was facing a window. I was lying on my side; the pillow my head was resting on was saturated in crimson. I moved my arm instinctively to wipe away the blood that was still oozing from my lips. I let out a low moan, which was just about all I could manage.

"She's breathing, she's back!" I recognized Jonah's voice from the shadows.

"Time for you to go," I heard Gabriel instruct, and I felt a small whip of air as Jonah left.

Behind me, Gabriel began stitching up my wound, and for the briefest second I was sure he paused. I felt the tickle of fingertips grazing my back; it was so quick I thought I'd imagined it as the sting of a thousand wasps jabbed me while he continued with his work.

But I knew the extent of the injury would dictate how long it would be before my skin would heal and my body would be back to normal, as if it had never happened. I would fall into a deep sleep, the length of which depended on how badly hurt I was and how much time my body needed to heal and recover.

For as long as I could remember, this is how it had always been for me.

A FEW HOURS HAD PASSED. I was cocooned in a comforting, thick duvet. My breathing had steadied. My mind was tired and my body ached, but I didn't want to drift off again. I couldn't turn my neck to look, but I felt a presence in the room. And even though I couldn't see him, the light flickering against the darkness of the windowpane told me it was Gabriel.

He moved silently around the bed, positioned an old wooden

chair next to me, and sat down. He studied my face and my expression before finally sighing and leaning in closer. With his eyes fixed on mine, he gently placed his fingers against my collarbone. I was intrigued by the look of wonder on his glorious face when he felt the cold chain resting against my skin and I watched him tentatively play with it for a moment before gradually pulling it upward. Only then did he remove his gaze from my own, rolling his head slightly and glancing down.

He lifted the ring, which was threaded through the chain, and placed it in his palm. I watched him as he gaped at the crystal sphere so prominently set at the center of the gold circle. It felt like an eternity before his eyes fell back to my own. He played with the ring lightly in his fingertips, while his stare flipped through the pages of my story, seeking out the chapter that held the answers he seemed to have lost.

Licking his thumb, he wiped the blood away from my stained mouth. Lowering his face to mine, he kissed my top lip, so tenderly it felt like little fairies dancing.

"We have a lot to talk about when you are ready." He smiled.

Now, strangely contented, I let myself float back into the darkness, and slept.

THREE

A BRIGHT LIGHT FILLED THE BEDROOM and I began to stir. Rays of winter sunlight shimmered against the window, accompanied by a crisp breeze sneaking in where it was slightly open. I sat up— straight up. I couldn't remember where I was or how long I had been here. I tried to recall what had happened to me, but my head was foggy. I hadn't died; I knew that.

My arm! I pulled my elbow from under the sheets, but it was fine, my skin smooth and pale as always. I twisted my body around to step out of the bed. My jacket and ballet flats had been placed neatly on a chair in the corner.

Not wanting to make a sound, I tiptoed to the edge of the room as quickly as I could. I had to concentrate hard, as my legs struggled to find the strength to keep me upright. As I bent to grab my shoes, a sudden, sharp pain hit me below my neck. I reached and felt a bandage taped onto my skin. Without much thought I swiftly yanked it off, frowning as the tape tugged. I found a mirror and looked over my shoulder to see a faint mark running across it where my broken skin had been stitched back together.

Then I remembered that I had been shot.

More carefully this time, I pulled my jacket over the torn top I still had on and dipped my toes into the muddied flats. Great—the massive blood stain on my jacket was a surefire way to draw attention. Gently, I peeled it back off and ran my fingers through my hair, which was also splattered in dried blood. Brilliant. I reached for the spare hair tie that lived on my wrist and flipped my blond hair into a giant bun.

Then it hit me. Gabriel. The subject of my dreams, my thoughts; he was here. We were here together.

I struggled out of the bedroom and hobbled across the landing, willing my legs to wake up. I made my way down the winding staircase but slammed to a halt when I got to the living room and three hugely surprised Vampires spun around and bared their fangs at me, with a ferocious hissing noise. I stepped back, feeling as though I had disturbed a nest of sleeping dragons, trying not to give them any more reasons to harm me. But instinct kicked in and I flung myself as fast as I could in the opposite direction, charging through a long hallway and out of a large—and luckily for me—open front door.

I tripped as I ran through and toppled to the ground. I rushed to regain my balance, pushing off the concrete with my palms, when a hand wrapped around my arm and pulled me up. I didn't dare look; instead I screwed up my eyes and started throwing my fists wildly into the air. I'd never had much coordination; today, it seemed, was no different.

He took me by the waist with his left hand and moved his right from off my arm, placing it across my back. I still couldn't bring myself to open my eyes and I squeezed them tightly shut.

"Hey, hey . . . look at me." I recognized Gabriel's voice. "Francesca, it's me."

Reassured, I slowly allowed my eyes to open, and there he was, clutching me tightly. I hadn't imagined him; he was with me.

"We have to go, there are Vampires inside—they'll kill us!"

Spurring into action, I tried to grab him by the hand and hurry him away from the danger. He didn't move.

"The Vampires in this house won't hurt you. Let me take you back inside, please."

I flashed him a puzzled look. It took a few moments for me to remember Jonah and these escaped Second Generation Vampires that he had told me about. Still, common sense was telling me to get far away from this house. Going back inside was the last thing I wanted to do. "Let's maybe just stay here. . . ." I tried to sound calm. I eyed a shiny Range Rover Sport that sat in the driveway.

"I don't want you out here, your shoulder isn't healed yet and the smell might attract unwanted visitors."

I looked at him blankly; then I understood. "Oh, right . . ." I lifted his hand with mine and rested it flat on my chest.

He returned my gaze, bewildered, as I slid his hand under my shirt, past my collarbone, and over my shoulder, where he had removed the bullet.

Startled, he withdrew his hand and reached for my wrist; sliding up my sleeve in one swift motion, he stared down. No mark, no Vampire bite, no bruise; nothing. He rushed to my other arm and repeated the action, making sure that he was not mistaken.

"How long have I been out for?" I asked.

His brow dipped in apprehension as he replied, "You've been resting a few days now."

"I didn't die, you kept my heart beating," I mused aloud.

"The bullet didn't hit any arteries or bones. You were lucky," he said. "But where are your stitches? I bathed your skin last night . . . they were there and now they're gone!"

"I only need a few days to heal. It's all right." Now I found myself comforting him.

"How are you even here?" he asked.

"I could ask you the same thing. I've known you before. I don't know when you and I were together, but I believe it was a long time ago indeed. And yet, it doesn't seem that you have suffered from the ages."

His lower lip quivered; he seemed sad. I waited, letting him contemplate, but he didn't answer my question. "Let's go inside, we can sit in the gardens at the back," was all he said.

Entwining my hand with his, as though it was the most natural thing in the world, he led me back through the country house. For now, at least, it seemed empty of Vampires. He guided me through the kitchen to the garden outside, where he sat me down on a cushioned rattan chair in front of the French doors. He made his way back inside the kitchen and returned with a jug of chilled lemonade and two glasses, pouring one for me.

I took a sip. It was real, fresh lemonade, nothing quite like it. The crisp, bitter flavor danced on my taste buds with a clean, dry finish.

The aroma filled my senses and, against my wishes, memories began to cascade in.

My eyelids started to flutter rapidly as my vision began to blur. I was no longer sitting on the patio with Gabriel. Instead, I was watching myself with him, munching from a picnic on a beautiful green, grassy verge, overlooking a lake. Wearing an almost military-style outfit, complete with a long velvet navy jacket, Gabriel looked incredibly handsome. Where this had been, I didn't know—when it had been, I could only assume was a very long time ago.

The sun was high and I could almost taste the summertime. We were clinking our glasses together and sipping the same lemonade. I was laughing at something he had said, and blushing. I hadn't watched this scene play out before; but there it was, within reach.

I moved my fingertips toward the image and the air seemed to undulate, like a pebble skimming over water, creating ripples before my eyes. The dreams and visions I had started to make sense. But I still hadn't put the pieces together. It was so frustrating, not knowing if what I was seeing was a true memory or merely my imagination. Like the past, which had become distorted and cloudy, my mind was in shadow, unable to separate reality from dream.

I turned my attention to the bushes farther back; something was rustling in among the leaves, spying on Gabriel and me together. Slowly, I moved my focus over to the disturbance. There was a young man holding his knees to his chest, his face hidden. I could only see him from behind; his shoulder-length hair was tied in a low ponytail behind his neck. His hands shook. My eyes were drawn to a large gold sovereign ring. I moved toward him, but came to an abrupt stop. It was as though I had hit an invisible wall.

Something was wrong.

The air seemed to pop and then it was black, empty: a void. The sun was no longer shining, the warmth of the light breeze had vanished, and darkness engulfed me. I froze, too terrified to move.

Thunder pounded through the stillness; something was approaching and fast. I searched for Gabriel and me, but everything about the memory vanished. Just as quickly as it had come, it disappeared.

Out of the nothingness, the creature stepped forward. The sight of me ignited the bonfires that burst from his globes as though he was envisioning the world aflame. I was able to see his stained face. He tilted his head ever so slightly, considering me.

I came back to my body. My hands were ghost-like in front of me. I felt my fists clench defensively, shaking uncontrollably as the creature snarled, bearing his fangs.

And he wasn't alone.

The thunderous noise underfoot had stopped, replaced with high-pitched squawks, piercing my hearing and surrounding me.

They were watching.

My gaze traced the quill-shaped lines of black ink that ran across his face. He had a hypertrophic scar stamped across his glabella, a spiral that coiled in the middle and branched out above the brow of his left eye.

He extended his arm and, with his clawed finger, signaled for me to move closer. I felt odd, compelled to do as he bid.

"Francesca!"

The darkness broke apart, cracks of light separating the black.

His burning flames extinguished, and he dissipated.

The fragments of light hung in the air until I heard my name again. With the second strike, they bounced and further shattered, becoming tiny shards. In one final swift movement, they disappeared.

I was back.

I looked down at my hand, scrunched into a tight ball. I'd caved in the lemonade glass, sharp pieces gouging into my skin.

"Francesca! Francesca!" Hearing Gabriel's voice was comforting. It soothed me until I barely felt the glass. "I'm here," he whispered more calmly, bringing his lips to my cheek. His voice, like a song, traveled through me.

I released my straining fingers, which had crushed the glass shards deeper into my palm. "How did you do that? How did you pull me back here?" I asked softly.

But Gabriel had already left. He rushed back to me, and placed ice cubes in my hand and wrapped a clean patchwork tea towel around my sliced skin.

My hands and legs were shaking uncontrollably, and my knees were knocking together. I was suddenly overwhelmed with a full range of emotions, coupled with complete exhaustion. It felt like I had climbed a mountain to reach this point. A mountain I could barely recall scaling—though the physical and emotional scars all sat below and on my skin from the lengthy journey.

Gabriel leaned in and placed his hands on either side of my chair, which was wobbling as I shook. I turned my face away from him, embarrassed. But he wouldn't allow it. "Hey . . ." Gabriel murmured.

His soft voice floated to my hearing, carried by a single breath that tickled my neck as he tilted his face to meet mine. I wasn't sure how he did it, but my body stopped convulsing.

Hesitantly, I rolled my neck so my eyes met his and I was surprised to see his bottom lip trembling. He gulped, hard. Gabriel stared into my eyes, and I watched his eyebrows dip—he looked sad.

His composure changed and urgently he lifted me up and wrapped his strong arms around my back and waist, pulling me into a tight embrace. I held my hands clamped together on his chest, his chin resting on the top of my head as the tip of my nose brushed his skin just below his Adam's apple.

Eventually releasing me, he placed his hands over the top of mine, rewrapping the towel firmly. He demanded, "You need to tell me everything."

I sat back down, and took a few minutes to gather myself while Gabriel sat patiently waiting. His blond curls were pushed back behind his ears, leaving a few unruly strands hanging above his shining eyes. His expectant stare reached deep inside of me. I felt exposed. "What do you want to know?" I asked quietly.

"Let's start with what just happened," he said. "You were sitting here one second perfectly fine, and the next thing you're completely frozen, as if you were in a trance."

"I was locked in a memory," I replied. "I have visions of things that happened in the past. Memories, I assume, when I'm asleep, dreaming. Sometimes when I'm awake it happens to me too, if I touch something that was familiar. . . . Sights, smells, sounds can all take me back."

Gabriel pondered. "You didn't look like you were experiencing a happy memory. You broke the glass from gripping it so hard. What did you see?"

"That was something different. I was watching you and me, having a picnic in the summer. But the memory dissolved and something, or rather someone, came to me."

My hands started to shake again, and my eyes prickled with a stinging sensation. A tear ran down the side of my cheek.

Gabriel appeared startled and began to hum low, comforting sounds. I felt calm instantly. I ran my fingers over my cheeks to dry them and panicked when there was blood on my fingertips.

I stared at Gabriel, confused. "Why are my tears blood?" I asked, as if he might possess the answer.

"Has that happened to you before?" he inquired as he tightened his grip, adding more pressure. It was starting to sting.

"I'm not sure."

He paused and seemed puzzled with the answer I had given. "Does it hurt?"

"A little," I replied, looking at my hand.

"Francesca—"

"Call me Cessie," I interrupted.

His lips curved up just a little at the edges, a sad smile.

"Francesca." Ignoring my request, he inhaled sharply. "We knew each other, we were quite close . . . a long time ago." He stopped to gauge my reaction, and I stiffened.

"I'm pretty old, I get that. But I don't age; I've been seventeen for a very long time. But I can die, it's just . . . I wake up again. My dreams, my visions are the only windows into anything that came before, and I don't pretend to understand them."

His face fell away from mine so I couldn't see his expression. He leaned back before he said, "When was the last time that you . . . died?" His wide eyes flashed up to mine. He seemed to hold his breath as he waited for my answer.

"Six years ago."

His shoulders slumped forward and I felt him tighten his grip around the tea towel. "So you don't remember me at all, not really. . . ." He trailed off.

"Maybe I don't remember you, but I never forgot you. Who were you to me?"

Glancing up to meet my eyes, I felt warmth resonating from his being, almost stroking my skin. "All that time ago, we were . . . well, we were close friends." He smiled.

"I see. If we were friends then how are you still alive?" I asked. "Are you a Vampire too?" I don't know why I even asked that; I could tell he wasn't. He was so different.

"No." He inhaled. "I'm an Angel." He waited for my reaction.

I sat silently. I hadn't known Angels existed—well, not outside of myth at least. But then, I had thought the same of Vampires until a few years ago. To the best of my recollection, I hadn't ever come across an Angel. I trod carefully with my next question. "If you're an Angel, shouldn't you be in Heaven?"

"Angels don't ordinarily live on Earth, that's true, unless the Angel is fallen," he answered. "If Angels choose to fall, they lose their connection to our world; their gifts cease. Rendered useless on this plane, they become mortal. Seldom is that choice ever made."

"But if choosing to fall means you become mortal, then I don't understand. You are the same as in my dreams, you look the same?"

"That's because I didn't fall. My situation is a little different," he explained.

"And these Vampires . . . Jonah? Are they somehow part of your different situation?" I pushed.

"Yes and no. I have been on Earth a long time and I have freed a number of Second Generation Vampires. They were human once; the life they have now was forced upon them. If I see a chance to grant salvation, I take it." He paused thoughtfully before continuing.

"Jonah was, well, a special case. When I came across him, he showed through his actions that he was capable of change. I offered him his freedom, and I try, just like with the others, to help guide him back to some sort of humanity."

"How long has he been with you?" I asked.

"Not long enough. He needs more time, and there are others involved—It's not that simple. He remains loyal to me in gratitude of my help. When he is able to leave, and if he wishes to, I will let him go."

He must have known I was about to pursue the conversation further as he quickly changed the subject. "How's your hand?" He peeled away the towel, raising my palm toward him. He met my eyes, disbelieving, when he saw that it had healed already. "How is that possible? You were—are—mortal." He stumbled over his words.

"It just is, I don't know why. Let me ask you, if we were such close friends, where did you go? Why did you leave me behind?"

He winced as the words left my lips and I sensed that I had asked the question he most wanted to avoid.

As Gabriel pondered his answer, Jonah bounded onto the patio.

"Hey, Cessie, you're up and about?" he asked, somewhat surprised.

Gabriel glared at him. I figured he was still unhappy about Jonah feeding from me.

"Gabriel." He nodded at his friend respectfully.

"Yeah, I'm a lot better, how are you?" I replied.

"All good." He seemed far more humble than when we had first met.

I stood, and both Jonah and Gabriel moved in my direction.

"Here, let me help you." Jonah scooped me up effortlessly. "You should be resting anyways." His arms were solid and they held me firmly.

"Put her down, Jonah, she's fine. She can walk." Gabriel's tone was far less gentle than the way he had spoken to me.

Jonah looked baffled, but placed me down.

"Francesca, why don't you take a warm bath and freshen up? Brooke will have laid out some clothes for you, you're about the same size," Gabriel said.

I scowled back at him—I still had plenty of questions.

"We'll continue this when you're done. I need to speak with Jonah. He's been recuperating himself, so we haven't had a chance to talk," Gabriel said, nodding at me.

I took "recuperating" to mean feeding.

Defeated, I reluctantly went back up to the room I had slept in and I ran a long, hot bath. The tub was wide and deep. I couldn't resist adding some of the salts that were placed tidily next to it. I unhooked my necklace and placed it carefully on the nest of tables.

Peeling off my clothes, I dipped my toe in but pulled it out quickly as it sizzled. I took a deep breath and tried again, this time stepping all the way in. I released my long, blood-stained hair from its elastic and let it flow down the nape of my neck and float on the surface of the clean water.

Sinking in as far as I could, I bobbed my head under and swilled my face. I rested for what felt like too long, before cleaning my skin and scrubbing my hair furiously. I reached for the white cotton towel, though I could barely see it, the room was so steamy.

I was anxious to return to Gabriel. I felt a powerful pull toward him and, strangely, out of the many questions I desired answers to, the only one I truly cared about was if he had loved me. I chuckled to myself, almost in disgust at my own indulgence. As if someone like him would have loved someone like me. He was exceptional, and I was not. But I knew his face, the way he smelled, and the way he had looked at me once before, in another lifetime. Mostly I recalled his smile, how it extended from the height of one cheek to the next; he was extraordinarily beautiful.

As I emerged from the tub, I dried myself off and wrapped the large, cozy towel around my pale skin. I moved into the bedroom and saw, as promised, a tight silk spaghetti-strap racerback top covered in deep purple roses hanging from the mirror on the dresser. For added warmth, a knitted hip-length cardigan was draped over the hanger. A pair of black skinny jeans and some stiletto boots sat on the chair. A pretty makeup bag and a hairbrush with some clips were also set out. I smiled. As far as I knew, no one had ever cared enough to look after me before.

Patting myself down, I set about trying on the clothes. They fit but were a little tight; despite my delicate frame, I had a curvy hourglass shape. But Gabriel had been accurate enough, this Brooke girl and I were a similar size. The boots were shiny and inviting, but the heel height was not, so I opted for my own flats instead. Wringing out my hair, I clipped it half up, half down, allowing the natural curl at the ends to dangle to my waist, leaving my side bangs to frame my face. Makeup was new; I didn't wear it ordinarily, but I didn't want to seem ungrateful, so I put a few strokes of blush across my cheeks and a little mascara on my lashes.

Eyeing the reflection in the mirror, I almost didn't recognize myself. I only ever wore practical clothes. Washing my face was about as much effort as I ever made to look presentable. I immediately felt self-conscious. Baggy jeans and flats meant that I blended into the backdrop; people never paid much attention to me. I didn't know how to wear clothes like this, I worried I would appear awkward in them. I closed my eyes and took a deep breath. Shaking my head, I scolded myself; there was nothing wrong with me—why shouldn't I look nice for a change? I attempted a more confident swagger toward the door.

I was ready to return to my conversation with Gabriel.

FOUR

As I paced out onto the landing, I could hear Gabriel and Jonah talking in the kitchen doorway. Their raised voices suggested they were arguing and so I loitered before I walked any farther forward.

". . . such power, I've never experienced anything like it. I knocked them down as if they were nothing."

"You'd been starved? Did they do anything to you that could have had that kind of effect?" I heard Gabriel ask quickly.

"Nope. I was completely weak and then she found me."

"You drank from her. You shouldn't have done that." Gabriel's tone was sharp.

"She didn't exactly give me a choice! And if I hadn't, we wouldn't be here now."

There was a pause, and I moved back toward the bedroom door.

"And while we're on the subject, are you going to tell me how it is you know her? What is she? She's not human, I know that."

"She is," Gabriel snapped back, though not terribly convincingly.

"I tasted her. She's something else. Who is she?" Jonah's voice lowered.

I couldn't hear the response; I started wondering if I'd been discovered, so I skipped down the winding staircase. As I reached the bottom, Gabriel's attention immediately switched from Jonah and focused on me for a few moments before that sumptuous smile spread across his face. Jonah spun around and nodded earnestly in my direction.

It was an intriguing sight to behold; the two of them side by side, such a contrast. Angel and Vampire—by definition, polar opposites. Impossible even.

Before I had a chance to speak, a male Vampire came charging through the hallway, slamming the front door so hard the floorboards under my feet shook. "We have to leave, they're coming!" His words tumbled out, barely coherent.

"What? Why would they track us? They fled when I fought them and they'll know there are more of us here," Jonah replied arrogantly. This was the Jonah I had first met.

"I sense Eligio," the other said. "He's coming with the clan."

"What's left of them," Jonah scoffed.

"There's more, it's not just Eligio. Another Pureblood and his clan travel with him, I can feel it."

That seemed to quiet Jonah.

"Two Purebloods? Two clans? That's an awful lot of effort to put Jonah in his place." Gabriel was thinking aloud.

Almost at the same second, all three of them glanced up at me.

"The girl?" the Vampire said, looking to Gabriel.

Gabriel contemplated this for a few moments.

"Erm, the girl has a name—Francesca. And who might you be?" I asked, a little annoyed.

He inspected me quizzically. "Michael. I'm sorry; I don't mean to be rude. The situation's quite serious and we don't have much time," he replied through gritted teeth.

"Francesca? But why? As far as they're concerned she just happened to be there. A human girl shot down seemingly by Eligio's own, assumed dead." Gabriel had a confused and somewhat worried look spreading across his face.

"Maybe they do want me. I ended a hell of a lot of them," Jonah offered, almost hopeful.

Michael's face screwed up and I sensed he was holding something back. I guessed their relationships were a little strained.

"I wonder how many of them I actually took out in the end. . . ."

"Enough," Michael snapped, baring his fangs.

"Hey, you're one of us now, you don't belong to your Pureblood anymore. You wanted out and we helped you," Jonah argued.

"I wanted Thomas to have his freedom more than I wanted my own. I've only been separated from them for a short time and I felt every single one of my clan's demise when you decided that they didn't deserve their existence anymore. Do you know how difficult that is?" Michael replied coldly.

"They aren't your clan anymore, that's the point. They have no desire to change. They're beyond saving. You said you wanted your humanity back, that's why you're here and they still belong to their Purebloods. Well, now some of them belong to the dirt. . . ."

That was too much for Michael, who launched himself in Jonah's direction. To my surprise Gabriel began to glow as he stepped in between them and both Vampires halted.

"Stop, right now. Michael, I will try to help Thomas, in whatever way I can, but right now we have to leave," Gabriel said. "How long until they reach us?"

"Minutes, not hours. But we need to go back for Thomas—he's my brother. I'm the reason he was turned; he was trying to save me. Now I must save him," Michael replied, stepping back from Gabriel. "If they are coming here, Thomas has surely been left behind, bound and chained. Now is the time to go back for him."

"We need to get Francesca away from here. I'm sorry. We will have to find another way, but trust me, I will help him." Gabriel's word was final.

Michael glanced at me with narrowed eyes, concluding that I was the reason Thomas wasn't with us now.

"Okay, gather the others, take them home. We'll follow behind." Gabriel hadn't even finished his sentence and the Vampire was gone. "Jonah, get Francesca to the car."

Jonah grabbed my hand and as we touched I felt a tiny spark pass between his palm and my own. I released him automatically and he gaped back at me. He'd felt it too. "Come on!" he yelled.

Shaking the moment off, we pelted through the front door and into the Range Rover. Jonah jumped into the driver's seat, ready to speed off.

"What about the others? There's only one car?" I quizzed frantically.

"They've gone on foot."

"But surely—?"

"We're faster on foot. We're only in the car because you wouldn't be able to keep up." Jonah winked at me.

I felt a blush sweep over my cheeks. In the cold light of day, he was just as attractive.

"Where's Gabriel?" I asked. "What's he doing?"

The thought of an army of Vampires tearing toward the house was terrifying and I wished that Gabriel would hurry.

"Tying up loose ends," Jonah answered.

"What loose—?"

"If they are coming for you," he said impatiently, "your blood is still all over the bedroom, your scent all through the house." He made this statement as if the rest were implied.

"I thought you said I had no scent?" I argued.

He hesitated before answering. "No, I think you were right. I was starved; I wasn't myself. I can catch your scent now." He raised his eyebrows and said, "Tasty . . ."

I dismissed his remark with a half smile.

Minutes later, Gabriel at last appeared, and as he jumped into the backseat, Jonah slammed the car into gear. Instinctively I reached for my chain; it wasn't there.

"Wait!" I shouted. I didn't have time to explain—I flung open the door and began running back to the house.

"Cessie!" Jonah yelled after me.

No!

Strange. It sounded like Gabriel's voice, but it was like I had imagined it.

As I approached the entrance, Jonah appeared and blocked me, grabbing my arm. I didn't have time to think about it. I forced my way around him and somehow, despite his strength, I found myself in the hallway with the winding staircase in front of me.

I sprinted up as fast as I could, telling myself we'd still have time to get away. The boards creaked loudly as I sprung up each one. Pushing the bedroom door open I charged through, snagging the cardigan on the bedpost, and raced into the bathroom.

There it sat, glinting and glimmering, its light reflecting off the glass table.

I scooped it up and quickly lifted it over my head, placing it back in its rightful position around my neck. At that moment, I heard a thunderous explosion. I spun around and, in a blink, there were flames engulfing everything, blazing up through the landing and filling every room and every crevice. The heat was so fierce that I thought I might melt before the fire reached me. I froze.

As the flames raced toward me, I felt the heat graze my face, but only for a moment; my feet swept past the carpet and my body was being elevated off the floor—Jonah!

We burst through the window; he covered my face with his shoulder, protecting me from the shards of shattering glass as we hurtled through the pane. He tried to brace me from the fall, spinning me, taking my weight on top of his as we crashed onto the ground below. Unfortunately, even he couldn't prevent us from being launched farther with the blast that followed.

I landed several yards away from Jonah, facedown in the grass. My ears were ringing and my hands failed me as I tried to prop myself up. Immediately Gabriel was at my side, and in one swift movement I was in his arms and being bundled into the back of the car. Jonah was already at the wheel and we flew away from the furnace.

What were you doing? Gabriel shouted.

Automatically I raised my hand to touch my necklace. "I left it inside."

Bewildered, his wide eyes met mine as he whispered, "I didn't say that aloud."

The car sped down the country roads. Gabriel, silently helping me into a more comfortable position in the backseat, began fastening my seat belt. The mood was tense and I could sense that Jonah was biting his tongue; he wanted to speak but followed Gabriel's lead.

"Are you all right?" Gabriel said, casting his eyes over me.

"I'll live," I replied.

"That's not what I meant. Are you hurt?"

"Perhaps a little bruised and embarrassed, but otherwise I'm fine." I surveyed myself. "Oh, I ripped the cardigan, I'm so sorry."

Gabriel looked confused. "That's the least of our problems. Brooke won't mind, don't worry."

"Thanks, Jonah. I think I owe you one," I offered in gratitude.

"Even Stevens now!" he replied playfully. "How did you get past me anyway? I'm pretty strong, you know!"

I thought I saw him flex his bicep as he asked, just to demonstrate his point.

Gabriel moved back to his own seat and, pulling out a map, he began studying it. But I knew he was focused on my response.

"I think you must have tripped or something, I'm not sure. I just got by you somehow." I wasn't entirely sure myself.

"Hmm yeah, I guess so; no person . . ." he hesitated, ". . . could get by me that easily."

His fingers met the dashboard and he started fiddling with the radio buttons. I thought about it for a moment and tried to recall. He had stopped me, hadn't he? He grabbed me and I couldn't move, but then . . . he was just out of the way and I was inside. As I focused on it, my head started to ache and I winced. Gabriel peered down at me.

Let him think he tripped.

His lips didn't move and the words floated around my mind, clearing the ache that was developing. I raised my eyebrows in surprise.

How are you doing that? I thought. I didn't say it. Could I communicate back?

Gabriel cast his eyes back down to the map. *When we met, I believed you were a mortal. When I found you, you were gone. You're obviously not and you clearly weren't. Whatever you are, he must believe you are human.* He continued scanning the fold-out map.

What do you mean, when you found me I was gone? If I was gone, how did you find me? And he already thinks I'm anything but human, I heard him telling you! I was getting angry now and I could feel my body tensing.

He is a Vampire, Francesca. I trust him, but he still has a connection to his Gualtiero, the Pureblood Vampire who changed him. We must be careful.

I felt upset, and an overwhelming sense of confusion started bubbling to my surface.

Why can't you call me Cessie!

Here he was, this memory, this ghost whom I believed I had a connection with, and he couldn't even call me by my nickname. I felt my skin radiating heat as my confusion swiftly transcended back into anger.

How the hell are you in my head telling me what to do when you've given me no explanations! When you left me! When you . . .

"Ahhh!" I screeched loudly as my thoughts were cut off by a violent ringing noise passing through my mind.

Gabriel clutched his temple, bowing his head down at the same second. He had heard the same deafening sound.

"Sorry, sorry! Not a fan of rock music, eh?" Jonah laughed, turning down the music bellowing out of the speakers.

I caught him glancing at me in the rearview mirror as he grinned. My eyes met his for a moment and his pupils widened in surprise. The creases in his cheeks ironed out into a smooth surface as his smile fell away. I covered my eyes with my hand as I felt them burning, wondering what he'd seen.

I glanced down into the footwell self-consciously, trying to calm myself. My eyelids stopped twitching after a few moments. Jonah switched the radio off altogether and said nothing.

Gabriel reached his hand out and cupped mine in his own. Instantly the knots in my body loosened and I felt calm again. Taking a deep breath, I said, just to him: *I'm sorry.*

Jonah continued to whiz around the winding roads at top speed, and miraculously the thick tires stuck to the road. Eventually I could see the highway. I glanced back at the countryside. Saying farewell to the rolling hillsides, I wondered if the rain that had begun pelting down furiously was an omen.

And sure enough, as I watched, the landscape became a whirlpool, and at the center of it, there was a transparent ball, bouncing and balancing, containing a terrifying image: a large group of Vampires standing next to the smoking remains of the house, observing. At the front of the row of obedient soldiers, two seven-foot-tall putrid figures snarled and shrieked an ungodly, deafening noise that reverberated through the trees.

Wearing long black cloaks, their bald heads covered in tattoo-like markings, they certainly didn't look like Vampires. They were so dark that I felt every inch of me tremble as I took them in. I couldn't watch them for long as something underneath their skin bubbled and traveled through their bodies, so that they seemed to disappear and reappear in and out of focus.

Standing slightly behind the others, I recognized the same Vampire who had stood face-to-face with me and then disappeared. He was furious. I tried to make out what he was shouting, and my body tightened as one of the putrid figures twisted his head, revealing his fangs. I was certain, as his stare shifted from his subordinate, that he could see me. Pointing into the air, he hissed a sound that made my bones feel as if they might splinter, and then the figures were gone.

Disconnected from my vision, I found myself panting shallow breaths.

Gabriel, sensing my unease, turned to me and took my hand once more. *What did you see?*

They are outside the house, they're furious that we have escaped. They will not stop. I don't know how I knew, but I did. They were coming for me and they wouldn't rest until they had what they wanted.

You mean they were *outside the house?* he corrected me. *You were seeing a vision of the past? But then, how is that possible, you weren't there, it's not a memory.*

I'm not sure. . . . It felt as though it was happening right now. And the two figures who stood at the front of the Vampire clans were nearly identical to the creature who came to me this morning.

Gabriel seemed to contemplate before responding. *Have they ever reached into your memories before this morning?*

Not in this lifetime at least. That was the first time.

"Since Jonah drank from me," I said aloud by accident.

"Sorry, what?" Jonah said.

I looked to Gabriel and he shook his head in discouragement, but I carried on. "I saw the Vampire clans outside the house. There were two huge figures with them, wearing black cloaks, and they were covered in tattoos."

"You mean you saw the Purebloods? But when? They weren't just standing around when we left," Jonah replied.

"They were Pureblood Vampires? Is that what they are?" I panicked.

Gabriel reached for my hand and squeezed it, taking the lead. "Francesca has an ability to see things. What she just described was a vision she had. Which means, if her vision is accurate, Michael was right. Two Purebloods and their clans are on our heels."

Jonah cleared his throat, hitting his chest as he said sarcastically, "Human, right?"

"Yes, Jonah, she is human. Just a bit extraordinary," Gabriel replied with a false confidence.

The car fell silent once again and no one said anything. Jonah careered down the fast lane, constantly checking his mirrors. I thought he was checking that we weren't being followed, but occasionally I felt his eyes observing my reflection.

"Where are we going?" I broke the silence.

"Back to the main house," Jonah replied.

"Which is where, Europe? America?"

"Buckinghamshire," Gabriel answered.

"Buckinghamshire? Surely that's not far enough away!"

"It doesn't matter how far away from here we are. Purebloods and their clans are all over the world. I was turned in Florida," Jonah replied coldly.

"Yes, but there are two Pureblood Masters not very far from here. I think I'd feel more comfortable if we went transatlantic."

"Cessie, we have a very secure property in Hedgerley. We live on the outskirts of the community. It's very safe, I promise you. We'll stay as long as we can before we move on. We can go to the States or Canada next if you still want to. Honestly, while we try to sort all this out, it's better for us to be somewhere we're already established—a place we know is as safe as possible. Trust me." Gabriel calmed me.

Gazing back at him, I faltered. "You called me Cessie."

"If that's what you prefer," he said, but it felt reluctant.

"And where will I live?" I asked.

"With us of course," Gabriel replied, flashing a cautious smile at me.

"It'll be nice to have another female around the place," Jonah joked, grinning cheekily as he watched my reaction in the rearview mirror.

"And the other Vampires?" I still wasn't comfortable with the idea of the others, and having to exist so closely with them.

"They won't hurt you. I promise," Gabriel reassured me.

I considered the idea and finally nodded in acceptance. I needed to be around Gabriel; he had filled my dreams for as long as I could remember and now I was with him. And, however odd, this was a family of sorts, and it was the best offer that had ever been extended to me.

"You should rest. We have a few hundred miles to go yet. And your shoulder must be killing you," Jonah suggested.

I looked to Gabriel, arching my eyebrows; he knew what I was thinking.

Don't say anything about that just yet, just for a while, especially now he knows you have visions.

"That's a good idea," Gabriel agreed. He reached for a blanket and began wrapping it around me so that I was warm and snug. His hand ever so slightly brushed the bottom of my bare neck and a tingle stirred through me. "Try to sleep. I'll wake you when we get there." Gabriel gently moved the stray blond hairs that had cascaded onto my forehead behind my ears and smiled.

As I closed my eyes, I couldn't help but feel conflicted. Gabriel was willing me to feel comfortable with the idea of living with these Second Generation Vampires. Yet at the same time, he sent me thoughts of warning about revealing too much about myself to Jonah. The only Vampire I might trust.

Strange, I mused, as I forced my eyelids shut.

FIVE

I couldn't sleep; adrenaline was pumping through me. I cast my mind back to the events that had unfolded over the last few days.

Here I was, going about my existence, pulling pints in a quaint little pub in the middle of nowhere, and now? Well, it seemed meeting Jonah had knocked my everyday life over. And Gabriel. I couldn't believe I had found him—the leading man in all my dreams, my memories, finally in the flesh. And an Angel no less. Although I suppose it made sense; if creatures like Vampires roamed the Earth then pure beings must, too.

I wondered why Gabriel was here, why he had come in the first place, how it was that we came to know each other, and why he had left me. I desperately needed answers. There was so much I didn't understand.

My body stiffened as the thought occurred to me: Can he hear what I'm thinking? I gently raised one eyelid, just enough to peek out and observe Gabriel scrolling through an iPhone. Very modern for an Angel. He didn't seem to be reading my mind; if he was, he was doing a good job of hiding it.

I thought you were sleeping?

The words somehow formed in my consciousness, swirling around my mind. Embarrassed, I flicked my gaze back down. The sounds of the road and the car disappeared into the background and finally ceased altogether. I let the silence engulf me. It was like I was in a tunnel, sealed off from the rest of the world.

Can you hear my thoughts anytime you want? I concentrated on my question, trying not to conjure anything else that he might be attuned to.

I'm not entirely sure why we can speak to each other like this in the first place. . . . Only Angel Pa— His sentence stopped abruptly, but I was still captured in the tunnel. The link hadn't broken.

Only Angel what?

He hesitated before he answered. *We obviously have a connection; something special.*

I fluttered my eyes open to try and read his expression. Confusion sat at the center of his dipping eyebrows. I quickly closed them shut again before he saw.

We can't read each other's minds. We're in sync somehow. I can call to you and you can respond if you are open to it. Or you can block me.

I have to want to hear you and vice versa? I asked.

I think so. Not "want" though; I think more willing and able. His response was fast, like he knew the rules of this game.

Can you see what I see? If I think of a memory or an image, can I invite you in?

I don't know.

Hmm. Maybe he hadn't played this game before after all.

I started to picture the memory I'd seen in Gabriel's presence over the lemonade. The two of us together, having a picnic—a relatively inoffensive image to test the theory on. As I recalled the scene as best I could, I felt Gabriel somehow. I knew right away that he was seeing it too.

Rather than showing him a picture in my mind like a postcard, I presented him with the memory. The sweet clove scent of the white dianthus and the fresh fragrance of the crisp, green grass surrounding us ... We looked so happy. But as the glasses clinked something strange happened.

I found myself observing the memory from Gabriel's perspective. I calmed myself for a second. He remembered it too after all; he had been there. I was still watching, but the emotions that rushed through me were not my own; they were his. It was the strangest sensation. I didn't get any feeling of happiness. I felt a bubbling of dread instead. Did Gabriel not like me? Was he pretending to? Flashes of still images started to devour the scene. They didn't belong to me.

Instead, extracts of Gabriel's memory started falling through. Another being, with feathered wings, glowing. The clips came swiftly tumbling out, one after the other. A crystal. It sparkled, dazzling me. A barn, with a pool of blood running toward an entrance.

The last picture startled me and I could feel Gabriel pulling away, trying to let go. But I wanted to see inside, to relive the scene the way he had. I held on to the memory as the blood trickled, gathering into a small pool. I felt his fear flow through me and I watched him desperately running to the open door. I resisted Gabriel's attempts to disconnect, but it was nearly impossible. Just as he was on the verge of reaching the wooden doorframe, the connection broke. I felt sick.

"Stop the car!" I shouted at Jonah, who remained oblivious to what we had been doing.

My request barked like an order. Being used to following such a demand without question meant that he abided without faltering. I didn't even glance at Gabriel. Unfastening my seat belt, I flung open the passenger door. I then dropped to my knees and threw up into the brambles nestling next to the concrete of the hard shoulder.

It took a few minutes for the world to seem steady around me again, and once more the thunder of the cars flying past—exceeding the seventy-miles-per-hour speed limit—unsettled my hearing.

Jonah remained in the driver's seat. Self-consciously, I wiped the bile from around my mouth with the sleeve of my borrowed cardigan. This Brooke girl was going to hate me; I had ruined most of the clothes she'd lent me within a couple of hours of wearing them. An outstretched hand appeared in my peripheral vision, holding out a bottle of water. I took it and swilled my mouth out. Attractive.

I turned my head to address him. "Why did you stop me?" I asked, not sure whether to adopt an annoyed tone or to feel guilty for invading a part of his memory that he didn't want to share. Damn it. Guilt prevailed.

"Not yet," he said.

He stooped behind me, stroking my back in a steady circular motion.

I didn't like this; I didn't like any of it. So much for a knight in shining armor! Vampires are scary, yes. Pureblood Masters, terrifying. But Gabriel was supposed to be . . . well, I didn't know, but definitely the good guy, thank you very much. What was he hiding? Perhaps I was better off on my own. Doubt spiraled around my mind uncontrollably. I was missing far too many pieces of the puzzle—a puzzle that right now I couldn't see being completed anytime soon. But Gabriel was an Angel. How could he be anything but honorable? I switched my train of thought: Maybe I had done something; maybe I had pushed him away, long ago?

"I felt what you felt. You were so angry. What did I do to make you hate me?" The question rolled off my tongue before I could stop it.

He paused for a second, staying still. Then I felt him lean in, lingering contemplatively, his mouth close to the top of my neck. His breath tickled my skin and I got goose bumps. "My anger was not directed at you, Lai," he said softly.

I was hoping for a bit more, but . . . Lai. Lailah. It hit me fast and hard. That was who he had known me as.

That had been my name. My first name. The only name. How had I forgotten it?

My eyes widened in recognition and began to fill, threatening to spill over. Everything about that name felt warm and inviting; happy. I had to catch my breath—I felt like I had been kicked in the stomach.

He moved his arm around my back and took my hand in his own, sliding his fingers in between mine, and squeezed. "Not yet," he repeated. His words washed over me like a wave breaking gently onto the shore, cleansing any debris and rendering it innocent once more.

He released my hand and I found my feet, twisting to face him. I strained my neck to explore his expression. He stood tall and I was average height, some five inches shorter. I simply nodded in acceptance. There were no words. I stepped back into the car.

I buckled myself in, and this time Gabriel retreated to the passenger seat next to Jonah. I slammed the door shut.

"That was some good hurling, Cessie! I'll try to make the rest of the journey a little less bumpy." Jonah winked at me in the rearview mirror, reminding me again that he could see my every expression. So I exchanged the bewildered look for a chirpy smile and a half-hearted laugh; it was the best I could muster.

The rest of the journey went quickly. I sat tentatively letting go of any thoughts for a while, simply observing the scenery as we sped past the traffic, eventually turning off the highway at an exit marked BEACONSFIELD. We moved across the roundabout, passing a sign stamped HEDGERLEY. It was quite a contrast when soon we were accelerating down a twisting country road, passing an old-fashioned white pub and cute terraced cottages with picket fences.

A lot of the buildings were clustered together; even the bigger detached properties were but a stone's throw away from the next. We zipped by them, until there was nothing on either side but woodlands. Jonah finally turned left and drove up a ridiculously long gated driveway, taking several minutes to reach the front of the house. It was spectacular.

The property was incredibly old, with beautiful traditional features. The front door itself was styled like an old church entrance and made from dark, sturdy oak; very grand indeed. There were several garages to the left-hand side and I counted seven windows on the face of the ground floor alone.

The engine cut and within a moment Jonah had opened my door and was extending his hand to help me out.

"This place is huge," I mumbled, overwhelmed, taking his hand and stepping out of the Range Rover. "Is this really yours?" I asked Gabriel in disbelief.

Gabriel stepped next to me, placing his hand affectionately on my back, and said, "Yes, and now yours."

We made our way inside. I followed Jonah's lead as he opened the door, walking into the huge hallway that extended maybe thirty feet ahead; solid hardwood ran throughout. I pushed my hair behind my ears nervously as I stepped inside, slowly absorbing it all.

"Oh, good, you're back, love!" a sweet voice chirped from the room at the far end of the hallway. She flashed toward us and I shifted uncomfortably. A Vampire. Of course. I knew they would be here, but it was still strange to see.

She swept past me as if I didn't exist and moved into a lingering hug with Gabriel, kissing him softly on the cheek. I couldn't help but furrow my brow, a surge of jealousy racing through me.

I looked to Jonah on my right, who rolled his eyes in reply. "Hanora, this is Cessie." Jonah forced the introduction.

She didn't move right away, but Gabriel took her arms from around his shoulders and turned her to face me. She was immaculate. Standing tall and slender at an easy five feet eight inches, her long dark brown hair cascaded in loose waves past her shoulders. Her eyes were a bright green with flecks of yellow, her skin was white as snow, and her face was perfectly symmetrical. She couldn't have been more than twenty in human years, but she made me feel like a disheveled child by comparison.

She eyed me, judging, instantly turning her pretty button nose up. "Nice to meet you, Cessie," she said with a smooth Irish accent. With a crooked smile, she extended a hand for me to shake.

I took it politely and returned the smile with a sarcastic one of my own. "It's Francesca, actually."

Our hands parted and Jonah coughed a little awkwardly.

"Jonah, why don't you give Cessie a tour of the grounds?" Gabriel asked.

I felt immediately rejected.

"Come on, we can start with the gardens out back," Jonah agreed, eagerly whisking me off down the hallway through an oversized eat-in kitchen and through a back door. It occurred to me that the kitchen was a pretty redundant room in this house.

"He wanted me out of the way," I huffed to Jonah as I bumbled over the decking and past the outside seating area covered with a canopy. My mind was in overdrive once again. I was expecting Vampires, but I wasn't prepared for a beautiful Irish one to drape herself all over Gabriel as soon as we walked in the door.

My annoyance receded briefly as I saw, outstretched in front of us, a beautiful woodland. Behind it, fields upon fields were tucked up in an icy blanket with a film of fog brewing on top. An idyllic setting, totally secluded.

"Wow," I mumbled.

"Twenty acres roughly," he said, answering the question I hadn't yet asked.

"Beautiful."

"Secure and well equipped. There are cameras everywhere and we know this village like the back of our hands, not to mention the booby traps," he returned. "Are you all right for a little exploration?" he quizzed, nodding in the direction of my shoulder.

I didn't answer as I began strolling down the slate path. "What's Gabriel doing?" I said, gazing toward the back door.

"Sorting some stuff out," Jonah answered. I rolled my eyes at him, knowing he was purposely withholding details. "Fine. He's holding a mini-briefing."

"With who and about what?" I inquired, shivering a little in the chill.

"With everyone who lives here. Letting them know you'll be staying and laying down the ground rules, I'd imagine," he replied. I slowed and he said, "You know, no drinking the girl and all that."

"Oh, great." I examined the setting ahead and viewed the opening to the woods. Nestled inside was another building. The path veered off and a track took its place through the trees. "Who's Hanora?" I tried to keep the quiver from my voice.

"What do you mean?"

"Who is she to Gabriel?"

He thought for a moment. He was slightly ahead of me so he slowed down. "She is Gabriel's oldest companion. He freed her back in the early nineteen hundreds. She was the first one he saved. They've been traveling together a long time, so they're, shall we say, close." His eyes glanced at me sideways, checking for my reaction.

His words stung. I didn't like the idea that Gabriel, my Gabriel, was close to any female. I felt betrayed. But how could I? It wasn't like he belonged to me. I still didn't know what he was to me or even what he had been to me in another lifetime. I gulped hard, but tried not to give anything away.

I rubbed my hands over my arms as the chill continued to sting me.

"You're cold," Jonah observed. "Here." He whipped off his dark leather jacket and stood in front of me. Placing it around my shoulders, he pulled the collar edges together. Glancing down thoughtfully, his pupils swelled a little larger, inviting me in. I was captured momentarily by his expression, a wicked grin spreading across his face. I knew he was dangerous, and not only because he was a Vampire.

He stepped a little closer and bent down suggestively, so he was almost nose-to-nose with me, his unwavering stare meeting my own. He held my gaze as he placed his hands into the pockets of the jacket hanging on either side of my body, brushing his thumb against my bare waist as he moved under the bottom of the shirt. I didn't falter. He moved in a little closer, his hips now touching mine. I was the first to break.

Self-consciously I jolted away, fluttering my eyelashes furiously, escaping the exchange. Bowing my face down I scratched at my head; he threw his own back and roared a little.

He snatched his hands out of the pockets and produced a pack of cigarettes and a lighter. Embarrassed, I hid my blush as he stepped back. Lighting his cigarette high in the air, he blew out the smoke through his nose. "Want one?" he asked, extending the box in my direction.

I inhaled, letting the secondhand smoke pollute my lungs, but shook my head. "I'd say they'd kill you, but I guess that doesn't exactly apply."

It took us about ten minutes to reach the woodlands. We entered the opening and the pathway led to a pretty but rather decrepit outbuilding. I lit up and Jonah offered to show me inside. "Gabriel's been doing some restoration work to it. It won't fall down now but it's a long way from finished yet."

It was small but perfectly formed. I creaked open the old wooden door and was presented with an entranceway that featured a beautiful tile floor with a sun design. Four rooms came off it—a sitting room, a bedroom, a kitchen, and a bathroom. It had been plastered and the plumbing was in but the rest of it was a shell. I wandered into the sitting room. A sheet hung over the fireplace, and I carefully peeled it back to reveal a newly installed log fire, ready for use. It felt so homey.

"It's incredible," I gushed.

"You're easily impressed."

I shrugged off his comment as I fell in love with the building. I bounced happily from each room. They were all bare, other than a sink and toilet that had recently been installed in the bathroom; but even so, it captivated me. I felt more comfortable here than I did in the luxurious house. It was far less alien, and a palace compared to the places I'd lived.

"How's your shoulder holding up?" Jonah asked, breaking my train of thought.

"Sorry?" We were back in the entranceway and my attention had turned to the tiled sun on the floor. It seemed to exude flashes of gold and white. I knew that was impossible, but it did.

"You know, where you were shot?" He squeezed the back of my shoulder where Gabriel had patched me up just a few nights before. I didn't flinch.

"What are you doing!" I stepped away from him, irritated.

"Funny, most people would feel something so soon after," he accused.

"I'm not most people." I didn't want to lie to him.

"Let me see it. I've been feeling guilty about it since it happened."

"No." I turned on my heel and started to make for the door. Gabriel had been quite adamant that I shouldn't reveal my particular gift to anyone, least of all a Vampire.

I was reaching for the handle when he spun me around, pressing me up against the wall so that I was forced to face him. Jonah was tugging off his jacket and the cardigan from around me, holding me by the waist, restraining me.

"Jonah!"

SIX

"Sorry, Cessie. I just need to see it. I won't hurt you."

Alarm rang through me. Reacting, I bolstered my weight into his chest, knocking him backwards a little, just as his fingers were gripped at the back of my shirt. He managed to tear the silk effortlessly, leaving it gaping open down my back. I huffed, aggravated, and he tilted his head, impressed with the strength I had exerted.

He eyed me for a moment but, within a flash, his hand was at my hip and he spun me around once more, my hands forced flat onto the cold brick wall. His body was flush with my own, his legs slightly parted, as he used all of his weight to keep me pinned, his hands clamped over the tops of mine. "You're pretty stubborn, Cessie," he murmured, his tone close to seductive.

I was so furious with him, yet a little chill of excitement flowed through me at the same time. He was playing me like chords on a guitar, in an attempt to change my tune.

"I just want a peek, that's all," he reasoned. Lowering himself down, his top lip skimmed my earlobe as he said, "No big deal."

I couldn't escape his grasp. I started to panic; I didn't want to have to explain to Jonah. I didn't even have an explanation.

He repositioned his left hand and I felt his weight shift across me. He reached for my hair and began to sweep it from my back. As it brushed my skin, I realized that I was seconds away from being revealed. He clasped my wrist. I forgot how strong he was; it felt as though he was nearly crushing my bones. I was about to scream when suddenly he let go.

I twisted to face to him, not entirely sure what had caused him to stop. I took a second to be thankful that my hair was still covering my shoulder blade. He had the strangest expression on his face: stunned.

"Who did that to you?" he said, his tone bitter.

I followed his line of sight. He was staring down at my lower back and up my spine where my skin was now exposed. I spun, immediately grabbing for the cardigan now discarded on the floor. He lunged forward and caught me midgrab, pulling me up and into him. Wrapping himself around me, he traced his fingers up and down the scar, which was protruding out of my skin, feeling it stretch from my lower back to the nape of my neck in anything but a straight line.

He was silent and when he pulled away from me, fury filled his expression. "I asked you who did that to you?" His voice roared, bouncing off the bare walls.

I wasn't quite sure what to say. I was uncomfortable; the scar was hideous and I was embarrassed that he had seen it. I needed the cardigan. I wanted it hidden. I snatched for it again, but he raced over, seizing it from my clutch.

"Cessie," he pushed on, deadly serious, and I had no choice but to answer.

"I told you I had known a Vampire once and the acquaintance-ship hadn't ended well." It was the truth.

Jonah's eyes flashed from his usual hazel color into deep red infernos. He looked ferocious. His whole body stiffened, appearing ready to erupt. "You're still alive?" He hesitated, a quizzical look spreading across his face.

I guess it was unusual to get out of the grasp of a Vampire with your life intact.

"Yes, and he, Frederic," I stammered, "is not." My eyes started to well up. I didn't want to think about this, about him. It was a painful memory and one I had no desire to revisit.

Jonah's muscles started to loosen and his eyes seemed less hard.

I wiped angry tears with the back of my hand, which now felt like ice. I was shivering—a mixture of emotion and the freezing cold. Jonah seemed to calm down and walked toward me. He rested the cardigan back around my shoulders over the top of my hair. I slipped my arms through it silently and then backed away from him. I was beyond mad, my cheeks flushing scarlet.

"I'm sorry," he offered guiltily.

I didn't want to talk to him. I didn't want to talk to anyone. I stumbled through the door, out into the woods. I stopped in my tracks as Gabriel stood directly in front of me.

What did he do? His thoughts filled me quickly.

I bowed my head, holding back the tears that threatened once more. Gabriel's eyes ran up and down my body hurriedly; I could feel him examining every inch of me and quickly his eyes set upon my wrist, which was bruising a lovely shade of purple. He looked to me again but still I didn't answer him.

Go back to the house and wait for me on the patio. I need to speak with Jonah alone.

I did as I was told and made my way back up the slate path slowly, to avoid falling on the slippery surface and to gain time to pull myself together. I didn't want to cause tension between them, but I was upset with Jonah. However, I felt more emotional over the memory of that Vampire, of that evening.

Reaching the patio, I sat down and waited. I remained there for what felt like a long time, when finally Gabriel returned and took a seat beside me. "I'm sorry about Jonah," he sighed. "He's curious about you, but that doesn't give him the right—"

I cut him off. "I'm fine, honestly. Let's just forget it."

Gabriel nodded dubiously before continuing. "I've spoken to everyone who resides here and they're all comfortable to be around you. They have sworn to me that they'll treat you as family. I trust them to look out for you, to help keep you from harm. I know it's difficult for you to be here, but I need you next to me while I try and work out . . ." He trailed off.

"Work out what? What I am? I'm just a girl! Okay, maybe I'm a tad on the immortal side, but I am still human—I can die."

"Yes, but you come back to life, and that's not exactly ordinary. It concerns me that not one but two Purebloods have come to seek you out. We need to know why."

I knew Gabriel was holding something back.

"They might have been tracking Jonah and I was likely a coincidence," I lied. It was me they were chasing. I knew this for certain after observing them in the vision.

"Jonah drank your blood and he was able to end a large number of Second Generations with his bare hands, alone. You're important to them and we must find out why. You won't be safe until we do, and I need you to be safe, Lai." His worried eyes shimmered and I became instantly agreeable. He cared about me, he wanted to protect me, and he wanted me here with him.

I answered with the most definite of nods.

"Come on, I need to introduce you to the family." He stood and offered me his hand, which I gladly took; I followed him into the kitchen. I wanted to hide behind Gabriel as we entered to a reception of several Vampires. "Cessie, you've met Hanora."

I flicked a quick glance in the girl's direction. She still seemed fairly aloof.

"This is Ruadhan, Brooke, and Michael, who you met this morning."

I greeted them with a nod of my head.

Ruadhan was the oldest in human years by far; he appeared to be in his late forties.

His Irish name and symmetrical features made me wonder if he were in some way linked to Hanora.

Brooke was curious. The nearest to my own age, she was small and incredibly skinny with shiny red hair cut into a long bob drifting at her shoulders. Plastered in makeup and with a *Vogue* magazine under her arm, she appeared every inch a Valley Girl. She was conventionally pretty, and I wondered how much of the venom that had turned them all had affected their appearances.

Michael was by far the plainest of the group. He was in his late twenties perhaps, and dressed in blue jeans with a shirt layered by a knitted sweater. All their clothes looked expensive, and their obvious wealth intimidated me. Michael's face was pale and shiny like the others', but his actual features were fairly indistinct. Simple brown eyes, a small bump in the arch of his nose. His build was average.

"It's a pleasure to meet you," Ruadhan offered first. "Gabriel has explained that you'll be staying with us from now on."

"Yes," I answered carefully.

"Well then, welcome, love!" he chirped. "I'm sure you'll like living here, it's a beautiful property and we're surrounded by glorious scenery. I would be delighted to show you around the village when you're ready," he offered kindly, and he seemed sincere. I liked him instantly.

"Thank you," I replied courteously. "That would be nice."

"Is it true that Jonah drank your blood?" Brooke's accusation sliced through the air.

"Urm . . . Yes. I didn't give him a lot of choice."

"Brooke, you know what happened. Cessie helped Jonah. He is still with us because she assisted him." Gabriel fired her an annoyed look that seemed to say "stop talking."

"Assisted him! Jeez! You're lucky you're still breathing! Honestly, who goes around offering themselves like that anyway!" she continued petulantly.

I started to sense that it wasn't my risky sacrifice that she was interested in; it was my connection to Jonah. "Really, there was no alternative," I defended myself.

A short, sharp snigger came from the far corner, where Hanora stood. And I couldn't help but feel that she was rather enjoying this little exchange. I didn't want to appear like an argumentative child, so I put an end to the conversation.

"Gabriel, would you mind if I take a nap? I'm a bit tired." It wasn't a lie. I was torn between starving hunger and an overwhelming need to close my eyes, just for a short while.

"Of course. I'll show you to your room."

"I look forward to getting to know you all," I offered uncomfortably as he whisked me off.

Politely, he stepped behind me and guided me through the hallway and up a huge staircase. He directed me to the landing, passing several doors as we went, eventually ending up at the far end. He turned the heavy steel handle and opened the room up for me. I stepped inside and observed my surroundings. The room itself was sizable, decorated neutrally in whites, which contrasted with the dark wooden beams that ran across the ceiling.

In the center there was a four-poster king-sized bed draped with expensive white-and-silver sheets. The hardwood flooring was mostly covered with a chocolate-brown rug that the bed sat upon, extending to a few inches in from the baseboards. I considered the ornate dresser, topped with a circular mirror, placed in the corner. It looked as though it once belonged to a prima ballerina or a lauded actress. I stepped farther in and saw an additional door, which I walked toward.

"Your en suite."

Behind the bed on the back wall ran enormous built-in closets and it occurred to me that I had no clothes, nothing at all. "I would never be able to fill that in a lifetime!" I joked, astounded.

Gabriel walked over and slid the mirrored door across, revealing several outfits, a dressing gown, silk pajamas, and slippers. "Borrowed from Brooke. She'll take you shopping so you can pick out everything you need yourself," he said, beaming.

"That's kind of her. I assume you had something to do with that offer. I get the distinct impression she's not my biggest fan."

"Don't mind her, she's still very young and she's quite protective of Jonah. He saved her, you see."

"Like you saved me a few days ago." Maybe Brooke and I had something in common.

Gabriel sighed. "If only I had been able to save you," he murmured. "I would have spared you a lot of pain and myself . . ." He trailed off. His gaze fell to my midriff. I shifted uncomfortably. He moved in and stood squarely in front of me and said, "May I take a look?"

"Did Jonah tell you?" I stuttered.

"He may have mentioned . . . I tended to your wound, I'd already seen—"

I stood uncomfortably still.

"There might be something I can do," he offered.

I met his eyes and searched them; it dawned on me that he had gifts of his own.

My feet sank into the rug as I strode across the room and gently shut the bedroom door. He watched me cautiously as I made my way over to the bed, flicking the flats off, letting them fall untidily to the side. I climbed onto the bed, plumping a couple of pillows on top of each other. I inhaled through my nose slowly. My top was still torn underneath the cardigan; all I had to do was slip it off. I did so, keeping hold of the front of the shirt across my chest as I lay down. I nestled my face in the side of the pillow, my hands close to my face. My loose curls tickled my exposed back at my waist.

I felt Gabriel sit down next to me. He stroked my hair tenderly at first before gradually sweeping it away from my skin. *Oh, Lai.*

I winced, changing my mind instantly. This wasn't a good idea; I didn't want him looking at it. I started to scramble up.

Shhhh, it's okay. His voice in my mind calmed me once more. I relaxed again. I felt his hands glide over my skin, his fingertips running up and down my scar. Goose bumps spread over me. His touch was so soothing; it was unlike anything else in the world. *What happened to you?*

I didn't want to revisit it, but I didn't want to hide anything from him. *I don't know exactly. A Vampire.* I was drifting off, deeper into the tunnel.

What was his name?

Frederic.

I didn't want to name him. There were black spots of him in my memory, even though it had happened in this lifetime, just over three years ago. Part of the story was missing, which made it difficult to recall the first few chapters. Although the details were sketchy, the wave of emotion that spread over me was pure desperation and complete, all-encompassing fear.

As I conjured his face, it flashed across my mind, and I jolted back. I felt Gabriel place both his hands across the ridge of my spine, easing me. But I couldn't control it; complete recollection came tumbling through rapidly.

Images of us working together in a patisserie seeped through first. I was laughing, he was laughing. He was my friend. Images of him leaving the shop with different girls, grinning like a naughty schoolboy as he went.

I had thought it was funny; I didn't know. I'd tucked it all away; I hadn't wanted to think of him again. I knew Gabriel was watching, able to see everything I saw.

What did he do to you? Gabriel's voice sang through my disturbing thoughts.

Why do you want me to see it again? Why do you want me to watch?
I was starting to panic. I knew what came next.

I have to know what happened to be able to take it away.

I didn't have time to respond before the memory flooded through my consciousness. I watched myself walking out of the exit at the back of the shop; I heard Frederic locking up behind me. I recoiled inside as I saw myself choke when the cruel steel sliced through my skin, scraping along my bone. I saw myself thud to the floor, my head hitting the curb.

For a moment, I couldn't see the scene any longer and I strained to focus. Then I suddenly realized I was no longer watching.

Somehow I was back in my own body. I was reliving the experience.

I couldn't get up. A trickle of blood crept past my vision and I tried to move my hands to my head but my arms were like bricks, dead weights down at my side. I heard the thick clanking of the chain fastened to the hook that was dug deep into my back, and he began dragging me across the ground at an accelerated speed. I screamed as I felt the hook etch through my skin as he pulled me along callously, the laceration traveling up toward my neck. I convulsed as it ripped through my nerves, tearing through the muscle.

He stopped running and I was facedown in the dirt. Only then did he stoop down to my level, and I watched the flames whirl around his prodigious pupils. This was the first time I could remember knowing and experiencing the cold brutality of the species known as Vampire. His razor-sharp fangs baring over me, he hungrily tasted the trail of blood from my forehead staining down to my cheek, but restrained himself from furthering his desire. I gasped for air. The blinding pain floated in a cloud, above me, outside my body.

Abruptly, his confident and malevolent expression changed. Snapping his mouth closed, hiding his gleaming fangs, he receded like a wild animal that had inadvertently woken a far greater beast. He shriveled and stumbled and then from the emptiness I saw her, moving straight for him. Her jet-black hair flowed loosely, cascading down her back. Her shriek filled the air. It was so dark that I could barely make out her silhouette as she circled around Frederic. Her chin tilted up, her face still covered with night. The red furnaces that replaced her eyes instantly blinded me. It was her, the girl in shadow.

Blackness. Darkness. Nothingness.

Excruciating, intolerable pain streamed down my back. My eyes flew wide open. I couldn't move, unable to speak, scream, or cry. I was trapped, suspended in time, halfway between memory and reality. I needed to vomit.

I was sure Gabriel was trying to break through, but I was alone; he had left the tunnel a long time ago. I struggled, willing myself to return. Gabriel's eyes were suddenly fixated on my own, his words falling over themselves to reach me, but it was like watching the TV on mute. I almost laughed; it was comical. Laughing, yes! He was funny. I think he'd always made me laugh. I wanted to be with him. He felt so warm, so easy, his arms so protective. . . . Oh, to be in those arms, so safe. The room seemed to be displacing, spinning behind him. That was odd, bedrooms weren't supposed to spin.

I didn't know what was happening to me, my brain was jumbled, the waves weren't connecting, everything was wrong. This was wrong! Panic rising, my throat tightened and I struggled to breathe.

I had to calm down. Yes, that was it, I had to just stop, stop trying, stop everything! I wasn't in France, I wasn't with Frederic, and I wasn't dying.

And just like that the whole room curved and then popped in; like a large bubble, it burst. My agony subsided along with it.

"I'm here! Can you hear me?" Gabriel was on me, with me, all around me. An aura of light exuded from his skin, caressing and holding me, like a blanket wrapping around my soul.

I trembled as I grappled for the pillows and hoisted myself up. Automatically I reached for my back; Gabriel's strong arm was already steadying me. A disobedient tear smeared across my cheek.

"Is it gone?"

He stared intensely at me, a bewildered and terrified look smacked across his face.

"No." He paused. "I lost you, Lai, I lost you to the darkness. You disappeared."

"I thought maybe you were detaching it somehow." It was my only explanation for the pain that was as real as it had been the first time I had endured it.

"I would never hurt you like that."

I believed him.

I jumped off the bed, tripping as my legs woke up. I revolved in front of the mirror. My skin was unchanged, the same violent damage marked me as it had for the last few years. My head lurched heavily and I felt dizzy.

I glanced back to the mirror and watched, astonished, as a trickle of blood drizzled down my forehead. I felt disoriented, woozy. I placed my hand across my head and presented the palm to myself, smeared with my blood.

I staggered back to Gabriel before my legs could crumple underneath me. I halted as I reached him, as if I had hit an invisible wall. I could see it now; he was caked in crimson red. All over his hands, his arms, his shirt, even smudged across his temple.

My blood.

I was going to faint; Gabriel caught me as I dropped to the floor.

SEVEN

STARTLED, I bolted upright.

Gabriel was at my side, dumbfounded. I was back on the bed. "It's okay, I'm here." His words washed over me and I felt reassured.

I wiped the stain from my cheek while he watched as the cut to my head began to recede. He was still immersed in reds. I sat motionless, trying to acclimatize back to reality, managing only shallow breaths. My heart was still pounding against my chest, my hands shaking uncontrollably. "Sorry, I'm squeamish. The sight of blood makes me . . ." I tried to explain.

Gabriel looked down at himself, peeled off his shirt, and threw it out of sight, exposing his toned torso. My eyes lit up and my cheeks burned a little in response. He must have thought I was embarrassed as, self-consciously, he leaped off the bed. I automatically reached for him, grazing his arm. I didn't want him to go. I didn't have to ask; he was already sitting back beside me.

"I don't know what happened. I'm so sorry," he began.

"It's all right."

"I had to see it play out so I could reverse it, but you stopped remembering. Everything fell into darkness," he continued, confused.

His face was strained, its glow dulled, as if the sun was setting, casting him in shadow. I knew then that the moment I stopped watching and inadvertently transported back into my body, he had lost the connection.

"How exactly does it work?" I asked.

"I'm not of this world. I have certain gifts here; they are very strong in this dimension. I had willed my powers away when I returned to Earth. My desire was to fall, to become mortal." His words cut through me, stinging, to the core.

"You wanted to die?" The very idea caused a lump to form in my throat. "Why?" I whispered.

"It's complicated. But I welcomed death, if that's what you'd call it. They would not grant me mortality for their own ends. But then from nowhere, there you were, lying in my arms. And I was thankful to them for refusing me in spite of their motivations."

Gabriel spoke in riddles a little more often than I liked.

"Who wouldn't grant you mortality?" I asked.

"The Arch Angels. Only they can decide if an Angel will be allowed to fall. Requests of such kind, now at least, are very rare." Gabriel shifted his weight, seemingly uncomfortable with the question I had asked.

"Are you some sort of healing Angel?" My knowledge of the supernatural was hardly up to speed and my mind was still throbbing.

"No, Lailah. I was an Angel of Death."

That shut me up.

He raised his eyebrows and smiled nervously, showing off those divine dimples. "Don't worry. I went rogue a long time ago," he added lightly. "Healing is just an ability all Angels, no matter what their job title, so to speak, possess on this plane."

I nodded.

His blond hair fell over his temple delicately and all I wanted to do was reach out and touch it, touch him. "So healing is just one of your gifts. You have others?"

"Yes, all Angels do when we are here on Earth." He didn't elaborate.

He shifted his weight nearer to me, and the warmth of his body temptingly radiated toward me. "I should have been able to take it away, but you stopped too soon. I don't know what happened. You were seeing the memory and I was watching along with you. I saw everything: your confusion, your fear, your helplessness." His eyes grew larger. He moved his muscular arm behind my back and placed his hand on my scar. His expression was indecisive before he asked, "Did you feel it?"

I shuddered as his words hit me and, as was becoming almost habitual, he pulled me in to his chest, his hand squeezing my waist, comforting me. He was so warm I sank into him, contentment flowing through me.

"No," I lied, saving him.

The lines in his forehead ironed out a little; he seemed relieved. I had lost the connection to Gabriel. He wouldn't have been able to sense anything from me, I guessed. I had to choose to let him in. Unconsciously I must have blocked him out in time to spare him that at least. Or maybe transitioning back into my body had automatically cut him out. I didn't know. How could I have been back in the past? Physically able to feel everything all over again? And if I were there again, did I have the power to change the memory, to do things differently? Or was I just trapped inside myself, unable to do anything but relive what had already happened?

"I was back here, in this room, beside you. Your scar began opening up and . . ." He stopped himself there.

"I know," I replied, feeling for the gash on my head that had already healed itself.

"But how can that be? How can something that has already physically happened repeat itself, in the here and now? I don't understand. . . ."

That made two of us. Only he was oblivious that when he disconnected, I stopped watching and began reliving it, locked in. He couldn't know. If he did, then it would be obvious to him that I had felt every inch of that hook.

Silence drifted between us.

"You were all alone, suffering at his hands." For a moment his face flashed, and as it cooled, sadness hung across his expression.

"I'm not alone now," I offered softly.

He peered down at me. Skimming my cheek with the back of his fingers, gently he leaned in, close enough that I could feel his breath against my cheekbone. "Jonah is outside," he mumbled, breaking the moment too soon.

Jonah didn't bother to knock, flinging open the door and marching toward us. Then he faltered, seeing me nestled so closely to a shirtless Gabriel.

"Jonah," Gabriel acknowledged him.

"I smelled blood."

Rising to his feet, ignoring Jonah, Gabriel directed himself just to me. "It's time I was leaving, Cessie." He emphasized my nickname as if reminding me that I had to remain hidden; that no one else in this house should be aware of my supernatural self. I wasn't about to disagree. For now, at least, I would wear my mask. I would continue to be Cessie.

Gabriel literally had to pry Jonah from my room, and I wondered for a moment why this Vampire, who had seemed so arrogant and disinterested in me at the start, was suddenly so concerned about me. I couldn't help but think that perhaps he just wanted another taste of my blood.

The door slammed and without Gabriel next to me, a sharp prickle of loathing stabbed my consciousness. I felt invaded again. I had to cleanse my skin. Snatching the silk pajamas and dressing gown from the wardrobe, I tiptoed to the bathroom and ran a deep, boiling-hot bath.

Removing my clothes, I stepped inside, immersing myself in the clean water. Using the rosemary soap, I scrubbed and scrubbed, peeling off what felt like one layer of skin until my knuckles ached with the effort. Flexing my hands in front of me, I was surprised to find dirt embedded underneath my fingernails, where I'd clung to the damp mud in my struggle against Frederic.

I took a deep breath and sank under the water. I opened my eyes and breathed out of my nose, watching the pockets of air bubbles swirling around me. I thought about Frederic once more, careful not to dissolve too deeply into the memory, for fear I would lose control again.

I went straight to the image of the blaze instead—the next thing I could remember after I was blinded by those fierce eyes.

Lighting up the clearing in between the trees, it was Frederic who burned. I could suddenly smell him. I didn't see it happen, but I didn't have to; everything inside me told me that it was him. She'd ended him, the girl in shadow. It could only have been her, considering the expression that Frederic had worn, evidently realizing her power just before it happened. I didn't know who she was; her face was always masked in the darkness. Nor did I know why she had saved me, why she seemed to appear in my times of crisis. Perhaps she followed me? Perhaps it was just some random, weird coincidence? And how had she healed me? The deep laceration had already closed and was scarring by the time the fire had faded out to ashes. I'd felt an odd sense of satisfaction as the flames had flickered against the blackness. I didn't die; she'd fixed me immediately, somehow.

Pushing my body back out of the water, I sucked in the air, scraping my wet hair behind my back. I had to change my train of thought to happier things. I thought about Gabriel instead. He had come so close to me. If Jonah hadn't interrupted, would he have kissed me? I couldn't work out what he felt toward me. I could only wait for him to reveal more of himself to me. I hoped he would soon.

Tiredness sneaked up on me, so I decided to take a nap. It had been another long and eventful day, and it wasn't even close to being over yet.

I patted my body dry, heat radiating from my skin. I slipped on the pastel-pink pajamas and stepped through the door back into the bedroom, drying my feet as I went. I approached the bed and saw that a tray sat at the bottom; a hot cup of tea, a cheese sandwich, pastries, and fruit tempted me. No sign of the chef, but I guessed it was Gabriel who was taking care of me. The warmth of the tea filled me and I enjoyed gorging on the fruit. As the crisp taste of the grapes danced on my taste buds, I felt revitalized.

I was so hungry. In a very unladylike manner, I scarfed piece after piece of fruit. A pocket of juice squirted out of my lips from the nectarine that I was chewing on, dribbling down my chin. I smudged my lips with the back of my hand. A thick, red liquid trickled down my knuckles, shocking me. Confused, I spat out the fruit. It looked perfectly normal.

Gripping the remnants of the nectarine in my hand, I nearly fell off the bed in my haste to get to the bathroom. The mirror was still steamed up, so I quickly wiped my sleeve across it. I shot backward. My mouth was oozing the same thick maroon-colored substance, tarnishing my pearly white teeth. What was it and where was it coming from? I couldn't fathom it. Then my thoughts rewound: hadn't the same strangeness happened to me while Frederic burned? I paused for a moment and thought back once more to the blaze, but this time I needed to inspect my hands. In my memory, I had been so entranced by the flames and the smell of the bonfire that I hadn't taken any time to observe myself except for the scar that had formed on my back. I needed to see my hands, I had to get back into my body, but I didn't know how to control it.

Emptying all thoughts from my mind, I let the images fill my memory and cautiously focused harder. I was still watching myself stand at the bonfire, not reliving the event. I was straining to see when the fire, roaring in the background, drifted into my concentration. I began to feel its heat spread over me. The sensation was intense and I allowed it to ride across my body, surrendering myself to the moment.

I found myself once more inside my body, back into the past.

It was so real again; the flames burned brightly and I squinted and coughed as the bitter, pungent aroma filled my lungs, reeking like melting paint. I didn't feel the same sense of awe that I did the first time I was here. I wasted no time; I threw my hands up to my face and, sure enough, they were covered in the ruby-red solution. I smeared the tips of my fingers against my jeans and ran them over my lips and gums, revealing the same substance. It resonated through me, perturbing my taste buds. It was addictively sweet, but also oddly metallic in my mouth. Then it hit me. This was blood, but not my blood.

Panicking, I willed myself back to the bathroom, back to the present and, sure enough, I returned to the exact same position that I'd left. Urgently, I swilled my mouth with the cold water from the tap, gargling and spitting it into the sink until the redness washed away and the water ran clear. I lifted my head up to the mirror but instantly withdrew when, for a split second, the eyes that reflected back at me glinted red in reply. I stumbled, unbalanced, and tried to regain some state of calm as I worked my way back to the bed.

Dropping onto the tray the remains of the nectarine that I was still clutching in my hand, it bumped and rolled and my gaze followed it. All the other leftover pieces of fruit were painted red. I gulped hard and threw them into the wastebasket.

What was happening to me? I couldn't help but wonder if being in such close proximity to these unearthly beings was in some way drawing out the abnormality that hid under my own skin.

EIGHT

I SLEPT FOR WHAT SEEMED TO BE only a few short hours; but when I finally got dressed and made my way down to the living room, Gabriel informed me that I'd actually been out for a couple of days. He made me a cup of tea and we sat down together on the tan leather sofa.

"You look very pretty in that dress," he commented.

I thought he was just being polite. I pulled a face. "Every outfit Brooke has lent me is either pink or purple and nearly all made of silk for some reason!"

I was sitting awkwardly, feeling uncomfortable, but grateful that the black skinny jeans I had borrowed in the first place were still intact. I'd pulled them on since the strappy minidress was barely covering me.

Gabriel chuckled. "Hmm . . . Brooke is very young. She likes to think of herself as being at the height of the trends."

"I guess my taste is a little old-fashioned by comparison. . . ."

I watched him as we bantered about the dress, or lack thereof. His blond curls were tickling his forehead, bobbing down past his ears, and his large, wide eyes were alert. His fresh, model-like looks certainly drew my eye, but it was far more than that. I felt an invisible pull toward him, like we were deeply connected; I just wanted to be near him.

I gathered he wanted to talk business by the way he continually cracked his knuckles, but as his eyes softened and his face relaxed, I could see he was enjoying chatting with me. Perhaps business could wait a little longer.

"Now, I want you to get back to some form of normality," he told me.

Perhaps not.

"This last week has been a strain on you to say the least. You've been through so much; I just want you to settle in and be happy." He smiled.

I nodded in agreement. I could definitely use some routine, but I still had questions.

He answered me before the words met the air. "I'm quite sure you still desire answers, and I will share those with you; but all in good time, Cessie."

When he used that name, I realized we weren't alone in the house.

I cast my gaze around the room, eventually settling it on the door, and Gabriel nodded his head in reply. I understood. We would have to keep this conversation light.

"So I have a few things for you." His face brightened as he reached over to the glass-topped coffee table and produced a bag of goodies. "First, an iPhone. The phone number is on the box. I've given it to everyone in the house and I have programmed in all our numbers for you," he said.

My eyebrows raised; I had never owned such an extravagant piece of equipment—well, not to my knowledge at least. "Thank you, it's fantastic!" I beamed.

Delving into his pocket, he produced a shiny gold credit card and handed that to me next. "I've had you added to my account. You need clothes and shoes and all those things that Brooke tells me girls need." He laughed. "She's promised to take you shopping, though I have to say, better you than me—she's a keen shopper!" His eyes glistened playfully.

"No, I can't take that." I had never relied on anyone to pay my way and I had no intention of starting now. I tried to give it back to him, but he refused.

"Seriously, please take it. Think of it as a gift. Think of it as a thank-you for helping Jonah," he pushed, but I still shook my head.

He leaned over and whispered, "Please let me feel as though I have done something for you, even if it is barely a scratch in comparison to the penance I have to repay."

Here we go, talking in riddles again. I stared back at him blankly, but I could tell he wasn't going to budge, so I conceded. "Fine, but I'll pay you back once I've found a job," I insisted, waving the card in the air.

"A job?" he replied quizzically. "When I say that we need to get your life back to normal, you must understand that you need to re-main hidden."

"Oh, well, I can't just stay here every day, I have to work."

He rolled up the sleeves of his posh royal blue sweater, as if to tell me that he meant business. His expensive attire made me feel even more inadequate, but I doubted dressing myself in designer clothes would fix that problem.

With a serious tone, he pushed on. "No, you don't. You can leave the house but only with one of us. We need to keep you protected; you're vulnerable on your own. I'm trying to make sense of some things, but in the meantime it's for the best if you remain here. If you must go out, I will insist that it's under the protection of one of us."

I readied myself to argue with him, to tell him that I was not a prisoner and I could look after myself.

"Though I hope you don't mind," he continued, "that will generally, mostly . . . always be me." The edges of his lips curved up. It only took the smallest hint of that luscious smile of his, creeping back up his cheeks, to cause me to change my mind and become instantly amenable. So I returned the smile. "But first you have to go shopping with Brooke. . . ."

As I glanced up to the door, Brooke stepped through it, right on cue. "Jeez! You're not supposed to wear jeans with that dress!"

She rolled her eyes at me, irritated, and I frowned at Gabriel. "Why do I have a feeling I'll regret this?" I grinned sarcastically.

"Regret what exactly?" Brooke replied. "Come on, we're going in to town."

She grabbed my hand, yanking me up. She surprised me, and I jerked away from her, but I caught myself quickly. If I was going to live here, I would have to get used to the fact that my roommates were Vampires. One way or another, I would have to learn to trust them. I turned back around to Gabriel and picked up the shiny new phone from the sofa.

"Not town," Gabriel warned, dipping his eyebrows.

"What? But Oxford Street calls!"

"No, stay local. Go to Windsor, there's plenty of shops there, it's perfectly adequate."

Gabriel was clearly the leader of this pack; they all seemed to abide by his rules.

Brooke huffed and made a disgruntled face. She seemed so much younger than she looked, which was odd for a Vampire. I would have thought that with more years behind them, even if their faces didn't show it, they would be more mature and worldly.

"It's not fair, just because she's being chased! Why do I have to suffer? I don't even want to go with her!"

"I'm being chased?" That caught my attention more than Brooke's clear disdain.

Gabriel stood up and paced over to the doorway where we were both standing.

"No, Cessie. You're not being chased," he replied calmly, easing me momentarily.

"Yes she is. I heard you talking to Jonah," she shot back snidely, clearly pleased with her eavesdropping skills. "You said that Eligio and his clan are still looking for her."

I turned to Gabriel for the truth.

"Cessie, what Jonah and I were discussing, *privately*"—he emphasized his last word and glared at Brooke as he did—"was simply that there is a chance that they're still trying to find you, that's all. Nothing more than what we already suspected."

I tapped my foot on the floor, irritated; he was holding something back, I knew he was. "And?"

"And nothing."

If there was nothing more to add, then why could I feel him blocking me from his thoughts? I didn't appreciate being kept in the dark.

"Brooke, go and pull your car out of the garage. Cessie will be with you in a minute."

She flicked her red hair, banging the door shut as she left.

"Well?" I said.

"It's nothing to be concerned about, but Michael has been feeling Eligio's presence a little stronger since we got back." Still he was trying to protect me, putting it as gently as possible.

"More than he normally would?"

"Yes; Michael's only been parted from his clan very recently, he's our newest addition. So his connection to his Gualtiero is stronger than that of any of the others."

"I don't understand. Does that mean that everything he knows, this Eligio knows too?"

"Not at all. Eligio created Michael, his venom will always be part of him, and as such, they will always sense each other to a degree. It's only when one or the other changes their proclivity that they essentially tune in to one another," Gabriel explained, trying to soothe me. "Michael can sense that something has changed within Eligio; he feels him stirring. But it could be anything."

I let out a breath. It could have been worse. After all, when I saw them outside the burning rubble of the house in Creigiau, there was no question in my mind that they would try to seek me out.

"But we have to be cautious. You're certainly precious." He smiled.

"Fine." I accepted his explanation, just in time to be startled by the impatient honk of Brooke's horn. "I better go, she's waiting for me."

Reluctantly I reached for the heavy handle, pulling the door back open.

Stay close to Brooke, and be careful. His words filled my mind and I answered him with a thumbs-up as I stepped through the hallway and out of the front door.

Brooke wriggled in the driver's seat, revving the engine of a brand-new Mini Cooper; pink, of course. I plonked myself down in the passenger seat and we sped off down the drive.

As we zipped through the gate, she grabbed a jacket from the backseat and threw it at me. "You'll freeze."

I pulled it on over the ridiculous dress. "So, Windsor? Shopping . . ." I said, trying to start a conversation.

"Nope, Oxford Street. You know, London?"

Ah. Gabriel would not be pleased, but I didn't want to put her out.

"And don't even think about telling Gabriel."

Brooke drove the car as if she were competing in the Grand Prix, eventually breaking the speed limit considerably. The landscape in London was vastly different from that of Hedgerley. I swapped views of endless greens for built-up concrete and towering buildings. Brooke blared some rock band or another and as the song hit the chorus, I recognized it to be the same band that Jonah had played in the Range Rover.

Turning down the volume, I said, "I didn't see Jonah this morning. Is he okay?"

Brooke's face strained for a moment before she replied, "He's fine. He's been out feeding more than usual, so he hasn't been in the house much since we got back."

She made no attempt to water down his eating habits; I quite liked how straight-talking she was. It was easy to see that she hadn't taken kindly to my arrival, but the fact that she cared so little about me actually endeared her to me somewhat. Brooke didn't give me a chance to respond, turning the volume back up and placing her large black Dior sunglasses over her eyes from on top of her head.

IT WAS DECEMBER and Christmas shopping was in full swing on Oxford Street. We'd been on the go for about four hours and though Brooke was laden with bags, I had only managed to muster up the energy to pick out a simple, long woolen coat and a pair of flat, plain shoes. I was entirely practical about clothing, living in sweaters and jeans. Brooke, on the other hand, was anything but practical when it came to her purchases, selecting only expensive designer shops to grace with her presence. I had spent some time complimenting Brooke on her various outfit changes, and she seemed a little happier with me and offered to take me to a coffee shop for some tea and cake.

As I sat in the far corner of Starbucks, mug of tea and pastry in hand, my attention briefly caught on a light bouncing off the window; but when I looked again, it was gone.

Brooke slid into the cushioned seat in front of me and watched, barely moving, as I added several sugars to my tea.

"Right, the next few hours we are dedicating to finding you some clothes. Gabriel will be rather displeased with me if I return you with one measly jacket!"

"One measly jacket? It's Chanel! Did you see the price tag?" I said. I was ashamed at having let Brooke coerce me into purchasing something so expensive on Gabriel's shiny gold card.

"Money is hardly relevant. We have bigger concerns."

"Such as?" I asked, taking a small bite out of the éclair that had tempted my appetite.

"Such as existing each day trying not to kill anyone," she whispered.

I almost thought she was trying to scare me off, so I replied showing as little emotion as possible. "But you do . . . kill?"

"Yes, sometimes it happens. We only feed when we have to—a must-need basis, if you know what I mean. Not for sport. It's the way things have to be. Gabriel wouldn't tolerate us otherwise. He's an Angel, you know," she added with a grin.

"I heard."

She looked annoyed that she hadn't been the one to deliver the news, but she pushed on. "So, human girl, what's the deal with you anyway?" she asked, fussing with her hair.

"No deal. Just wrong place, wrong time, I guess," I said, trying to be casual.

"Been there!" She laughed, but sadness turned the edges of her lips.

I didn't think now was the time to ask her how she had come to be a Vampire.

"Hmm . . . So why are we hiding you? What's so special about you, that you have Purebloods on your heel?" She lowered her tone. "And why is Gabriel so protective of you?"

I could have smiled when she said the last part; it made me happy to think she knew he cared. "I guess he feels that keeping me safe is only fair. As you say, he's an Angel; he's obliged to do the right thing."

I almost wondered myself if that's all there was to it, despite our history. Maybe he was just obliged; he had commented that he had a penance to pay.

"I'm not sure why they're trying to find me. Perhaps they're mad that I helped Jonah escape? As I said—wrong place, wrong time."

At the mention of Jonah, Brooke's limited attention span perked up. "Well, I guess we have you to thank for that. We wouldn't have wanted to lose him." She moved her neck and rubbed her shoulder.

"Are you and Jonah an item?" I asked, attempting to flatter her. I didn't think they were, but I hoped to encourage her to drop her guard.

"Oh, well, no. But we are closer than you could imagine! He actually saved me from . . . well, you know. I'm sure he wants me, and maybe we would be together, if we could be." She quickened her sentence defensively.

"I'm sure, but he's a bit older than you though, isn't he?"

"Depends how you look at it. I guess so. But that's not why we can't be together."

She ended her sentence abruptly, as if she had said too much.

Can't? I blew on my tea and sipped it, casually slipping in a "Why?"

"Just the way things are. Vampires"—she lowered her voice once more—"can't be with other Vampires, physically. It's sort of forbidden. But you know a Vampire could never be with a human either. Not really, it'd never work out," she said, pretending to look through the tops of her shopping bags.

"Well, what human would want to go out with Jonah!" I said. I giggled, trying to break the tension; I was afraid she might close up.

Feeling less threatened, she attempted a smile.

"Why is it forbidden?" I pushed, taking another bite out of my creamy bun.

"You're new to all this so I'll cut to the chase. You'll never see many girls—well, girls like me. Very few are created, or so I'm told.

If a male and female were to give in to their desires they would likely end up"—she pointed at my cup—"you know, what you're doing now, from each other."

"And that's a problem?"

"Because of what runs through our blood, yes. One feeding off the other is one thing but that sensation would lead to both feeding from one another. At that point, neither would be able to stop. The power of each individual would be transferring, mixing between the two. Ultimately one would be ended. The males are more powerful so inevitably it's the female that gets it." She was enthusiastically explaining now, enjoying my reactions.

"Right, so it's forbidden by who?"

"By the Masters; it reduces their numbers. Though Ruadhan told me that sometimes they would allow it—manipulate it, even, on purpose—if they wanted to strengthen a particular male in the clan. Not like Jonah could take up with a human either," Brooke continued. "It would take a lot of willpower to avoid the same end occurring for the unwitting girl."

She made sure she got that in.

"I'm surprised you got off so lightly, you must not have whet his appetite enough!"

I recalled the flash in Jonah's eyes as he had fed from me. I was sure I did more than whet his appetite, not that I was about to reveal that to Brooke.

"So you can never experience love?" I asked. By my reckoning, this tale was applicable to Brooke as much as it was to Jonah.

She almost snorted at me. "Love isn't an emotion that comes easily to . . . Vampires," she whispered again.

The coffee shop was bustling with tired shoppers. They chatted loudly, surrounding us in a cloud of half-heard conversations. I looked over my shoulder and when I felt safe that no one was listening in, I carried on. "But you love Jonah?" My statement tumbled out before I had a chance to stop and think.

Brooke looked like I had hit her in the face. It was the most honest expression I had seen her wear yet. She sat silently and I didn't dare break the silence first. I was half expecting her to throw a fit. I was suddenly thankful she kept the dark glasses on, masking her eyes. To my surprise, she lifted them instead, and spoke softly.

"Yes, maybe. It's more difficult for him. I never served a Gualtiero; Jonah did serve for some time. Perhaps I am closer to my humanity because of it. I'm sure, deep down, he must feel the same, but he knows how this works and he would never risk me like that."

As she said it, I nodded with empathy; though I couldn't help think that she had somewhat deluded herself. The Jonah I knew didn't exactly fit the "knight in shining armor" persona that she seemed to have created for her own fantasies. I thought she must have been lying to herself to avoid his rejection; that, I could genuinely sympathize with. I guess it was a lot less painful to accept than the truth.

I finished my tea and crumpled the paper that the éclair had sat in. I stood up, preparing myself for the rest of the shopping onslaught.

We moved fast from shop to shop and I picked up several practical pairs of skinny jeans and a few pairs of boots, including a black pair of something Brooke had referred to as "Uggies." Apparently, if I had to be practical I could at least be on trend, or so she insisted. Legs aching, my fingers sore from the plastic bags that dug into the palms of my hands, I was ready to give up and insist on calling it a day when a little boutique shop on the corner of the road caught my gaze.

The word MADEMOISELLE neatly swirled above the door.

Brooke tried to move me along, but before she could convince me, I had stepped through and was already scanning the racks of vintage clothing.

It was one floor, with only a few racks, but the items hung individually, each unique and distinct. Fingering my way through the lace tops carefully, I finally felt at home.

"This stuff is hardly vintage! Everything looks ancient!" Brooke said.

"It's beautiful," I replied, picking up an ivory-lace buttoned top.

I turned it around and saw that the back of it was absolutely stunning. I was saddened momentarily at the fact that I would have to wear a slip underneath to cover my scar.

Within fifteen minutes, I had literally filled the changing room with the most delicate fabrics and designs that I had ever seen. The clothing ranged from lace tops to muslin day dresses, though I had to agree with Brooke—most of the items looked incredibly dated. I popped on the lace blouse that had first caught my attention. Slipping it on over my curves, it rested neatly on my shoulders, molding to my contours perfectly.

I let my golden blond hair fall down my back, but slid in some pins to scrape the left side up. I then placed a black shawl around my shoulders, completing the look.

"Well, it's old-fashioned, but it is elegant on you," Brooke commented.

I didn't need convincing. I felt immensely happy in the outfit, even though I had teamed it with black skinny jeans; they seemed to modernize the outfit and bring it back into this century at least! I paid for my selection at the counter and begged Brooke to let us be finished.

"Ralph Lauren first. You need some sweaters; it's freezing cold in this damn country if you hadn't noticed!"

Eight identical sweaters in an array of colors, eight shirts, five blouses, and two more jackets later, she was dragging me through a shop called Selfridges, at which point I gave her full permission to pick out everything else without my approval; yet she continued to drag me around each section. This girl could seriously shop.

Two more hours and I had everything from peplum dresses to something called harem pants.

As I sought refuge in the shoe department, Brooke stole the opportunity and began wedging my feet into a pair of Christian Louboutin platforms.

"Okay! Enough! *Please* can we go now?" I said, throwing off the shoes and grabbing for my flats that were the ugly stepsister in comparison.

"Fine, but I am getting these for you; you need some heels. You do know you're a girl, right?"

"I don't do heels, Brooke. I do flats; plain and practical. When would I ever wear five-inch sandals exactly?"

"First, they are six inches, and they're stiletto peep-toes, not sandals. Second, you will thank me . . . at some point."

At that, she called the enthusiastic saleswoman back over and started pointing out a selection of stilettos to wrap up.

My jacket pocket started to vibrate and, surprised, I shoved my hand inside and produced the iPhone; I'd forgotten about that.

TIME TO COME BACK, IT'S NEARLY DARK, the text read. The name popped up as "Gabriel."

I had no idea what time it was; I had barely seen the outside today.

I typed a reply: *TRY TELLING BROOKE THAT.*

A few minutes later she returned and handed me yet more bags and the credit card, which I remorsefully zipped up in the pocket of the borrowed jacket.

"Frickin' Gabriel wants us to call it a day, come on," Brooke huffed.

Reluctantly Brooke ventured for the exit and, to my delight, we left the shop. As we began to walk down the street, I briefly paused to take in the beautiful Christmas window display that was now lit up. But Brooke snatched my arm and dragged me away before I had time to truly appreciate it.

I don't know how we managed to fit all the bags into the Mini; there certainly wasn't enough trunk space, so we made good use of the backseat. The headlights were the only things illuminating the street that we had parked on.

Brooke had already placed the sunglasses back over her eyes and I wondered why she wore them; it was winter after all. My toes were vibrating and had swelled in my shoes. The balls of my feet sighed with relief when I took my weight off them and collapsed into the passenger seat.

Traveling back, music blaring once more, I pondered on the conversation we had shared. I felt sorry for Brooke. If she fell in love with another one of her kind, which she already had, she could never be with him, not fully. Nor could she risk developing feelings for a mortal; she might end up killing him. That must be a bitter pill to swallow. I wondered when she had become a Vampire, questioning what kind of life she had lived prior to being changed, and who and what she'd had no choice but to leave behind.

As the buildings became spaced farther apart, I realized we weren't far from Hedgerley, so I loosened the seat belt around my chest and turned the music down so that I could thank Brooke for her time.

"What?" Brooke snapped, before I had a chance to speak.

"Sorry?" I said.

"What. Is. It?" she enunciated. "I like that song!"

"I just wanted to, you know, say thanks for taking me shopping."

Brooke wiggled her nose, causing her huge sunglasses to bob above her preened eyebrows.

"Can you see the road properly with those on?" I asked.

"Vampires can see in the dark, Cessie," she said.

"Oh, like cats."

"Christ! You'd do well to remember that we're deadly predators, not house pets."

I bowed my head and whispered under my breath, "I do remember. . . ."

I knew she heard me by the way she tilted her head, but she chose not to ask.

"I do bear a striking resemblance to Anne Hathaway, though—when she played Catwoman. Only hotter." She snorted. "You don't need to thank me for my personal shopping services, more for my benefit than yours."

"Oh, how so?" I asked, stretching my legs out in front of me.

"I have to be seen with you. Plus, Gabriel said if any of the locals see you with us, they have to assume you're a relative. And let's be honest, right now you look more like our maid than a member of the family. You stick out like a sore thumb."

The car jolted as Brooke swapped lanes, weaving in between the speeding cars.

I peered down to my scuffed shoes. She was right, I didn't fit in, and I definitely didn't look good enough to be seen by Gabriel's side.

Brooke took her eyes off the road, long enough to see my cheeks blush red in embarrassment.

She softened, in a way that only Brooke could. "Don't worry, Cinderella, you've got your glass slippers now, thanks to me. Just make sure you wear them."

Shrugging, she turned the music back up to full volume and began singing out of tune along to Jessie J's "Price Tag"—the irony was not lost on me.

NINE

GABRIEL SEEMED A LITTLE UNHAPPY when we reached the front door; nonetheless, he helped us carry all the bags inside.

"There's a cup of tea waiting for you on the kitchen table," he told me as he began taking the many shopping bags up the stairs to my room.

I made my way eagerly through the long hallway to the back of the house. Remembering my manners, I twisted around to once again thank Brooke, but she was gone; hanging up her prizes already, I was sure.

Sipping the warm cup of tea, the combination of the sugar and caffeine brought me back to life quickly. I hadn't even managed more than a few sips when Gabriel appeared and took a seat next to me.

"Did you have fun in Windsor?"

I bought some time by blowing on the tea to cool it. "Brooke was in her element shopping. I'm sorry, I think the credit card took a bit of a beating," I detracted.

"In Windsor?" he pressed again.

I said nothing.

"It's okay, I know you were in town."

I fidgeted a little and watched his straight face, not giving anything away.

"Yes. I'm sorry, I didn't want to upset her or anything and we were perfectly safe," I apologized bashfully.

"I know you were. I followed you."

"You followed us?"

"Do you honestly think I'd let you out of my sight, given the choice? Ever?" His face smoothed and his eyes glinted, almost testing for a reaction.

"Oh, um . . . why didn't you just come with us then?" I asked.

"I wanted you to spend some time with Brooke. You're of a similar age, or at least on the surface of things," he whispered. "I thought you should get to know each other, maybe strike up a friendship."

"That's wishful thinking; she's still not overly fond of me," I replied, clutching the handle of the sturdy white mug.

"Well, you also needed clothes and I'm afraid I'm not much use in that department. Plus she took you for tea, that's a good sign," he said.

A smile crept across his face and I went gooey inside.

"Maybe. She opened up a little, about her relationship with Jonah. And she told me that Vampires could never be with each other; that one would kill the other." Now I was testing for a reaction.

Gabriel pondered on that for a moment. "She's right. When one drinks from the other, a sort of fever starts. The blood fuses together and they absorb the other's power. They become attached, forever. Until one of them ceases to exist, no one and nothing would ever compare." Gabriel's shoulders slumped and he skewed his face to the side, frowning. He seemed contemplative.

"Wow. That was a straightforward answer."

"You asked a straightforward question." He stopped for a moment and caught my eye; he kept me suspended there for what felt like an eternity.

Part of me wished I could crawl deep into his eyes and curl up and sleep in them forever.

"So how is it one comes to kill the other? By your reckoning, if anything, it sounds as though they fall in love," I said.

"Either the one that drank the other becomes so obsessed with getting their next fix that ultimately no matter how deep the connection is, they will end up drinking the other to an end, or far worse; if they both drink from one another, the process is far more accelerated because neither can resist going back for more. One would always overpower the other. It's actually very sad. I have never known any Vampire able to connect with another and maintain a relationship without a violent end being the outcome. From what I've seen, their addiction always wins," he explained.

"You make them sound like drug addicts!"

"It's a far truer portrait of the situation than the fairy-tale love story you were opting for," he said.

I finished my tea and placed my mug down on the thick wooden table, bringing my hands up and playing with my nails self-consciously. I couldn't help but feel under the microscope with Gabriel, as though he was taking in my every movement, every glance. We sat in silence for a few minutes reflectively.

"Go ahead," he said.

"I'm sorry?"

"You wanted to ask something. . . ."

He was finely tuned in to me, and with his encouragement, I

said, "And what of that and Angels?" I kept my head down. I was teetering into potentially soul-crushing territory here.

"What of Angels?"

"Can an Angel love a Vampire?"

Hanora's face flashed across my mind. I had no desire to look at his expression. I was afraid of what he might be about to say, though his initial silence told me that I had caught him off guard. Whatever he had been expecting me to ask, it wasn't that.

Wasting little time, he tipped my chin up toward him, so I had no choice but to return his gaze. "That's not my business. This Angel's concerns are vested only in one individual."

Her name is Lailah.

I felt the cloud blow through my mind, replaced by his words, which danced—sparkling and shimmering. If it were possible, they were almost turning into colors, swirling, my mind awash with golds and silvers.

Bringing his hands down he placed them over my own, cupping them tightly, his warmth heating them instantly. His face was entirely serious. A long vein in his neck jutted out a little as he tensed. I tried to keep my poker face on for a few more seconds, but I couldn't help a smile creasing the edges of my lips.

I have so many questions. . . .

I was suddenly on the verge of tears. I felt so close to him. I knew him deeply, but I couldn't remember how. It was so frustrating.

"Shhhh," he soothed me through his pursed lips; he could sense my feelings. I knew because I could feel his washing over me.

Soon, Lailah, soon. I promise.

Gabriel left me hanging, again, but I slept well thinking of him.

As a glimmer of winter sun perforated the bedroom curtains, I woke gently. I felt happy, until I remembered the abundance of clothes that needed hanging up and sorting out.

I showered, brushed my teeth, and with Brooke's words from the car journey ringing in my ears, even ran a little makeup across my cheeks before I decided to brave sorting through the mountain of fabric. Finally, when the last pair of boots had been set neatly in the wardrobe, I picked out something to wear for the day. I opted for black skinny jeans, but was keen to wear the best find of the day—the beautiful lace blouse.

I grabbed for a pair of black knee-length Ugg boots and popped them on the bed. I made for the door and turned the key in the lock before rummaging for a matching bra and panties set and, of course, a camisole to cover up my scar. I slipped off my dressing gown and, stepping into the frilly undies, I began reaching for the bra when I suddenly stopped. The smell of rich fruits and sultry woods breezed through the air. I recognized the scent; Jonah wore it.

I spun around, covering myself with my arms in the process, and sure enough he was standing behind me, leaning against the wall. "Jonah!"

I snatched for the dressing gown from off the floor, but he traveled over so quickly he had it in his hands first.

"You want this?" he replied, handing it to me.

I flung it around my body and tied it up tightly, pushing my damp hair behind my ears. "Can I help you with something?"

"Well, if you're offering . . ."

He stepped into my space, overstepping the mark. I raised my hands and pushed his shoulders, and to my surprise, he fell back a little. He gathered himself rather quickly.

"Calm down! I'm just messing with you, Cessie!"

His smirk seemed to suggest he was pleased to get a reaction out of me.

"The door was locked."

"I'm a Vampire. Plus a locked door is too tempting to resist."

I scurried around to the other side of the bed, putting a little distance between us.

I was about to ask him to leave when I noticed his eyes seemed to have changed color—the hazel shade was diluted with flecks of maroon. Then I remembered what Brooke had said: he had been feeding a lot these last few days. I felt a chill run down my spine.

"How many people have you killed?" I demanded. I wasn't usually so assertive, but after what Brooke had said about there being occasional casualties in order for them to survive, I suddenly had to know.

"No light souls, I promise. Only the dark ones."

His words cut through me. I didn't care if they were good or bad. The very idea of him drinking from unwilling victims made my stomach churn; but I was well aware that I was wearing nothing but a dressing gown and underwear, so now didn't seem like the right moment to get into a heated debate.

He, on the other hand, was sporting a rather unusual russet red–colored rugby shirt with the collar flicked upward, which contrasted against his skin and eyes perfectly. His hair, which as I had come to know him was always tousled and flawlessly out of place, was no different this morning. He was stupidly good looking, and I felt a pinch of excitement low in my belly, and my cheeks began to burn in embarrassment.

"Dime for your thoughts?"

I shook the musings from my head, and gave myself a good dressing-down mentally.

"It's 'penny' for them, and trust me, my markup is higher than a penny."

He smirked at me before replying in a low murmur, "Name your price." Tilting his head, he winked at me and wetted his lips. His upturned smile was goading me, daring me even, to play his game.

"Again, did you need something?" I said, gesturing toward the door.

I'd never liked playing games.

Straightening himself he replied, "Only to say that I thought I would take you into the village, show you around."

He wasn't asking. He never seemed to ask.

"Thanks, but Ruadhan's actually on duty today. Gabriel's already arranged it."

Momentarily, I caught a look of disappointment flit over Jonah's face, but it only lasted for a brief second.

"Wouldn't you rather someone a little less ancient and a lot more fun take you sightseeing?"

Jonah seemed irritated that I hadn't jumped at the chance of spending some time with him. Judging by the lines on his forehead as he screwed up his face, you could tell that he didn't enjoy, and wasn't accustomed to, having to work for attention. This was someone who was used to being in charge, getting what he wanted the way he wanted it and whenever he wanted it.

"The last time you did that, I ended up pinned up against a wall, so I think I'll pass."

"Fine." He made for the door and I immediately felt guilty for reminding him that I hadn't quite let go of the incident in the cottage.

"Jonah, perhaps you could take me for a drink sometime? I hear there's a pub near here?" I softened, wanting to show a little more willingness.

He glanced at me over his shoulder as he went for the handle. "Perfect. It's a date."

I thought he almost sniggered and it quickly dawned on me that he had fooled me into agreeing to go drinking with him, rather than escorting me on a mundane tour. I was annoyed with myself; I would have to learn to be sharper.

I turned my back to him, and just before he pulled the door, he just couldn't help himself. "Nice butt, by the way!"

Argh! I was so cross with myself; he was way too cocky. He definitely needed taking down a peg or two, even if he was pretty gorgeous.

I was more cautious dressing after he left, trying to put my new clothes on under the dressing gown, just in case he decided to make a reappearance. I did however take a moment to check out the reflection of my bum in the mirror.

I towel-dried my hair and picked out a mini Mulberry satchel handbag, courtesy of Brooke. I popped the new iPhone and credit card inside, along with the house keys Gabriel had handed to me before I had retired.

From the dresser drawer, I checked on my assortment of fake IDs, including my passport. Ruadhan had ventured into the house in Creigiau after Eligio's clan had attacked Jonah and me, rescuing my only belongings from my backpack. Gabriel had sent him back provided the coast was clear; he didn't know what I had left behind. As I imagined Ruadhan searching the levels, I wondered if he had left the property in the same state as the one Gabriel and his Vampires had, as we sped off toward the motorway a few days later. I hoped he hadn't. Such a waste. However I was pleased to have my documentation; I'd need it if we had to leave the country quickly.

And so, I was ready to face the day.

I wandered down the hall, passing several doors as I went. I hadn't actually inquired who was staying in each of the rooms. I had hoped Gabriel had put me next to his. I reached the top of the stairs and Gabriel stood at the foot of them, waiting for me.

"Morning." He beamed.

He looked as luscious as ever; he had styled his blond curls behind his ears today, though a few stray strands still tickled his forehead. I bounced down the many stairs to the foot, where he was leaning his elbow against the wall at the bottom, one leg bent behind the other. I was about to greet him when his grin faltered and his face seemed to fall. I stopped at the last step, positioning me almost at eye level with him. Shuffling uncomfortably, he stared at me with that familiar puzzled look on his face.

"Um, everything okay?" I said.

"Yes, of course." He picked himself up quickly. "Where did you get that blouse from?"

"Oh, this one was my choice; we found a little vintage shop. You don't like it?" I said. I started to feel terribly self-conscious, even more so when Gabriel didn't answer.

Automatically I turned and began making my way back up the stairs. I needed to check my reflection.

"Wait!" He grabbed my arm and brought me back in to him. "It's quite lovely, really. I was taken aback to see you wearing a style like that. It just reminded me of, well, you."

He hadn't meant to say the last part. I wasn't an idiot.

"It's old-fashioned, I know; I just liked it. I'm sorry I reminded you of me." I was deflated.

We continued to stare each other out, neither of us flinching; finally he broke into a laugh at my stubborn expression and, even though I attempted to keep the frosty exterior going, I couldn't resist and I started laughing too.

"Being reminded of you, the you I knew, is never a bad thing. You just caught me off guard. I was expecting something a little different, that's all."

He recovered well and I was quick to forgive him as he stroked my arm with the back of his fingers. I got goose bumps almost immediately at his cool touch. It was strange that sometimes he felt so warm and other times he was ice cold. It was like he could control his temperature to suit.

Joining me on the step, he ran his palm underneath my hair and pressed his opened hand across the keyhole cutout of my blouse, bringing me in a little closer. Grazing my lower back as he swept his hand downwards, he leaned in to me, sweeping my waist-length curls out of the way.

"I think the detail is meant to show off your back. I hope you're wearing a top underneath because it's chilly and not because you are trying to cover up your scar?"

Gabriel had a way of hitting the nail on the head. That was, of course, precisely the reason.

"I don't like it. Even though my hair covers it, I feel more comfortable this way."

Sighing, I watched him become more troubled for me. "Come on!" he said, lightening the moment. "I have something to show you."

He found my hand and he led me right down to the back of the house, into a grand library, full of bookcases filled with all types of literature. At the far end, in the bay window overlooking the grounds, sat a beautiful custom-made wooden chessboard placed upon a mahogany table with two leather chairs on either side. It reminded me of an old man's den.

Sitting me down on a dark green chair, he made his way over to the corner of the room, pulling up a floorboard mysteriously. When he returned, he was clutching a heavy box that he placed carefully next to the board before sitting down opposite me. Opening it, he proceeded to place a set of red and white ivory chess pieces into their rightful positions on the board. He didn't rush and took his time to put each figure carefully in its correct square. The pieces were hand-carved and quite remarkable, having been kept in immaculate condition, despite their obvious age. He tilted one of the rooks up to me, displaying the stamp underneath on its base.

It read: *Calvert, 189, Fleet Street.*

For a second, it seemed to mean something to me, but I was grasping at a loose thread; no change there. For once Gabriel answered, looping the thread and tying it neatly in a bow.

"I bought this set in 1839, from a small shop in London, as a gift for you."

I felt my eyes widen—1839!

Too quickly the words tumbled: "How old was I when you met me, how many lives had I lived? Do you know?"

"You were mortal then. I met you when you were sixteen. I celebrated your birthday with you when you turned seventeen, just the two of us," he said.

"What happened to me?" My heart pounded hard, thudding against my chest.

"You died, Lailah. You were gone and so I left. How and why can wait. You need answers, I need them too."

"But where did you go, where have you been all this time?"

"Where I went isn't important. You said you never forgot me. Well, now I want you to remember what it was that you never forgot. I want you to have those memories back. The rest will come, in good time."

He could tell me more. He knew everything about me, back then at least. There was a reason why he wasn't revealing everything to me. It was as though he was trying to anaesthetize me, to soften the blow.

I slouched back, swallowed up by the broken leather, and waited.

Finally, he moved, slipping his hands together in a prayer-like shape, resting his elbows on his knees, watching me. I was confused to say the least; I didn't know what he was expecting.

I broke the silence first, nodding at the chess set. "It's very beautiful, but I don't know how to play."

Was he waiting for me to start?

Gabriel remained mute, his hands covering his lips making it difficult to read him. His mouth, I had noticed, had come to give him away on occasion. If he had a tell, it was his lips. Still he said nothing. I tuned in my other senses; he wasn't communicating to me through my mind, but as I focused in I could feel a level of expectancy rising within him.

He left it a little longer, then outstretched his strong arm and placed his hand on mine, positioning it on top of a pawn. As he curled my grip around the cold, silky ivory, the room started to vibrate and pop all around me.

I found myself zooming through a tunnel of light, and at the end, the exact same chess pieces. Images began seeping in, but I was reluctant, so they didn't come easily. I thought I heard Gabriel in the distance encouraging me to explore them, so I eased myself and stopped trying to escape.

As soon as I accepted the vision, I found myself staring at an image of Gabriel and my past self. We were perched over the chessboard. This was my memory; brushing the pawn had triggered it. He must have hoped it would.

Gabriel was kneeling behind me, hand on top of mine, moving the pawn up and diagonally along the squares. I was giggling and he was cheek-to-cheek with me, talking, explaining the rules. We were in a barn. Horses were tied up below us. The board rested at the very top of a high pile of stacked hay bales. We were having fun and a stream of summer sunlight filled the space through the open doors. Delight and excitement overwhelmed my past self and it rushed over me as I watched.

My outfit was a little over-the-top compared to current standards: a light cotton pastel-blue day dress with petticoats and big puffed-up sleeves. My face was the same; even my hair retained warm, vibrant shades of blond blending delicately together. Other than the clothing, I didn't look any different.

I observed him gently moving my hand and the pieces across the board in different ways. I felt myself knot inside as his hand touched my own. Just as I was acclimatizing to the scene, smashing hooves clipped against an uneven ground. The sharpness of the clatter from a rearing mare scratched my eardrums, and the image splintered. The broken shards of a glass sheet fell all at once.

Hiding behind it was a new memory.

Again it was the two of us, our attention drawn over the heavy wooden board underneath an ancient oak tree. Autumn leaves cascaded down, forming a messy pile covering the grass next to my feet. We sat opposite each other, contemplating our next move. I watched and many minutes seemed to roll by before I finally picked a white knight and moved it carefully to a new spot. Gabriel wore a cheeky smile as he instantly took it with a bishop and presented me with my impounded piece. I tossed my head up to the sky with a disgruntled sigh; Gabriel placed the knight back on the board and reshuffled his bishop to where it had been. He seemed to be trying to show me where I had gone wrong and where I should have placed my piece.

It was odd; all my visions tended to be in silence, except for the occasional sharp noise. I never heard the voices. I had learned now to interpret body language and movement.

Watching memories was gripping, but being overcome by the strong emotions that they brought with them still felt unusual. All I felt watching the memory was pure rapture, and I couldn't recall knowing such happiness in my current life.

I stretched my arms out in front of me and the tips of my fingers tingled as the air swelled around them. I was on the outside looking in. I had time to take in the memory for a few more moments but

Gabriel couldn't resist any longer; he had jumped into the tunnel, tuning in to my private channel, and watching once again.

As he joined, my memory broke apart into tiny segments, and as if blowing gently through a plastic tube, he manipulated the image, creating a series of tiny bubbles all reflecting the story that had disappeared somewhere inside me once upon a time. The bubbles drifted and vanished from sight.

My memory, now blown away, became replaced instead by images from Gabriel's consciousness. He presented me with a slide show, but this time the photos whirled around, spinning and twisting.

They depicted similar moments of playing the game, always just the two of us in each other's company. One of the images floated directly in front of me, tempting me. I reached out, trying to capture it as the picture paused just long enough for me to succeed. I poked my fingertips through its seal and it welcomed me by playing the story for me to watch.

I was sitting once more atop the haystack, hiding in the far corner. Gabriel sat behind me, my back lying flush to his chest, resting in his arms.

The white king lay horizontal and the other characters were scattered in a small heap next to the thick wood. An overwhelming sense of joy filled me and I realized that I was starting to feel what Gabriel had felt in that moment. I was suddenly intensely aware of a sensation of desperate longing. Had he joined in, so I could feel how he had felt and experience this the way he had?

I wasn't sure, but I became, in that split second, more certain than I had been about anything else. He had loved me!

I homed in on us, Gabriel weaving his fingers through the ends of my long hair, my eyes closed. Skimming his hands down my arms in front of him, he tickled them, grazing his fingertips along my pale skin.

He breathed into my neck as he nuzzled into me lovingly. I viewed him stroking my face, engulfed in light and happiness. My former self opened her eyes and I knew that I had been pretending to sleep. As he gazed adoringly into my eyes, a tremendous ache gripped my heart. He had pined for me so deeply.

The tips of our noses brushed together before finally our lips met. It was a deep lingering kiss. The kiss of two lovers. It was so strange experiencing the emotion of our first embrace from Gabriel's perspective, but not at all unsettling. I was elated by it on every possible level. As our lips parted the memory froze, suspended in that last image.

Lailah.

Time to go back. I didn't want to leave; I wanted to see what happened next.

Lailah. He was calling me out, back to the now. But I preferred it there, in the past. By all accounts, it seemed far less complicated.

It's time to come back. . . .

I still held on, staring at that last image.

Lailah . . . He called my name differently this time, reaching and pulling me out.

I found myself back in the library, hand still cupping the pawn, Gabriel's still resting on top. I flicked my wide eyes to his.

Entirely enchanted by him, I couldn't stop smiling.

TEN

"WE WERE A COUPLE BACK THEN?" I asked finally.

Removing his hand from off the top of mine, he shifted in his chair, taking his time to respond. "Yes and no. The first time I met you, I was completely and utterly captivated and intrigued by you."

"By me?" I found that difficult to believe. I had never considered myself anything special and Gabriel was so unique and beautiful.

"Yes, by you. Don't seem so surprised! You were innocent and so full of life. Everything about you captured me. I manufactured ways of bumping into you, and reasons for us to spend time together. But even back then there were . . . complications."

His smile fell away and the creases in his forehead made a reappearance.

"What complications? That you were an Angel?"

"Well, that was an issue in itself, but you didn't know I was an Angel. I was going to tell you, tell you everything, but I was too late." His face dropped and his body tensed.

Perhaps it was wrong but I tried to connect to him; I hoped he was still open from what we had just seen together. He instantly seized up.

"What are you doing?" he asked. I could tell he wasn't happy, but his words were still soft.

"I just want to understand. Why don't you show me what happened?"

"There are some things I never want you to see, and I won't be the one to show you."

He seemed to be trying to protect me, but I couldn't help feeling frustrated. This had been my life as much as it had been his. I was entitled to know all of it, not just the bits he deemed appropriate to share.

His expression cooled as he gathered himself. "There were a number of situations that made things difficult. I don't want to go through all that now. I just wanted you to feel the happiness we shared back then. You need answers, but that's enough for now."

I screwed up my face to protest, but I knew Gabriel meant what he said, and if that was all he was ready to reveal today, that was it. Instead, I tried to be grateful for the memories and feelings he had given back to me.

"That said, I think I should teach you to play again."

The grin returned to his expression and he nodded at the soldiers who were prepared for battle in front of us. His face lit up brightly again as I conceded.

"Ruadhan will take you for a tour of the village at twelve, so we have a couple of hours."

"You kept this all those years?" I asked quietly as I concentrated on the pieces in front of me.

I was immediately drawn to the knight.

"I hid it for all those years, yes." Gabriel unbuttoned his cardigan and rolled up his sleeves. He meant business.

"Let's start with the characters, shall we?"

He spent the next hour naming each chess piece and explaining how they could move and what the rules of the game were. Although it all seemed new to me, I found myself moving some of the pieces instinctively.

As he continued the chess lesson, my mind wandered and his words echoed around it. I was mortal when he met me. Then I had died and returned, a different girl than who he had fallen in love with all those years ago. I was changed forever and I couldn't be sure myself if any remnants of the innocent Lailah were left.

I watched how delicately Gabriel handled the pieces. I could barely bring myself to take my eyes off him. Finally, checking his watch, he signaled that it was time to finish our game for the morning.

He began packing the characters up and I cradled the knight in my hand; the cold ivory was so smooth to touch. I hid it carefully in the box and Gabriel placed it back under the floorboards.

He wrapped his arm around my waist and whisked me from the library to a patient Ruadhan, who was standing at attention in the kitchen.

"Hi, Cessie, you ready to go for a walk?" he said.

"Yes, that would be lovely." I grabbed my jacket and looped my satchel over my shoulder before turning to say good-bye to Gabriel. "What will you be up to while I'm gone?" I asked.

I wondered if he would follow on this particular outing.

"Ruadhan will take good care of you. Michael and I have some things to catch up on."

I took that to mean that he trusted Ruadhan, unlike Brooke. And I had to remind myself that he was working to make sure the Purebloods and their Vampires were not hot on our heels.

"Okay," I replied, sending a grateful look his way.

As we left the kitchen, Gabriel called, throwing me an apple.

I caught it one-handed.

"A late breakfast snack?" he suggested.

I actually wasn't hungry, I'd never had much of an appetite, but I tucked it away in my handbag anyway.

As we stepped onto the driveway I could sense Gabriel's reluctance to let me go, but clearly he thought it was good for me—even if he didn't like it. And he needed time to strategize with Michael.

We made our way down the drive and onto the road. It was a long walk to the village; I was quickly learning this group liked to maintain its distance and privacy. I took the opportunity to take in Ruadhan properly. In his late forties in human years, he was certainly very elegant, wearing a tweed jacket over pressed trousers and leather shoes. His dark hair had flecks of gray running through it at the temples and he had bushy eyebrows of the same color. His pale skin had faint freckles across the cheeks and over his nose, and he had a small bit of stubble on his chin.

We made idle chitchat until we eventually reached the local church and cemetery. Guiding me around, he explained his Irish Catholic heritage.

"Do you still believe in God, after what happened to you?" I asked as we moved slowly down the church aisle. Ruadhan was admiring the images in the stained-glass windows.

"If anything I believe now more than I ever did. The Purebloods came from Hell, and Gabriel came to us from Heaven," he said.

He bent his head in silent prayer at the foot of the altar before we ventured back outside.

Drifting through the cemetery in winter was eerie, but Ruadhan took his time, reading the inscriptions engraved into the headstones. "It's amazing, isn't it? To think I am more than a hundred years old, but yet here I am, and here they are." He looked down at me. At over six feet tall and burly, he was quite impressive.

"But that is the normal order of things, Cessie. You will grow older and you will die one day, and that's how it's meant to be."

He seemed humbled. Little did he know, I was actually far older than he was, and as far as I knew, I could never have an end of any kind.

We left the cemetery and walked down the narrow street, passing by a wide property that looked as though it dated back to the Tudor period.

"That was used as a school in the nineteen hundreds. It's been converted into a house since," he explained.

I could tell. It was an old-fashioned one-story building from a bygone era, with windows stretched from the bottom right to the very top. I could almost hear the excited children running and giggling as they stood in the playground waiting to go inside.

Opposite was a row of terraced cottages; they were all painted white with a short picket fence running the length of them. They were small, but looked very cozy. The properties were more clustered along the main road, but you could see farther back that the houses got bigger on the streets that continued off this one. We approached a tall sign that swung and creaked in the chilly wind; it featured a picture of a horse's head surrounded by the words THE WHITE HORSE.

"Local boozer," Ruadhan said.

We neared the entrance and the prospect filled me with pleasure: another single-story brick building, which looked more like someone's home that had been converted than a purpose-built public house, with its old-fashioned black and white beams and array of benches outside sheltered by enormous umbrellas. Of course, no one was actually using them because it was freezing, but inside you could hear that the place was brimming with people.

Ruadhan offered to take me in and treat me to a Sunday lunch.

"Sure. That would be lovely, thanks," I said as he chivalrously held the first of two doors open for me. I still didn't have much of an appetite, but I wanted to go in and escape the frost for a while.

Stepping inside, I was suddenly reminded of the life I had been living up until recently. While the building and the thought of the families inside enjoying their Sunday dinners had initially made me feel warm inside, that sensation was quickly replaced with the cold reminder of the loneliness that I had come to associate with my existence in these places.

It was tightly packed and ahead of me was a large wooden bar with an overworked barman trying desperately to attend to five raucous customers at once. There were logs burning in an open fireplace, heating the whole room, which instantly took the edge off the chill. The room felt even more snug thanks to the low ceilings, and I noticed Ruadhan wasn't far from hitting his head on the thick beams that ran the whole length of the room.

"If you walk down and to the right, there's a set of double doors.

They have another seating area out there covered by a tent with heaters; we're more likely to get a table in there."

"Okay, great."

"What would you like?" he asked.

"I'm happy with anything, I'm not that fussy."

"Aye, and what about to drink?"

"Just a juice, please," I replied, and began squeezing through the standing patrons to reach the double doors.

Sure enough, a table at the far end was available, so I ventured over to claim it. I peered out of the clear plastic of the tent onto the sloping gardens at the back and glowed as I watched the children playing on the swings and running about with their dogs. It was charming and rustic; just how an English pub should be.

Ruadhan spotted me at the end of the tent and, joining me, placed a pretend saltshaker that said TABLE 6 on it. Drinks in hand, he passed me a cranberry juice and plonked a pint of Guinness in front of himself.

I noted it curiously before asking, "Do you eat and drink normally?"

"Drink, yes; eat, no. Being a, well, you know . . . alcohol is actually far more intoxicating than it is to normal folks like you. Food, well, you know the score there. Luckily for you I have had years of practice on this stuff!" He laughed heartily as he guzzled his pint, leaving a frothy white mustache on his top lip. I giggled and wiped it away for him with a napkin.

"So tell me, Cessie, where are you from? Where are your parents?"

I hesitated a little before I replied. I had instantly liked Ruadhan, and I felt guilty for being dishonest with him. So I tried to stick to the truth as best as I could, just omitting some of the detail. "Well, not much to tell. I was orphaned, if you like. Always been on my own as far as I can remember. I was working in a pub in Creigiau when I came across Jonah on my way back home. You know the rest. . . ." I trailed off, taking a sip of my juice.

"Home? I went back there; it was more of a shell if you ask me. What's a nice girl like you doing staying somewhere like that?"

I'd forgotten that he had gone back in search of my things.

"Well, I don't have any family. I wasn't making much money, and that house was just sitting there. . . ." I said. "And what about you? I bet you have a much more interesting story than mine." I wanted to change the subject, but he seemed unnerved as he shifted uncomfortably in his seat.

"I'm from the Emerald Isle originally. 'Course you probably gathered that." He paused for a moment, slurping his beer while he considered the rest of his story. "I wasn't a young man when I was turned, and served for over ten years before Gabriel found me. He saved me from my Gualtiero and he helped me rediscover my humanity."

His face became drenched in regret and sorrow; I would have thought being saved would evoke a different emotion. I leaned in, hoping he'd tell me more.

"Gabriel saved me, but I had trouble adjusting. When I was changed, I was taken away from my wife and daughter. Gabriel told me I couldn't risk returning to them. He said I wasn't ready. But I didn't listen."

He stopped there. I shouldn't have pushed but I couldn't help myself. "Did you say good-bye to them?"

"In a manner of speaking. Gabriel was right, I wasn't able to control myself." He rubbed his eyes.

"It wasn't your fault," I whispered. "You didn't ask to be what you are."

Ruadhan blinked, and the flecks of green in his eyes started to swirl. He certainly appeared to be far more able to restrain his impulses than Jonah.

"That may be true, but what I am now is . . . I would have ended things myself, but I have a debt to Gabriel for risking himself for me."

"That's the only reason you go on?" I said.

"Yes. I have assisted him in freeing the others. I hope in some way that my support will allow me some small form of redemption. Though I know when my final end comes, I cannot be saved past this existence. But I've got a duty to Gabriel to help him in any way I can."

I struggled with the idea that this wise and caring being would simply stop existing when his end finally befell him.

"So you go on for him? Only him?"

"Yes. When he no longer needs me, I will ask him to be the one to finish this. I'm evil, we all are—our choice or not. Nothing evil should be allowed to exist in this world. We belong in Hell, right alongside our creators . . . the Purebloods. I hope to help send them back to the darkness from whence they came, before my final day does come."

"Even your Gualtiero? Do you not still have some form of connection to him?"

His eyes blazed momentarily before he answered me. "Especially my Gualtiero. If you believe nothing else you hear while you keep our company, believe me when I tell you that if I were ever presented with an opportunity of ridding this world of one of them—any of them—I would not hesitate. In fact, I pray that I am given the opportunity."

His words cut through the air between us.

We sat, neither of us talking. I felt the weight and enormity of Ruadhan's guilt and loss now weighed heavily on my own heart.

My lunch finally arrived: several lamb cutlets—undercooked and dribbling blood—together with roast potatoes, Yorkshire pudding, and vegetables, all submerged in thick brown gravy. I realized suddenly that I was in fact quite hungry after all.

"Looks grand, that!" Ruadhan laughed. "A hearty meal for a hearty girl!"

I went straight for the lamb; it was chewy as it hadn't seen the oven long, but delicious.

Ruadhan placed his hand on my arm as I cut into my meal. "You know, you remind me of my daughter."

I stretched a small smile as he moved his heavy hand from me. "How did you find Gabriel?" I spoke softly despite the outside seating area brimming over with people and the noise filling every available inch.

"He found us, all of us. Hanora was the first he saved. I was shortly after." He leaned back in his seat and folded his arms together, and suddenly seemed very fascinated by his pint glass, his eyes not moving from it for a while. "Gabriel seems to believe that there are Gualtieros and their armies looking for you."

I was surprised by the turn in conversation.

"He trusts me implicitly and I him," Ruadhan continued. "He isn't telling me everything, not yet. And I get that; there'll be a good reason for it. But he has told me that they want you and he doesn't understand why. He's got us on full alert, patrolling the village in shifts. You clearly mean something to him."

It was more of a statement than a question. I munched on my carrots while I considered my response. "Why that is, your guess is as good as mine," I said.

It wasn't a lie; it was the truth. Ruadhan seemed content with my answer, for now at least. We passed the rest of the conversation on lighter topics.

By the time I had finished my lunch, I was stuffed. We made our way to the exit and Ruadhan settled up before escorting me out of the pub.

Deciding that it would be wise to walk off the meal, we proceeded to trek across the many different trails and roads around the village. I didn't mind; it was a change to be out in the fresh air, even if it was frosty. The new Chanel jacket was too fancy for the outing, but it kept me sufficiently warm as we walked for what felt like miles. I still didn't have my bearings among all the fields, streams, and tall trees.

It was almost six o'clock; we had been going for over four hours and the night was drawing in. Letting out an unwanted yawn, I covered my mouth with my hand.

"Oh dear, sweetheart, have I worn you out? I'm sorry, I rather forget sometimes. . . . Not used to the company of a mortal! Your legs must be aching!"

As I looked up to reply, I waffled.

"What's wrong?"

Against the darkness Ruadhan almost sparkled like the stars in the dark sky.

"Our kind are created out of darkness," he said. "We are strongest when it's dark."

I wondered about my Angel. "And Gabriel?"

"He is born out of light, he feeds off the sun. On Earth, his gifts peak at sunrise and weaken at sunset."

It made sense. Whether day or night, Gabriel was almost impossible to take in, unlike anyone or anything I had ever seen. My knees weakened as I pictured his face.

"We should get back. He'll be waiting for you."

"How far do we have to walk?" I asked, hoping we weren't miles away.

"Not far. Can you manage, or would you prefer a lift?" He smiled.

"Um, we can walk."

Half an hour later we were near the property, and I finally gave in, letting Ruadhan carry me the last bit of the way. Sure enough, at the front door, Gabriel was standing there smiling widely at me, displaying his perfect white teeth.

"She's all yours!" Ruadhan laughed, lifting me from his shoulders and placing me in Gabriel's arms, leaving us alone together.

"Did you have a nice time?" he asked me, his dimples set deeply into the sides of his cheeks.

I stretched my body in his arms and raised the back of my hand to my temple, attempting my best damsel-in-distress routine. "Funny, I never ever thought I'd need rescuing from a Vampire because he was forcing me to exercise!" I laughed, burying my head into the crevice between his shoulder and his chin.

Gabriel held me effortlessly as though I weighed nothing at all.

"Well, now you've been rescued, or rather, returned for a refund, what can I do for you?"

I paused and considered some things I'd like him to do, but I resisted enlightening him.

I hopped down and shivered as I removed my jacket. "Tea . . . !"

ELEVEN

ONE CUP OF TEA and several chocolate cookies later, I lay my head in Gabriel's lap, my tangled hair covering my face. My boots were strewn by the side of the sofa, and I felt myself drifting off.

Sweetly playing with the curls at the ends of my hair, Gabriel proceeded to stroke the length of my arm, finally circling his fingers inside my palm. I was only dozing, yet I was very aware of his hands and what they were finding.

Lightly, he undid the top few buttons at the back of my blouse. He rested his hand on my shoulder, holding it there tentatively before running it around to just under the left side of my neck. Moving aside my crystal ring, which was dangling at the bottom of the cold chain, he spread his whole hand out.

I realized then that he was searching for my pulse. I was worried that he would feel it beating at a hundred miles an hour as his skin touched mine.

I tried to think of anything else, but no amount of distracting thoughts could stop my heart from thudding against my chest at his touch.

"Your heart's racing," he whispered in my ear, gradually moving his hand to my head. I guessed he was checking that I was feeling all right.

Nervously I sat up, relocating his hand away from my forehead down to my waist, and—caught in the moment—I released a few buttons from the top of his crisp shirt.

Fluttering my eyelids closed I placed my hand over his chest in return. He wrapped his hand over the top of mine, pressing it down more firmly. It was like his soul was enveloped around me tightly, and I imagined cupping his light, watching his purity dance in the palm of my hand.

"So is yours," I murmured back, keeping my eyes shut.

As the dancing light subsided from my mind, I repositioned his shirt back together and returned to my dozing position. Now content, I began to nap.

I WAS RELUCTANTLY WOKEN AN HOUR LATER. As I stirred, Gabriel informed me that he had to leave with Michael to "see to something."

"There's fresh food in the fridge if you want some supper, and plenty of milk and tea," he said as he paced toward the door, with an edgy-looking Michael in tow.

There was something about Michael I didn't like, something that wasn't quite right. Gabriel had told me that he was important; his connection was the deepest and freshest with a Pureblood. He could detect changes in his Gualtiero's behavior, such as his moods, and apparently being in this position made him an asset; however I couldn't help but think that our best asset was also our Achilles' heel. Michael was the most recent Vampire in the group to have been separated from his Gualtiero and clan. Gabriel hadn't spent long guiding him back to some form of humanity, and I had a bad feeling about Gabriel being alone with him.

Just as Gabriel and Michael reached the doorway, I shouted, "Why don't I come with you? I might be useful?" I tried to stop my suggestion from sounding like a plea.

Gabriel turned to me and smiled. "No, you stay here, curl up with a good book and rest. Michael and I will be fine, won't we?"

Standing behind Gabriel, Michael half turned in my direction, making sure Gabriel could see his enthusiastic thumbs-up to me, with a sweet smile spread wide across his face.

But as Gabriel walked through the door, Michael's grin fell away and he stared at me with a blank expression, and in a low murmur said, "As Gabriel said, enjoy your time. . . . I'm sure we'll find a use for you soon enough."

A shiver made its way up my spine, and as Michael followed Gabriel through the hallway, I paced after them.

"Gabriel, I really think you could do with another pair of hands. If you won't take me, at least have Ruadhan go with you? His are strong and, well, Irish—you always need a pair of those!"

Just then, Hanora appeared. Bumping me out of the way, she started trailing them, swishing her perfect hair as she went. "I couldn't agree with you more, but it's mine he needs. Don't worry, I'll look after him, I always do," she shouted down the hall back to where I was now standing still.

I wasn't sure if that was worse, but at least if she was there he wouldn't be alone with Michael. I tried to make myself feel happier about it. The sinister undertone in Michael's words only made me feel more wary and suspicious of him.

As the front door slammed shut, Ruadhan appeared, a book in his hand. "Are you okay, sweetheart?"

"Yeah. I wanted to go out with Gabriel, but he's taken Michael and Hanora with him instead."

"Business," Ruadhan said. "Best for you to stay here, where I can keep an eye on you. It's not safe out there."

"Do you know where they're going? What they're doing?" I asked.

Ruadhan shifted his weight from one foot to the other. "As I said, business. Nothing for you to worry about. You'll stay indoors, maybe get an early night?" he suggested.

"Doesn't seem like I have a lot of choice in the matter." I forced a smile.

"I'll be in the study if you need anything." Ruadhan went to leave, but then hesitated.

He stepped closer, and to my surprise brought me in to his chest for a hug. Awkwardly, I returned it, and he kissed the top of my head and said, "Night, love."

I didn't want to go to bed yet, so I decided to stay occupied by raiding the fridge.

It was a huge fridge/freezer, which was ludicrous given that until now it had probably never been used.

Gabriel had stocked it well for me. There was an abundance of yummy things to eat: eggs, cheese, pizza, chicken, fruit juices. I wasn't hungry, but I needed to busy my hands, so I decided to make a sandwich. I placed the bag of green shredded lettuce, together with the cucumber, tomatoes, precooked chicken, and bread on the counter next to the sink and went about washing the vegetables in a colander. To draw out the process, I chopped the lettuce into smaller pieces, placing it neatly into a clear glass bowl.

"Hey, Cessie." Jonah's voice traveled from the entrance of the kitchen.

I swiveled around. "Hi, you all right?" I replied.

He sat down at the table, watching me as I aired out the greens. "All good. What you up to?"

"Making a sandwich. . . . Not really hungry, though."

"Then why are you bothering?"

"To keep my hands busy, to take my mind off wondering what Gabriel and the others are doing."

"Well, if you want something better to do with your hands, I can think of far more exciting options than mangling veg—"

The scrape of his chair over the tiles as he stood up made me cringe, and I readied myself to bat him away. To my surprise, he rustled about in one of the cupboards and placed down two tumblers next to me, pouring a large amount of neat vodka into each.

"I don't really drink," I said.

"Humor me, have a glass. You never know, you might enjoy my company. Seems I've got a bit of ground to make up."

I supposed one glass couldn't hurt, but one. I still wasn't completely comfortable alone with Jonah. I set down the sharp knife and the tomato I was butchering and made an effort to lift my spirits. We exchanged a "cheers," tapping the tumblers together, and I sipped at the clear substance that reminded me of paint stripper.

He downed his glass quickly. "Jeez, Cessie. Not much fun, are you?"

I scowled at him and took another sip. I creased my brow as it hit my throat. It was difficult to resist spitting it out.

Rolling his eyes, Jonah produced a bottle of Jack Daniel's and refilled his glass.

I eyed him curiously. "You smoke, you drink, I saw your reflection in the rearview mirror . . . not exactly fitting the usual Vampire stereotype here," I stated.

"Nope. Interestingly, as you may have noticed, we don't explode in sunlight either."

"I guess I don't understand," I said.

Jonah chugged back his shot, and his expression hardened as he clutched the base of the tumbler, setting it down on the counter. "Vampires were human once. Our Pureblood Masters turned us; they infected us with their venom. By the time they were done, virtually everything about who we were before was erased. Our very DNA coding changed, and we became something else—marauders, bound with immortality and abilities to aid us in our subservience. But, like all things—immortal or not—we still have a physical form and we need fueling. We exist on blood; blood is the giver of life, after all. That bit is accurate enough."

I shuffled uncomfortably, not sure what to say. "Well, looks like TV has mostly got it wrong."

Jonah filled his tumbler once again. Swishing the brown substance around he said, "People have it wrong. It's simply a game of Telephone over many years. Humans who encountered Vampires told each other about these beings who they couldn't comprehend. With no explanation, factual accounts were reduced to stories, and over time became nothing more than myth." He stopped for a moment, and when he continued his tone was lighter. "The whole Vampires-can-fly thing is a good example. We can't fly. But perhaps someone, somewhere, saw a Vampire jump a vast distance. The story gets recycled over and over, until eventually that Vampire was flying, not jumping. Stake through the chest thing is right though, so don't try to test that theory on me." He grinned.

"Noted." I nodded. While this was all very interesting, I was worried about Gabriel. "So where have they gone, do you know?"

Jonah lit a cigarette before necking his drink. "Michael received word from Thomas. They've gone to meet him," he said.

"What?" I stammered. My grip around the tumbler tightened. "Why are you sitting here giving me a 101 on the life and times of Vampires, when you know that? It's insane! It's a trap!" I exclaimed.

"Oh, for sure. They know Thomas failed to escape and they used him as bait to try and capture Michael back—you know, when they caught me instead." He snarled. "If he is still around since this little rendezvous was organized, after his attempted desertion, it would only be because they still deem him useful in some way."

"So why have they gone? Come on! We have to go!" I had already slid my glass along the shiny surface and begun rushing in the direction of the door, when suddenly Jonah was blocking me, his hands on my shoulders.

"Trust me, if they needed us, we would be there. My job tonight is to keep you here and safe. Gabriel's no fool, he's got no intention of getting caught in the middle of an ambush. You need to trust me."

I couldn't take Jonah's word for it; I needed to find Gabriel, but preferably with Jonah, Ruadhan, and Brooke in tow. So I tried again. "The second they get near Thomas, that will be it! Why would they risk themselves like that? And how can you sit here while they do? Gabriel saved you, all of you. You owe him!"

Jonah held his cigarette in the corner of his lips, his hands still firmly placed on my shoulders. He puffed out a stream of smoke from his nose and stepped back, surrendering his hands as if I had a loaded gun that I was about to shoot. "We need to know what the Purebloods and their clans are doing. Thomas will know their movements at least. Gabriel's fully aware of the risks involved, but it's a chance he's prepared to take to find out what they are planning. You are forgetting a very important fact: he's not a Vampire. He has his own talents, and a good plan. He is safe," he said.

"Then why has he taken Michael and Hanora with him? If he's so safe, he wouldn't need them!" I argued.

"He doesn't need them. They won't be anywhere near when he meets Thomas, they will be meeting someone else."

I furrowed my eyebrows, confused.

"A friend, delivering a message from him instead. Thomas's Gualtiero plans on ending him in the worst possible way; he knows this. There's no saving him now, nothing we can do for him. But Gabriel can offer him something. Peace in his final moments, in exchange for information. Not a bad deal considering the alternative."

Jonah raised his cigarette back to his lips, inhaling deeply. "If you go out there, assuming you could convince me to take you, it will end badly for all of us. I'd be right next to him if I thought there was any chance they might not come back."

There was nothing I could do. There was no point leaving because I didn't have the faintest idea where they had gone. I had no choice but to sit it out and wait for them to return.

Huffing noisily, I returned to my chopping board and my drink. I gulped the last of the alcohol, hoping it would relax me. Jonah was back by my side; whether it was out of duty or through choice, I didn't know and I didn't care.

I took my frustration out on the tomato and Jonah raised his right eyebrow in response. "Your attempt on that tomato's life might mean more if it weren't, well, just a tomato . . ." he said.

I continued chopping. I tried to block him out and let my mind wander. I wanted to see if I could feel Gabriel's presence, see if he was anywhere near our private tunnel. He wasn't.

"Gabriel seems to think you are at the epicenter of everyone's interest. You want to tell me why that is?" he asked, refilling both our glasses, stubbing the remains of his cigarette out and lighting another immediately.

Chucking the greens into the bowl, I maintained the silence. A few minutes passed and he was refilling his tumbler once again.

I nodded toward his glass. "Ruadhan tells me alcohol has a far greater effect on Vampires?" I asked him with raised eyebrows.

He flicked his collar up as he jumped up onto the work surface.

"Careful of my tomatoes!" I couldn't help stifle a giggle as he nearly sat straight on top of one.

"That's better! Half a smile! You know the evening will pass quicker if you chill out a bit."

I thought about that for a moment. He was right. Counting the seconds wouldn't make them go any faster.

"I work in a bar uptown, I can hold my liquor. Looks like you need an induction though—your pupils are all lovely and dilated!" Jonah said.

I shrugged at him. "I only drink sometimes to sleep," I said. "I almost don't even dream. . . ."

"What's wrong with dreaming?" Jonah asked. "I miss it. We don't sleep." He filled me in on more Vampire particulars.

"My dreams would make even your hairs stand on end."

His lighthearted expression turned to concern. Stubbing out his cigarette, he exhaled the last bit of smoke from his lungs. "What are you, Cessie? I know you're not human. I've watched you, you look at things as though it's the first time you have seen them. And your eyes . . . Has Gabriel seen those eyes?"

I wasn't sure what he meant.

"You really should get another hobby, something other than stalking me."

He paused, refusing me a reaction. "I tasted you. Your blood is bitter but tinged in sweetness at the same time. You're some sort of living, breathing contradiction."

I didn't answer. The alcohol was doing a fantastic job of numbing me, and I let his inquiries pass me by. I didn't owe him an explanation, even if I had one to offer. And what Gabriel did and did not know about me was none of his business.

"Who are you?" he persisted.

"Cessie."

"And who is Cessie?" he said.

"I don't know, Jonah! I don't know!"

Tears of frustration started to well in my eyes, but I pushed them back. I was still no closer to understanding what had caused them to be bloodied when I had shed a tear on the patio.

"Hey, hey." Jonah took my hand and I snatched it back and continued chopping the tomato aggressively.

"It really will all be okay." His tone lowered as he purred the words.

I refused to meet his eyes. I could feel them boring straight through me.

Would it be okay? I wasn't so optimistic. How could I be sure of anything when I knew so little?

"Cessie . . ." He reached for my hand again as I scattered the chopped tomato into the bowl. He caught it, holding it tight, and I felt comforted for a moment.

He guided me in between his legs, which dangled over the counter. "You are unique, Cessie. Clearly everyone thinks so, and I don't disagree."

I hadn't seen this side of him before.

"Thanks . . . I think." I bowed my head, not wanting to meet his gaze.

He brushed the loose hair away from my eyes and gathered all my long strands over my shoulder. He fingered my wrist and, slipping off the elastic band, he bent down and tied my hair into a side pony.

As he leaned in, he purposefully brushed my cheek and a surge of electricity ran up the length of my body. My heart belonged to Gabriel, I knew it always had. Yet Jonah only had to touch me, ever so slightly, and my body practically convulsed, willing him to put his hands to better use.

"There you go, beautiful," he said.

I flicked my gaze up to his own and he grinned naughtily, winking at me.

Sighing, I stepped out from between his parted legs and moved back to the chopping board. The vodka was kicking in, as if I needed it. Jonah's company seemed to have the same effect on me that the hard liquor did.

I picked up another tomato and positioned it centrally on the wooden chopping board. Jonah jumped down off the counter and stood behind me. "Your buttons are undone."

His hand moved up my back and glided across the nape of my

neck. I lost my concentration and sliced deeply into my finger, only managing to graze the tomato.

"Arrgh!" The blood flowed instantly from the split in my skin.

I spun around to locate a towel, but found Jonah toe-to-toe with me instead. His pupils were twice the size that they had been a minute ago and I knew it wasn't the alcohol.

He knelt down, his eyes fixated on my own.

Softly at first, he molded his lips around my fingertip, then gradually moved his mouth and tongue down the length of my finger. Rooted to the spot, I didn't even blink; in fact, I think I actually stopped breathing as I watched his eyes begin to burn. He didn't take his gaze away from me as he swirled his tongue and lapped up my blood.

As I watched him, excitement stirred inside me. So when he shifted his entire hardened body against my own, I didn't push him away.

Finally he withdrew, my fingertip lingering at his lower lip.

Engrossed, I surveyed him as he observed the tear begin to heal itself, magically gluing back together. He said nothing. Instead he slid his fingers in between my own, squeezing them so that they were clamped together.

Leaning in until the tip of his nose touched mine, his orbs flicked between hazel and red and his face glowed a little; it was a diluted version of the being I had saved that fateful night.

I remained perfectly still, unwilling to concede first, searching his eyes. He held me there suspended; he was calling the shots and I let him. Our bodies could barely be any closer, as if I were a magnet drawing him toward me.

I knew these seconds belonged to him.

I felt myself becoming hotter, a burning sensation rising from the pit of my stomach. As his lips brushed my cheek, I heard his fangs crack as they fractured into place. They immediately found my neck and proceeded to scrape my soft skin, preparing to burrow their way in.

Maybe it was the alcohol, or maybe I had lost myself in the moment, but there was something inside me that yearned for him to stab me with his fangs and consume every inch of me. I could feel my eyes widening in anticipation and my sockets began to itch.

But the sensation was quickly ended by Brooke's voice yelling urgently from the doorway. "Jonah! What are you doing?"

Brooke caused the taut rope in between us to snap clean.

I began to remember myself. Jonah didn't flinch; he remained poised at my throat. Brooke was on Jonah's back within a split second, desperately struggling to pull him off, but he was far stronger than she was. I grabbed his shoulders and thrust my weight into him, and to my surprise he was thrown backward.

Brooke clutched him tightly, shouting for Ruadhan.

"Get off!" Jonah bellowed.

The counter steadied me as my legs wobbled. His eyes had a few remaining flecks of red swirling in them, but he wasn't lit up the way he had been on the night we met. He was excited, but I could see he was regaining control of himself and I felt relief wash over me.

Jonah shrugged Brooke off easily, tossing her to the side as if she were nothing. She stared at him, crestfallen, as she saw that his eyes were alive for me, not her.

She stiffened and turned her attention to me, enraged.

I made for the double doors leading to the patio area outside, mumbling something about needing some air.

I learned something very useful in the seconds that followed—a lesson once taught to me by Frederic, the first Vampire I'd ever encountered. It had slipped through the net in my panic.

Never turn your back on a murderous Vampire.

TWELVE

As I reached for the handle and pushed it down, the sudden force of a thousand rocks hit my back, sending me sailing through the windowpanes. There was no time to protect my face as the glass shattered, slicing effortlessly into my skin.

Facedown, I slammed against the icy paving stones, and it felt as though I were being stabbed with a thousand knives.

No time to consider my options; she had me by the top of my arm, dragging me up.

My vision was hazy in the night's blackness, but I could see Brooke's red eyes glowing, and they widened as she consumed the space around me. I was petrified. She was a girl scorned, and I couldn't see an escape from this. I didn't know how badly I was bleeding. Riding on a wave of jealousy, I was sure that her intentions had been to only give me a good beating, but I conceded that the smell of my blood might be too tempting to resist—for any of them. The true danger of this scenario hit me square in the jaw: Gabriel had left me in a house of Vampires.

The bone in my arm crunched as she gripped it tightly. Just as suddenly she released it and I heard her hit the floor hard as Jonah pounced on top of her. Two sturdy arms eased my fall as I crumpled. Ruadhan was behind, steadying me. Brooke screamed and wailed as Jonah pinned her beneath him. The noise whirled around my mind, disorientating me.

Ruadhan left me propped against the garden furniture and helped Jonah calm the sobbing Brooke. My left arm lay heavy at my side; I could tell she hadn't broken it, but she had at least fractured my bone. I willed it to heal quickly; I needed to protect myself if any more of them turned on me.

My stomach seemed to be pulsating; I placed my hand over it and discovered a large chunk of glass digging deep inside with very little protruding out. My whole body seized up and I was momentarily glad that I had drunk some alcohol; it was helping take the edge off the pain.

I placed my hand across my stomach to conceal the injury and waited. It took some time but eventually Ruadhan and Jonah pacified Brooke to the point where Jonah was able to lift her off the ground. Supporting Brooke's weight, he positioned her arm around his shoulders. She would heal quickly, from whatever hurt her; that was one thing we had in common. As she cried into his chest like a little girl, he turned back to me. He looked uncomfortable, as though he wanted to check I was okay. He wished he was with me, but he couldn't be; I could see as much in his strained expression.

As they left, Ruadhan returned to my side and began picking at the loose hairs that were sticking to my cuts and grazes. "I'm so sorry, love! I'm going to get some water—I need to clean you up." Rising to his feet, he left me.

I tried to lift off the floor with my hands, but subdued a squeal as my arm bowed under my weight. My bone was not healing as fast as I needed it to. I removed my arm from my torso and took a closer look at the sharp piece of glass that was lodged firmly to the left of my belly button. Pulling it out here, with no Gabriel and three Vampires in close proximity, was not a brilliant idea.

Hiding it once more, I began picking out the little shards of shattered glass that had cleanly sliced their way through my jeans and lace blouse. Ruadhan appeared and insisted on plucking a barbed piece from my eyebrow. His face remained composed, almost clinical. He didn't even wince at the spurts of fresh blood as he pulled out piece after piece. The feeling in my arm was returning and I knew the fracture had almost healed. I allowed Ruadhan to wipe my face clean with a white cloth, and then he started treating me with ointments and creams. It was in vain; the scrapes and cuts would fix themselves, but I couldn't tell him that.

"I'm sorry," I said.

Ruadhan replied with a quizzical look, scratching at the stubble on his chin with his spare hand.

"It's my fault. I've come here and things have changed for you all. I have made your existence . . . difficult." I teetered.

Ruadhan patted my neck lightly and I grimaced as the cloth made contact with a deeper laceration. He moved in closer and took in the state of my skin. "Jonah was about to drink from you, I can see where his fangs dug into your flesh," he observed.

"But he didn't, he never pierced my skin. Please don't say anything to Gabriel—I don't want to make things worse."

Ruadhan ignored my plea, shrugging. "Brooke will be very regretful of her actions tomorrow," Ruadhan said. "The two of them have a, well, complicated relationship, but she would never have killed you. I just think you should know that."

"I know," I lied. I had no idea how far she would go to keep Jonah for herself. "Thank you, Ruadhan," I said somberly.

"Love, you have nothing to thank me for. Can you get up?"

"Yes, you can leave me. I'll be fine."

"Let me help you to your room," he insisted, scooping me off the ground.

I didn't want him to see the wound in my belly. As long as the glass was still lodged in my skin no blood could flow out; he wouldn't be able to sense or smell it, unless he saw it.

"I'm fine, Ruadhan. Please, I just want to be by myself. Go and see to Brooke, Jonah might need your help," I insisted.

Reluctantly, Ruadhan allowed me to slowly pace through the house and up the stairs. As I shut the door behind me, I slumped down against the wood, grabbing my side, desperately trying not to let out a loud cry. My arm, now feeling back to normal once more, meant I was able to use my hands to grasp the rug as I crawled across it to the side of the bed. I struggled to reach for the fluffy dressing gown that I had hung over the end. I dragged it down the sheets and painfully moved my body to allow it to twist around me and knotted the belt.

Inhaling a deep breath, I prepared myself to stand and move to the bathroom. There was no way I was going to stay in the house while I pulled it out. The smell of my blood would overwhelm the air. I had to get out to the gardens without being noticed, but I would need towels to apply pressure; the last thing I needed was to bleed to death.

Using the bedpost to heave myself up, I staggered to the bathroom.

I became increasingly concerned with the amount of time I was wasting. I had sent Ruadhan to Jonah and Brooke, but how long would Jonah wait to appear in my room? Not long. I couldn't trust myself around him. When he drew me in, I lost all sense of who I was and what I wanted. He stirred emotions deep within me that I never even knew I had. I didn't want to endanger my life and I certainly didn't wish to jeopardize my relationship with Gabriel, whatever that had been and whatever it was becoming.

I couldn't stay in this house anymore.

As I mulled the few options available to me, the small, dilapidated cottage in the woods came into my mind. It could afford me the privacy I desperately needed. I had to remove myself from Jonah—and from the situation here.

I grabbed some bath towels and wobbled to the door and, closing my eyes, I prayed I would make it outside unseen. Easing myself across the landing, there was no sign of Jonah, so I tiptoed down each stair, trying not to make the boards creak underfoot. I got to the bottom and leaned against the banister for a moment, then staggered down the hallway to the kitchen.

I took in a sharp breath when I saw Ruadhan at the far corner of the room reaching for a dustpan and brush. I guessed he was on clean-up duty. He spun around, surprised, but strangely he looked right through me. I threw my hands in front of my face. I was there—why couldn't he see me?

I didn't have time to explore this peculiarity further. I was aching and needed to get the hell out of this house. As Ruadhan wandered over, I made for the door and stepped through the frame and over the shattered glass, still barefoot. I turned back and watched confusion spread over Ruadhan's face. He knew something was there, but I was invisible to him.

I made my way down the frozen stones, to the front door of the little house. I was filled with relief when I pushed the handle down with a squeak. The cottage was dark, but the door to the kitchen was ajar and moonlight streamed through it, stretching into the hallway. The sun shape in the tiles seemed to twinkle where the light hit it. Tired and worn, I collapsed against the brick wall with my legs sprawled over the art. I rested for a while, delaying the painful action of wrenching the glass from my stomach.

I thought of Gabriel and opened myself to him, if he were there. He wasn't. Had something gone wrong? Or was he deliberately blocking me out while he met with Thomas?

I removed the dressing gown, and laid it over my legs for some warmth. My jeans sat low on my hips, the blouse covering the top of them. Still, I unbuttoned and unzipped them, squeezing them down even lower, eventually exposing the top of my frilly underwear. I carefully peeled my once beautiful top back and reluctantly tore it so that my midriff was fully exposed. Squeamishly, I forced myself to assess the damage.

The glass was lodged in deep, but right now it was keeping me from bleeding out. Once I removed it, blood would rush to the wound and I would have to hope that applying pressure would keep me conscious long enough for it to repair itself. I wasn't in a position to stitch it up; I'd have to push the skin together and hold the towel down hard.

Plan ready, I fingered the bath towels that I had dumped next to me. Gripping the top of the shard, I counted to three. I figured it was similar to removing a Band-Aid; snatching it out quickly would be best. When I reached "one," I inhaled deeply and tugged it with all my might.

As the shard of glass—now digging into my palm—glinted against the small stream of light that fell across my midriff, I let out an almighty scream. I couldn't help it. My breathing became shallow and I tried to fight past the excruciating pain that burst through me. I bit down on my arm to stifle my voice, and dropped the piece of bloodied glass, which plinked as it bounced off the tile. I didn't dare gaze down; grabbing for a towel, I pushed my skin together and wrapped the white cotton around my stomach, front to back, as tight as I could.

I reached for another towel, but the painted sun, which seemed to be coming to life, distracted me. It filled with sparkling dots, which raised and danced above the floor. As I watched it, captivated, a surge of warmth filled me. I couldn't take my eyes off the silver and gold whirling around me. Without looking, I fingered the towel and pressed it down into my navel, exerting as much force as I could muster.

The gem I wore around my neck grew hot; the swirling colors seemed to be drawn to my ring, coming ever closer. I was no longer sure if I was awake or dreaming. It was one of the strangest yet truly incredible sights I had ever witnessed. While I watched it, the ache in my stomach numbed and a sense of calm swept over me. As the light from the moon outside softened and moved, the colors and sparkles disappeared with it and I was left in the darkness once again.

My feet were like two blocks of ice—I couldn't even feel them anymore. My ring grew cold and my body began to writhe in pain again. I reached out for Gabriel, but he was still absent. My thoughts slipped away from me and hard as I tried to stay awake, my eyes closed shut. I passed out.

From the depths of my mind the blackness cleared and an image of a bright light bubbled and swelled, filling every inch of my consciousness. It was almost blinding; I was transfixed. I didn't know if I was dreaming, but as the light dulled it was replaced by a figure: Gabriel.

Next to Gabriel, a wave of burning ash flew past in the winter wind. Shrill shrieks consumed the landscape beyond, and I realized then that Gabriel had ended Thomas, just as Jonah promised he would. I watched as Gabriel flickered and left the scene just before a mass of Vampires began hurtling over to him.

The vision jolted and bounced like a scratched DVD; then it seemed to fast-forward: Gabriel was back in the house with Hanora and Michael behind him. Looking alarmed, Ruadhan was throwing his hands in the air and talking fast. Gabriel flew from room to room. Hanora, Michael, and Ruadhan followed suit, splitting in different directions, all finally congregating back in the kitchen.

Jonah had now appeared, but Gabriel refused to face him. The only one missing was Brooke. Gabriel was at the back door, kicking what remained of the double doors, and I almost shouted at him to stop as he lifted the dustpan full of glass. He picked out several pieces, running his fingertip over the rims, presented with the remnants of my drying blood. Gabriel's face turned to pure anger. I had never seen him so full of hate. I wondered if I was dreaming.

Gabriel flew over to Jonah and grabbed him by the neck. Ruadhan placed his hand over Gabriel's outstretched arm, seemingly trying to defuse the situation. Brooke appeared seconds later, pleading with Gabriel and thumping his back, but he was a statue. He refused to let go. I watched as he came in and out of focus, light and color swirling, and I panicked. I had entered this vision watching him end another Vampire, Thomas, and he was shining in that same ominous way.

Gabriel, stop! I found the voice in my head, though I had no idea if he could hear.

I surveyed Gabriel as his expression changed and, releasing Jonah, his face turned apologetic. Jonah shifted his body, ticked off but not afraid, and simply nodded in Gabriel's direction as a sign of respect or understanding, I assumed. He walked away from the Vampires out onto the patio.

Lailah, where are you?

I was about to answer when, without warning, the picture evaporated and I not only found myself thrown into darkness, but also found my thoughts fading, and I was losing consciousness once again. It occurred to me in the last few seconds of awareness that I might well be dying.

My eyelids were heavy and refused to open, as though they were glued together. I desperately tried to gather my thoughts but my head throbbed. As feeling began to come back to my body, I became aware extremely quickly that I was suspended in Gabriel's arms. He had reached me in time. His face was buried in my stomach and I felt a strange sensation blow through the pain. I tilted my head and opened my eyes in time to witness light cascading across my midriff, spilling out into the space around me. It was like he was parting a vast sea. As his breath met the wound, the pain subsided and then departed. I didn't know how, but he was fixing me. As the last breath exhaled from his lungs, he paused, watching my skin close back together, sealing itself.

He laid me down flat so that I covered the sun etched into the floor, and he searched my face. His eyes were bright, glowing at me. For once he looked a bit messy; smears of dirt covered his forearms where his skin was exposed, and his once crisp white shirt was muddied. But how clean he was didn't exactly concern me.

"G . . . g . . . a . . . br. . . ." I couldn't find my voice.

Choking back the blood that had filled my lungs, I stopped trying to speak. I coughed violently and a rusty colored haematic liquid bubbled out from the corner of my lips.

He reacted immediately: cupping the sides of my cheeks with both hands he moved his mouth over mine. As he leaned down and grazed his top lip against mine, the same resplendent glow was gifted from him to me. I could breathe easily again.

He hovered for what felt like an eternity before caressing my skin with his soft hands and placing the lightest of kisses on my mouth. He broke from me, still lingering at my lips, waiting for my response. His hands were on my cheeks and I covered them with my own. I tangled my lips with his, gently at first, but as his top lip met my lower, I crushed myself against him. His kisses became deeper and more urgent, as though he thought I might disappear at any given moment. My hands found the back of his head, pulling him closer. Dragging my fingers through his brilliant blond curls, I felt as though I was cradling creation; he was painting me by numbers, coloring me in from top to bottom, quite literally breathing life through me. It was magic. He was magic.

I returned his urgency and wrapped my legs around his waist, easing him toward me. He didn't object and I found myself guiding his smooth, perfect hands from my back down to my sides. He skimmed my skin gently and finally grasped my hips, hugging my body tightly with his own. We were entirely entwined. His aroma was a mixture of yuzu and sandalwood; he tasted like citrus.

I ran my hands up under his shirt and felt his broad shoulders, then ran my fingertips down the length of his spine. His hand traveled down to the opening of my jeans and he tickled my navel, bobbing his finger in and out contemplatively. An elated tingle raced through me as he pawed the top of my panties. Using my hips, I tried to encourage him to wiggle me free. My whole insides seemed to light up at his touch; there was no question in my mind that we were connected in some profound way. Kissing my neck, he found my now cold ring resting on my collarbone and, regarding it hesitantly, he seized up.

Moving away from me, he placed his hands on my waist and held them there, eyes still glowing. He tugged my jeans up and re-buttoned them. I didn't know what to say, so I said nothing.

"Let's get you back in the warmth, back to the house. You'll catch your death out here," he said.

What? Why had he stopped? I was utterly perplexed. I had felt him—he wanted me as badly as I wanted him, but yet again something was holding him back. I eyed him with bewilderment.

"I'm more likely to catch my death in there actually. I'm not going back inside." My words were fierce, covering my disappointment.

"Stay here, don't move," Gabriel said, springing up.

I waited for him to return, freezing to the bone and completely dumbfounded. But I did as he asked. He was only gone a few minutes before reappearing carrying a thick duvet and pillows. He wrapped me up tightly inside and I turned my back to him, hurt.

He nestled in next to me, under the quilt, and placed his sturdy arms around my body, nudging his nose into the dip of my neck. Pushing my tangled hair from my face, he grazed his fingers over the lacerations scratched into my cheeks. I curled in embarrassment; I was a mess. He was so perfect, and I was a fool to think he would want me.

"Don't worry. The way your body works, I'm sure they'll be gone by tomorrow," he whispered lightly.

He confirmed my fears: I *was* a mess. I struggled to keep my tears from falling and closed my eyes self-consciously.

Intertwining my bare feet with his own, he bound them together, expelling waves of heat, bringing them back to life. I was grateful to him for that.

The image of Gabriel glowing in light swept through me. I wasn't sure if what I had seen was real; though deep down I knew it was.

You ended Thomas. I saw you.

He didn't reply, but he was listening.

I didn't think Angels were killers, especially for their own gain. I tried again, hoping to provoke a reaction. Although I was sure that I was misplacing my anger, it was his rejection that truly upset me.

I granted Thomas an ending he would never have received otherwise. His last moments were filled with light. I did what was asked of me.

I left it at that and, warmed by the heat that radiated from Gabriel, I fell asleep in his arms.

He had rejected me only minutes ago, yet lying here, he locked me in as if I were the most precious and expensive jewel in the world. I didn't realize it yet, but I had, and would continue, to cost him everything to keep me safe.

And he didn't yet know what I truly was and who I would become.

THIRTEEN

I sat up to find the door to the cottage ajar and a chilly breeze seeping through. Gabriel wasn't next to me anymore. Wrapping the duvet around my body, I made my way to the door. I was taken aback by what I saw. The silhouette of Gabriel was positioned in the stream of light that was rising from the horizon. His body was illuminated and flashing gold, while twinkling star-shaped crystals exuded from his skin. He floated above the grass, absorbing the waking morning. As the sun rose higher in the sky and night gave way to day, his glow changed and his full form came back into focus, but he hesitated before he turned around to greet me.

"I was created and born from light; on Earth the sun fuels me."

It was a straightforward answer to a question I couldn't recall asking.

He paced the length of the slated path and met me at the entrance. He peered down at me and placed his thumb and index finger under my chin, tilting my face upward to meet his eyes. He ran his gaze over me, finally touching the corner of my eyebrow softly, and I flinched a little.

"All gone, but that cut might take a little longer," he said.

I scratched my head, tousling my blond hair, which added to my messy appearance.

"You are especially striking in the sunlight," he said, observing me as several rays of light warmed my face.

The winter sun was blinding and I squinted to watch Gabriel's expression as the light rose above his form and cascaded over me.

He pulled my body, still wrapped in the thick duvet, in to him and leaned down, resting his chin delicately against my temple. Running his nose down my cheek, I felt his breath against my skin, soaking up the fragrance of my hair. "Citrus," he murmured.

"Sorry?" I whispered against his cheek.

"Your scent. It's never changed."

I almost laughed, for I was sure he must have smelled himself; his essence had reminded me of the same.

"Gabriel," I started with a serious tone, "tell me where you come from."

He thought about my request before replying, "Okay, Lailah."

Squeezing my hand, he led me back through the building to the sitting room.

Helping me to the floor, he lifted the sheet from over the new fireplace and stoked some logs on the fire, allowing it to blaze warmly. Once he was sure the room was comfortable, he knelt down beside me.

"Our world has many names. Mortals on Earth call it Heaven; some call it the first dimension; but its real name is Styclar-Plena." He paused as I took in the information.

Styclar-Plena. Its name alone sounded extraordinary.

"Existence of our kind evolved from a large crystal sphere that floated at the center of what became our civilization."

I looked at Gabriel, confused. He answered my unspoken question.

"How it got there, we don't know. Some speculate that it was a star that fell, but no one really knows for sure. But beautiful, stunning creatures grew and flourished in its light, the beings existing in pure splendor. Life for our kind first began tens of thousands of years ago, by your understanding of time. It was in the peak of my ancestors' history that the silvers and golds exuding from the crystal began to dull and weaken. The crystal seemed to be running out of energy."

His brow creased as he continued the story. "The light began to recede, and creatures and beings began to vanish where the darkness took its place. Our kind were not just born from the light, but needed it to survive. Not many still existed when the great leader Orifiel, who had begun to fade and wither, saw a silver sparkle forming just on the edge of the brightness."

I was captivated. "What did he do?"

"He watched it flutter; he had never seen any such thing before. From the fading crystal, he carved a small piece and held it in his hand for comfort. He started moving toward the silver cracks that were forming in the air. It is told that when he reached them, they mesmerized him, willing him nearer. The crystal carving in his hand began to glow once more, and resonated heat. He stepped into the swelling air and passed through to another dimension; we know it as the second, and you know it as Earth."

Listening intently as Gabriel relived the beginnings of his world, I felt completely honored to be the chosen audience. "How come they had never seen it before?"

"How do you see light against light?" he replied, seemingly impressed with my question. "It was only as the darkness crept forward that for a few moments in time, the faint crack of a bright, shimmering silver contrasted against the void. He explored the new world and found landscapes, rivers, and animals. He glowed as the sun that penetrated the Earth's atmosphere warmed his face, and he realized that he could exist in this new world. Humankind was very young then; they hadn't even begun to make a mark on their world. Orifiel traveled as fast as he could, trying to find something, anything, that might help keep our dimension living."

"Why didn't he just rescue the others and bring them to Earth?" I said.

"Though Earth had its own beauty, nothing could compare with the majesty of Styclar-Plena. He discovered mortals—humans that grew from children into adults and eventually ceased to exist. Death, the end of things, was not a natural cycle for those in the first dimension. Our ancestors did indeed grow, but the stages of their life were vastly different. Time moved there at a far slower speed than on Earth. Once our beings and creatures became all but a day old, which on Earth is the equivalent of nearly twenty years, they remained fixed, frozen in time, and their forms—immortal. It is in that first day of our graced life that each of our kind is brought to the crystal. It is the only time in our existence that we are permitted to touch it. In that one day, all the history of Styclar-Plena is revealed to us and our purpose made clear. The story of our origin, our heritage, and the days that followed are unveiled to us in a series of images and memories."

"So you touched the crystal?" I asked.

"Yes. I can't even begin to explain its magic. An all-encompassing feeling of calm, contentment, and acceptance flows through every inch of your being."

It sounded magnificent. It reminded me of how I felt in Gabriel's presence. He almost started to glow as he recalled his experience.

"Orifiel became aware, very quickly, that he had gifts that were unusual in this dimension. He could do things that mortals could not. He was far faster and stronger; he had the power to influence; he could make himself invisible to them should he choose, to name but a few. And it was while Orifiel searched for answers that he stumbled upon a young woman who was dying. As she passed, he witnessed a light so white and pure, which was remarkably similar to the light from our crystal. The brightness ascended into the air and floated above the woman's body. He noticed that none of the humans who surrounded her could see what he could. The light seemed to be drawn to his carving from the crystal. The essence traveled toward Orifiel and as it did, the crystal once again came to life, becoming bright and bold and luminous in his hand. Suddenly waves of silver formed like hairline cracks in the air, just the same as when he had passed through. They appeared in front of him and Orifiel returned to our dimension with the woman's essence."

"He stole her soul?" I asked, a little unsure.

"He didn't steal it; he simply guided it to where it wanted to go. I witnessed, through the images, Orifiel returning with her energy. It seemed to dance and almost sing as it traveled into the crystal sphere that dulled where he had left it. The sphere immediately lit up once more, and the gold and white sparkles outstretched. It was in this moment that Orifiel realized that he had found the key to our survival. He returned with others of his kind, and they learned how to harness the energy that left a mortal's body in death and lead it through the second dimension back to the first, Styclar-Plena. Using carvings from the crystal they were able to command these gateways to open, and from there, life in the first dimension flourished once more, and was even more majestic than it ever had been. It was as if this was the way it was always meant to be. The light spread farther and wider and our world grew vast and deep."

He looked at me and encouraged me to ask the questions that hung on my lips.

"So what you're saying is that when a person dies here on Earth, beings from your world, from Styclar-Plena, open these gateways and collect their souls and use them to, well, fuel your world?"

I was trying to make sure I had it clear.

"Essentially, yes. But it is a wonder for the souls that feed the crystal; they continue to exist in a form of beauty, different from anything on Earth, as brilliant light . . . love. Humans don't have it far wrong; it is a form of Heaven, only their souls don't continue to exist in the same way—they live on, but as something else. Another being, a structure, air . . . Their essence is transformed by the light and they still go on existing."

Gabriel paused to make sure I understood. Then he continued. "But as the days passed and the ages moved forward, a more structured society was born out of necessity. Now, so that Styclar-Plena would continue to flourish, select beings were appointed by Orifiel, to ensure the survival of our world. They were later given the name 'Angel.'"

"Like you?"

"I am an Angel, but I am an Angel Descendant; I was not one of the first. I have existed for nearly two hundred years in Earth terms, which is still very young when it comes to my kind," he answered.

"Though I only inhabited Styclar-Plena for that one day before I was tasked." He stopped abruptly. His body stiffening told me that it was not a comfortable subject.

"How are you a Descendant?"

"There were only a few of our kind who could fulfill these duties. They were the most human-like of all. There were only forty left after the day the darkness fell: twenty male and twenty female, including Orifiel himself. Not enough by any stretch to move souls to our plane. So they did what no other being in our dimension could do. Having seen how the human race populated, Orifiel devised a similar solution. Through the exchange of light and energy, a male and a female Angel would conceive a child. Around the same time, another male and female Angel couple would also create a child in the same way. A special ceremony was then held and, harnessing the bright white light and energy from the crystal, it touched both unborn Angel children in their mothers' wombs, bonding them together. One light, split into two."

"An Angel Pair?" I mumbled.

"Two Angels, fated to be each other's mate; fated to work together in their tasks on Earth, in the same rank, guiding and supporting one another; fated to share a love like no other."

"But why would they want to do that?" I said.

I could feel an unsettling feeling rising inside me; was Gabriel half of an Angel Pair, and if so, where was she?

"In the beginning, only one Angel Descendant was conceived at a time, not linked to any other. But as time moved forward, Angel Descendants began to fall, choosing to exist on Earth as mortals— and to die."

"But why?" I asked.

"Parted from Styclar-Plena in order to carry out their tasks on Earth, they grew weary. It was at the loss of so many that chose to fall that Orifiel decided to pair up the Angel Descendants. So although Angels had the duty, and to a degree, the burden of sustaining our world so that others could exist in paradise as they had once before, in return Orifiel gave us something none of the Arch Angels possessed: the immediate connection to another via an all-encompassing love, a love that bonds the two souls together for eternity. It no longer mattered how long they spent away from our world, as long as they had each other, their lights continued to shine brightly. These Angels then worked up the ranks, put in place by Orifiel, together."

I looked at Gabriel, saddened. He didn't love me after all; he was fated to someone else. I didn't want to ask him about her; I couldn't bring myself to.

"And you were an Angel of Death?"

"Yes. There are nine different ranks of Angel, all of which are tasked with continuing to collect the pure energy of souls from Earth, but in different ways. Some Angels are messengers, visiting Earth and influencing mortals to make the right choices, to find their grace, so that when the time comes their energy is pure and an Angel of Death can collect it and move it across the dimensions," he explained.

"What if a person's soul is not pure? What if they are bad people?" I asked.

"If the soul is tainted, it is darkness, not light, that leaves a mortal's body. Styclar-Plena was born from light, and light is what keeps all its inhabitants living a pure and beautiful existence. We have no use for dark souls. Their energy exists on the Earth until the scavengers appear and snatch it for the third dimension." He raised his eyebrows, waiting for my reaction.

"The third dimension?" I stared back at him, bewildered.

"It is believed that Orifiel's passing between the dimensions created rifts. The more that Angels moved between our world and this one, the more fissures formed, creating a passageway between Earth and another dimension which sits on the opposite side of our own. We call it the third dimension; mortals on Earth call it Hell. It's from the third dimension that Pureblood Vampires have emerged."

I tried to understand. "Did they already exist in . . . Hell?"

"We don't fully understand how they came to exist. I was taught that when the dark souls left a human body, they would linger and then move toward an opening. Orifiel, during his investigations, followed one and watched as it levitated over a black crack in the atmosphere. He believed it to be a doorway to the third dimension. The more the Angels visited Earth, the more these cracks appeared. At first it didn't seem to have an effect on anything, but during the time when so many Angel Descendants fell, Orifiel lost track of them on Earth. They were separated from Styclar-Plena and had become mortal, so they became lost. There were rumors that some of the fallen Angels had passed through the doorway, to the third dimension, but Orifiel couldn't determine if that was the case."

"But how could Angels, beings born out of light, exist in darkness? Wasn't it the darkness that began killing your world in the first place?" I pressed.

"They were fallen. They had lost their light and gifts when they fell; they became mortal. But their souls were still created and born out of light. If they did move across, who knows what would have become of them. Soon after this, Orifiel learned of new creatures—terrifying, dark, and evil—which were crossing over to the second dimension and existing on Earth. The Arch Angels watched over them and observed them killing mortals using their fangs to bore into human flesh and drinking the blood until the mortals were empty. What was even more disturbing was that these humans didn't release any light or dark energy, so it was as though these monsters were consuming their souls along with the blood."

I shuddered as Gabriel continued.

"For a while, they were like savages. It was almost as though they had stumbled across the rifts and passed through to the second dimension. They were merely surviving here with no purpose or goal. But then they started creating Second Generation Vampires. They became ordered and collected. The Pureblood Vampires started building small armies of humans that they had infected with their venom and turned into Second Generation Vampires. The Purebloods sought good, clean souls; it seemed as though the venom worked in a superior way, changing the mortal not just into a Vampire with powers, strengths, and gifts of their own, but it made their external features enhanced and flawless. It made it easier for them to hunt and bring the mortals back for them to feed off or change as they saw fit." Gabriel took a breath.

"So what you're saying is that they target dark souls to feed from and pure souls to change?"

"It appears that way. They seem to survive on blood and the dark energy released from a tainted soul. Mortals who are pure take far better to the change when a Pureblood fills them with their venom. When they are changed they become connected to their Gualtiero, their Master," he reminded me.

"And what of these scavengers?" I asked.

"It seems that more and more creatures are creeping into this dimension. The scavengers appear the same way we do, to collect the souls of humans who have died. Only they seek out dark souls." Gabriel seemed riled at this idea.

"So basically, to ensure the survival of Styclar-Plena, your kind transfer light souls to fuel your own world. And in doing so have created cracks in these . . . dimensions, so that we now have evil penetrating Earth, and murdering human beings? And worse still, Angels know that for every doorway they open, more rifts occur and yet they still come?"

How could the inhabitants of Gabriel's world be so careless?

"They didn't do it intentionally, Lailah. But this dimension in itself is a hard place to live. While Earth has its beauties, it's also so full of darkness. Styclar-Plena is a miracle, pure and excellent, where there is no such thing as suffering or pain. I could try to describe it to you, but I could never do justice to its magnificence. They deem the few lives of humans to be a worthwhile sacrifice for the many lives in Styclar-Plena, and for the world itself." Gabriel's eyes glazed over with a sense of longing. I wondered how much he missed his home.

"Let me into your memories, show me," I pleaded, my eyes filling with tears.

"I can't, Lai. Humans can never pass through the gateway to Styclar-Plena, they would lose their physical form the moment they touched it, and if they were a pure soul, would exist only as light. You're immortal, but I don't know exactly what you are. So for now, you can't experience it in the same way that I can. If I showed you from my memories, I fear you would drift in and not return. I couldn't risk it; I might lose you, only this time, not to the darkness, but to the light."

I must have appeared crestfallen, so Gabriel attempted to compensate.

"Can you imagine the icebergs in the North Pole, with the sea that runs underneath so crisp and unspoiled, that it reflects everything that surrounds it? So still; no breeze, no movement. Perfect. You seem to breathe not air, but the taste of fresh fruit, crisp and refreshing, and it consumes you. Looking up, there is no sky; just a blanket of stars and moons, and worlds swirling against a clear film. If you can imagine that, then you are a thousandth of the way there."

I closed my eyes and tried to picture it, and strangely the image came to me so clearly that I didn't have to struggle to imagine it. I was staring out into the landscape that Gabriel had just described. It was as if there were no sky and no ground at all. It was as if I was always meant to have seen it.

Later, I would come to realize the full enormity of the life I had been robbed of. But for now, I shook the wonder off and considered the cost. "You say the Arch Angels deem the deaths of humans to be a worthwhile sacrifice in order to keep Styclar-Plena, and its inhabitants, in existence. But they are not sacrificing anything of their own. So it is not their sacrifice to make, is it?"

FOURTEEN

GABRIEL HAD OFFERED NO REPLY to the question I had asked of his kind. He suddenly seemed nervous, and somewhat distracted. Twice he started a sentence that he didn't finish.

Pacing in a circle, thinking, Gabriel eventually tried to convince me to return to the main house. I promptly and stubbornly refused; I wasn't ready to face any of them. So instead Gabriel fetched some water and breakfast for me, returning with the chess set in hand.

"I'm not really in the mood. . . ."

He looked almost hurt. "There's time to start a game, while you eat."

He began setting up the board and pieces in between us. I munched on the fruit, surprising myself at how hungry I had become. Despite trying to keep my manners in check, I wolfed down the chunks of red apple and licked my fingers. Gabriel gestured toward the board, nodding at me to begin.

I set the fruit down and wiped my sticky fingers against my red-smeared jeans, crossing my legs, not entirely fulfilled by his offering.

Shifting uncomfortably on the uneven concrete I reached over and carefully lifted the heavy board, twisting it around so the pieces were changed.

Gabriel raised his eyebrows.

"Today I get to be the red family," I said.

It was a statement of intent. Today, I would be firm and get answers to my questions. Today, he would tell me everything.

Moving a pawn forward two squares, I was careful not to scratch the aging pine.

I was ready to begin with my inquiries, but he beat me to the punch.

"Lailah, I have to leave."

His words ripped through me. The brave and bold person I was planning to become withered right there and then. "Wh—what?" I stuttered.

"The message Thomas left last night—the situation is worse than I'd thought. The Pureblood Masters have convened and an edict for your capture has been issued. All the Purebloods and their clans have been called, they are combining all their armies to seek you out."

His brilliant blue irises opened and expanded into the shrinking white sclera that surrounded them. His expression was held deliberately and perfectly still. I let the information sink in.

"All of them?" I stifled in disbelief.

"All of them."

I rubbed my cheeks pensively. "Did his message say anything else? Did he say why?"

"No, but he warned that his own clan, his Gualtiero—Eligio— is hunting us while the rest come together. He wants to be the one to find you. He wants the glory."

"So when you say you need to leave, you mean *we* need to leave?"

"We all must leave, but on different journeys," he said. "You will go with Ruadhan. He will hide and protect you."

"Where are you going? Where are the others going?"

He fingered a pawn and took his gaze away from my own, moving the piece one square. "I need to find Malachi. He is a very wise fallen Angel. I don't know why the Purebloods want you, but I do know this: they are not the only ones." He cast his eyes back to me, pursing his lips as he finished his sentence.

"What do you mean?"

Was this what he had been keeping from me?

"The Arch Angels want you too. It seems the highest beings from both dimensions are looking for you. We know you are some form of immortal, but I have no idea why they all have such a heightened interest in your existence. We need to know; perhaps then we will understand."

My stomach tied into a nervous knot.

"Go to the Arch Angels," I implored. "Go to your people, surely they will help!"

He turned his face away. "They want you dead, Lailah. We cannot go to them."

How did he know that? Why would they want me dead? Nothing he was telling me made any sense.

"You will go with Ruadhan. I'll seek out Malachi, he may have information. Until I know exactly what you are and why they want you, I cannot fully protect you. I will come back, I promise you that. I would go to the ends of every world to keep you from harm. I owe you nothing less."

He reached over and grazed my cheek with his fingertips and for the first time, I didn't feel comfortable in his presence; I pushed back. What had he done that had landed him in my debt? I didn't know, or couldn't remember. It didn't actually matter, and I silenced the voice that dared me to ask. I had a suspicion that I wouldn't welcome the answer.

"And what of the others?"

Where would Jonah, Brooke, Michael, and Hanora go?

"They'll leave together. I can't be sure I can trust them with you. Especially after what happened with Jonah last night."

I tensed; I didn't want to confess my near betrayal. Hesitantly I replied, "I cut my finger. Jonah reacted and Brooke walked in."

I moved, releasing another pawn. The game provided a useful distraction.

"And what did she walk in on exactly?" Gabriel persisted, removing a stray blond curl from his vision.

I felt my face flush and I shifted uncomfortably. "It's your move," I muttered, keeping my attention locked on the board.

He slid another pawn quickly across the checkered box and his attention was back on me. "Lailah, what you do is your business. All I ask, for your own sake, is that you do not put yourself in harm's way. Jonah is a Vampire, that's something you shouldn't forget, regardless of how much you . . . enjoy his company."

His voice trembled a little; he suspected that I had feelings for Jonah.

I moved another pawn. "Well, I—"

He cut me off. "As I said, it's not my business."

His dry reply was nonchalant; perhaps it didn't hurt him because he was merely paying me back for whatever he believed he owed me in the form of his protection, nothing more. I couldn't be sure he felt anything romantic toward me, at least not the me that stood before him in the present. I accepted that he might just be hanging on to an echo of my past self. One thing I was certain of was that nothing was ever clear-cut with Gabriel.

"The others have readied themselves, and I need you to prepare a bag. We need to leave," he said, with a chill that blew through his voice.

"I have a backpack ready," I replied. "I don't need to pack."

I moved a rook and, holding my finger on it, narrowed my eyes and crinkled my forehead. "Gabriel, I . . ."

I wasn't sure how to tell him that I loved him, that I didn't want him to leave me. I was frightened, and not of the Pureblood Vampires, but of losing Gabriel all over again.

His face smoothed and he took my hand from over the board and slid his fingers in between mine. "Don't be scared, I'll never let anything happen to you." He misinterpreted the reason behind my fear.

He parted his hand from mine, moving his bishop into play.

I suddenly filled with an uncomfortable impatience. "Why are we playing chess?" I blurted.

"Because I wanted to start a game we could finish when I come back to you. Something to look forward to," he offered.

The fire burning next to me was starting to scorch my skin and I shifted away from it.

"Why can't I come with you?" my voice pleaded in a slight squeak.

"They will suspect I will look for Malachi, it's not safe," he replied.

I didn't know if he was referring to the Purebloods or the Arch Angels.

"If these superiors of yours want me erased then why don't they just come and do it?"

He grimaced. My words stung him. I felt it.

"They can't. They watch over the other Angels bound by their own rules. Finding you isn't that simple. They have no claim to you."

I perched my finger on top of the red knight and my body shook, disconnecting my train of thought. My fingertip tingled as it stamped the smooth mane and the knight seemed to enlarge. "I feel something toward the knight," I said, my voice shaking.

Gabriel grinned. "It was always your favorite piece. You said it reminded you of your own horse . . . Uri."

As he said her name, my skin began to tingle. I felt myself slipping back through a tunnel of memory: I was watching myself pelting through thick, green grass on top of a fantastic white mare. We were galloping across a wet field, stormy clouds forming above us. I watched myself pull the horse to a halt, while a galloping stallion came into view, eventually coming to a stop next to us. I was surprised to see that the rider next to me was not Gabriel. As he dropped the reins, he brushed his long, dirty-blond hair back from his face. Catching the stray strands, he placed them neatly behind his ears. The gold ring on his finger caught my attention and for a brief moment I thought I recognized it. As I began to scan his features, the scene suddenly felt strange and I was forced to look away.

The image spun and whizzed in front of me as the thundery clouds swallowed up the daylight. I panicked. It was the same sensation I had felt when I had sat with Gabriel, lost my memory, and become trapped in a vision of a Pureblood. I felt my heart racing and I desperately tried to leave and return to the present.

As a wave of heat from the log fire brushed my cheek, I began to relax. I was in the room again, Gabriel sat opposite me; his lips moved, but strangely the words didn't reach me. He was mute, and it occurred to me then that I was suspended, caught between Gabriel and the dark clouds.

Gabriel's expression darkened and he catapulted forward. I desperately reached for him, and just as I was on the verge of meeting his hand, I slipped away.

I left him, falling back through the tunnel against my will. The cottage, the chess game, and the flicker of the flames were all gone. Something, someone, was dragging me back in.

I was faced with a backdrop of emptiness. The Pureblood appeared in front of me, huge and towering. He took his time striding toward me. As he neared, I recognized his coal-black tattoos, two opposite rows from the center of his form. They were plastered across his face, broadening as they ran down his neck, two faultlessly symmetrical quills, black liquid keratin stained against his skin. The raised lesion prominently embossed between his orbs. It was the same Pureblood I had seen in the vision when I was drinking lemonade with Gabriel. He was back. This time he was alone.

He grew closer, seeming to change position without moving. I encouraged my legs to stretch out into a sprint, but my body was unwilling to shift an inch. He circled me; disappearing and reappearing. Finally, he extended his terrifying clawlike hand and moved it over my eyes and nose, stopping at my throat. He squeezed it, just enough to prevent the air from finding my lungs. He seemed to cackle, tormenting me. His sharp-razor fangs protruded over his lower lip.

As I gagged, I considered his expression in all its unholy glory; it made me want to die on the spot. I couldn't move my neck to avoid his glare and more panic rose inside me as his black pupils mutated, forming a revealing clear film. In his eyes I glimpsed a reflection of a dark silhouette—the girl in shadow. Where was she?

Petrified, silent tears poured from my eyes and I forced them shut. Just as I felt my arms and legs growing limp, he dropped his hand from around my throat. Gasping for air, I shivered as he ran the tip of his split lizard-like tongue up from my jaw to my eyelashes, tasting my tears. He pulled my head back by my hair, and with the serrated talons extending from his knuckles; he sliced a tuft of my loose curls. Grasping the stolen strands, he threw me down.

I was confused as I watched him raise them to his orifices. As he took in the fragrance, the wavy curls appeared black. Perhaps everything he touched turned to night?

He tilted his head from side to side, his bones cracking, and I found myself elevating from the ground. He raised his arm up and I ascended; he was controlling me.

"You belong to me!" he roared with a sonorous voice.

Each word quaked in a language I didn't recognize, but I understood him nonetheless.

I felt an anger brewing inside the pit of my stomach, unlike any emotion that I had felt before. My blood seemed to boil and blacken, and my hands formed into claw shapes, daggers breaking through my knuckles.

I didn't know what was happening, but as I grew hotter my teeth shifted and fractured. I felt myself slipping away when a lightning bolt flashed across the blackness. It splintered into forks, vibrating my name and crushing the metamorphosis rising inside me. I cooled as my name was sung to me in the second strike. I didn't see the creature disappear; I was focused on the lightning that was illuminating the space, now filling the void with light. The ground dissolved and I dropped into nothingness.

My eyes opened. A blurred but bright spark spread across my vision. A beacon, leading me home. The illumination glowed, expanding until the light made up Gabriel's figure. I choked, my body released, and I gasped for air.

"Where were you? Lailah! Are you okay?" Gabriel's words struck me repeatedly.

I said something and he stared back at me confused.

With soothing tones, he said, "Lailah, I don't understand what you are saying." He was running the back of his hand over my blazing cheek and my attention pricked, witnessing his skin dripping crimson with the stain of my bloodied tears.

"She is mine!" I hissed in a voice that didn't belong to me.

Gabriel didn't flinch. Placing both of his hands on either side of my face he came in nose-to-nose with me. I closed my eyes shut; I didn't want him searching my swollen and blackened orbs.

"She is under my protection! I will end you if you harm one hair on her head!" Gabriel yelled.

I knew the creature was still listening, imprisoning my consciousness. I was a vessel.

"Know her for what she is, Angel, and you will release her to me!"

It was over. A black hole inside convinced me that what the Pureblood had said was true. I didn't know what I was, but I wasn't who Gabriel thought I was. Not anymore.

"Lailah," Gabriel began.

I leapt off the floor and grabbed for my throat; piercing stabs jabbed through my lungs and over my skin where the Pureblood had touched me. I scratched and scratched at my neck and I screamed long and hard, hoping that the sensation boiling within me would escape.

Gabriel's body was hard as marble; every muscle now clenched and jutting from under his skin. He grabbed my wrists quickly, forcing them down to my sides. I shook my head violently. Why was this happening to me? What did they want with me? What was I? Intense anger bubbled under my skin.

"Look at me! *Lailah!*" Gabriel was shouting louder now, but I refused to give in to his wish. The last thing I wanted him to do was peer into my soul through these eyes. I didn't own them and I had no idea what he might find.

With a dark and inhuman strength, I shook my arms away from him and forced his hands off my wrists. I bolted through the room, running over the painted sun and toward the entrance. Just as I reached it, the heavy door flew open and Jonah filled the doorway.

"Stop her!" Gabriel yelled.

I peered up at Jonah for a split second and took in the surprise stamped across his face. My eye sockets were burning and bloodied tears still streamed down my cheeks.

Jonah's arms wrapped around me, forcing me in to his chest, holding me prisoner.

"I can't let him see me like this. . . ." I whispered, and his body eased in reply.

Feeling confident that I was secured, he let his guard down. Taking advantage, I heaved him off me and made for the path.

I couldn't run very fast; my legs were weak and I was disoriented. Hoping that no one else would find me, I stumbled through the door into the kitchen of the main house. Speeding along the hallway, I passed by Hanora, who was hovering on the edge of the lounge looking curiously toward me, but it seemed as though I was invisible to her.

Somehow I made it out of the house. I ran along the roadside. I blocked Gabriel; I didn't want him sensing any part of the feelings that were surging through me. I scoped the landscape for somewhere quiet to calm down. I needed to be alone. Across the road there was an opening to a trail in the woods. I headed toward it, but smoke filled my vision as something hard knocked into my side. Stumbling, I flashed a glance back to the car that had caught me as I raced across the gray lane. I watched the stunned expression of the driver as he ground to a halt, the hood dented and concave. Unconcerned, I charged to the trail. The driver lowered his window, but I had already gone into the woods so I failed to hear the profanities.

My legs slowed me, so as soon as I found a tree with a trunk large enough to conceal me I slumped to its roots. Shaking, I tried to compose myself, but the heat fizzing through my body was still raw and aggressive. Beads of sweat tumbled from my forehead and I was painfully aware of the fact that I was still streaming tears of blood. I felt so dizzy. I moved my arm back and forth and it came in and out of focus, as though it didn't exist in this world. I forced my eyes shut and tried to think of happy things, good things. Gabriel. The two of us playing chess, wrapped around one another in the barn, the softness of his lips brushing my own . . .

As the images rolled repeatedly on a loop, my body began to cool and I stopped feeling nauseous. I placed my hand over my crystal ring hanging at the bottom of the chain, hiding underneath my blouse. Feeling the soft edges of the crystal across my palm instantly comforted me.

Just then the heavens opened and torrential rain poured down, quickly soaking me through. I raised my head and let it wash over my face. I sobbed. Ordinary tears merged with the raindrops, forming an alliance.

Curling into a ball, I cradled myself, arms wrapped around my legs. I didn't know where I was, or how dangerous it could be outside unaccompanied.

Lailah, where are you? My being filled with light and suddenly I wasn't alone.

I didn't reply.

You can't be outside by yourself. Tell me where you are.

I disconnected. I knew it was wrong. I knew I shouldn't be out here, and I didn't want to be alone, but I was afraid of my own self. I needed more time to be sure that the Pureblood wasn't coming back. I didn't want Gabriel to ever see me like that again. So I imagined building a wall in front of the entrance to the tunnel. Visualizing it, I placed the last brick in the gap and silence fell. I squeezed my legs more tightly into my chest and rocked myself.

I MUST HAVE FALLEN ASLEEP as the rain battered down. Once more the winter reached the core of my bones and, wearing only jeans and my ripped blouse, I was frozen through.

The day was nearly over; the sun was starting to set through the thick mist that surrounded me. I panicked. I knew I wasn't safe. Would they have all left without me? Were they searching for me? I didn't know, but only now did I feel a twinge of guilt. How long had

I been out? It only felt like moments, but the sun retiring to sleep once more proved I had been gone too long.

I squeezed my eyes shut, forcing the haze to clear and attempting to knock the wall down. He must have been waiting for me.

Lailah, please! Where are you?

I responded by conjuring an image in my mind of the scenery around me and the large tree under which I was sitting. It couldn't have been more than a minute later that he literally appeared right beside me. He wasted no time scooping me up off the bark and thrusting my body against his. He clung to me, allowing no space between us, pushing his hand into my soaking hair. Eventually I removed my face from his chest and stared up into his eyes; they were enlarged with worry and brimming over with sadness.

"I'm sorry," I whispered.

"You have nothing to be sorry for."

His reply was firm and convincing, but now the anger had subsided and I was starting to feel like some form of human again, I was confused. Worse still, I was completely vulnerable.

"Never block me out again, you hear? I'm trying to protect you, to keep you safe. I need you to be on my side for me to do that. Do you understand?"

I nodded apologetically.

In the moment of my innocence, I forgot myself. "You loved me once before. . . ." I sniffed.

"Yes." His answer was swift.

"I'm not the same person you knew," I said. "I have changed; I haven't even the slightest clue who Lailah is. She's a stranger to me. I don't know who I am, I never have."

He didn't reply immediately but pulled me closer, kissing the top of my forehead. "You're wrong. When I look at you, I'm met with the same person. Your smile may have weakened and your eyes may have grown weary, but you are no different from the beautiful girl I fell in love with. And somehow, if it is even possible, I feel more connected to you now than ever before."

Despite the force with which he exerted his words, I couldn't help but feel that he was trying to convince himself more than he was me.

He tilted my chin up toward him, but kept his hand spread tightly in the arch of my lower back, his eyes daring to reach deep down within me. He touched my cheeks gently before bending down and placing the lightest of kisses against my lips.

"Lailah," he said. "I need you to decide for yourself what it is you really want."

I read between the lines. What he actually meant was that I needed to decide who it was I really wanted.

My lips trembled. "Your face has been the only constant I have ever known. I would bet good money that ever since the day you left, I've been able to feel you. It's an extraordinary, inexplicable yet inevitable force that I can't deny. I may not know what I am, but one thing I am certain of is that whatever it is I may be and whatever it is I may want, none of it matters without you." I began to sob, but I had run dry of tears.

"Ah, but Lailah." He stopped, his hand clenching into a ball-shaped fist against my spine. "Lailah," he repeated. "I would never let inevitability dictate your happiness. Wherever your path is meant to lead, you deserve and you should command the choice to decide. In your decisions, inevitability doesn't rule you." I watched his jaw lock, though it did nothing to harden his features.

What was it that I wanted? Normality? No. Though I had envied it, my destiny was not aimed at "normal." I knew I wanted Gabriel. But to really know why that was, first I had to understand what I was and perhaps more importantly, who I was now.

I breathed in the smell of the damp soil. The rain continued to lash down. Gabriel's shirt was stuck to his chest. The white fabric had become transparent and the muscles along his torso were clearly visible. His scent of citrus had diluted with the rain, but I could still taste him. He rubbed my shoulders repeatedly, finally reaching for my hand. I gave it gratefully.

We had reached stalemate; there was nothing left to say. Not yet. Before either of us could calculate our next move, we would have to be still and patient for a while longer.

Filling my body with heat through his touch, Gabriel instructed, "Come on, we have to leave, it's almost dark." His tone was urgent.

We emerged onto the curb in front of the driveway to find the metal bars of the gate bent and discarded. Hissing shrieks deafened my self-pity into silence.

They were here.

FIFTEEN

GABRIEL'S EYES SNAPPED TO ME and I met them with alarm.

"You need to go, Lailah! Now!" He lifted me and ran until his gaze finally settled on an old, rusted Ford parked in the distance. He yanked open the door, quickly bundling me into the driver's seat. He touched the ignition with his index finger and the engine kicked in. Neat trick. "Drive as far as you can. Do you have your cell?"

"No," I replied, stifling my shock.

Thrusting his iPhone into my palm, he ordered me to leave and I hesitated, mounting a protest that never managed to leave my lips.

"You have to go now! I have to help the others and you need to leave!"

I knew arguing would result in wasted minutes, so I nodded as he slammed the door shut and I put the car into first gear and pulled away. I looked for him in the rearview mirror, but he had already disappeared. I hit the brake and it squeaked in reply; I then jiggled the old gear stick into neutral. Did he honestly think that I would run away? Leave him and the others to perish at my hunters' hands? Perhaps he didn't know me that well after all.

Grinding the round leather knob into reverse, I pulled backward down the road, accelerating fast, finally plummeting to a halt outside the gates. I took a deep breath and made my way to the discarded pieces of metal strewn over the smooth concrete.

The sun had set and was replaced by a half-moon that hung low in the sky, watching me walk into impenetrable uncertainty.

A glint of light reflected off my crystal, spilling out over my blouse; it caught my attention as it bounced off a jagged piece of metal. Scooping up the bar, I ran my fingertip along the edge. It was deadly sharp.

Now armed—well, sort of—I realized Gabriel might feel my presence, so as I drew nearer I built my brick wall once more. As the hissing, shrill shrieks pierced my hearing, the hairs on my arm stood on end, and I once again wished that I could remain concealed.

As I tiptoed through the door, I was greeted by the sound of shattering windowpanes and the blast of hurtling bodies, causing my legs to tremble in response. Edging underneath the staircase, I crouched down—unmoving—in the corner, weighing my immediate options.

Formulating a plan against a Vampire attack was far outside of my experience. Noise filled every gap around me; it could only be moments before I would be faced with one of them. I heard a pub regular say once that the best form of defense was attack; albeit he was an overweight lump of a man, and he was talking football tactics, but it was the best I had. I mustered my courage, but just as I was about to charge from under the staircase, I heard Michael's panicked voice coming from the lounge.

"What are you doing? I led you to her, we had an agreement!"

This confession caused my skin to crawl. Michael was the reason they were here. He had told them. He had betrayed Gabriel. He had betrayed all of us. The response that met him was simply a series of harrowing high-pitched noises; I knew it was a Pureblood Vampire. This had to be Michael's maker, the most deadly force inside this house, his Gualtiero—Eligio.

Despite that fact, I found myself rising from the ground and catapulting myself into the hallway. Michael certainly didn't deserve my help, but then if it hadn't been for me he wouldn't be about to meet his end either.

My fingers gripped the wooden doorframe. I began to raise the jagged metal in my free hand, but just as I was about to dart forward, thick layers of flashing hot ash and dust smothered me as if I had been caught in a volcanic eruption. I was too late.

I didn't have time to wipe away Michael's remnants. Repositioning my body and regaining my balance, I spun around as a spine-tingling scream reverberated upstairs. Without thinking, I flew up the staircase, but fell as the house vibrated and rocked. Jumping back to my feet, I followed the sound. I didn't have to open the bedroom door; half the wall was missing as though a demolition ball had smashed through it.

Brooke was cowering in the corner of the room, sobbing, covering her eyes. Jonah was protecting her, engaged in a death match. He hurled the Vampire into the other wall. The Vampire plummeted through it, but bounced back within a millisecond.

His fangs hung like deadly daggers from his mouth. In an instant he had Jonah pinned on the carpet and was ready to rip him apart.

My mind emptied and I sprinted over to the Vampire, and with all my might I plunged the metal bar into the creature's left shoulder blade, breaking through the muscle and bone, straight through to the other side of his chest. My aim was so precise that I just missed stabbing Jonah, who lay underneath him. The Vampire screeched and spun around. But before he had a chance to meet the gaze of his killer, he exploded into burning ash and dust.

Jonah jumped up and grabbed me by my arm, which was still extended in front of me, shaking. "What are you doing here? You have to go!" he shouted.

His eyes locked with mine; an instant connection swelled between us. I broke it and nodded over to Brooke, who was lifting herself up using the wall to leverage her body. "Take her away from here," I said. "Look after her."

I hadn't intended for my words to sound so final, but my inner voice was reasoning that this was most likely the end. If I were to ever meet Jonah again, I would likely not remember him. I turned my body reluctantly from his and moved back in the direction of the gaping hole in the wall.

He grabbed my hand and pulled me toward him. Reaching for my waist, he held me tightly and protectively. "You're coming with us," he whispered.

I realized he was afraid for me. I shook my head. "Where is he?"

Jonah's shoulders slumped; he knew I wasn't about to leave without Gabriel and he didn't have time to try and convince me otherwise. If Brooke stayed here any longer, she would surely perish. She was no fighter.

He blew hot air from his mouth and cracked his jaw from side to side. "Last I saw of him, he was on the ground floor."

"What are you waiting for? Go!" I commanded, and unwillingly he charged to Brooke, lifting her easily.

He perched on the ledge of the window, but before he jumped he said, "I'm coming back for you."

I was already making my way through the broken pieces of plaster, but his words fell around me and I knew that he meant it.

As I reached the landing, three Vampires stooping below flashed their red, bloodied orbs at me, their prize. I had nothing to defend myself with, I had no hope; all I could do now was call to Gabriel.

I need you—

The adrenaline that was pumping through me began to grow hotter as I lost myself to the Vampires' enraged eyes. As my blood boiled beneath my skin, my cry for Gabriel gave way to a shadow that flickered to the left of me. I broke my stare away from the Vampires growling below me as her long dark hair stroked my skin.

She was back.

All three ascended into the air, up to the banister rail that ran the length of the landing. I tripped backward, shocked, as from behind her I watched blades slice through her knuckles. She made a low howling noise that seemed to come from deep inside her. The girl's form matched the color of the night that had wrapped itself around the house, masking her into little more than a faint silhouette. It was only through the blur of flame caused from an explosion below, which lit her arms now poised away from her waist, that I saw the ink of her tattoos.

Two of the Vampires hesitated on the tip of the railing, unsure of their next move. But the other, undeterred, hurtled forward, flying above her head. She raised her hand; he was only inches from her face, plummeting down, when suddenly he stopped. She held him suspended above her, cricking her neck from side to side—almost contemplatively—before she reached her bladed hand up and struck his chest, crushing through his bone in a clenched fist. The shriek that burst out of the Vampire's lungs sent shock waves through my whole body.

The girl only twitched a little as she whispered, "Shhhh . . ."

I couldn't see her expression, but I could tell she was smiling.

As she opened her hand from inside his chest, she slowly sliced open his blackened heart and he burst into a waterfall of thick oil. It poured at such a speed that it hit the floor and splashed back, splattering my skin from where I took in the scene, disbelieving. Whatever she was, she was far more powerful than any Second Generation Vampire.

The same realization must have hit the two malefactors that were still perched on the ledge. Their features filled with awe and both turned at the same moment, rushing to escape. She wasn't about to let them leave. She toyed with them, willing them nearer with a gesture of her finger. She wasn't just saving me, she was playing a game that she evidently enjoyed. That thought terrified me more than anything else.

I whimpered as she tore their throats out with her teeth, finally ending them. Spitting blood from her mouth, she began to move down the length of the staircase without even glancing back at me.

I trailed behind her, afraid to see where she was going and who she might find next. She traveled down the long hallway; the flames that were spreading quickly through each room didn't concern her. She didn't seem to notice the stifling heat or choking smoke that filled every corner as I made chase.

I finally caught up with her in the destroyed kitchen. I needed to see her face, needed to speak with her. I extended my hand to her shoulder, and just as I was on the cusp of touching her, an all-encompassing light spilled through the doorframe from the garden, striking her, and she evaporated into thin air.

I fell where she had stood, my knees grazing the kitchen tiles and my hands spread out on the other side of the doorframe, scraped by the grit of the pebbles underneath them. The light dissolved immediately and as I shook my head back into some form of comprehensive thought, my stomach somersaulted.

Gabriel lay several feet away, covering Hanora's body entirely with his own. I moved my lips, but stopped as the air around me began to warp, like the atmosphere underneath a rocket when it takes off.

In slow motion, I was forced to observe his strong arm move behind her back as he smoothed her hair away from the wounds that ran down her blackened neck. Her eyes flew open and with every frantic bat of her eyelashes her orbs grew bigger, brimming with desire. She pulled him close by the collar of his torn shirt into a long lingering kiss. I didn't see him pull away as his lips touched hers. The moment spiraled, and the invisible hands of the clock ticking in my mind resumed normal speed.

Suddenly, like two race cars slamming into each other head on, our connection collided. For a flicker of a second, I felt a sense of love pass through him.

Instantly he twisted around, his surprised eyes capturing mine.

I sprung my body up by the palms of my hands. As I teetered back to my feet, I resented Gabriel desperately scrambling away from Hanora to get over to me. I wanted to run far away, and this time from him.

I didn't have long to listen to the moan of my heart as it tore in two: I was elevated off the tiles by a tremendous hand lifting me by the back of my blouse. I squirmed as the pain of his fangs swiftly bore through the skin of my neck. It was like boiling water cracking a frozen car window, splintering down every last vein inside me. His poison was paralyzing; even my thoughts seemed to slow.

The creature dragged me backward through the kitchen, though he was careful to weave me past the destruction toppled all around. I watched Gabriel racing to follow, but it was like he had hit an invisible force field that he couldn't get past. He was pounding against hidden walls, unable to penetrate them. I didn't have to see my captor to know that it was Eligio; I could feel his darkness pulsating through my arteries.

The Pureblood was suspending Gabriel as he stole me. I wanted to blink everything away, but my eyes remained wide; I was completely immobilized.

Suddenly, my figure fell as the creature was knocked away from me. I couldn't turn to see what was happening. Whoever now had the Pureblood's attention had allowed Gabriel to break through and he hurtled past me. My body bounced against the tiles, as an incredible weight struck them from behind me. I wished I could scream, move, run, anything! Jonah appeared and hauled me into the corner. Cradling me into his body, we formed a perfect ball, just as the brightness of a white sheet—just like the one before—flashed next to us.

Patterned red and white plates rained down over us, bouncing off Jonah's back. The porcelain clattered, shattering next to me into a thousand pieces; they might as well have been my heart. As the glow faded into nothingness, the poison evaporated from my veins. Eligio was gone and I was still here, thanks to Jonah.

SIXTEEN

"You all right?" Jonah was slumped beside me, panting.

I extended my unsteady hands in front of me as life began circulating through them once more, and attempted to wiggle a finger. "Yeah, I think so," I said, casting my gaze to him.

He was sporting a white polo shirt with the collar pointing up, teamed with dark denim jeans that were torn and ripped from his efforts. He ran his hand through his thick, matted hair, tugging at the back as he watched me watching him.

His eyes were cooling, reverting back to his regular shade, and the concern that edged the downturned corners of his lips brought me some comfort. Jonah cared about me, he came back and had saved me. His intense stare pulled me in. He was an itch I needed to scratch somewhere I couldn't quite reach.

Ignoring my common sense and desperately needing someone to embrace me, I dismissed all thoughts of Gabriel, Hanora, and everything else. Rising from my knees, I burrowed my face into his shoulder, his waiting arms wrapping around me. I let him hold me and as I looked up to his eyes I found myself edging nearer to his dry lips. He took a deep breath, nervously anticipating my next move.

"You don't owe me anything," he began.

But the sheer fact that he wet his lips told me that he wanted me.

I met my mouth with his, and pushing my inner turmoil to the pit of my stomach, I gave him the sweetest of kisses. He didn't need any more of a green light. Placing both his hands against my cheeks, he parted my face from his, his thumbs exerting a gentle force against my cheekbones. His expanding pupils oozed black, like a knocked-over inkpot, overpowering his hazel flecks. Taking control, he crushed his mouth against my own more fervently, and I could tell by his urgency that he had been waiting too long to kiss me.

He was wrong; I did owe him something, and I was quite certain that this was his preferred method of payment. He was surprisingly soft and oddly he tasted sweet, like cinnamon. He was fast becoming my guilty pleasure.

In this moment of time, where only he and I seemed to exist, I suddenly became aware that Gabriel was getting near to us. I sensed him, and then heard his footsteps growing quicker and louder, striding through the mess.

Watching Gabriel kiss Hanora only confirmed everything that I had suspected about his feelings for me. Anything he claimed to feel for me was simply him desperately searching for someone I used to be, not who I was now. After I died, he had clearly moved on. Perhaps now I needed to as well.

Reluctantly Jonah pushed me away, bobbing his head to the right; he had heard Gabriel too. Planting a last quick kiss on my parted lips, he removed himself, putting a decent amount of space between us.

Gabriel came behind me. Securing his arms under my chest, he pulled me to my feet. He inhaled my hair as he clung to me tightly. Jonah stood up and shook off the shattered shards of porcelain from his shirt. I wiggled out of Gabriel's grasp and stood next to Jonah.

"Eligio fell back into the third dimension," he began. "He was able to command the rift."

I looked to Jonah and noticed his brow crinkle with trepidation.

"That's new," Jonah replied.

Gabriel reached for my hand and pulled me back in to him. "I told you to leave. You could have been killed or worse. . . ."

His eyes sprinted down the length of my body, which was still trembling. Not only was I soaked through, but now I had a mixture of Michael's remains and several other Vampires' covering me. This fact dawned on me quickly and, disgusted, I threw myself over to the tap, now absent of any sink, and began splashing the water, scrubbing my hands and face.

The smell of burning paint and the fumes of the stifling smoke had evaporated; the house was no longer blazing to the ground and it was free, for now, of any enemies.

With my back to both of them, I said through gritted teeth, "Luckily, Jonah was here for me." I tried to drop Jonah's name like an anchor, to emphasize my point.

"I didn't know you were here," Gabriel replied quickly, keeping it clean for Jonah's benefit. He still didn't trust him with the secrets we were keeping. "Not until—"

I cut him off swiftly. "Speaking of which, hadn't you better go and see to Hanora?" My words were cutting. I tried to infuse as much bitterness as I could muster into each one. I spun around to meet his eyes in order to gauge his reaction.

He looked back at me, puzzled. "She'll be okay, she's a Vampire. Her wounds will have healed by now."

Swinging in through the doorway, kicking a large chunk of plastic that had once belonged to the fridge from her path, Hanora appeared. Her skin that had blackened from the impact of an explosion was fresh and white once more. "My ears burning, love?" she said.

Her words were delicate and decisive, and unlike me, she didn't appear as though she had just been caught in the middle of World War Three. Her tiny frame was back to its annoyingly perfect self, her glossy waves cascading down and framing her slightly freckled creamy skin.

I couldn't be in the same room with her. If he wanted her, he could have her. Though the very thought made me want to throw up.

I dug my way past the battered, broken pieces to the hallway, passing Gabriel, my head bowed deliberately. I had to see if my documents were still in the dresser upstairs. It was time to go.

There's nothing between Hanora and me, Lailah.

He was quick to speak to me, but the very fact that he didn't utter the words aloud where she could hear irritated me. I stopped for a second, my heart pounding and jealousy gushing through me.

So to make sure he knew precisely what I had seen, I remarked: *Didn't look like that when you were kissing her. You love her, I felt it.*

As I was about to continue, Ruadhan—unaware—interrupted, bounding up to me.

"Cessie love! What are you doing here? I thought Gabriel sent you off? We need to get Brooke and Michael, we have to make a move, folks, it's not safe."

Hanora and Jonah shifted forward to meet him, but I traveled past to what was left of the stairway. As I attempted to climb it, I addressed all of them. "Michael's gone. I'm wearing half of him." I gestured to my grayed blouse, caked in his soot.

At that point, the house fell quiet; the rushed conversations were immediately swallowed up by my revelation. Gabriel looked perplexed as he came after me up the stairs, but I carried on climbing.

"Eligio ended him. Seems cutting a deal with a Pureblood isn't always the cleverest move. Michael told him where we were, that's how they found us." I partly needed to inform them, but also wanted to add a hint of a warning, just in case anyone else was considering doing the same thing. Though I genuinely didn't believe any of them would. . . . Well, except possibly Hanora.

My attention flashed to Jonah briefly, who had braced his hand against his temple, digesting the news.

I worked my way into what had been my bedroom. The wardrobe was smashed and the bed had been torn apart. I clambered over to the ornate dresser in the corner, which surprisingly was still intact, almost. As I slid open one of the drawers, it scraped against the sides. I found the envelope, removed my fake passport and driver's license, and then banged the drawer shut.

"Can I help you?" I asked Gabriel.

I sensed that he was hesitating on the landing; I kept my back to him.

He strode across the room and, confidently now, he stood behind me. "You didn't experience me feeling love for Hanora. Our connection found one another, that's why you felt what you did. I don't love her and I have absolutely no reason to lie to you."

His words were matter-of-fact, unemotional, certain.

"Then why were you lying on top of her and why'd you kiss her?" I asked, still facing the now shattered mirror on the dresser.

He pulled my body in to his own, cocooning me in his warm, muscular arms. He placed his chin on the top of my head and sighed. "I didn't, I was covering her from the light. I was ending Vampires. If the light had hit her, she would have been ended along with them. I was protecting her. And I didn't kiss her; she kissed me—there's a difference."

I felt myself waver. I didn't have any reason to distrust what he told me and, after all, I had witnessed Hanora pulling Gabriel in to her. As my resolve began to weaken, immensely helped by how he held me so dearly, a vibration went off in my pocket. I pushed my hand deep inside and found Gabriel's cell; I still had it.

Hanora's name appeared at the top of the text.

TIME TO GO MY LOVE

IT WILL BE NICE TO SPEND SOME TIME ALONE

I broke from Gabriel's grasp and chucked him his phone. A bewildered look spread across his face as he caught it. "Lailah?"

Snatching my backpack, which still remained fairly unscathed underneath the debris in the far corner, I managed to tug out a jacket. I looked back at him as he read the message that I had seen. "She's going with you." It wasn't a question.

He nodded at me softly.

"Well, I hope you enjoy your alone time. Thanks for your help, I'll pay you back, but I think I'll be leaving now."

I didn't look back, I couldn't. My insides felt as though they were being scrambled with a whisk. I jogged down to the opening of the house, ignoring Jonah and Ruadhan, and proceeded up the long driveway. I'd have to find somewhere else to wash and change my clothes; I wouldn't stay here another minute.

I hadn't even made it halfway down the driveway when Gabriel caught up, standing above me with his six-foot height, preventing me from moving any farther. "Do you really think I am just going to let you walk away?"

I stared back at him with hurt, puffy eyes. "I don't think you get to decide, and why are you bothered anyway? You have Hanora, you've had her for a hundred years! You've known me ten minutes! All I bring you—all of you—is trouble."

He tried to take my hands, but I shrugged him away and stepped around him. It didn't stop him blocking me once more and reaching for my arms. "I'm not letting you leave on your own. I'm telling you the truth when I say there is nothing between Hanora and me." He huffed, rubbing my wrists gently.

"Really? Well, I think she has other ideas. You won't take me with you, but you'll take her. Why?" I demanded.

"Because I can't trust her with you. It's safer if she travels with me." His brief explanation rushed through his lips.

His dimples dipped and I took a mental picture of his chiseled but soft features. I was upset with him, but it occurred to me that I didn't know if I would ever see those dimples again. I bobbed my thumb into their creases and I smiled at him as if it were the last opportunity I might have. It was most certainly night now, but that didn't stop his glow from exuding, framing his body ever so gently.

"You know best, I'm sure," I said, unable to remove the sarcasm from my tone. One thing I had come to learn about myself was that I didn't let things go easily. I certainly had no intention of changing now.

Gabriel inhaled deeply and pulled me in, despite my obvious reluctance. He smoothed my hair and squeezed me, pressing his warm hands to the small of my back. As he breathed in my fragrance, I stole a last opportunity to remember his smell of citrus fruits.

"Come on, Cessie! Time to go!" Jonah's voice broke the silence.

Gabriel didn't move, so I gently stepped back from him and acknowledged Jonah, who was standing behind us, several bags at his feet. I had to suppress a gasp as Jonah glistened against the moonlight hanging high above us.

A screech of burning rubber and Ruadhan was beside us in the Range Rover. Lowering down the passenger window, he joined in a little more politely. "Sweetheart, are you ready?" he asked.

"Erm . . . I think I'm going to go it alone from here, but thank you. Thanks to all of you. I can't let you risk yourselves for me any longer."

I shuffled uncomfortably; Brooke and Hanora had also appeared—though I didn't actually mean what I said where Hanora was concerned. Gabriel's body became rigid, ready to protest, but Ruadhan beat him to it. In a flash he was at my side, picking me up and placing me into the passenger seat.

"Ruadhan, I . . ."

"Little love, we haven't got time to argue. You're coming with me whether you want to or not." He sounded like a father scolding his unruly daughter, as he hustled my backpack from my shoulders.

Hanora moved in next to Gabriel, taking his arm in her own—sending me a message, I was sure—and gazing longingly up to his face. Gabriel's eyes never left mine. I hoped she saw that.

A hard wind of jealously hit me. "Fine, but not without Jonah," I spat, and I watched Gabriel flinch.

"No problem with that!" Jonah said, throwing his bag in the trunk.

"Well then I'm coming, too!" Brooke shrieked, gesturing to Jonah to add her oversized suitcase into the trunk.

Obediently he chucked her belongings untidily into the space. Within seconds, they were in the back seats and I watched Ruadhan and Gabriel exchange unhappy glances. Any other time I think there may have been a debate over the traveling companions, but right now there was no time; every lost minute was an opportunity for Eligio to return.

As Ruadhan put the car into first, Gabriel tapped on my window. "Your cell." He handed me the iPhone. I reached for it, skimming his skin, which made me wobble inside. "Keep it with you, call whenever you want. . . ."

His wide eyes made mine run like a watercolor painting caught in the rain.

Please don't be angry with me, I will come back to you as soon as I can.

I didn't have an opportunity to reply; Ruadhan was flooring the accelerator and we made off like bandits into the night.

As soon as he was out of sight, I regretted the things I'd said. I wanted to tell him that I loved him, that I was prepared to fight for him, for us; I wanted to tell him that I trusted him, but that wouldn't have been entirely true. There were still things that he was keeping back and I was skeptical as to why he hadn't shared them with me yet.

As that thought crossed my mind, I felt a twinge of guilt; I hadn't exactly told him everything either. I hadn't been forthcoming about the girl in shadow; I hadn't informed him that she had been here tonight. I could have told him, I could have explained how she appeared in my time of trouble and that I had no idea who she was.

I remembered her long dark hair streaming down her back, which had brushed my cheek. But as always there was a gap, a hole in my memory. All I could recall was that she appeared, and then . . . nothing. Did I see her disappear when Gabriel's light overflowed from the porch, or was I imagining that? Of course, Gabriel had hardly given me the chance to tell him, given how I had found him. Still, I knew I wouldn't have been able to explain the girl to him. To add to that, there was a strange, unsettling feeling swelling in my subconscious as soon as I began to think of her.

A warning not to think too hard, I had decided.

Brooke interrupted my inner turmoil. "Erm, Cessie . . . I'm sorry about last night. I was just, well, trying to help you. . . . Anyway, no harm, no foul. You look fine." Her apology was barely half-hearted, I could only assume it was given at Jonah's insistence.

"It's okay. . . ."

"Well anyway, by way of seeking your forgiveness . . ." she half chuckled, "I packed some of your clothes this morning. I figured you'd abandoned most of my hard work when I saw that tired-looking backpack of yours. . . . So don't worry where we're off to, at least you'll be dressed in style. . . ." She trailed off as Ruadhan slammed the truck into a deep bend and zipped around the winding roads, heading for the motorway.

"Oh, thanks. Where are we going exactly?" I looked over my shoulder to anyone for an answer.

"Ah . . . *Oui, oui!* Carcassonne, South of France," Ruadhan joked. His Irish-accented French was awkward, but I appreciated him trying to raise my spirits.

I looked at Jonah and he replied by stretching in my direction. "Don't worry, Cessie, he's gone. Frederic is dust. You said so yourself."

I shivered at the mention of his name. I guess offering that tidbit in the cottage had given away where I had been at the time.

"Something I'm missing?" Ruadhan's tone lowered to a murmur.

"No, no," I said. "I just had a slightly bizarre experience with a Vampire in Nice a couple of years back is all." I didn't want to have to explain myself for a third time.

I scratched my back underneath my coat and blouse, feeling for the elongated scar. Sure enough, it was still there—a constant reminder of that night, of that Vampire I had foolishly befriended.

"Well, don't you worry, love, you have us," Ruadhan said without taking his eyes off the road. "We'll keep you well hidden while we wait for Gabriel."

I half thought Ruadhan mentioned Gabriel for Jonah's benefit as I caught him glimpsing at Jonah in the rearview mirror. I wondered how much Ruadhan really knew.

"Any particular reason we're going to France?" I asked, trying to take the conversation away from my Angel.

"We have a property in a village called Neylis," Ruadhan replied. "It's an hour or so by car from the airport, the middle of nowhere by all accounts. However, should we need to leave quickly, we can be in Andorra in no time, over and into Spain. We can connect to Africa via Perpignan or Marseille—"

Brooke interrupted him. "And we can get to Milan—shopping in Italy is amazing!" she chirped.

I found her upbeat attitude surprising considering the danger she had been in only an hour ago. "You've been?" I asked.

"To Milan, yes, but not to Neylis. Bit too quiet for my liking, but this lot likes to keep us separated from the rest of civilization!"

"I wonder why," I muttered under my breath.

I wanted to ask about Gabriel, but I held back. I would talk to Ruadhan when we were alone.

No one spoke for a while and when we hit the motorway, Ruadhan encouraged me to sleep, but my body was still buzzing, fueled with adrenaline from the mammoth events of the day.

"What happened to Eligio?" My inquiry met with no reply, so I turned to Jonah.

"Seems when Gabriel struck him with light he fell into a rift to the third dimension and it closed, Gabriel's light sealing it." Jonah seemed relieved.

"Why didn't the light kill him?"

"It's not powerful enough to end a Pureblood the way it does the rest of us. But it is weapon enough to have some effect," he answered.

"How did Eligio open the rift into this world? Was he waiting for more of them to come through?" I pushed.

Ruadhan coughed, signaling to Jonah to stop, but I gestured for him to proceed.

"Don't know," Jonah said. "We didn't think they could command the rifts like that. He was dragging you toward it; he opened it to take you through with him." He stopped there and my stomach turned over.

Ruadhan butted in. "Jonah doesn't know that for sure, Cessie, he's surmising."

"But Gabriel told me that light souls are taken through the cracks by Angels and that dark souls seep through the rifts to this third dimension. Surely I would just disappear if I were taken through into their world?"

I didn't quite get it. If I were to pass through either rift, to either dimension, my energy would feed through, if it matched either. Gabriel had led me to believe that my soul was pure and good, so Eligio and his kind would gain nothing by destroying my human form if they took me. Jonah must have it wrong, I decided. He didn't know as much as Gabriel, and Ruadhan had been talking about Heaven and Hell, not different dimensions. I had convinced myself until Jonah piped back up.

"Perhaps you have a dark soul, perhaps there's something about you that makes you different, so that you wouldn't just evaporate like the rest of us. . . . Maybe you'd keep your form. . . ."

Ruadhan slammed the truck over to the hard shoulder and came to a swift halt. Releasing his seat belt he twisted to Jonah, directing a menacing expression his way. "That's enough! She's not one of us! Gabriel has made it quite clear that she is an innocent and furthermore this little gem is human! Stop scaring the poor girl!"

With that, he snapped back to the wheel and pulled back out into the road. I glanced at Jonah, who met me with raised eyebrows and a grin creasing his cheek.

As I let the words sink in it dawned on me that Jonah's theory, as uncomfortable as it made me, didn't feel that far off.

SEVENTEEN

THE ROADS WERE QUIET so the journey didn't take long. Ruadhan had booked a room at the hotel adjacent to Stansted Airport, so we could all change out of our bloodied clothing. Jonah stood outside the room, guarding the door while I showered. Ruadhan and Brooke went to the ticket counter to sort out our flight.

Emotionally drained, I unzipped my backpack and pulled out a fresh pair of skinny jeans, a T-shirt, and a hoodie. I hesitated as I scooped the items up, placing them into a neat pile on the dresser, and rummaged for the smartphone inside my pocket. No missed calls, and no messages. I threw my phone onto the bed and made my way into the bathroom.

Stripping off and stepping into the shower, I ran the water as hot as I could, steaming up the tiny room immediately. I scoured my skin in an attempt to rid myself of the Vampires' remains that painted my neck and arms. Allowing the water to run down my face, I twisted, letting it soak through my hair. I dug into my scalp with my nails and made a mental note to thank the good people of this establishment for providing soap and shampoo. As content as I could be that the Vampire I had conversed with only yesterday was now safely down the drain, I carefully tiptoed out of the shower, wrapping myself in the fluffy yellow towel. Once covered up, I continued through to the bedroom.

I found Jonah waiting for me, perched next to my cell, scrolling through my lack of messages.

"Spying on me?" I inquired, not bothered about my appearance. It seemed our relationship had gone beyond the realms of childish embarrassment.

"Nope, just waiting for my turn to wash down. Seems I'm quite dirty." Winking, he stood up and handed me my phone. "Fancy helping me clean off?"

He moved in a little closer. I hesitated and blew out a small puff of air. "What's with you? One minute you're, well, soft—almost kind— and the next . . ." I wasn't sure how to finish that sentence.

He tilted his head and laughed a little, his seductive mouth curving up at both ends with a dazzling smile. "Now don't go around telling everyone about my softer side, I'd prefer to keep my 'bad boy' persona intact!"

He squeezed my shoulder as he stepped past me, but stopped and hovered. I clenched my towel a little tighter around my chest. He leaned in and tugged my heavy hair above my neck, detangling my chain.

His fingertips tickled the nape of my neck as he slid my ring back down to its rightful place: at the center of my collarbone. He held it there for what felt like too long and I finally engaged him, unable to avoid meeting his eyes with my own any longer. He didn't say anything; he didn't need to. His mien had turned back to calm, tender. I paused as I inhaled the sultry wood scent that drifted out of his pores.

"Where'd you get this, beautiful?" he asked, twisting the chain above my gold circle.

"Not sure, I've had it as long as I can remember," I murmured.

He scratched his head and said, "Well, it looks like an engagement ring to me. Something we should know?"

A strange sensation of déjà vu floated over me. I had never considered it, but he was right, it was an engagement ring. I shook myself and as his words sank in I repeated, "We?"

"Me and Gabriel. By the look of that rock we both have competition."

I opened my mouth, but Jonah cut me off by kissing the top of my head roughly and caressing the back of my arm with his palm before walking off to the bathroom.

I stood in silence, trying to concentrate on the misplaced memory, but Jonah broke through the crux of the issue. "Offer's still open, beautiful. I could use you in here."

I replied by grabbing the handle and slamming the door just as he was stepping into the shower, catching an eyeful of his bare back.

"Now who's spying on who?" he shouted playfully.

IN RECORD TIME WE WERE READY to board the plane. Ruadhan was on constant lookout, making sure that we were not being followed and that there wasn't anyone—anywhere—who might mean me harm. The queue for the flight was long and Ruadhan insisted that we board last as he swept the line for anything unusual. I left my place in line and went to find him.

"You okay?" he quizzed, looking over my shoulder. He wasn't taking the operation lightly.

"I have a question. . . ." I trailed off. It didn't quite seem the time or place, but then when was?

"What's worrying you?"

"There were two Purebloods and two clans in Creigiau that came for us. But only Eligio and his clan came to the house tonight, right?"

He pondered this for a moment, never stopping his scan of the immediate boarding gate. "Seems Eligio thought he would go it alone. The note Thomas left for Gabriel indicated that he would; there was only his clan attacking us, but then . . ." He teetered off.

"Then what?"

"There was another Pureblood with them; I saw her moving through the hallway."

I hadn't seen any other Pureblood; I hadn't even seen Eligio . . . well, not entirely. Then I heard him properly. "Her?"

"She was prowling through the house. I tried to reach her, but I was struggling to end the Vampires that were surrounding me. Kids, really—well, compared to me. But there were too many. . . ."

It struck me like a bomb exploding at my feet. He'd seen the girl in shadow. She must have passed through the hallway to get to the kitchen; that was the next recollection I had of her after she had appeared. And it made complete sense. She was dark to the core and it conveyed through to her physical form, always shrouded in blackness. I recalled that Frederic had halted at her presence. She was stronger than him. She'd ended him. But then I thought that she had disappeared as Gabriel's light had soaked through her being. Where had she gone and where was she now? More importantly, if she was one of them, then why had she been protecting me all this time?

"Love, are you okay? You've gone a bit green."

"I . . . I just need to use the bathroom."

I stumbled backward, finally spinning myself into a sprint to the nearest sign for the ladies' room. I found it tucked away in the corner, but stopped before entering, dropping down in a heap on the ground. Burrowing my head in my lap I tried to stop the multitude of worrying thoughts from racing around my head, bouncing off one side of my brain to the other. My forehead ached when I tried to concentrate on the image of her.

I jolted, releasing my hands, and as I watched the people rushing past ahead of me, through the mass of bodies he stood like a monument, unmoving, in front of the giant wall-length windows at the opposite end of the room. His eyes blazed red and his dirty-blond hair was swept back, allowing me to absorb his sharp features. I didn't move. I think my heart stopped as he began slowly pacing through the horizontal traffic of bodies, in a straight and purposeful line, coming right for me. It was the Vampire I had met the night Jonah and I had come under attack; the exact same one I had seen in my vision, disbanding from the Purebloods outside the blazing house in Creigiau. Still he wore dated clothing—a frilled white shirt tucked into straight-legged trousers—and as he neared, the sockets that held his flaming orbs broadened.

From just a few feet away he extended his hand, beckoning me to meet him in the middle. I didn't dare move or flinch; if I ran there would be bloodshed. As he was on the cusp of reaching me, his eyes left mine; he was intrigued by something below my neck. I followed his gaze to my gemmed ring. Only then did he stop. His expression turned from menacing to intrigued.

"Jeez, do you gotta run off like that? We're gonna miss the damn flight! Come on!" Brooke had emerged at my side, hauling me off the filthy floor.

I snapped back to where he stood, but he was gone, as if he had never been there. How had he disappeared so quickly?

Searching the crowds with my eyes, I couldn't find him. As Brooke whisked me to the boarding gate, I reasoned that I might have conjured him myself, a figment of my imagination. I didn't know anymore. I didn't know anything.

She handed the flight attendant our boarding passes and passports and we met with Ruadhan and Jonah, who were waiting at the door. Jonah peered down at me, sensing that something wasn't right. He gestured to Brooke and Ruadhan, and they walked ahead, leaving him to tighten his arm around my shoulders, steadying me onto the plane.

The flight was full and we had only just managed to get seats side by side. Jonah placed our luggage into the compartment above. I searched ahead to find Ruadhan and Brooke scattered on aisle seats a few rows ahead. I stiffened a smile at Brooke as she looked back unhappily at the seating arrangements. She wanted to be next to Jonah. Ruadhan made the same motion a few minutes later, with an equally disgruntled face but for different reasons. He was worried about me.

Jonah fastened my seat belt for me and I wriggled the iPhone free; still no messages. My connection to Gabriel was still present but like a horizon you moved away from—it was becoming a tiny dot in the distance. It seemed that the farther apart we were, the weaker our connection became. I couldn't feel him near my invisible tunnel and I decided that the very fact he had handed me my phone meant he wouldn't be able to meet me in my mind. Apparently that little trick didn't work long distance, at least not properly.

For the first time in what felt a very long while, my thoughts were my own again. It felt desperately lonely.

"You gotta switch that off, we'll be on the move soon." Jonah took my rejected phone and handed it back to me; the screen turned black. "Cessie—"

I cut him off. "Just . . . just hold me, please." I snuggled my face into his chest and obediently he slid his arm behind me. I got away with my silent sobs, but my chest-jerking gave me away.

"Shhhh, beautiful."

I fell asleep nuzzled into Jonah. Bizarrely, on this frosty winter night, he was the only thing that would keep my soul warm.

HE WOKE ME AS THE PLANE came into a bumpy landing, hitting the tarmac and bouncing up and down before coming to a complete stop. I pawed my tired eyes with curled fists and reluctantly peeled myself from Jonah's chest.

"Did you get some rest?"

"Don't sleep, remember," he said. He smiled a sweet, sincere smile that put me at ease.

"Right. Thanks for, well, you know . . ." I offered, unbuckling my seat belt.

Ruadhan and Brooke waited for the seats to empty before finding us and we traipsed down the aisle, the flight attendant wishing us a pleasant stay as we made our way down the steps.

Brooke attached herself to Jonah, so I held back and joined Ruadhan.

"We'll be out of here in ten minutes, it's a shed of an airport. I've got a rental waiting for us. We'll be in Neylis in less than an hour and a half."

It hadn't occurred to me that the French security might have a problem with my passport. Jonah and Brooke had gone through no issues with theirs, but when I stepped up to the window the old French woman with graying hair eyed my passport and me for a prolonged period of time.

She called over another staff member, who looked me up and down, at which point Ruadhan stepped in. When her tone didn't respond positively I was rendered speechless: I witnessed him capture her stare, speaking extremely slowly in her native tongue. She then nodded, repeating what he'd said, and signaled for me to move on. The wrinkled lines of her crow's feet ironed out as she moved on to the next foreigner.

"What did you do to her?" I whispered, pacing quickly to the baggage claim.

"Vampire ability, the power of influence . . . One of the few traits we have in common with our Angel friend."

"What was wrong with my passport?" I asked, taking it from Ruadhan's large hand and dropping it into the top of my backpack. I couldn't remember how I had obtained it, sometime in a life gone by. Of course, it was fraudulent.

"Some confusion over your photo, she didn't think you were the same person. I told her . . . young folk dye their hair, wear contact lenses and whatnot." He rushed over to the conveyor belt, grabbing the first of Brooke's suitcases coming through and chucking it to Jonah.

I bowed my head, confused; I looked the same as my photo. I didn't have long to ponder on the mistake; Ruadhan was like a bat out of Hell taking my hand and dragging me to the waiting car. In exchange for a credit card swipe, Ruadhan received the keys to a matte black sedan. A few moments later, a bright yellow bumblebee-striped Mini Cooper convertible appeared.

Brooke dashed from the entrance to swipe the keys out of the young lad's hand with an extended smile. "Come on, Cessie, you can ride with me!"

Obediently I stepped forward, but Ruadhan's long arm moved over my chest, yanking me back. "No, the little love is with me. You take Jonah and follow. Keep your eyes on your mirrors, make sure no one's behind you that shouldn't be."

Her face soured. "Ruadhan, I apologized. I won't hurt her, freakin' hell, you can't tell everyone what to do!"

Ruadhan didn't grace her with a reply.

As Jonah found his way to the car, suitcases in tow, she stopped complaining. Riding alone with Jonah wouldn't be so terrible after all.

I opened the door and Ruadhan chuckled under his breath. "Other door, love, they drive on the wrong side of the road here, you know."

"It's the right side!" Brooke shouted at him, deliberately emphasizing her American accent.

I slammed the door shut.

"You ready?" Ruadhan asked.

I nodded as he pulled away from the curb, switching his lights on. The clock on the dashboard informed me that it was 6:27 a.m., and I found my thoughts wandering back to Gabriel. I switched on my phone and waited to see if any messages would load. They didn't.

"He'll be halfway over the Atlantic by now, he won't be able to call you yet." Ruadhan tilted his head in my direction as if he were reading my mind.

"Oh . . . Do you know when he'll be back?"

"When he's found who he needs to find and he knows what he needs to know." Shrugging, Ruadhan circled several roundabouts, finally hitting a long stretch of road. I peered out at the side mirror to check that the Cooper was following us. Sure enough, they were there.

Ruadhan broke the silence between us. "I need you to keep your distance from Jonah."

I let his words drift between us before I replied. "Says who, you or Gabriel?" Snuggling deeper into the seat, I rubbed my coat sleeves.

"Gabriel has concerns. . . . Jonah's unusually taken by you; he drank from you and Gabriel's worried he might try again."

"He had the opportunity two nights ago. He didn't," I argued.

"No, but if Brooke hadn't walked in, well, who knows . . ."

What actually worried me more was that night, in the kitchen, I was on the verge of asking him to do so.

"He's a Vampire, sweetheart. He, like the rest of us, feeds on blood. Sometimes that urge supersedes even the strongest of wills."

"He's not a monster! He risked himself to save me, and I for one am most grateful for that."

"I'm not saying he's a monster. By all accounts, he's a good lad. He's trying his best to overcome the hand he was dealt, but he has many people's lives to pay for. In the eyes of God, in a thousand lifetimes he'd still be hard-pressed to have redeemed himself."

We continued down the motorway, breaking the speed limit

and passing row upon row of plane trees. The branches were pointing at me like old, decrepit fingers poised accusingly. What it was
they were accusing me of, I didn't know.

"You know about the dimensions?"

"Yes."

"Then how is it you believe in God?" I was walking a tightrope,
but I had to know what he knew.

"However Gabriel puts it, whatever science is involved and by
whatever name you would call these dimensions, to me they are
Heaven and Hell. The mythology stems from what people witnessed
all those years ago; different people interpret things differently. I still
believe there is a God."

"Have you asked Gabriel if that's true?" I was losing my balance
on the tightrope.

"He's not able to explain to that degree. He's an Angel, and I am
one of the Devil's. I understand and accept that." He nodded, rubbing
his hairy chin, the other hand placed rigidly on the steering wheel. He
didn't know about the crystal, about Orifiel, about the reason behind
the existence of Angels.

Ruadhan had been deeply religious before he was turned, I had
gathered as much from the conversation we had shared in the church
back in Hedgerley. Shattering someone's faith like his would never
be easy and even if you could, why would you want to if it gave a
purpose to his existence and provided some sort of comfort?

I swerved the conversation back to Jonah. If I was going to be
spending some serious time with him, I needed to know more about
him and his intentions. "How did Jonah become a Vampire? What
happened to him, Ruadhan?"

"Would it help you understand him, help you understand the

danger?" He was not one to gossip, but if it served a purpose he might tell me.

"Yes."

He contemplated before he began, and I sat up straight in the passenger's seat, ready to listen.

"Jonah has been with us just shy of seven years. He grew up in New Jersey, and by all accounts he was a perfectly normal lad—captain of the football team, and all that. He was granted a scholarship to Florida State and started in the autumn. He hadn't been there long when he received a call to say that his family had been in an accident; they had all perished."

He stopped there and I inhaled a sharp breath. "Poor Jonah . . ." I trailed off. "What happened?"

"A car accident . . . drunk driver knocked them clean off the road. From the account Jonah gave, it sounds as though they didn't suffer. But he couldn't accept it. Especially his sister. She was the baby, he loved her more than anything. He never went back to Jersey; he stayed down in Florida, but he went off the rails. Spent most of his time drunk, squandering his inheritance away in bars and by gambling. He got kicked out of college."

"How do you know all this?"

"He told me once; some of us have shared our stories. He's still haunted by his past life. He's not the only one. . . ."

"How did he come to be a Vampire?"

"He was found by a Second Generation, slumped behind some dumpsters outside a biker bar, and was dragged back to their Gualtiero—Emery. Jonah was a light soul, and so Emery chose to turn him. Jonah took to his new role like a moth to a flame, enjoying his new powers. He moved up the Gualtiero's ranks quickly, and was out stealing humans for him within a matter of weeks. Within months he was one of Emery's most prestigious soldiers. Jonah took orders only from Emery and did his bidding directly. That is unusual with an army of so many."

The rounded streetlamps that lit the borders of the mountains reminded me of army helmets. Ruadhan drove fast but steady; sheer drops into the forest on any other day might have scared me.

"So how did he come to travel with you, with Gabriel?"

"He savagely murdered and pillaged, Cessie. Worse still, he enjoyed it. Emery held him in such high regard that he would turn females specifically for Jonah to feed off, to grow stronger. He granted him the freedom to hunt for his own human meals and Jonah always sought out pretty little things like you. There's your second warning sign."

I tried to stop my heart banging against my chest as I imagined him feeding off young girls, chasing them down for sport.

"What was the first?"

"The very fact that he is a Vampire."

I didn't say anything for a while, letting this new information sink in. "You didn't answer my question—how did he come to travel with you?"

Ruadhan was trying to highlight the evil in Jonah to scare me away from him; I would have to do more than scratch the surface in order to understand the entirety of his story.

"That's not really important, is it, love? What's crucial is that you recognize the danger and keep your distance."

"It's important to me."

Looking at my expectant face, reluctantly he continued. "He was hunting with some of the others and found a house on the beach. Inside were a mother, father, and daughter. The girl was the same age as his sister and had the same disability."

"Disability?"

"She was blind."

"Oh . . ." I trailed off.

"He told the Vampires to leave, but they wouldn't. Some went, taking the parents back to Emery, but a few stayed, turning on the girl. She was not worthy of presenting to their Master, so they set about tormenting and killing her. Jonah had to make a choice, and for whatever reason, he decided to turn on his own kind and tried to save her. Gabriel and I found them at the moment Jonah broke through the door, carrying her in his arms."

"What happened to the girl? To Jonah?"

"She, well, she died. . . ." Ruadhan went quiet and I sensed he was not telling the whole story. "Gabriel and I ended the three Vampires who made chase, but we offered Jonah a choice: return to his Gualtiero, or leave with us and try to regain his decency. He chose the latter."

I pondered on this for a while. "He felt love for the girl, like he did for his sister. It broke through the darkness of his soul, long enough for him to decide. And he chose redemption. Why would you warn me off him, when he's so clearly trying to find himself again, trying to be a good person?" If anything, Ruadhan's story had caused me to feel a surge of compassion for Jonah.

"As much as he tries, like the rest of us, he is still dangerous."

"Then why aren't you warning me off Brooke, or off you? You're all the same, aren't you?" It was a bold question, but I had to ask.

"Essentially, yes. But he is the only one of us who has drunk your blood. He's showing signs of being drawn to you and it can only be for that reason."

"But Brooke told me that it is only truly dangerous if a Vampire drinks from another Vampire, that's when a connection is fused."

"Yes, but human blood can still be difficult to resist. You may have been the first light soul Jonah has ever drunk from." He put it in layman's terms.

"But then theoretically he should be put off by my blood. If I have a light soul surely I would just repel him?"

The further Ruadhan tried to explain, the more I started to concede that Jonah might have been onto something earlier.

"True, darkness feeds darkness. He shouldn't be drawn to you, but for whatever reason he still seems to be."

I could see that Ruadhan hadn't fully considered this, but then he wasn't entirely enlightened on my individual circumstances. I might exist in a human form, but I was immortal. And who the hell knew what kind of immortal I was or how it had come to be. I didn't break the rules because I was some sort of weird, abnormal exception.

"Well then, I'd stop worrying. Perhaps he just wants to be my friend!" I didn't want Ruadhan looking over his shoulder every time Jonah and I had a conversation.

"Perhaps . . . We'll see."

EVENTUALLY THE MOUNTAINOUS, curved roads came to an end and Ruadhan highlighted the Pyrenees Mountains, which were coming into view as the light of the early day began to glimmer. The mountains were quite something, but what was even more appealing was that I felt nothing toward them. This was the first time that I was seeing them and I enjoyed the newness of the sensation.

"It's pretty brisk up there," Ruadhan said. "They're covered in snow some three thousand meters above sea level, like." Ruadhan knew a lot. Over a hundred years of reading and an interest in history and geography would do that to you.

"They are stunning, Ruadhan, really," I replied with genuine interest.

We passed a sign for Neylis. I wasn't surprised by the isolation of the place—there weren't many houses around. Gabriel chose remote properties, and unique ones; our destination was an impressive barn conversion. I was too tired to ask for a tour. I needed to sleep. Ruadhan turned off the engine, unlocked the ground level with a key from underneath a plant pot, and led me to a bedroom in the basement of the property.

"You've not been here for a while?" I asked.

Remarkably there were fresh sheets and towels placed neatly at the end of the bed.

"Gabriel had someone here a few days ago, readying it for our arrival," Ruadhan explained as he placed my backpack down neatly next to the head of the bed.

"A few days ago? I thought he only decided yesterday morning that we were leaving?"

"He decided several days ago, but Michael persuaded Gabriel to stay on a bit longer in Hedgerley. I guess we know why now."

As groggy as I was, Ruadhan's comment startled me. "Michael was lying all this time about his Gualtiero's stirrings, wasn't he? He knew they were near, but he wanted to get Thomas back in exchange for me—"

"Seems so," Ruadhan cut in. "He didn't count on Gabriel striking his own deal with Thomas and ending him first. Thomas, at least, must have had the sense to know that there's no such thing as a deal with a Pureblood. I guess Michael was pretty cut up about it. I reckon in the end he just wanted revenge."

"I cost him his life," I murmured, pulling the quilt back.

Ruadhan drew the curtains, blocking the rising sun, before tucking me in like a small child. "No, love, the darkness inside him cost him his existence," he said, his voice gentle. "His life was taken from him a long time ago; you need to separate the two."

I was quite certain Ruadhan was also reminding me that the same rule of thumb applied where Jonah was concerned. So he got the last word in the end, and I was too tired to care.

Still dressed, I fell asleep as soon as my head touched the pillow.

EIGHTEEN

I COULDN'T BE SURE HOW LONG I SLEPT FOR; the thick velvet curtains blocked out any sense of day or night. My phone buzzing inside my pocket woke me.

Wearily sitting up, I yanked it out and saw a text from Gabriel. The message was simply a description of where the chess pieces had been when we had left our game.

I was surprised to find the set neatly placed upon the table in the corner of the room, waiting for me. I followed Gabriel's instructions, carefully positioning the ivory statues back in the checkered boxes.

Cautiously this time, I moved the knight two up and one across to the left—where I had originally intended—this time fingering the round base. I texted him back with my move, nothing more. The phone vibrated in my hand as he speedily replied. This time it was his move, continued with a note.

CASTLE ON THE RIGHT FOUR SPACES FORWARD.

ARE YOU OKAY?

I contemplated my response. Moving one of my pawns, I spent far longer considering my answer to his question.

THIRD PAWN FROM THE RIGHT ONE SPACE FORWARD.

WE HAVE ARRIVED AT THE HOUSE, HOW ARE YOU AND HANORA?

I couldn't help putting her name on the message—my way of reminding him that I was still upset about the situation. He didn't reply instantly. I perched at the foot of the bed, waiting.

WE'RE IN THE STATES. I HAVE SEPARATED FROM HANORA FOR NOW

IN SEARCH OF MALACHI ALONE. KEEP SAFE. STAY WITH RUADHAN.

DON'T LEAVE THE HOUSE. I'LL BE IN TOUCH.

I was disappointed at the lack of emotion; I guessed he was giving me space.

Rummaging through my backpack, I changed my outfit for some sweatpants, a T-shirt, and a jacket. I just wanted to be comfy. I found the bathroom and splashed water over my face, waking myself up, and ran my fingers through my long hair.

The glint of my crystal gem in the mirror above the basin reminded me of the interest that had spread over the Vampire's face as he had regarded it. I took it off and sat on the tiled floor to study it further. The jewel was certainly unique; I had never seen anything like it. The gold band was delicate in comparison. I tipped it upside down and for the first time I noticed that the round, thick base underneath the stone had some sort of marking on it. I had to squint, but I was sure it was the symbol of a swan. How had I never seen it before? I guess I had never had a reason to look at it that closely.

As I rolled it back and forth in my palm, my mind wandered back to Gabriel, and how he had considered it while I recovered after I had been shot. When he kissed me and held me in the cottage, this very ring had caused him to seize up.

What did this ring actually represent?

As I pondered that, I slid my hand under my T-shirt and touched my navel, now unmarked. When Gabriel had filled me with light it had healed, not leaving even the faintest of reminders that anything had ever perforated my skin. I could almost hear the faint sound of his breath blowing gently, skimming my midriff as he stitched me up—quite a contrast to the noise that had filled the room when I had been shot. Why hadn't he just breathed this magical light of his across my shoulder that night?

I needed answers and so I decided to leave my lonesome fortress and text him. Okay, it was a cop-out, I should call, but leaving your fortress and jumping off the top of the castle were two entirely different things.

YOU HEALED ME WITH YOUR LIGHT WHEN YOU FOUND ME IN THE COTTAGE, WHY DIDN'T YOU DO THAT WHEN I WAS SHOT? WHY DID YOU STITCH ME UP INSTEAD? DO YOU KNOW WHERE MY RING CAME FROM? DID YOU GIVE IT TO ME?

I hit send before I had a chance to change my mind. I stayed nervously on the floor, waiting for his reply. A few minutes later my phone started to ring. I hadn't considered that he might call. I nearly let the voice mail pick it up, but I answered at the last second.

"Delete that message from your phone." Gabriel's words were hurried.

"What? Why?"

"Because it's dangerous."

"What do you mean? Why is it dangerous?"

He paused and I heard him breathing heavily down the line, which was crackling.

I shifted the phone away from my ear, long enough to realize that my reception wasn't very good in the basement.

"The light, the energy I released, doesn't heal humans or anything of this world. If one of the others reads your messages, they will know you are not what I have said you are."

"I don't get it, who does it heal?"

I was quick; his reply was not. Finally it came. "Angels."

Now it was my turn to be quiet.

"This isn't a conversation I want to have with you over the phone, it's not safe. When I find Malachi he may know."

"When did you start to think I was . . . ?" I stuttered.

He paused. "The day we left Creigiau. I don't understand how that could be, but I will find out. Please delete that message."

I gulped, hard. "And what about my ring? Did you give it to me?"

The line crackled, but his answer came through. "I didn't give it to you, Lai, your fiancé did."

Then the line went dead.

My initial shock was followed by a wave of embarrassment that made me cringe. Stupid, stupid girl! Why would you ask that? Why in the world would Gabriel propose marriage? But if it wasn't him who had been my fiancé, then who was it, and what had happened to him?

Picking myself up off the cold floor, I began circling the room, my mind revving like a car with a fresh tank of gas.

Gabriel thinks I am an . . . Angel. He healed me with his light, a light which I know can end Second Generation Vampires because they are created from darkness. But Eligio tried to take me through a rift into the third dimension. There would be no point if my soul was light, I would simply disappear.

Jonah said my blood was different and it made him impossibly strong. He suspects I'm not human. But Vampires feed off dark souls, not light ones. I weighed these facts, but nothing made sense. And then to add even more confusion, that girl—my protector—shrouded in shadow. Ruadhan had seen her with his own eyes, and said she was a Pureblood Vampire. But then why would she be following me? Why would she destroy Second Generation Vampires to keep me alive? How was it that I could never recall what it was she did? I remembered her arrival, but then everything else that followed turned into a black spot. Did she wipe my memory somehow? But why would she bother?

Then there was Gabriel. He found me in my first life, when I was some form of human. I died and he left, but where did he go? How had I met my end and then been resurrected into whatever I was now?

No closer to working anything out, I decided to venture up the staircase and find the others. The gaps between the boards were far apart so I used the rickety banister to help me up.

I found myself on the ground level of the property; an open-plan-lounge-cum-kitchen/dining room presented itself to me, with a glass panel that ran the length of the far wall, overlooking a garden. The design was a strange mixture of a hundred-year-old barn converted and mixed together with contemporary fixtures and fittings.

I rather enjoyed walking over the uneven, sloping wooden floorboards that ran throughout the property.

The exposed beams above, and half-plastered, half-brick walls took me back to a simpler time. A retiring sun was setting on the horizon; only the brightness of the solar lights outside and the lit lamps in the house gave me the opportunity to appreciate my surroundings.

Past the kitchen lay four bedrooms, a family bathroom that was void of any windows, and a study that was crammed to the ceiling with books. I slowly made my way up another staircase, which lacked any form of railing. This gave me access to an attic room that was short on head height, but had two laptops set up, with desks and a craft table. Three large loft windows slanted downward and as I peered up at the graying sky, safe behind the glass seal, I marveled at the clarity of the night's backdrop. The twinkle of a thousand stars waking up and coming into focus against the dark navy was beautiful. I half wished I were up there with them.

"You shouldn't sneak up on people like that," I whispered, unmoving, keeping my eyes locked on the stars.

The faintest creak of a floorboard had given him away. Jonah placed his hands on my shoulders and squeezed them. "Sleeping Beauty finally wakes."

"How long have I been out for?"

"Oh, just a couple of days."

"My phone woke me up." I shrugged.

"Gabriel?" he inquired, but he already knew the answer to that.

I twisted around to address him properly, though no amount of familiarity ever seemed to stop the surprise on my face as he stood out against the blackness. He was magnificent. "Hmm, yeah. Listen, I

can't thank you enough for your help. Well, for coming to my rescue."
I shifted my weight a little awkwardly. "But I have a lot of, well, issues
I need to work through. I need a friend right now, more than I need
anything else. Think you can help me out with that?"

His stance didn't change, but his perfect lips curved into a delicious smile. His eyes copied the stars, glinting spots of a sizzling
sparkle. "Whatever you need."

I nodded, surprised I didn't get a little more fight out of him. I
carefully moved back through the attic, and Jonah followed. He was
forced to stoop to avoid hitting his head against the sloped ceiling. I
hesitated, rocking from the balls of my feet to the base of my heels as
the reason for his vague response occurred to me. Whirling around,
I positioned my mouth next to his earlobe, and for once, not having
to stand on my tiptoes to meet his face, I whispered, "Ruadhan's listening, isn't he."

Pressing his palm against my cheek, gently moving my hair
back, he murmured in my ear, "Yup."

His breath tickled my bare neck and a tingle rippled the full
length of my spine. I couldn't help returning his naughty grin, but I
tried to disguise it by rolling my eyes at him and carried on down
the stairs, being careful not to lose my balance.

Ruadhan stood waiting in the kitchen, a glass of orange juice
poured for me. "You look fresh, love, the sleep did you good. We
were worried about you, but Gabriel said to let you sleep. I hope you
don't mind, he asked me to leave you with the chess set."

I nodded and chugged the juice, realizing how thirsty I was.

He gestured to follow him into the living room and presented
me with the wall-mounted flat screen, pulling out a drawer full of
DVDs. "So, we'll be here awhile. Gabriel thinks it's best if you stay

in the house and on the grounds. But don't worry, there's plenty of grub, drink, and movies to keep you occupied!" He scratched his stubble almost apologetically.

I looked over his shoulder at Jonah, who winked at me, as if to say not to worry about it.

"Thanks, but I'll decide what's best for me from now on. Gabriel is thousands of miles away across the Atlantic, having a ball with Hanora, I'm sure. Do you really think I'm going to let him have all the fun?" I tilted my head, attempting to be assertive.

Before he had the chance to argue I called for Brooke, who, in a flash, was snuggled in the dip of the corner sofa, one leg over the other and hands behind her head.

"Yo!"

"Film tonight, shopping tomorrow?" I asked.

One thing was for sure; I wasn't about to be a prisoner.

Not anymore.

"There's not really any shopping around here. The market should be open tomorrow in Mirepoix, that one you were telling me about, Ruadhan."

"I was actually trying to educate you about the history of the town, not about the shopping facilities!" He huffed, irritated.

I plonked myself down a seat over from Brooke, maintaining a safe enough distance.

"Sounds good, what time do we leave?" I asked, directing myself at Brooke only.

"No, Cessie," Ruadhan said firmly.

"I know you're looking out for me, but I am my own person, and I'll decide what I do and where I go from now on."

Grinding his teeth together, he threw his arms up in the air and said, "If you insist on going, we all go."

"You can visit that Saint Maurice Cathedral you were harping on about. See, I do listen," Brooke said victoriously. Leaning in to me, she added, "I listen, but I really don't care."

I couldn't help but giggle; she was quite a character when she wasn't trying to kill me.

"Jonah, stick a movie on, and bring Cessie some popcorn," Brooke said, flapping her hands at him lazily. "Oh, and some of that wine in the fridge for us . . ."

It never failed to amaze me that he gave in to her every whim with no argument. The most he managed was a sarcastic grunt and I was sure that was for my benefit. Why Jonah, of all of them, took orders from Brooke was beyond me.

Very kindly, Ruadhan brought over a knitted blanket. The light scent of countryside wafted over me, reminding me that I was far from the city. He excused himself to the study. More reading, I assumed.

Popcorn and wine now in our hands, Jonah pressed play on the remote. I couldn't help but turn to look at him, sitting still on the opposite end of the sofa, as the opening title sequence to *The Highlander* began to play.

Winking at me in reply, he tilted his head a little, attempting to read my thoughts. Luckily for me, only Gabriel possessed that particular gift. I shook it off. I didn't belong to a race of immortals trying to kill another race of immortals, though I got the underlying statement he was attempting to make. He knew there was far more to me than what met the eye; he didn't believe I was an ordinary human girl. He wasn't wrong and I could only assume this was his way of reminding me that he wasn't buying it.

Trying to avoid being noticed, I slyly shifted under the blanket to check my phone. No messages. Remembering what Gabriel had said, I opened up the last trail and deleted it.

I managed to make it halfway through the film before nodding off again. I blamed the wine and the fresh air.

NINETEEN

THE NEXT MORNING, as the sun rose from the east over the mountains that surrounded the barn, I was startled to find myself slumped against Brooke. She had her arm over my shoulders; she had stayed with me all night.

"Ah, good, you're awake. Now I can get up!"

My eyes swept the room. "Where are Ruadhan and Jonah?" I asked, tying my hair back with the elastic around my wrist.

"Ruadhan's still reading and Jonah popped out to get you eggs for breakfast. The nearest neighbor is a few miles away, but he's pretty fast and they have chickens."

"Thanks for, erm, not waking me. I'm sorry; I didn't mean to fall asleep on you." I apologized, still wary of the redheaded Vampire.

"Listen, Cessie. I'm sorry I lost my cool with you the other night. I, well, I just overreacted. But I understand now that you're not interested in him like that. It might've taken me some time, but I know where your affections lie." Her expression was triumphant, like a naughty girl with a secret.

I straightened myself underneath the blanket. "You do?"

"You like Gabriel, I get it. You're barking up the wrong tree with him, though. Unattainable is not an exaggeration! But I get that you can't help who you fall for. Look at me. I can never have who I want, but you learn to live with it. And the way you're heading you might not be living much longer so at least you don't have that worry!" She chuckled.

I didn't find her funny.

"So you want to try this friend thing?" I continued. "It's been a while since I had a shopping partner." I strained to make it sound more appealing than being my friend actually was. Brooke was by no stretch my first choice either, but she was all I had, and it was better than nothing. Well, maybe it was better than nothing. I wasn't quite sure.

She must have felt the same way as she replied, with a lack of enthusiasm, "Well, we're stuck in the middle of nowhere together so we might as well make the best of it. Plus it couldn't be worse than listening to Ruadhan waffle about the Cathars."

"The who?"

"Don't ask." Standing up and taking out her massive sunglasses, she placed them over the ridge of her perfectly upturned nose.

Jonah appeared moments later, though he was so fast I didn't see him come through the sliding doors at the side of the kitchen. "Boiled, fried, or scrambled?" he asked, juggling three eggs in his hands.

"Soft boiled with soldiers?" I answered.

He peered at Brooke, who merely shrugged her shoulders in reply before dashing out of the kitchen, I assumed to change.

"It must just be an English thing," I said. "You boil, I'll do the bread."

I made my way over to the work surface and fumbled about creating some neat slices. As I began buttering I couldn't help glancing over. Jonah was wearing his usual dark jeans and white polo shirt combination. Today, however, he'd added a layer in the form of a fitted sweatshirt, the bright orange wearing him. It clung to his washboard stomach and broad shoulders. I tried to cast my wandering eyes back to the butter before he saw, but Jonah never missed a trick.

"You seem to like color. I thought I'd take the opportunity to be bold."

"Suits you," I lied.

Sitting at the large table, he watched me dunk my bread into the yolk with some interest. "I don't get why you call the bread 'soldiers.'"

I grinned. "'Cause if you cut them and line them up, they resemble a formation of soldiers."

As I moved the bread into an ordered formation on my plate, my bottom lip began to quiver and I was brought back down to the inescapability of my situation. "How many of us will see past the final stand in this battle?" I wondered aloud.

I thought back to Michael. I felt responsible for his demise. I could only hope the others wouldn't come to such an end because of me.

I threw down the last piece of bread, my appetite suddenly disappearing. I scraped my chair against the floor; it made a nails-against-chalkboard squeal. I continued my way to the basement to wash and change.

MIREPOIX WAS A THIRTY-MINUTE DRIVE, but of course, we did it in fifteen minutes. The sun was strong, with a clear blue sky as its peaceful backdrop as the clock struck ten. But it was cold, very cold.

I had showered and for once taken the time to blow dry my hair so that I wouldn't catch a cold. Brooke had insisted on French-braiding the top half of my hair and folding it neatly with gold bobby pins, allowing the length to dangle down to my waist, up-turned where the loose curls hung. She had also taken it upon herself to dress me for shopping. I had tried to remind her that we were not in Paris, but she seemed to enjoy playing dress-up with me, like I was the Barbie doll she never had; though I suspected she had probably possessed the largest collection of all her friends as a child.

She'd put me in a lace blouse with cap sleeves, tucked into a high-waisted, turquoise pencil skirt, finished off with a tan leather belt, which she wrapped around the top of my skirt. I had refused the Alexander McQueen heels and she just about let me off with pointy tan flats from Topshop instead. I did my best to hide my scar while I had changed. Finally, a tote bag made of tweed was flung at me—essential, apparently, for the markets. It was only due to my insistence that she let me wear a light jacket over the top. She may have thought the outfit was compromised by a coat, but the weather strongly disagreed.

We pulled up to a small parking lot and I stepped out, ready to absorb my new surroundings. "It's quite a bit windier here," I observed as my hair blew in what felt like all directions.

"Ah, yes, it's always a few degrees chillier here, I'm not sure why," Ruadhan answered as he clicked the automatic lock to the sedan.

"It's down there, I can see people!" Brooke began excitedly, tipping her giant sunglasses and pacing ahead. Ruadhan caught her up, redirecting her down a narrow cobbled street.

Jonah met me at my side, extending his arm out for me to walk with him. Smirking, he said, "Brooke dressed you, I see?"

"Hey, you're the one who resembles a pumpkin right now!" I giggled, slapping him gently on his chest. "Crikey!" I yelped, shaking my hand out; his chest was rock hard.

He winked and said, "Careful, I'm pretty ripe!"

"Hmm, you don't say." Removing my arm from his, I cracked my knuckles back and forth. "Anyway, I have it on good authority that this is acceptable wear for shopping in a quaint market. Such is the world according to Brooke."

"You look very . . . refined," he replied softly, the hazel in his eyes softening as his black pupils widened.

Pacing a few feet or so behind Brooke and Ruadhan, I took the time to appreciate the sweet terraced town houses with their brightly colored shutters. In fact, I was slightly too engrossed—

"Watch out!" Jonah reached for my waist and hoisted me from off the ground, into his protective arms, saving me from being knocked over by a speeding bicyclist. Caught off guard, and surprised by the sudden closeness, I took a second to catch my breath before I peered up to meet his eyes.

"Careful, Cinderella," he murmured.

"Cinderella?" I repeated in a whisper.

"Well, given this pumpkin just turned into your carriage—"

I shook my head in disdain and said, "If you're going to promote yourself, you should aim a little higher than a carriage." I pointed to the ground, signaling for him to place me back down.

Obediently Jonah did as I asked, but he pulled me in next to him tightly, cradling my hip with his hand. I didn't want to get run over so I didn't protest; it felt nice and secure.

"Nothing wrong with the carriage. The carriage gets Cinderella safely to her destination." Jonah flashed me a cheeky grin.

"Yeah, it delivers her to Prince Charming," I said, raising my eyebrows.

"Oh. I hadn't considered that bit. . . ." Jonah trailed off. "Okay, I'll go back to being the pumpkin, you go back to being Sleeping Beauty. We'll work something out."

For all intents and purposes, the street had only a few residents strolling up and down. They had scarves tied around their aging hair, wicker baskets in hand full of baguettes, cheese, and something else that smelled like old feet as it wafted past me in the draft. Coughing, I made a suitably unimpressed face and Jonah laughed at me.

At the top of the street, a main road presented itself and, on the opposite side, a bustling square with market stalls formed a rectangle in front of a medieval section of joined properties. Ruadhan and Brooke met us at the roadside.

"The market is bordered by thirteenth- and fifteenth-century houses. Look, you can see the top levels are properties that local folk and tourists with vacation apartments own. Underneath there are shops and cafés." Pointing up and waggling his finger around, Ruadhan was like a proper tour guide.

"Ahhh, they are quite something," I answered, impressed by the medieval houses that seemed to be floating in the air, seemingly supported only by wood and concrete arches below. Despite their age, it was amusing to see that it hadn't stopped the residents from painting their shutters in bright blues and reds—not quite in keeping with the brown wooden crosses and elongated beams on the face of the properties, presumably designed by some celebrated architect of the era.

"Boring . . ." Brooke whined impatiently.

"Okay, okay. We'll all walk around the market together. . . . Cessie." Ruadhan handed me some bills and I shook my head in protest; I didn't want his money.

"Listen, they don't take Visa here! Pick some bits up for yourself for dinner, and anything else that takes your fancy, love."

"Ahem!" Brooke huffed as I reluctantly took the paper from Ruadhan.

He handed her some cash, and she snatched it out of his hand so quickly a passerby might have thought it was a magic trick. Jonah had money; I'd seen him cleverly hit an ATM at the airport. I was starting to think I should have drawn some from the card Gabriel had given me. It was bad enough that I felt financially indebted to Gabriel; now I could add Ruadhan to that list. Fingering the notes in my hand, I felt awkward and I frowned knowing full well that he wouldn't let me hand them back. Money that was not carefully earmarked for absolute essentials was not something I was used to possessing. Every penny I had ever earned had been spent with caution. I was not in the slightest bit comfortable being given money for nothing, and I was even less happy at being encouraged to spend it frivolously.

"Don't you want to look around the cathedral?" Jonah asked, turning toward Ruadhan and cutting off my train of thought. He pointed in the direction of the grand building in the distance.

"I wouldn't mind taking a look, in a little while," he replied.

Jonah's expression gave nothing away. I couldn't help but think he wanted to snatch a few minutes on his own with me, but then I could be wrong.

We began traipsing around the market stalls. It didn't take

Brooke long to realize that this was not her type of shopping; there were no designer clothes anywhere to be seen. The only fabric on offer seemed to be that of 1970s-style vinyl tablecloths.

The market was alive and bustling with locals and tourists alike. We walked through the food section first. The meat counters made me want to gag; freshly slaughtered and nothing like what you'd find in the supermarket. As the coppery smell of blood drifted over me, I looked to my Vampire companions, anxious for a moment that the scent might have caused a reaction. Catching Jonah's eye first, I was relieved to see that his irises were still hazel in color, and he tilted his head curiously at me in reply.

"Problem?" he asked as we continued to stroll.

"No. I mean, are you okay?" I said, darting my gaze between him and the meat dangling from the steel hooks.

"*Please—*" he sneered, stopping. "Dead animal blood? Doesn't work like that. Sorry, beautiful. Gotta be fresh, from the veins of a human whose heart is still beating."

"Oh," I said thoughtfully.

Picking up his pace again, he added, "Besides, you eat with your eyes. I need to like what I see first." Jonah winked at me.

I wasn't sure what to make of that, so I shrugged it off.

We moved on swiftly, eventually coming to a stop at a bread stand, where I bought a baguette and a couple of croissants. I stood in line to purchase some brie from the cheese stand.

We'd only been shopping for fifteen minutes and already Brooke was getting agitated. "Man, this place sucks! You'd think we'd gone back in time forty years. Oh, jeez, look at that stand! Old women's nylon negligees! Ugh!"

I think she actually stamped her feet on the ground.

Ruadhan rejoined us, having done his perimeter check.

"We good?" Jonah asked.

"Aye, all tourists spilling out of the coffee shops. It's safe."

Apologizing to the Frenchman who was attempting to sell me a window-washing service, I joined the conversation. "No one knows we're here. If they did, they would have hit the house by now," I pointed out.

Ruadhan nodded.

"So, Ruadhan, go and see your cathedral. Market hopping is no place for a man." I winked at him; I'm not sure why. Spending too much time with Jonah lately perhaps.

He considered my proposal for a few moments before agreeing. "You'll stay with Brooke and Jonah, you won't separate. Your word?"

"I promise, now go! We'll come and find you when we're done."

"Jonah, make sure you take the little love to see the Maison des Consuls. The rafters are carved with some amazing portrayals of animals, monsters, all sorts! You can't come here without seeing them. It's just around the corner there." Ruadhan gestured like a proper Irishman, giving directions that weren't necessary.

His enthusiasm was genuine; I could tell he loved places like this, steeped in history and culture. He was in his element.

Before finally leaving, Ruadhan took Jonah off for a conversation, pointing at various points in the square—exit points, I imagined.

"Do you want to get a coffee or something before we drag ourselves around the rest of this dump?" Brooke was disheartened; it was obvious by the very fact that she was prepared to let me stop for a drink.

A few minutes later, the three of us were fighting for an outside table at one of the many overcrowded patisseries looking onto the market. Jonah ordered us all a coffee, though I would be the only one actually consuming the caffeine.

"Well, this is a total bust!" Brooke spat angrily as I sipped my latte.

"What do you think are the chances of Ruadhan letting us go up to Paris for the day to do some real shopping?"

"Not gonna happen," Jonah said.

I looked out at the congested stalls and walkways, which were jazzed up by green and red holiday tinsel, brightening an otherwise drab, graying backdrop. As Brooke mounted a protest, I watched Jonah's attention fall away from her, and from me. His eyes were scanning the market, and his body suddenly tensed. The checked tablecloth edged away from me as he dug his fingers down, pulling at it.

"Jonah?"

Nearly knocking his chair over, he was suddenly on his feet, his eyes tracing the pavement below. The Frenchman sitting behind him mumbled something; you didn't need to speak the language to understand that Jonah jolting the back of his chair had irritated him.

"Stay here, don't move. Brooke!"

"What?" she replied, oblivious to Jonah's urgency.

"I said don't move!" He bolted from the table and I lost him in the crowds within a matter of seconds.

"What's his deal?" She was annoyed that he'd cut off her objections.

"I'm not sure. . . ."

I was trying to work out what had caught his attention when a looming darkness seemed to stretch itself over me. "You know what, I think we should maybe go and find Ruadhan."

I got up and Brooke followed suit.

"Hang on, we need to go pay. Wait here." She was up and in the shop before I had a chance to change her mind.

The moment she was gone, a haggard old woman appeared in front of me some distance away, gesturing at me to come to her. I hesitated and she willed me on again, more urgently this time. I could stay and wait for Brooke, or I could go and see what she wanted. She was human, I could tell. In her eighties and with a hunched back, she wouldn't be able to harm me, so I ventured onto the cobbles; but as I neared she moved through the crowd. I called after her, but she just kept walking. So I followed. For an old woman, she walked fast. I briefly lost her among the many shoppers, but as I rose to my tiptoes, I found her fidgeting awkwardly underneath a sign for La Maison des Consuls. Well, at least I would keep my promise to Ruadhan of visiting the Council House; I'd accidentally broken the first one I'd made him.

As I approached, it seemed as though it was the one place in the square that no one else occupied. Drawing near to the old woman, the air stung me with its frost. And maybe it was because of the arches, but it looked darker than the open-air market.

As I reached her, the sound of a busker filled my ears. He was playing a violin of sorts; a sad and desperate tune freed itself from the strings across which his bow glided. Hunched over, the old woman grabbed my hands in her papery palms, and her yellowing, unclipped fingernails dug into my skin. Her odor was drenched in death; the stench was like rotten eggs and spoiled milk all tangled together, permeating my tongue. It was nauseating.

She spoke in French, not stopping for breath.

"Madame, I don't understand. I never learned how to speak French!"

I wanted to cover my nose and mouth, but she still had my hands held captive in her own wart-infested grip.

Finally she let go of my hands and threw her own up in the air in annoyance. She reached inside her old moth-eaten cardigan and pulled out a velvet pouch, which she dangled in front of my face.

She spoke again in French and I shook my head.

In the end, she pushed the pouch against my chest and pointed her finger past me. "De-a-meo-n! De-a-meo-n!" Shouting in broken English, she knocked me as she scurried past.

I watched her leave, then turned my head back to where she had signaled; there was no one there. Scanning the rafters above me, I jumped as the garish carvings of deformed faces stared down, as though they were watching me.

I opened the pouch. A thick gold-banded ring with a coat of arms etched into the center dropped into my hand. A swan, with a castle above it, glowered at me. It took a moment, but I remembered it. I had seen it before. As I ran my finger along the curve, I felt dizzy. Stumbling forward, I found myself on the ground. The disfigured faces were screaming down at me, adding to my panic.

I lost myself. I was in my tunnel and images swirled and danced across my vision. Moments passed and eventually one came into focus.

A boy, maybe ten years old, was playing in a field. His long, browny-blond hair whipped past his face as he ran through the thick green grass. As I followed him I saw a young girl the same age, with blond curls down past her waist, making chase. As she caught up with him, they toppled to the floor, playing. It took me longer than it should to see that the young girl was, in fact, me. I was startled; I had never seen myself so young.

Then the summer disappeared, replaced by winter. Only now the boy and I were older, maybe fourteen. It was nighttime and we were snacking outside of a barn, the same barn in which I had seen myself with Gabriel playing chess.

Sitting with our backs against the wall, sharing a blanket, the boy was pointing up at the night's sky toward the stars. I tugged the blanket away from him and he punched me playfully on the shoulder and we rolled around the floor giggling. He was my friend.

The scene was replaced by a series of still images depicting my childhood—our childhood.

Finally it rested on an image of him, older, maybe sixteen. I watched us as he read to me, his face partially hidden by the book. His stallion grazed on the land behind him. I had to look past him to see a familiar mare—pure white—lying on the ground: Uri. Moving the book from his face and placing it down beside him, he shuffled his hand in his pocket. The white of his flared cuffs emphasized his tanned skin. He produced a ring. It was my ring. The gem gleamed against the rays of the sun, which were cascading in strips. As he gently slid it down my finger, his own ring—a thick gold band with the crest of a swan and castle—came into focus. It was the same ring I was holding now.

Maybe my body jolting stopped the image, maybe it was my rising emotions, but it popped and dispersed. Instead, I watched the boy sob behind a dense green thicket. I strained to see what he was watching, what was upsetting him so much, and then I saw it: Gabriel and me picnicking, playing chess, laughing and smiling.

No!

I think I shouted it to myself. Either way they were gone. We were all gone.

I was back on the cobbles, my palms sweaty, causing my grip to fail as I tried to grapple to my knees.

For a second I thought it was one of the faces from above that petrified me, but he, although much like a statue, was living and he was standing right in front of me.

This time I didn't have to consider it. The Vampire who came nose-to-nose with me when Jonah and I had come under attack; the same one I saw leaving Eligio and his clan; the very same Vampire who approached me in the airport.

He was once my fiancé.

Though his eyes now blazed with flames of red, and though his skin had changed to a porcelain milky white, they were one and the same. Only he had been human—mortal, when I had known him before—and now he was a Vampire.

Remaining poised, anger filled his expression. He knelt next to me and pulled my necklace out from under my blouse, cupping my ring. Tugging it toward him, the air rippled and the sound of the fiddler's sad song faded into nothingness. Time was suspending itself and as it did, I felt the tug of the chain once more. But this time I was back in the barn and he was yanking it angrily away from my neck. I wasn't watching; I was reliving.

The light at the entrance couldn't have seemed farther away as I lurched forward, turning my back to him. But he pulled me backward, twisting me around to face him. I met the same eyes, only they belonged to him when he had been human. Streaming furious tears, his face flushed. He looked desperate. Gently I exerted some force against his shoulders, pushing him away, though I was hardly in control; I was merely trapped inside my body, my actions, and my choices in that pocket of time.

My legs scrambled, catching the inside of my underskirt, as I attempted to flee. The smell of the damp hay and the once familiar scent of horses filled me.

That's when it happened: a deadly blow to the back of my skull. I heard the crack as I fell to the floor. I blinked my eyes so fast that my eyelashes were getting tangled up and he was there, lifting me up. Pure horror and regret lined his brow and he was shouting. Though it was muted, his lips shaped my name over and over again. Casting my eyes away from him, I noticed blood pooling from my body; it spilled down the sloping ground toward the entrance.

So this was how I had died.

There was no pain. I couldn't feel any of it. Gabriel's name floated around my mind; I must have thought of him in my final seconds.

Before everything fell into darkness—before I stopped breathing—the image became concave and popped.

I found myself breathing the same air as the Vampire again as he considered my gem sitting in his hand. The chords of the violin filtered back into my hearing, though they were slow, as though they were being sieved.

Automatically, I grabbed the back of my head. Crimson blood trickled through the lines in the palms of my hands.

Presenting them to him—and without thinking—I said, "Ethan, you killed me."

His eyes were immediately flashing at mine as if I had been the one to deliver the blow. He pursed his lips, hiding his dangerous fangs. His angry expression subsided, to be replaced by one of mourning. The vibration of heavy feet racing across the market set me free of our exchange and when I looked back at him, he had vanished, like a puff of smoke. I guessed ghosts of the past were entitled to do that.

Remaining on the ground, I crossed my legs and cupped his ring as at last a piece of the puzzle snapped into place.

I don't know how long Jonah had been beside me, but I finally gave him my attention.

"Cessie! Cessie! You're bleeding!" His gaze found its way to the splatters over my hands and he pulled them in to him, following the scent up my arm to the marks smeared down my neck. Resting his cheek over my hair, he absorbed my fragrance. When he removed himself, his own skin blemished with the stain of my blood, he looked utterly panic-stricken.

"Give it a minute, it's disappearing."

Not only did my body heal itself ordinarily, having transitioned back into my body when I had relived the terrible memory of Frederic's attack, I knew that the damage receded quickly when I returned to the present.

"What happened?" His eyes darted speedily around the immediate area, but he couldn't be distracted long, his interest drawing intently back to me.

"Nothing. It's just an echo of a two-hundred-year-old injury, it can't kill me again." Where I'd felt empty, a state of calm spread into the void. Perhaps it was the effect of the blow in the present, or perhaps I was just oddly relieved to finally have something—anything—of my own to understand, even if it was horrific. I think it was the latter.

Jonah breathed heavily, his fingers fumbling through my hair. I could see desperation, disbelief, and desire all surfacing through his worried eyes.

I glided my arm over his, pushing him away from my head impatiently. "I said it will heal."

Scooping me off the ground and steadying my weight against his frame, he demanded, "I think it's time you filled me in, don't you?"

TWENTY

BROOKE'S ARRIVAL HAD BROUGHT a halt to Jonah's inquires, and once back in the confines of the house, I made every effort to keep in the company of Ruadhan and Brooke. I wasn't entirely sure how to play this; I needed to talk to Gabriel before I could delve into a revealing conversation with Jonah. I would have to tell him something, but how much and exactly what, I was unsure about.

Luckily the split in the back of my skull had receded quickly so neither Ruadhan nor Brooke were any the wiser. Convincing Jonah that no one had been in my presence, that no unearthly being had caused my spilled blood, hadn't been quite so easy. He knew someone or something that shouldn't have been in the market had been. He had sensed it.

I texted Gabriel, asking him to call me as soon as possible. Then I made my excuses and went for a nap in the basement bedroom.

I must have drifted off thinking of him, for as I slept an image of his blue eyes opened up in my mind. At first I was excited to see his face. He was in a bar, tucked away in a quiet corner, and he wasn't alone. I watched as he talked quickly and I peered past his image to see a far older, light-haired man who was listening attentively while scratching his head, an intrigued look on his face.

I was dreaming, but I was confident that what I was seeing was real, either from the past or perhaps of the future. It was difficult to know.

The man Gabriel conversed with looked fairly ordinary and nondescript; if I hadn't known Gabriel was searching out a fallen Angel I would have assumed this being was human. Gabriel paused briefly to pull his iPhone from his pocket and I watched as he read the message that I had sent him. He bundled it back into his jeans' pocket and continued talking.

Now the fallen Angel rubbed his stubble and began to speak. I couldn't tell what he was saying; as ever, the picture was muted. As he spoke he waved his hands about in the air, expressing himself with dramatic effect. The conversation seemed to go on for a very long time. I started drifting away but then the fallen Angel's body suddenly stiffened at something Gabriel had said, rekindling my interest. He gawked at Gabriel, his tumbler slipping toward the table a few inches from where he grasped it. I wondered what Gabriel had told him that had caused his reaction. He stood up and made his way over to a pay phone, sliding in some silver coins, with his back to Gabriel.

When he returned he wrote something down on a napkin, folded it carefully, and handed it to Gabriel. Nodding respectfully as he uttered a few last words to him, Gabriel seemed to thank him in reply and then was up, striding through the bar and out of the doorway.

I watched him leave, but I found myself unable to follow, so instead I turned my attention to the fallen Angel still sitting at the table. Now alone, he held his face in his hands, and swayed from side to side.

After a moment, he made his way over to the bar. I watched him neck a brandy as if to steady his nerves. The bar woman seemed to inquire genuinely after his well-being, and this time he spoke slowly enough for me to read his lips: "Nothing. Just the end of all worlds."

I wished for Gabriel and, like a genie in a bottle, he appeared in front of me against a different backdrop.

He was fumbling around in his pockets and finally produced a key. He stood in a walkway leading up to a seedy motel room opposite a dusty highway. I tried to call his name; maybe I could speak to him? But he didn't hear me. I remembered then that he was far away and I couldn't communicate with him. I wanted to tell him what I read from the fallen Angel's lips, and ask him what was happening. Why hadn't he called me yet?

He turned the key in the doorknob and I followed him into the most basic of rooms. He pushed past the sofa and, searching hurriedly, made his way into another room. He called Hanora's name hastily, and I watched his lips curving in and out over the three syllables that made up her impressive name.

I thought he'd said that he had separated from her. Were they sharing a room together? I think my heart stopped as he halted inside the doorframe and I looked around, observing Hanora strewn over a bed and wearing little more than an enticing smile.

I bolted upright in my own bed. And as the haze dispersed, my thoughts fell to Gabriel and Hanora, throwing the fallen Angel's words far back into the deep recesses of my mind. I wasn't quite sure what to do.

Anger filled me, displaying itself in my burning cheeks. I reached for my phone but stopped. If my dream was the present, was the moment happening right now? Would I interrupt them? I found his name and pressed the call button. I didn't know what I would say, but I had to reach him, tell him that I knew what he was doing, that I had been right all along and that I never wanted to see him ever again. I didn't get the opportunity. He canceled my call.

Furious, I leapt off the cotton sheets. Ripping away the glamorous clothes that were molded around my body, I chucked on jeans, T-shirt, and sweater instead.

Exiting through the garage off the utility room, I marched through the grounds. Where I was going, I had no idea, but I needed to move, to argue with myself in private. It was dark now—I'd overslept; my late afternoon nap had inadvertently turned into an early night. Though it was the early hours of the morning, day was not far away. The planes of grass were slippery; it must have rained during the night. I didn't care if I fell. I hoped I would fall and keep falling away from here, away from this life.

I stomped for over a mile, searching for explanations as to what was truly going on with Gabriel and Hanora.

In the distance, I spotted a horse; in the vast stretch of land, it was the only living thing for miles. I made my way over, and as I finally neared the mare, she didn't shy away. Running my hand down her silky black coat, she nuzzled into my side. I didn't know what she was doing here or who she belonged to, and I didn't care. Well over sixteen hands high, I still managed to hoist myself onto her back, clutching her long mane. I squeezed her sides and she began to trot. Throwing my weight into my bottom, I urged the mare into a canter. It felt freeing to ride through the fields by myself, the crisp silence calming my mind of every erratic thought.

We neared a forested area; hundreds of deciduous plane trees were grouped together, each one having long lost its leaves with the onset of winter. Their branches resembled splintering claws, seeming to direct me inside. Their thick roots were graying, as though they had been drained and were dying. I half wondered if they were marking an entrance to some sort of house made of gingerbread, waiting for an unwitting person to stumble inside and be consumed by a wicked witch. I considered what evil might lurk—hidden—within.

At the opening to the forest, the mare sidestepped, shying away from the trees as though something inside them was spooking her. I squeezed my left leg to her side, pushing my weight down harder, in an attempt to encourage the mare to stay still.

A cold chill ran from my neck down to my toes and suddenly I was mindful that I was out in the wide open and all alone. It occurred to me that any number of my ghosts could be poised like chameleons inside; the girl in shadow, the Pureblood that invaded my visions, maybe even Eligio.

Then the obvious dawned on me. Ethan.

We had unfinished business. I needed to talk with him, alone. Clearly he sought the same opportunity. He must have answers, I just didn't know if he desired my life in exchange for them.

"Ethan?" I chanced in a soft whisper, my voice traveling on the wind rippling through the trees.

It was met with stillness, and the mare underneath me waited anxiously. I was about to guide her toward the opening when the arms of the branches began to sway, stretching from the back and moving toward the opening.

I held my position, mustering my bravery. The branches stopped moving and I was sure for the briefest of seconds that I saw a pair of dulled, red eyes lingering from behind their fort.

"We need to . . . talk," I stuttered.

My courage was dwindling, though I didn't believe his intention was to kill me. My memories had led me to believe that we had been close, once. That he hadn't meant to end my life. But then, he was human when I had known him; now his eyes burned and his soul was submerged in blackness. What had become of him, and how?

The mare began pacing nervously backward. I patted her neck and felt the wetness of the steam rising from her coat. As though she was able to sense that whoever or whatever had been inside the forest was now edging closer. She knew that this game of hide-and-seek was over before it had really begun.

A stray twig in the bush snapped as a heavy weight fell. That was all it took. I was thrown off balance as the mare reared with a panicked snort. I braced myself to hit the ground; instead a pair of arms wrapped around me, breaking my fall. The mare bolted and was gone before I had a chance to see where.

"You never belonged to the Scouts? 'Be prepared,' remember?" Jonah's voice cut through the eeriness of the now motionless backdrop and I was momentarily relieved that it was him.

Sitting in his lap, I searched the trees ahead of me. Ethan was gone. But I would find him again, or more likely he would find me first.

I scuffled about, tilting my head up to meet Jonah's face. "Where the hell did you come from?"

"Behind you. After yesterday, you think I'd let you do a runner in the middle of the night, all by yourself?"

"I get the feeling you've always got one eye on me, regardless of the day's events. Do you remember what I said? You know, about finding another hobby?"

He wrinkled his nose and said teasingly, "You gonna get off my lap now?"

"Yes!"

I stumbled to my feet, dusting myself off in the process.

"Any particular reason you decided to take a random midnight stroll, steal a horse, and go galloping out to the middle of nowhere?" He vaulted from the grass, far more impressively than I had.

"No," I lied.

"Come on."

He signaled for me to jump on his back, but I protested with a firm shake of my head.

"Err, no thanks, I'd rather walk. You go on ahead, I'll follow."

"And miss the opportunity to play question time? I think not! We'll take a walk together and you can tell me what happened to you yesterday, and all the other days of your two-hundred-year-long existence."

Arching his eyebrows at me, he stretched out his arm, pawing through my knotted hair. He was feeling the now closed-up scar that had formed a bump on the outside of my skull.

I paced next to him, subdued, weighing my options. I had wanted to speak with Gabriel, but now I didn't care. As I thought of him and Hanora my stomach did backflips.

"Can I?" Jonah asked, gesturing to my shoulder blade—the one I had managed to keep hidden from him since it had been stitched up.

There was no point hiding it now, so I nodded and came to a stop. Lifting the sweater over my head, I pulled down the collar of my T-shirt.

Almost apprehensively, he swept my curls across my neck and brushed the back of his hand over my cold skin. "How long did it take to heal?" he asked.

"Not long, only left the faintest of scars this time."

He released my hair, but before I had time to squeeze the sweater back on he asked, "This time . . . how many scars do you have?"

He trod carefully with his questions, softening them for my benefit.

"A few. The one down my back is the worst. But at least I know how I got that one."

Without asking, he slid his fingertips up the length of my spine and I winced.

"If Frederic wasn't gone, I would end him myself. I would take my time." His tone flipped to sinister and I didn't doubt that he meant every word.

I pulled on my sweater and walked back toward the house.

"You gonna tell me what happened to you in the market?"

There it was: the first potent question of many, and I decided there and then that I would tell him. Never mind what Gabriel thought; he was obviously too busy with Hanora to be bothered. I would, however, omit the detail about Ethan. If Jonah knew there was a Vampire here he would insist on moving us on, and I wanted to connect with Ethan. We shared a history and I now had an opportunity to discover the detail firsthand. Hopefully including the part where I woke up immortal.

"I have visions of the past, memories of times gone by. They are windows into my own lives, events I can't remember."

"You said that the wound wouldn't kill you again. That it was two hundred years old."

"Sometimes when I have a vision, I don't just watch the past. I don't know how, but I fall back into my body and I relive it. Today, I had a memory of my first life, when I was mortal. I relived the very moment I was killed. Somehow the physical trauma transitions into my present reality, but the damage seems to recede. I feel it, but it doesn't affect me in the here and now to the same degree. That's why it didn't kill me again." I was whispering. I wasn't sure why. It was just he and I alone.

"And you've lived for two hundred years?" he asked, his face absent of any emotion.

"Near enough, that's what Gabriel tells me. When I was killed, I woke up again. Only I was different, I was changed. I became immortal, and before you ask, I don't know why."

Lightening to gray, the day was dawning, and I shivered. Jonah removed his jacket and secured it around me, taking the edge off the chill.

"Thanks."

"So you knew Gabriel back then?"

"Yes. When I died he left. He thought I was mortal, finished. I found him again when I found you." I pulled Jonah's jacket tighter. "Every time I die, I wake up. I don't remember anything about the past. I have some fragile recollection of who I am, who I was. . . . The memories, the visions are the only insight I have. Some days, they seem more of a curse than a gift."

Today was one of those days.

"You don't know what you are?" Jonah asked.

I felt my eyes well up. It might have been the question; it might have been my mind conjuring images of Gabriel against my will. Regardless of the situation, he always teetered on the fringes of my consciousness.

"Hey, it's okay. You don't need to get upset," Jonah said, rubbing my arm with his firm hands, and I allowed him a small smile.

"You can't tell the others. Gabriel knows—he's gone off to try and piece it all together. The others . . . well, they mustn't know."

"Our secret, I promise." His reply was definite and unwavering.

We strolled for a while, lost in thought. I broke the silence first. "Ruadhan and Gabriel have warned me away from you."

"I know," Jonah said. He hovered as if he wanted to tell me something.

"What is it?"

"Nothing, it can wait; after all we have nothing but time. That goes for both of us apparently."

"I beg to disagree. Seems the hands on my clock are about to stop ticking."

"You reckon because they seek you out it's the end. I got news for you—your story's just beginning." Jonah was confident, knowing. And strangely, that remark made my heart feel even heavier.

He smiled widely in an attempt to lighten the mood and, without asking, whisked me up, throwing me on his back, and we sped down through the fields. Looping my hands together around his neck, I clung on tightly.

Despite my troubles, I felt exhilaration racing through me as we moved faster than lightning back to the front door.

TWENTY-ONE

CLINGING TO JONAH AS WE POUNDED across the landscape had somewhat emptied my mind of all the heavy thoughts that had been weighing me down. I jumped to the ground as we neared the house and he swung around to face me.

"Fun?"

"Very!" I said.

"Listen, Cessie, I don't want to add to your complications, but . . ."

"But what?"

"It's just . . . you and Gabriel. I get that you have a history, but you know that can't work, right?"

I was about to answer when my phone rang. I pulled it out of my pocket. Gabriel.

I left it; I didn't have anything to say to him.

"I'm hungry," I told Jonah. "I'm going to grab some breakfast."

I made my way to the basement entrance, up the stairs, and into the kitchen. He didn't try to pursue the conversation any further. Instead, he took up a seat on the corner sofa, flicking on the TV.

Gabriel must have called ten times as I made myself tea and toast. I guiltily continued to ignore him.

Eventually, Ruadhan came and sat next to me at the table as I munched on my slightly burnt piece of bread.

"I've got Gabriel on the line for you."

He handed me his cell and, now cornered, I took it off him reluctantly.

"Yes?" I said.

"Take yourself somewhere private."

Nodding politely at Ruadhan, I pushed my chair back and heaved open the glass doors, which led into the garden, sliding them firmly closed behind me.

"I'm alone." I tried to sound standoffish.

"I have a lead. I'm traveling to Boston to try and find an Angel called Azrael. I think he may have the answers we need. I should reach the city in a few hours. I'm hoping he's still there. Then I'm coming to get you." His words were quick. "Are you okay?"

"What about Hanora, where is she?" I asked bitterly, ignoring his question.

"Lai, she's the last person you should be concerning yourself with."

"True, you're concerning yourself with her enough for the both of us."

"I don't understand?"

"I dreamt of you in the bar, with Malachi. Then I saw you walking into a motel room." I paused. "For a friend she has a funny way of greeting you!"

He didn't say anything. I took his silence to confirm my worst fears.

"Well?" I could feel the blood rushing to my cheeks.

"How much did you see?"

"What does that matter? I didn't need to see much to know what you were doing."

"Lai, you've got it wrong. You need to trust me, okay? I know it's hard, being apart, but I will be with you soon. Please, just have some faith in me." He sounded sad, but he hadn't exactly gone out of his way to explain what I had witnessed.

I was finding it difficult not to burst into tears, so I finished the call. "I have to go."

Needing a few moments to gather myself, I wandered over to a seating area built out of stone, but as I was about to sit down, a huge bushy tree—balancing precariously against the high wall—distracted me.

"Everything okay, love?" Ruadhan stepped out onto the decking, but his face fell when he saw what I was looking at. "Ah, you found it then?"

"Why is there a tree from the mountains in the garden?" I asked.

"I got it for you! It's a Christmas tree, a real one!" His smile sat high on his cheeks. "Just because we're in hiding doesn't mean we shouldn't celebrate, now does it! I picked up some decorations in the market, so let's take it inside and get started!"

He was so sweet, I didn't want to disappoint him by wallowing, so I forced a smile as he hoisted it onto his shoulder and carried it through to the living room.

An hour later, the entire household—Brooke included—was well under way with the decorating; though we had spent the first thirty minutes arguing about the color scheme of the tree.

Brooke felt that the tree should be contemporary and elegant, which meant no tinsel and just the one color: silver. Jonah had strangely suggested a two-tone scheme of black and white.

I, on the other hand, was just desperate to layer it with everything we had.

"You're making it uneven!" Brooke snapped at me.

"Hey, the bottom's my area, you worry about your own," I said.

"Now, now, girls," Ruadhan said. "It's looking grand!"

I wasn't so sure. Unable to reach a compromise, we had split the enormous tree into three sections to decorate as we each wished. Given they were Vampires and they could jump ridiculously high, I'd ended up with the bottom layer. On the plus side, it was the widest compared to Jonah's, who'd pulled the short straw, getting the very top.

Ruadhan had opted out of having his own section. Instead, he had the pleasure of selecting an ornament for the highest point, which he had yet to reveal.

While we worked, he made up some mince pies and mulled wine to get us in a festive mood. Given that I was the only being in the house who actually ate regular food, I had a feeling I was going to end up disliking mince pies once I'd forced down the large batch that he was halfway through creating.

Decorating the tree, coupled with the sweet smell of mulled wine drifting from the kitchen, reminded me of the only Christmas I had ever spent in any company.

A few years ago, I had been traveling through Scotland, and I'd been lucky enough to meet Mrs. Kynoch. She was the proprietor of a B and B, and had been kind enough to give me a job cooking and cleaning in her establishment during the busy seasonal period, in exchange for full board.

I'd decorated the tree there with an eight-year-old girl who was staying with her parents. She had enthusiastically rammed every last ornament and piece of tinsel onto the green branches that she possibly could. Through the eyes of a child, that tree couldn't have been more beautiful. But it was the joy she'd shown as she dressed it that made it truly special to look at. For every piece that twinkled only reflected the happiness of the girl who had placed it there.

On Christmas Day, I had sat down with the guests and eaten a full turkey dinner with all the trimmings. We'd pulled crackers, sung songs, and danced like no one was watching. It was the only Christmas, until now, that I hadn't been totally alone.

While I hadn't expected to be spending Christmas this year with a group of Vampires, I was suddenly grateful that I was. No matter how strange, they were a family. And as long as I was with them, I was part of that, part of something. Just as I had been, once before.

"I'm done!" Brooke chirped victoriously, bringing me back to the task at hand. Brooke stood back to admire her middle layer, and I had to admit, it was pretty.

"Hmm, Ruadhan, you got any more of these clear fairy lights?" Brooke asked.

"Maybe. There's another boxful in my room, have a rummage."

She was gone in a split second.

Jonah plopped down on the floor, his legs crossed, observing while I crammed star shapes and reindeer—two at a time—onto the lower shoots.

"Not sure what look you're going for, beautiful. I'm starting to think Santa's workshop exploded and somehow landed on your part of the tree!" he teased.

I laughed, and I was surprised that I had managed to put my concerns and hurt feelings to one side, for a few moments. "I don't know how they do it across the pond, but in the UK, well, the more Christmassy the better!" I said.

I reached down to pick up a piece of red tinsel and brushed Jonah's hand accidentally as he passed it to me. A short, sharp shock tingled under my skin, but I ignored it and carried on.

"Thanks," I said quickly, scrambling around the tree, bobbing and weaving the long strip through the foliage.

Dusting myself off, I stood and admired the conflicting decor.

Jonah's baubles were dangling neatly and I tilted my head as I pondered his choices.

"Dark and light can be a striking contrast. Don't you think?" he said, crossing his arms and standing beside me.

"I guess; looks like it's a bit undecided though, the way it's all mixed up. Why don't you split it into two halves, so when you stand behind the tree it's black, and when you're in front it's white?"

"I don't know, I think it takes a certain eye to appreciate the two blended together—"

"We're out of fairy lights!" Brooke zoomed back into the room and stomped her feet.

"Ah, never mind," Ruadhan called from the kitchen. "Come, let's put the finishing touch on the very top."

He slammed the oven door and strolled over.

Reaching into a small cardboard box, he lifted out an ornament of an Angel dressed in white, complete with a wire halo above its head. I raised my eyebrows, surprised.

"You don't like it, love?" he asked.

"No, no, it's not that. It's just funny, with the halo and wings and all . . . it's not really . . . accurate." I stopped myself. If Ruadhan believed the Bible, then to him, this was how he saw things. So I veered off. "Just thought you might pick something else."

"Well, now. I think in this family it's only right we have an Angel. After all, we have our very own to thank for us all being here, together." He gestured over to me, so I stepped toward him and he handed me the ceramic figure. "And, as the newest addition to our little family, I think you should be the one to place it on the top, sweetheart."

I turned to the towering tree, which nearly brushed the ceiling, and considered that we couldn't possibly have a ladder tall enough for me to climb in order to reach it.

Bear-hugging me from behind, Ruadhan leapt into the air, hanging off a beam on the ceiling, and I remembered I had something better than any ladder.

Unfortunately, as I attempted to pop the Angel on the top of the tree, I leaned over too far and unbalanced the both of us. As Ruadhan lost his grip on my waist, I fell headfirst into the pine, knocking it over as I went down with it.

"Ahhhh!" I screamed, plummeting.

Jonah, as ever, was the fastest to react. He jumped into the air, meeting me halfway to the floor, and landed on his back with me on top of him.

I gawked in horror as the tree came crashing down.

Brooke was speedy, just about managing to stop it from hitting the flat-screen TV on the wall and saving some of the decorations in the process.

Before I knew it, I burst into laughter. Ruadhan was still hanging one-handed like an uncoordinated monkey from the beam above; Brooke was struggling to balance the enormous forest tree, shouting profanities; and Jonah had me sprawled out on top of him, pinning him to the floor. I rolled off his chest and cried with hysteria.

"What is so freakin' funny? You've ruined my glass snowflakes!" Brooke wailed. She only made me laugh harder.

Ruadhan landed on all fours and helped Brooke pull the tree back up to a standing position, observing the Christmas massacre strewn everywhere. He glanced at me wiping my eyes and started bellowing a deep, hearty laugh. Even Brooke started to giggle, though she moved her hand over her mouth to try and mask it, trying her best instead to maintain a deep scowl.

Jonah sat up and, for the briefest second, his hard bad-boy exterior faded away as he looked at me. Shaking his head, he laughed in a way I had never heard him laugh before. It was a beautiful, happy sound—one I was sure I would never be able to forget.

"Well," Jonah said, gathering himself. "If anything I think it's only improved your section of the tree!"

SEVERAL HOURS AND FAR TOO MANY mince pies later, I lay on the sofa, hand on belly, trying desperately to come down from my sugar rush.

Ruadhan finished drying the plates and bobbed over to me. "You certainly enjoyed those mince pies, love!" He beamed as I nodded. "I'll make you some more!"

I suddenly wished I hadn't looked so satisfied. That would cost me later, I was sure.

"Listen, Jonah's got to go out this evening," Ruadhan said, his voice quieting. "He needs to . . . well, he needs to refuel. And I was thinking of going to the Église de rupestre de Vals. It's a remarkable church in a small village, about forty minutes from here by car. This near to Christmas there's a midnight Mass and I thought perhaps you'd come with me?"

I understood. Ruadhan didn't want to risk even a remote possibility of me being alone with Jonah.

"Actually, I think I'd rather just stay in if you don't mind. No need to worry about me, I'm fine. Jonah can go out, Brooke and I can just watch a movie. I promised I'd call Gabriel later this evening as well," I lied.

"Hmm. Well, as long as Jonah's out. And you'll stay indoors, yes?"

"Yup."

"No more midnight strolls?" His words hung in the air for a moment. He knew I had left the house; nothing seemed to get by him.

"If you insist." I smiled.

BROOKE AND I SAT ON THE SOFA sorting through the massive DVD collection, when Jonah appeared from nowhere. I did an internal gasp when I saw him. He was dressed in dark jeans that were turned up at the bottom, showing off military-style boots; a deep V-neck T-shirt that allowed his collarbone to jut out; finished with a rich leather belt, which sat low on his waist. His jacket was black leather, and he wore several cross-shaped pendants on long worn cords around his neck. He hardly looked ready to race through the woods.

Leaning in to Brooke, he handed her a business card and shook his phone at her. She huffed in reply.

"Cessie, I'll be back in a few hours." He winked at me and several DVDs dropped off the coffee table and hit the floor as a gust of wind blew through the door when he left.

"What's on the card?" I asked Brooke, who was already on her feet.

"Oh, in case of emergency. Only the name and address of the club Jonah's gone to." Springing over, she yanked me from off the sofa. "Come on, we need to get ready!"

"I thought he was going out to, you know . . . feed?"

"He is, he's gone to a club to find some dark souls, and we're not gonna sit here and let him have all the fun! Besides, Ruadhan won't be back till the early hours, he'll never know. Now go take a shower, you've got fifteen minutes and then we're out of here!"

She left me to contemplate my options, though I doubted I had any choice in the matter. So I made my way to the basement; as I did a message buzzed on my phone.

ROOK ON THE RIGHT FOUR SPACES FORWARD. I MISS YOU

Grudgingly, I moved the piece on the board but didn't reply to his message. The hurt that I had briefly burrowed away hit me with full force and suddenly I felt rebellious.

Ten minutes later Brooke was in my room, eyeing up my jeans-and-white-top ensemble. "No! No! No! We're going to a *nightclub*, Cessie! Here." She flung a pile of clothes down on the bed and said, "But first we need to sort out your makeup."

Within minutes she had painted my face, caking me in a layer

286

of white foundation and creating a smoky look across my eyes by adding thick eyeliner and layers of mascara to my lashes. She smudged just a hint of blush on my cheeks and colored my lips with a bright red liner and lipstick to match. She let me leave my hair down but straightened my bangs, making them sweep across my eye so that I could barely see.

I didn't protest. I'd let her have her fun; at least that's what I had decided until I saw the clothing she had selected. "Oh, no, come on!" I protested. "I don't want to look like a dominatrix!"

"What do you mean?" she asked, adjusting her own leather outfit.

"Trust me, the type of clubs Jonah goes to, you'll look out of place if you don't wear what I'm giving you!"

I looked over the low-cut black top that gathered just below the belly button (with no back to speak of), the tiny leather skirt and stiletto heels, and shook my head. "Compromise: I'll wear the top, but can't I wear that other skirt you got me? You know, the floaty black one?"

She rolled her eyes, but found it for me anyway. It was short, maybe seven inches at the front, but it did have a longer, transparent train that wrapped around the back and sides. I reached for a slip and she snatched it off me in disgust. "As I said, less is more, believe me."

"But . . ."

She'd grabbed me before I had a chance to move, tugging my T-shirt over my head. I grasped my bare chest as she began tying the two strips of the plunging halter top around my neck. She paused for a second as she brushed my hair out of the way of the sueded silk. "Crap. How'd you get that?"

She didn't give me a chance to answer.

"Doesn't matter, your hair covers it anyway. We don't have time to argue, you're wearing it and that's that."

I was momentarily grateful that Brooke was so impatient and self-involved; at least I didn't have to explain myself. Throwing me the pair of six-inch patent black Louboutin stilettos, she was quick to remind me of her earlier statement. "Like I said, you'll thank me later!"

She allowed me a quick glance in the full-length mirror in her room, and I was taken aback to see my reflection. This was so not me; I felt uncomfortable in such an outfit, and I could barely walk in the shoes. But Brooke was going to get her way.

I slipped my iPhone, credit card, and ID into a little black patent clutch, and then we were in the bumblebee car, speeding down the road.

"So where's this club?" I asked her, fidgeting uncomfortably in the passenger seat.

Brooke handed me the card from the dashboard. The top line simply read: LE BARON, LIMOUX.

TWENTY-TWO

I TOTTERED NEXT TO BROOKE as we made our way from the car to the entrance of the club. The line to get in was long, but that didn't faze Brooke. Walking straight up to the doorman, she whispered in his ear and locked eyes with him. Whatever she had said did the trick; he let us straight through, unhooking the black velvet rope and ushering us inside.

We wobbled down a corridor. Well, I wobbled, until blaring music filled my ears. It was a large space for a club outside the city. In front of me were a hundred bodies crushing each other on the dance floor and a layer of fashionable women and trendy men up against the bar.

Brooke pushed through to the front of the bar, every man in view staring at her. She was certainly something to behold—her petite figure hugged lovingly by the skintight leather, her flaming red bob tickling her jaw, and her perfect white skin creating a striking contrast. She made her way back to where I stood. I wondered why we were dressed so scantily.

Brooke handed me a Bloody Mary and said, "Cheers!"

"We'll never find Jonah in here!" I shouted, trying to be heard over the Lady Gaga remix.

"Oh, he's here. He'll be in the basement," she bellowed back, scanning the talent around us.

"Basement?"

"Yup. There's a strip club below for members."

I thought maybe I had heard her wrong.

It didn't take long before a couple of local guys made their way over to us, offering a top-up on our drinks. Nodding, Brooke allowed them to buy us another round.

For over twenty minutes, she flirted and laughed, seemingly taking a liking to the dark-haired boy who was in his early twenties and dressed too trendily in an open black shirt and designer jeans. She soon abandoned me to go to the dance floor with him, leaving me with "the friend."

"What? Sorry, I can't hear you!" I yelled back at him while bouncing to the beat. He tried again, but I only feigned interest.

Making my excuses, I strolled away, looking for some sort of entrance to this basement Brooke had told me about. Maneuvering around the gyrating, sweaty bodies, I finally settled my eyes on a tall, stocky man in the far corner. He was suited, booted, and guarding another velvet rope, only this one was a deep red. Fluffing my hair, I attempted a confident swagger over to him, though it was more difficult given the height of the heels I had been forced into.

"*Membres seulement,*" he said, not even looking at me.

"Sorry." I cussed myself for never learning French. "I need to go inside."

I finally caught his eye and he studied me for a moment. Then he lifted the rope and ushered me through.

Carefully, I walked down the large concrete steps. When I reached the entrance I was taken aback. Brooke had been right; the basement was definitely a private member's area. Music was humming and beautiful girls—dressed in corsets and thongs—were giving lap dances to elegantly dressed men.

The bouncer at the bottom of the steps regarded me, and I thought for a moment that he was going to refuse me entry. Instead, he collected a glittering eye-mask from behind him. It shimmered with the red and white diamanté encrusted all over it. He gestured for me to place it over my face. I didn't refuse. Feeling now a little like a sparkly version of Catwoman, I made my way to the bar.

Next to the bar was an elevated stage with a pole in the middle. A girl with legs up to her armpits was twirling around it, topless, showing off her finely toned midriff, her long brown hair flowing down past her bare bottom. I don't think her thong actually knew what a thong was.

Casting my eye around the space, taking in the grand double vaulted ceilings, I quickly realized that all the women were wearing masks of different colors.

Leading to the stage was a small dance floor with a silver disco ball that caught the light, making me squint as it bounced back at me. Beyond the dance floor stood a grand piano, which was, for now, absent of a pianist. An abandoned full-face mask sat on its lid.

There wasn't an empty seat in the house, so I leaned against the glass top of the bar, scanning the room. I couldn't see Jonah.

The barman brought over a bright red cocktail without asking for my order and smiled at me. He was pleasant looking, only slightly taller than me, with fluffy dark hair and piercing blue eyes. They were a million miles away from Gabriel's luminosity, but then he wasn't an Angel.

I shook Gabriel from my mind. Tonight wasn't about him; besides, he was probably cozying up to Hanora.

"Thank you," I said, offering him my plastic, which he refused to take. Apparently if you were a member, which he seemed to think I was, you didn't pay for your drinks.

I twisted myself back around, scanning the room, when my phone buzzed. I opened my clutch and read a message from Brooke. She was checking that I was okay and telling me that she was having a fab time with Pierre. I replied a quick, YES AM FINE. CALL ME IF YOU NEED ME, and went back to sipping my cocktail.

Just then, one of the lap dancers moved away from an older gentleman and I caught sight of Jonah.

A dark-haired girl with a heart-shaped face who was wearing virtually nothing sat on his lap. He was whispering into her ear and she giggled, pulling away from him teasingly.

My stomach jolted and I gulped hard. A fast shock of jealously streaked through me. It shouldn't have—I wasn't in love with Jonah; I loved Gabriel, despite everything I feared he was doing.

So why then did I want to throw up?

Jonah brushed his lips to the girl's neck, but stopped as his eyes caught my own. I watched them enlarge as he met my stare. Could he recognize me, even with the mask? I turned my back to him and drained the remnants of my red mixture, calling the bartender over for another.

"Ah, vodka?" I forced a smile.

"English?"

I nodded in reply.

"And extremely beautiful . . ."

"Hey, you're stealing my line!"

The barman poured a large, neat vodka and scuttled away quickly, surprised by Jonah's sudden appearance.

His chin nudged into the crevice of my neck, and his breath tickled my bare skin. A flutter of excitement rose inside me.

"What are you doing here?" he asked.

I didn't flinch. "How'd you know it's me?"

He inhaled long and hard before saying, "I can smell you a mile away."

He lingered before finally removing himself and took a seat next to me. Cupping my cheeks with his hands, he nudged my mask to my forehead and grinned. "So, you felt like dressing up tonight?"

"Brooke thought we should have some fun."

"She's here?" he asked, gesturing to a different waiter to fill his tumbler.

"She's upstairs with a guy named Pierre." I trailed off. "She's having a good time."

His forehead creased with annoyance. I found myself nervously playing with my hair, caught behind the elastic of my sparkly mask.

"Maybe not as much as you though," I added for good measure, not meeting his eyes.

His head tipped backward and he let loose a burst of laughter. "What's wrong? Don't like me spending time with other women?" he teased.

"No, of course not! You can do what you like." I sputtered, barely in control of my own words.

There was a minute's pause between us.

Jonah finally spoke. "You look, well, delicious tonight."

I glanced coyly in his direction and, as always, had to stifle a small gasp as I watched his eyes sparkle for my benefit.

"But it doesn't matter what I think, does it? Your interests lay elsewhere."

He was testing me. It took me a moment too long, but I nodded.

As his fingers skimmed down the soft skin of my arm to my wrist, circling around and around, he said, "There's nothing I can say, or do . . ." His voice lowered to a deep murmur as he ran the tip of his nose softly to my earlobe. ". . . to change your mind. . . ."

His lips were now pressing against my neck, leaving only the smallest gap to allow his words to travel to my ear. I began melting quicker than an ice cream left out in the sun. But just before I fell completely out of my cone my phone vibrated. I raced for it, a perfectly timed interruption. Shuffling around in the clutch, I lifted the phone out to see Gabriel's name appear on the screen. Jonah placed his hand on mine, pushing the phone down.

"He's not right for you, Cessie."

Despite the feeling in the pit of my stomach that yearned, it irritated me that he would make such an assumption.

I shot him a displeased look, and he seemed offended. "Have fun," he said abruptly.

I grabbed for his arm as he glided away from me and he turned back with a quizzical expression.

"Don't. Well, please, don't drink from her." I pretended it was because I was a good person, saving her from him, but it was hard to convince myself of this lie. The very thought of him drinking from a girl that attractive made me ache deep inside, somewhere I couldn't identify. And it was a sensation that screamed to me that *I was* jealous, even though I didn't want to hear it.

He thought on my request before replying. "What does it matter to you?"

"Just please, promise me."

He considered me a while before nodding firmly. Striding back to his seat, he gestured to the girl, who had been drifting nearby, watching our exchange over by the piano.

She swiftly took up her position on his lap, but not before sending a look of triumph in my direction.

I read the message from Gabriel: CALL ME.

I flicked the text away. I would call him later. I wasn't a puppet he could pick up and put down when he felt like it, tugging my strings however he so desired.

I was about to make my way back upstairs to find Brooke when a man took up the barstool next to me.

"What are you drinking?" he asked.

I looked at him, startled. He was a good-looking guy, maybe in his early twenties, with gelled blond hair swept from his face and large green eyes and a wide smile. His shirt had a patterned lining of swirling blues and whites, nearly as white as his bleached teeth.

"Vodka," I answered, throwing a quick glance back over my shoulder. Jonah was now receiving a lap dance; I was slightly disappointed that he hadn't seen.

"Are you here alone?" the stranger inquired, an uneven smile forming across his lips.

I thought about it for a second before replying. "I'm here with a girlfriend, but I think she's abandoned me for the evening."

"Well, that's just my good luck. I'm Bradley. Judging by the accent, am I safe in assuming you're a Londoner?"

"Yes," I answered, recognizing that his accent was similar to my own.

"I'm only passing . . . a fleeting visit; my dad owns this place. I wasn't going to come tonight, but now I'm rather glad I did. What brings you down here? Not many women choose to spend their evening in this part of the club, unless they're working of course."

At first I thought his eyes were wandering to my cleavage, but I realized he was staring at my ring.

Before I had a chance to answer, he continued.

"That's a remarkable crystal you have there," he pondered. "May I?"

Without waiting for my agreement, he lifted it from my skin and, squinting, he rubbed it in between his fingers. I was taken aback; he was far too close for my liking. As he grazed the perfect edges of my crystal, everything felt all wrong inside.

Over Bradley's shoulder, I glimpsed Jonah's blank expression. He inclined his head, observing this little exchange, now ignoring the dancing girl's efforts. So despite the sickening sensation that was rising to my throat as Bradley leaned in for a closer inspection, I placed my hand on his back and let a little laugh slip through my lips. "Sorry, I'm ticklish. . . ." I lied, grinning.

"Where did you get this?" he asked, returning back to my eyes.

"An old fiancé, apparently," I said, relieved he had released it.

Losing interest in my gem, his interest pricked instead at the mention of my seemingly single status.

"Well, I'm rather glad the fiancé is past tense. Let's dance." He wasn't asking.

With a wave of his hand the brunette swinging energetically around the pole stopped, and a middle-aged man took up the piano stool and started to play.

Grabbing my hand, Bradley hauled me onto the parquet floor. The light fabric of my skirt swirled and floated as he spun me away from him before pulling me back in. An incredibly beautiful rendition of Adele's "Make You Feel My Love" sang its way through the keys of the grand piano.

Bradley twirled and dipped me like a pro. But his controlling grasp on my body felt anything but gentleman-like.

"You are certainly something," he said, his eyes making their way unashamedly down the length of my exposed skin.

I gave him a disinterested half smile out of politeness; I didn't want to be dancing with him. He felt cold, confident, and certain: arrogantly convinced, and wrongly so, of me tonight. I noticed a gold wedding band on his ring finger, greeting me with its chill as, uninvited, he pressed his hand down my neck.

He slapped his hands on my waist, as if I belonged to him, and forced me in closer so that we were cheek-to-cheek.

"You're married?" I asked.

"Yes."

That was all the excuse I needed. I pushed him away, but he grabbed my hips and pulled me in.

"You shouldn't be dancing with me!" I glared at him.

"I can do whatever I like. Relax, enjoy yourself."

Managing to release his hand as he spun me, I briefly glimpsed Brooke with the French boy in tow. He stood behind her, looking bemused, at the bottom of the stairway. She beamed at me, seemingly happy to catch me dancing with a wealthy-looking guy.

I shouldn't have responded so obviously, flashing my glance straight from her to Jonah, who was engrossed entirely by the stripper, his back to Brooke. She followed my stare and I watched her wobble for a moment as she took him in. She nodded at me and, seizing the French beau by the collar, she strode back up the stairs and disappeared.

I thought for a second that I saw Jonah glance up, and I couldn't tell if he had seen her. Bradley was behind me in seconds, scooping me back to him and throwing me into an unwanted dip. Shuffling uncomfortably out of his grip again, I twisted around, trying to find Jonah. He was gone.

As the emotional song came to a wavering end, he led me back over to the bar and commanded another vodka for me, setting himself up with a line of shots.

Jonah's girl was perched on a stool, eyeing me as if I was something she'd trodden on. Speaking loudly in broken English to the barman, she was telling him that she was waiting for her customer to return. I could only assume that she wanted me to know Jonah was coming back.

"I need the bathroom," I said to Bradley. "Will you excuse me?"

I broke away from him, but as I jumped off the stool, he grabbed my wrist tightly and replied, "I have the next dance."

I made my way to the WC, weaving between the rotating bodies. I yanked the door open and found three cubicles inside, all of which were empty. I splashed water on my face to cool my cheeks and rearranged myself in the magnified mirror, smoothing the top and yanking down the stupidly short skirt.

My phone buzzed. Brooke was calling me.

"Hello?"

"Cessie, come back upstairs, they're playing some great tunes! You're missing out!" she shouted, though the music in the background sounded faint and distant.

"Where are you?" I asked.

"Upstairs of course. Come back, I'll meet you at the bar!"

"I've lost Jonah. Shouldn't we find him?"

"Jonah? Erm, no. It's fine, I just saw him. Listen, don't worry, he'll meet us later. Please come back upstairs!"

Brooke's sudden interest in my company was strange, but I decided to play ball. I wanted to escape Bradley anyway. I might as well go and see if I could convince her to leave; I suddenly wasn't in the mood for what this place had to offer.

And I was ready to call Gabriel.

I opened the door and as I scanned the space ahead of me, a small corridor—hidden almost out of sight—caught my attention. Written in French but with the English translation underneath, something about the DO NOT ENTER sign enticed me toward it.

Placing the mask back over my face, I stepped forward. Cloaked in darkness, a vast array of doors ran down the long stretch of carpet. There was no bouncer here; this was a strictly private area, where members came not wanting to be seen.

I'd passed three doors when I heard the faint moan of a woman, and I hesitated, stopping outside one of the rooms. Maybe I was emboldened by the vodka. But I gave in to a sudden urge, and I kicked the door. It swung open obediently, bouncing loudly off the wall as it hit the exposed brick.

On the opposite side of the room, the dark-haired girl was

pinned against the plasterboard wall, her leg wrapped around Jonah's hip.

He immediately released his grip, bowing his head down in my direction, but never bringing his face up to meet my eyes. He knew it was me.

The fact that he refused to meet my gaze told me he was ashamed that I had caught him with her. Though I couldn't be sure in that moment exactly what it was I had found him doing.

If he was feeding, he had broken his promise to me. If she was in the middle of putting out, I highly doubted he'd want me to know, let alone see that either.

I reeled backward as though I had been punched square in the jaw. My insides coiling in a tight knot, I was suddenly overcome with anguish. Why? Why did he make me feel like this?

It felt as though the answer to *that* question was hidden in plain sight.

"Cessie—" Jonah began in a low voice.

My name fell to an empty doorway. I was already falling over my feet, hurrying to get away; I didn't want to talk to him. I wanted to go home.

TWENTY-THREE

I MARCHED SWIFTLY, my eyes fixated on the EXIT sign next to the bar. I muddled through the smoke-filled air across the dance floor, but my wobbly sprint came to an abrupt halt as a hand grabbed my arm firmly.

"Now then, you still owe me a proper dance. And this time maybe don't speak." There was nothing polite about him, especially the way he emphasized "proper" with a dreadful undertone.

Bradley had already yanked me backward, showing no sign of releasing me. He blew a puff of smoke from a Cuban cigar that he held lazily in his right hand, and his eyes glowered expectantly. I could tell by his dilated pupils that he had consumed too many straight shots.

"Maybe another time," I replied, attempting to loosen his grip. I didn't want to cause a scene. I just wanted to leave.

"Come now, one dance and a drink won't kill you—I've hardly gotten to know you yet!" His grip had tightened, and I began to feel flustered. He wasn't referring to swapping childhood memories, of that I was quite sure.

As he maneuvered his chest flush with my own, I started to manufacture an argument, but I didn't have time to propose it. A strong and protective hand found mine, and with one swift tug, I was pulled away from Bradley's grasp.

"I'm gonna have to take this dance." Jonah's eyes prickled, and as Bradley began to protest, he stopped, taking in Jonah's fierce expression.

"Oookay," he said as he stumbled away with no objection.

Jonah took me lightly by the waist, twisting his fingers under the hem of my skirt, and stroked my hips as he began to sway me in time to the music. "Can't go anywhere without attracting attention to yourself, can you?"

I remained silent.

"Cessie, look at me, please."

Bowing his head down to meet mine, he pushed the twinkling sparkles to the top of my head. After a moment, I gave in and accepted his hazel eyes, which flickered with the subtlest strobes of red.

"I didn't sleep with her." His voice was sharp and definite.

I hadn't wanted to ask; if I had then he would know I gave a damn.

"It's all right. Really. I don't pretend to understand what you need, how you go about, that is . . . Well, it's not my business." I felt like I was fumbling my words.

"It's not difficult. What I need is the girl who's standing right in front of me. I'd say that truly makes it your business, doesn't it?"

He spoke in a low, seductive murmur, and I had to do everything in my power to stop my knees knocking together. Releasing my body he twirled me around before pulling me back in, placing his hands underneath my long hair and across my bare back. I inhaled sharply, grabbing for his hands and throwing them down from my jagged, bumpy scar.

"Don't touch me there!" I snapped, exhaling abruptly.

He stood perfectly still, watching anger and embarrassment spill over my expression.

Against my will, he placed his hands back, this time running them up my scar rebelliously. My long hair draped over his strong arms, tickling his skin in return.

Whispering in my ear, he said, "There isn't an inch of you that isn't irresistible to me."

A few of the other members had joined us on the dance floor. A lounge singer now accompanied the piano with a rendition of Lana Del Rey's "Born to Die." I crumpled a little and placed my face against Jonah's chest.

The words of the song stung me, and I wavered, uncertain, not sure who they referred to anymore: Gabriel or Jonah.

Jonah reached for my chin and angled my face up toward him. He wasn't meant to make me feel like this. I began to let my defenses down for just a minute, caught up in the music, in his eyes, in the moment. I struggled to stand upright; I winced, unbalanced, as the stilettos slowly killed the balls of my feet.

Sinking deeper into Jonah wasn't helping; he'd suddenly become quicksand, and the more I struggled to fight him the faster he pulled me down. Without asking, he scooped me up in his arms and ran the length of my lower leg with his index finger, leveraging my feet out of the patent heels, gradually popping me back down to the floor, barefoot.

Placing my feet on top of his boots to gain a little height, he lowered me back down. "I like you just the way you are . . . hair up, hair down," he murmured, twisting my sweeping bangs, which cascaded across my eyes, so that I could see him clearly.

His left hand remained softly stroking my cheek. "Lipstick on, lipstick off . . ." he continued, suggestively pressing his thumb gently into the center of my lower lip. "Eyes . . . black holes . . . red warning lights . . ." His words growing quieter, he kissed my eyelids gently and I closed them, drawing a breath.

"He only glimpses part of who you are," he said, lingering.

His lips caressing my earlobe seductively, he whispered, "I see you, all of you. I can still taste you even now."

I let his words drift over me, comforted by his palm placed protectively at my back. He brushed the tip of his nose to mine. When I didn't protest, he married his lips with my own and I squeezed gently in reply, a silent confused tear falling against my cheek. I inhaled his warm and inviting aroma, which reminded me of the woods in summer.

As he crushed his lips a little harder, the sweet flavor of his kiss seemed to subside, instantly changing to a warm metallic taste. My eyes flew open and, pulling away, I gagged as her blood spread across my tongue.

"Cessie?"

Pulsing with disappointment, I pushed him away.

"You drank from her?"

He answered me with a stare that gave nothing away.

"Did you kill her?"

He looked irritated that I would make such an accusation.

"No," he said.

"Was she worth it? Did she taste that good?"

"Not as good as you, beautiful." The corner of his lip turned upward.

I was such an idiot! He didn't give a damn about what promises he made me or whether he kept them. He was beholden to no human, no creature, and certainly not to me.

Watching his eyes watch mine, I delivered a final blow—one that I was certain would bring this conflict to an end. "He's everything you're not and could never and will never be!"

I broke away from him. I wedged on my heels and ripped the mask from my forehead, chucking it on the bar. I felt a draft whip my neck; I didn't have to look over my shoulder to know Jonah had left.

I followed an EXIT sign to a back door and stumbled into the black of night. I had to get back to the main entrance of the club and find Brooke. I began tottering forward, but I didn't get far before a hand grabbed my shoulder, pulling me backward.

"Jonah, I don't have anything else to say to you!" I hissed.

"Lucky for me, I'm not your friend Jonah," Bradley sputtered.

"I thought you were someone else. You'll have to excuse me, I need to go."

"Now, now, what's the hurry?" He wasn't about to let me leave.

Taking me by the length of my curls, he dragged me farther down the building's side until we came to an isolated area, cut off entirely from the rest of the club. Ancient cobwebbed beer barrels stacked on top of the concrete cut off the track into the trees.

"You're hurting me; let go!"

He hurled me up against the cold brick wall and pressed against me. "You still owe me a dance. . . ." He trailed off as he inhaled my hair.

I froze. I wasn't expecting to run into trouble with a human this evening.

"I figured when I saw you leaving that perhaps you'd prefer a private one." He grinned menacingly as he placed the palm of his sticky hand through the soft fiber of my top, resting it on my chest.

"Take. Your. Hand. Off. Me," I said firmly.

Puckering his lips, he stared defiantly back.

He smeared his clamminess around to my back, tugging my hair down, smelling my neck. My body shuddered with disgust. He grazed my scar as he moved down my back and the slightest look of surprise bounced between his beady eyes. "What's this? Seems you're prone to danger. My kind of girl."

He slapped his other hand on the inside of my thigh, running it higher. The fury that filled me was immediate—how dare he touch me!

"I'll let you in on a secret," I whispered. "It was a Vampire that gave me that scar, and I'll tell you something else. I killed him." The words fell out of my mouth.

"A what?" He seemed to halt for a moment, but then shrugged off what I had said. "Calm down; trust me, we're going to have some fun."

As a disobedient, angry tear stained my cheek, his expression changed to astonishment. My tears were blood.

Suddenly unsure of himself, he pulled a sharp knife from his pocket. Using just the one hand to flick it out, he rested the blade against my throat. "Ohhh, you're something else entirely. I thought I'd had every kind of girl there was to have, but you, you're different."

The cold blade dug into my skin, splitting the top layer.

"I said, get your hands off me!" I squeezed out the words through gritted teeth.

He swung the blade to my cheek and bolstered his body against mine, murmuring, "Now, why would I want to do that?"

As he started tugging at my skirt, I answered him. "That Vampire might be dead, but the one standing behind you isn't."

He stopped momentarily—that was all the time Jonah gave him.

He was flat on the ground before he had the chance to see who had put him there, his knife clattering as it bounced off the cobbles.

Jonah turned his face back to me, his eyes ablaze.

He kicked Bradley hard in the stomach. I felt no pity for him. Scraping him off the ground, Jonah plunged his fists repeatedly into his face until Bradley's blood stained his knuckles.

The sight of the red caused something to stir in me, despite the blackness of the night; I could have sworn I saw a shadow move across my vision.

Everything stopped, creating yet another hole in my memory.

I was slumped, palms placed firmly against the brick—steadying myself—when I came back. I twisted around to see Jonah crouched over Bradley's lifeless body; metallic red splatter incarnadined the cobbles. The gory scene was visible only by the faintest flicker of an old bulb flanking the exit door a few feet away.

"What did you do?" The flaming anger that had swept over me had fizzled out.

I ran over to Bradley's side. It was a gruesome sight; his face was unrecognizable, swollen and coated entirely in blood.

I stumbled backward and Jonah was immediately at my side.

"Get off me!" As I shoved him, a strange, sweet cinnamon smell met me and I snapped my head to his neck. I grabbed his shirt away from the vein throbbing just above his collarbone, and a lump rose in my throat. A multitude of lacerations scarred his skin. Bite marks. Someone had drunk from Jonah.

"Cessie." His voice was monotone and calm, as if that might make me the same in return.

Before I had a chance to think, my attention was drawn away from him as I heard something crunching through the trees behind us.

"Jeez! What the freakin' hell happened here?" Brooke cried. "So that's why you told me to bring the car around. Why won't you ever let me have a go?" she snapped at Jonah, taking in the scene.

Dried blood circled her lips as though she'd been snacking messily on some summer berries. Looking from her to Jonah and back again, the obvious dawned on me.

"You drank from him . . . from Jonah?"

Brooke's jaw dropped.

"It's more complicated than you would think," Jonah said.

"What do we do? She can't know!" Brooke's voice filled with alarm. "They'll come for us! Do something!"

I turned away from the pair; the sound of her fangs cracking into place unnerved me. That was all the warning I needed, and, flinging my stilettos off, I ran.

Before I knew what was happening, my body was elevated off the ground and I was trapped in Jonah's strong arms. We ripped through the trees, evidently traveling some distance, and finally ended up in a clearing behind a vineyard.

As he came to an abrupt halt, I was sure he smelled my hair as I kicked and threw my arms about.

Eventually placing me down on the ground gently and steadying me on the grass, he said, "I created Brooke."

His hazel eyes were uncertain.

I was shaking. Removing his leather jacket, he wrapped it around me in response. I shrugged it off, chucking it back to him.

"I made her how she is," Jonah continued.

"How is that possible? You're a Second Generation, you can't create Vampires!"

"I'd drunk from my fair share of female Vampires, so I was strong, fueled by their powers and strength. She was human, and I changed her. I'm no Pureblood. Seems as much as I would never be as powerful as my maker, she would never be as strong as a Second Generation."

The crosses that he wore around his neck caught the glint of the full moon. Sidestepping the glare, I dug my bare feet into the mud.

"Why would you let her drink from you? Surely she'll end you?"

"She's not strong enough. She may be a Vampire, but she's got nothing on me. I had to break my promise to you tonight to not feed, and for that I'm sorry. But you need to understand, Brooke would have killed that boy if I hadn't." He ran his hand through his thick hair, sweeping his eyes from side to side as if he was trapped.

"What are you talking about? Don't blame her for your greed! You drank from that girl in the club because you wanted to, regardless of how I felt about it!"

I paced away from him, but there was nowhere to go. We were on the fringes of a field backing onto the tall vines, somewhere between nowhere and . . . well, nowhere.

Reaching for my hand, he pulled me in to him. "Brooke can't

control herself, and she's hungry. I drank from that girl so Brooke could drink from me. She can't exist off human blood alone, not in her form. She drinks my blood, she feeds off my strength. If I drink from a human first, she gets what she needs the same way I do. I had to. She'd have tried to drink from that innocent French boy otherwise and he would have died. Do you understand?" His tone was becoming more urgent, like he needed me to grasp it.

"I get it, Jonah, but what I don't understand is why you would condemn a human being to your existence? What right did you have? Was it to feel important, or did you do it just because you could? They're right about you; you are black all the way through."

Batting his hand away from mine, I turned my back to him, crossing my arms.

"You really think I'm evil, don't you?" he said softly. "That my word means nothing? That I relish the fact that I made Brooke what she is? I'm really not like your Angel at all, am I. . . ."

I felt myself hesitate. I had always thought Jonah was trying his best to find his humanity again, that he was dealt an unfair hand for which he was trying desperately to redeem himself. But I couldn't get past this. Brooke was more like me than I had first thought—forced into an existence that she didn't ask for.

"She loves you, Jonah. Every time she drinks from you, she becomes more and more connected to you."

At the end of my sentence, as if by magic, she appeared, standing ahead of me.

"And he will never feel the way I do, because he can never drink from me. He's too strong and he'd end me. But he looks after me, he sacrifices his own hunger for mine, and he protects me. And you do love me, in your own way, don't you?"

Jonah must have nodded behind me, as she smiled in return.

"You gotta forget that you know this. If the Purebloods ever discover what Jonah has done, they would hunt us down and end us both. They don't know about me and that's the way it has to stay."

I wondered if they even knew it could be done. But she was right, she was born into this life through Jonah; none of the Pureblood Masters would know of her existence. If they did, they would end her. And if they thought that their Second Generation Vampires could create a new breed, they would certainly exploit that fact to add to their armies.

"How can you even tolerate him, knowing what he did to you?" I asked. "How can you love someone who would take your life?"

"He saved me," she said, shrugging.

From what? I wondered.

Standing quietly for what felt like an eternity, they waited for me, and finally I broke my silence.

"Fine. I won't speak of this again, but, Jonah." I turned around to face him. "What you did, there is no excuse. I don't care what you were or how you try to make amends for it now. She might tolerate you because she has no choice, but I do. You need to stay away from me."

I could no longer believe in him.

My sides twinged as I watched his face, cold and frozen, glower back at me, his eyes wide with regret.

"Cessie, you don't understand—"

I butted in, "Don't! Just leave me alone!"

By the time he'd thrown his jacket back on, his sorrowful expression had molded back to one that was hard and uncaring.

"Did you bring the car like I said?" He directed himself at Brooke only.

"Yes."

"Take her back to the house," he ordered. "I need to go and clean up the mess left behind."

With that, he was gone, the vines shaking as he sped through them.

The mess he was referring to was the torn-up pieces of the body that once belonged to Bradley.

How could I have been so wrong about Jonah?

TWENTY-FOUR

A TERRIBLE SINKING FEELING stewed in the bottom of my stomach as I sat perched on the end of my bed. Two days had come and gone since the night of the club.

Ruadhan had greeted us at the door when we returned that night, very disappointed with my behavior; he had made sure that I knew it too. We spoke nothing of what had happened and I wondered if Ruadhan and Gabriel knew about Jonah and Brooke. I hadn't even seen him since I'd left with her from the clearing; he was obviously granting my wish.

I hadn't managed to get Gabriel on the phone. I hoped he was deeply embroiled in Angel-business and not Hanora-business.

As that thought crossed my mind my phone rang and I felt a nervous flutter as Gabriel's name appeared on the screen.

"Gabriel . . ."

"Lai. I'm coming back."

"Did you find out—well, did you get anything useful?"

He paused. "Yes, I think so. He wasn't in Boston. I've been three steps behind him, but I finally caught up with him today in Montreal. He's traveling back with me. He seems to know what you might be, but he won't say until he sees you for himself. We'll be with you no later than tomorrow night." His voice was hurried.

"Does he know about the company you keep?"

I wasn't sure how comfortable an Angel would be in a house of Vampires.

"Yes. He's not altogether happy about the situation, but he is, well, accepting. Listen, I have to go. Is everything okay? Are you all right?"

His words were smooth and caring and I felt safer just hearing his voice.

"We're all still in one piece, but I . . . I feel terribly alone. I miss you," I said, letting my hurt feelings take a backseat to my overwhelming need to connect with him again.

"I miss you too, Lai; we'll be together again very soon, I promise. And once we have all this sorted, well, we have forever to figure out the rest."

I heard a female's voice in the background.

"Is that Hanora?"

"Yes. I should go."

I felt betrayed all over again.

"Right, you *should* go. To *her*."

I hung up.

I COULDN'T STAY IN MY ROOM FOREVER. Showered and dressed in jeans and a plain T-shirt, I climbed the stairs up to the living area.

I found Brooke throwing her phone and her lipstick into a bag before pulling her arms through a denim jacket.

"She emerges at last!" Brooke smiled hesitantly at me, tidying the stray bangs around her forehead and eyeing my modest attire. "Really?" she scoffed. "I know you don't care about your appearance, but for my benefit could you at least try to look less like a homeless person!"

Ignoring her, I asked, "Where is everybody?"

I headed for the fridge and helped myself to some orange juice.

"Ruadhan's in the study, where he always is. Jonah hasn't been back since we left him." She was careful with her words in case Ruadhan was listening.

Grabbing her car keys from off the table, she eyed me curiously. "Jonah's texted. I think you hurt his feelings, if that's possible. He wanted to make things easier on you and give you some space. I'm heading out for a drive now, to see if I can find him."

Good, I was glad I had hurt his feelings. I hoped he stayed away and that I never had to see him again. I had been so foolish thinking that he had anything good inside of him.

"See you later, Cessie." She put on her massive sunglasses and began to walk out of the sliding doors.

"You know it's winter. I don't think you need those ridiculous glasses." I couldn't resist getting my own back and poking some fun.

She turned and faced me, lifting the glasses from her eyes.

"I don't wear them for fashion."

Her expression was serious.

"Then why do you wear them?" I shot back, washing my glass in the sink.

"Old habits die hard. When I was human, well, I always wore a pair. I couldn't see. Later!"

I stood, paralyzed, and watched her leave. The glass slid out of my hand and shattered in the sink. Brooke had been blind. She was the girl in the house, the night Ruadhan and Gabriel found Jonah. Ruadhan said she had died and she had, but Jonah brought her back; he turned her into a Vampire.

The terrible things I had said to him flew through my mind. Ruadhan said she reminded Jonah of his sister. A sister he hadn't been able to save. So he'd saved Brooke instead. It all made sense, the way he treated her so delicately, catering to her requests and protecting her from a life of hardship.

I darted to the doors, but she was already gone.

I sped back to my room and threw on some sneakers and grabbed my phone. I needed to find Jonah. I had to apologize.

I ran and ran, shouting his name. I tried his cell repeatedly, but his phone was switched off. I hadn't the first clue where he'd be, or if he would even want to talk to me if I did find him, but I had to try.

I'D WALKED AN HOUR away from the house; green fields spread out as far as the eye could see. Finally a stream with a small brick bridge caught my attention. The sky was overcast and the chill in the air made the hair along the bare skin of my arms stand on end. It was so quiet out here.

So few people; so few anything.

I made my way to the bridge. The air grew damp, making me cold and uncomfortable. I called Jonah's name once more and then, like magic, a figure appeared next to the stream. I was too far away to make out his face, but I decided it had to be him. "Jonah!"

The figure dissolved and reappeared with his back to me at the center of the bridge. I ran toward him, thinking of what I might say. I hoped he would forgive my unkind words; I hoped he would accept my apology.

As I neared, he disappeared again.

"Jonah?"

I peered down at the water. A thin layer of ice had formed on the top of the stream and I hesitated as I urged my feet to move forward. The side of the bridge was only as high as my knee. A bramble snapped on the other end and I knew he must be waiting. As I made my way across, the wind suddenly whipped at my cheeks and in a blink he stood directly in front of me.

Only it wasn't Jonah.

"Ethan?"

He was still wearing dated clothing, and his dirty-blond hair was swept away from his face, tied in a loose ponytail behind his neck. He studied my expression, before he raised his finger to my lips and made a low shushing noise.

"Lailah . . . you're alive."

He used my name, my first name, my only name.

I nodded, his finger still pressed against my chapped lips.

"You should be long dead and so should I."

He spoke in the smoothest and most elegant South East accent I had ever heard; even the wealthiest men I had met from London sounded common by comparison. His black pupils were dilated and I couldn't tell if he meant me harm or not.

I should have been scared, standing nose-to-nose with a Vampire, but instead I felt sadness. The images I had seen flickered through my mind, of a time when he was just a boy, and I was just a girl. When we were both someone else, and something to each other.

I was able to see beyond his deadly exterior now, to the friend I had once known.

"You owe me some retribution." He forced an unhappy smile.

So he did mean me harm.

I spared a second to peek down at the icy stream below as the thought of jumping crossed my mind. His eyes flashed from mine to over my shoulder. The rickety bridge wobbled underneath us with the slamming of heavy feet, and I was thrown to the side as another body launched over me, knocking Ethan onto his back. I regained my balance just in time to see Jonah glance at me, while Ethan, growling, pulled him down by his ankles.

As Jonah's body fell to the ground, his tremendous weight knocked into me and before I could grab onto him—grab onto any-thing—I tripped and fell over the ledge.

Jonah's hand reached out for me but, trapped by Ethan's grasp, he wasn't nearly close enough as I slammed chest-first into the icy water.

The sound of the world around me gave way to an inaudible force of nature as the undercurrent swept me downstream. The fall had winded me and now water filled my lungs as I gasped for air. The sheer pain of the freezing cold ate its way to my core, as though it were stripping me of my skin.

The ice formed a thick covering here, and I desperately hit it, as my body traveled against my will, to no avail. My eyes were open but the water was murky. I realized with heavy dread I was going to die and I would be right back to square one: a blank page in an unfin-ished novel.

I clung to my fragile life. As the impossible task of staying alive raced through my mind, so too did an image of Gabriel's face, imprinted in my memory till the true end of my days.

First my arms failed me and then I could no longer feel my legs. I became unable to hold off the darkness that was filling me. As the water slowly suffocated me, static pulsed in and out of my mind like an old, broken TV failing to pick up reception.

But then something—someone—grabbed my arms and propelled my body out of the water, breaking through the white seal. I couldn't open my eyes, I couldn't breathe; I was barely aware of anything around me.

"Cessie! Cessie!"

The voice was distant; I thought I might be underwater still. Only the superhuman strength of a Vampire shaking me violently could break through my semiconsciousness. I might be immortal, but I was cursed with a delicate human form.

Fresh air traveled through me as I felt lips parting mine. The water in my lungs was heavy, and I choked, leaning to the side and coughing up the dirty liquid. My rescuer rubbed my back painfully hard, helping me expel it.

Eyelids twitching, the blur in my vision began to refocus. The bridge looked far away, covered by fog. Now sitting on the bank of the stream, I began to tremble uncontrollably.

"You're okay, beautiful, I'm here. . . . Just breathe."

There was a softness to him and, in my confused state, I could have almost mistaken his comfort for Gabriel's. Jonah pushed my soaked hair back from my face, scooping it behind my shoulders.

"I'm so sorry," I began, while he rubbed my bare arms, trying to warm me. "I should never have said the things I did."

"You were right, Cessie. I'm no better than them," Jonah said, taking my icy hands in his. "Don't worry, take your time. That was quite a fall."

I absorbed his glowing hazel gaze. I reached my fingers to his cheeks and stroked them softly. "You're not a monster, you were saving her. You love her like you loved your own sister."

He jerked backward, his brow creased with a sense of incomprehension.

"Ruadhan told me what happened. The night you decided to change. The night you saved Brooke from them. I didn't know it was her until now. I had to find you, tell you how sorry I am for judging you."

He paused contemplatively and was cautious as he spoke. "I didn't know it then, but if I'd let her die, if I hadn't intervened, then they—Gabriel's people—would have come for her and she'd have existed somewhere else, somewhere better. Instead, she's like me, an empty vessel with a stolen soul. I took her goodness and made her dark; for that I can never be forgiven."

"But you didn't know! You did what you thought was right."

Smelling the damp grass beneath my body, I knew my lungs were clear once more.

"Jonah, please accept my apology."

I hung my head, ashamed, and he fingered my tangled hair in return.

"Do you know who that was back there?"

I kept my head down. I had briefly forgotten about that little secret of mine. "His name is Ethan. He was the one who gave me this." Pulling out my chain, I played with my ring; the chill inside me was receding and I could feel its shape against my skin.

"Your old fiancé was a Vampire?"

"He wasn't when we were engaged. I don't know what happened to him. He pounced on me the night you and I met. I didn't recognize him then. He was with me in the market."

"I knew something, someone, was there with you. Why didn't you tell me? Come on, you're in danger, we need to move."

He started pulling me to my feet, but they wobbled underneath me.

"No, no! It's okay, he's alone. I know he is. We have unfinished business. I need him. . . . I need to know what happened to me."

I tugged at Jonah's arm as he tried to drag me off.

Twisting around to me, his voice raised, he said, "And how do you reckon he would know that?"

"He was the one who killed me."

Jonah's eyes grew larger, his gaze burning.

"He might know what happened to me after, what I am, why I'm like this." I hoped Jonah could see that I didn't want to go back to the house, not yet.

"Cessie, you're a Vampire. You don't need him to tell you that!"

The words shot from his lips too fast for him to reclaim them, and I fell backward.

"No." My voice cracked louder than the ice had when I'd fallen through it. "I'm not a Vampire."

Inspecting me carefully, considering his next move, he said, "Maybe not like me. You're more powerful than I am, but you are certainly some form of Vampire."

"I think I would know." I stifled a worried laugh under my breath.

The clouds above me seemed to be misbehaving, swirling and

parting, making way for some impending rays of daylight. Yet they soon changed to a duller gray; a formidable downpour was getting ready to burst.

"I drank from you. You are nothing like anyone else I have ever tasted. Not even remotely similar to a human, and different than a Second Generation Vampire. Your blood fused with mine and made me so strong and so fast, like . . ."

"Like what?"

"Like a Pureblood."

I turned away from him, but I did so too fast and I became aware of a stinging sensation in my waist. My back to him, I lifted my T-shirt and, sure enough, there was a large gash running across my skin.

"What's wrong?"

The fragrance of my fresh blood took no time to reach his senses and he darted forward, placing his hand over the cut.

"It will heal," I said through gritted teeth as I watched the fireworks set off in his eyes.

Lifting his stained hand to his mouth, he licked a trace of my blood slowly and thoughtfully.

Suddenly and hurriedly he yanked my top back down with his free hand, furiously revolving his face away from me.

"Jonah, it's okay. You won't hurt me."

Dropping his fingers from his lips and gripping his hand in my own, he seemed locked in concentration.

"Is it painful?"

"What?" His eyes flashed to me.

"Not being able to, well, you know—"

I watched his Adam's apple plummet as he gulped.

"Yes." He flicked his eyes down to my waist and then back up to my face. "It's like a thousand suns burning inside me and the only way to put them out is to . . ." He didn't finish his sentence.

"A human's blood wouldn't do that to you?"

He shook his head.

"And the female Vampires, is that how you'd feel before you ended them?"

He shook his head again.

"I have fed on female Vampires and, yes, I've drained them to their end. They don't compare—not one bit—to the way you've made me feel. Still don't believe you're some sort of Vampire?"

"I have never drunk human blood. I've never killed anyone!"

That was true as far as I knew.

"Really? What about that guy outside the club?"

My turn to gulp hard. "You killed him, not me."

"No, I'm pretty sure you killed him. Though you knocked me out before you did, so I didn't get the pleasure of watching you work, but we were the only ones there. You don't remember?"

I kept my hand held over the cut, hoping to stop the smell of my blood wafting further in his direction.

Sure, there were many things I didn't remember; there were enormous almighty holes in my head. I was a scratched record; broken. I didn't exactly know what I was, but of one thing I was certain: I was not a killer. If I was, how could Gabriel ever love me? I shook my head. Why was Jonah saying all this? Why was he messing with me?

Without warning, Jonah's fangs burst out with an almighty crack. Lifting his wrist to his mouth, he gauged rips as he tore through his own skin and drifted in close to my body. Taking me with his muscular arm, he yanked me close, so there was no gap between us.

"What are you doing?" I muttered.

My initial angst was rapidly overtaken by the sudden sensation of a billion butterflies in my tummy, and they were far from being nervous. Expelling pure adrenaline, with every frantic flap of their wings, a feeling of electric anticipation raced up and down my body.

I realized then that I was hungry for him to touch me.

He lifted his wrist to my mouth. The sweet scent of cinnamon tickled my taste buds as I breathed him in. It was as though I was back under the water again and he was the air I so badly needed.

"Taste me," he murmured.

I fixated on the red trickling down his arm, and whimpered in reply, "What . . . Why?"

"If you are what I think you are, you'll . . . enjoy me."

I locked my eyes with his and said, "If I am what you say I am, I would surely end you."

"Perhaps, but at least you would know the truth."

Moving his hand up my T-shirt and scraping past the gash, he rested his palm on my lace bra, grazing my breast. A shudder of excitement filled me; a snap of desire exploded in a way I'd never felt before. I wanted to taste him—have him—more than anything.

My knees began to buckle, and Jonah pulled me in closer.

"He can never be with you. But me, you can have me any which way you like. I want you," he said, grazing my earlobe with his shiny fangs.

Moving my cheek next to his I panted hard, my mouth watering. As I lingered, his intoxicatingly sweet aroma filled me and a heat rose in my throat. Obediently I moved his wrist to my lips and contemplated his request.

The clouds that had threatened a downpour finally opened and torrential drops hit us both. Taking my time, I peered up at the gray clouds, still grasping Jonah's wrist tightly, allowing the rain to wash over me. They didn't put out the fires that were burning inside me. As I brought my face back down, I caught the darkness inside him waging a war across his eyes.

"Please," he whispered.

The demon inside was getting the better of him; seemingly the demon inside of me was, too.

Nearing the bloodied slices across his wrist, I ran the tip of my nose along his skin, avoiding the tear. I cupped my cheek with his hand, and then found his lips instead.

Bringing both his hands now over my cheeks, he pressed firmly. I was tired of fighting and exhausted by my life, so I let myself get lost in the darkness that now filled me and was overflowing.

Emptiness replaced everything.

I WAS BROUGHT BACK by a white dot at the end of the void. It grew until it overcame the dark. The sun. Its light blinded me and I crumpled in the grass.

I lay on my back, met by the frost beneath, and Jonah perched beside me, looking perplexed.

"Cessie?" He seemed calm, almost motionless.

Leaning over me, he placed his hot hands on my collarbone. I realized then that my top was torn and practically falling off.

"What happened?" I asked, taking in the red crimson splattered around his mouth. "Did you drink from me?"

He slumped next to me, his infernos extinguished by the cold, accusing words that fell from my mouth.

"What's the last thing you remember?"

"You, you cut your wrist, but I kissed you. I told you, I'm not like you."

I didn't see or sense any bite marks on my skin: even the cut across my waist had repaired in record time. I considered for a moment that the blood around his mouth did not belong to me. "What happened?" I insisted again.

Staring at me blankly he answered gently, "Nothing, beautiful, it's okay. I think maybe you're not ready yet. . . ."

"Not ready for what?"

"Nothing. Don't worry, come on."

"No," I stated, sitting up. "Not you as well." I shook my head in frustration. "You're going to tell me what I missed, Jonah."

Ignoring me, he reached for my hand and slid his fingers in between my own, lifting me off the sloping stream bank.

"How about you start with what happened to my T-shirt!" I said, flustered, throwing my hand down from his.

Again, he didn't answer; instead he grabbed his discarded jacket from off the ground and placed it over my shoulders.

"Did Ethan come back?" I offered him the most hopeful explanation I could think of.

I scoured the scenery intently.

That would make sense. We must have gotten into an altercation. That was why my top was torn and why Jonah had traces of blood smeared on his skin. I must have fainted or something.

While he didn't seem willing to fill me in, apparently he wasn't prepared to lie to me either. "Nope, he did a disappearing act when you fell in."

"Then why is my top barely in one piece?" I practically hissed. "Why is there blood on your cheeks and around your mouth?" I was getting angry, and Jonah was pacing away from me. "Tell. Me. Now," I enunciated, and Jonah stopped in his tracks.

He let the silence drift between us for a moment, and with his back to me he bowed his head toward the ground.

"Jonah!" I shouted.

Looking over his shoulder, finally he said, "I think the question you should be asking is why is there blood on *your* cheeks and around *your* mouth."

He was right; I wasn't ready to hear that.

TWENTY-FIVE

Christmas Eve. Gabriel was due back this evening and I was nervous.

I was striding up and down the living area, trying to take my mind off the fact that he had an Angel and Hanora in tow. I was dreading the conversation we were certain to have about him and her.

Making his way to the kettle, Ruadhan proceeded to brew me a cup of tea. It was now midday, and Jonah and Brooke had been gone for hours. She had nagged him to drive her to Toulouse in the hope of finding some decent shopping haunts, and as usual he had bent to her will.

Despite Brooke's cool-as-a-cucumber persona, the look of relief on her face when she'd returned to find Jonah back safe and sound made it plain to see how worried she'd actually been. I half suspected that for once she didn't really want to go shopping, and that she was using it as an excuse to mask her need to be alone with him for a while.

Jonah had seemed preoccupied since he'd rescued me from my

fall, and after what he had said to me, I was more than happy to let him be.

"Shouldn't Gabriel be here by now?" I asked Ruadhan.

"Aye, soon enough. He's bringing one of his own with him. Don't suppose *he'll* be pleased to find us lot when he gets here."

"I'm sure Gabriel's told him."

"I reckon he knows about Hanora, given they are traveling together. I doubt Gabriel's explained about the rest of us," he said firmly. "It's not exactly an Angel's place to be mixing with our kind, let alone roaming around freeing us."

Shifting from left to right, I contemplated my next question. "Ruadhan . . ."

"Yes?"

He had his back to me as he poured the boiling water into the small teacup.

"How long have Gabriel and Hanora, you know . . ."

He finished pouring and, setting the kettle down, he turned to me, leaning his elbows on the island in the kitchen that separated us. "It's not like that between them, love. Believe me, there are enough reasons!"

Shifting over to the fridge, he added some milk and I made as much noise as I could pulling out a chair at the dining table, inviting him to sit and tell me the story.

Hesitantly he joined, drifting at my side.

"It's not my place to go speaking about other folks' business."

I wanted so badly to hear what Ruadhan knew, and he saw it in my face.

Sighing, he plonked himself down across from me. "I told you Gabriel saved all of us?"

I nodded briskly.

"Hanora was the first, best part of a century ago in fact. But she rejected him. She was distressed at being parted from her Gualtiero, and it took her an awful long time to accept the new life he was offering her."

"Why'd he bother? He should have just let her go back if she felt like that."

"They'd have ended her if she had tried to return. She'd escaped, disbanded, remember. He worked with her, helped her overcome the connection she still felt to her Master. Eventually she came around, but seemingly all that time she spent with him, well, let's just say she mistook his interest in her."

I gulped hard. I had to be careful; I couldn't let him see how deeply I cared. Ruadhan wasn't stupid. I was sure he was aware, to some degree at least, about my feelings toward Gabriel.

"But they were together for a while at least?"

"No. Never. He's an Angel, born from light. She's dark. The two don't mix like that," he said.

"Why?"

"Love is light. Hate, evil is darkness. Polar opposites. It would never matter what she did, even with a being such as Gabriel, he could never love her like that."

I swallowed harder. Jonah said he thought I was dark, that I was some sort of weird Vampire. If I was, surely by Ruadhan's rules the same outcome would apply. No. Jonah was crazy. . . . I wasn't a Vampire.

My stomach turned as I realized that no matter how much I attempted to convince myself otherwise, after what Jonah had said down by the stream, it was becoming difficult for me to deny that he was onto something.

"Didn't stop her trying, mind! She's one of those that wants what they can't have, you know? I think the fact that he's turned her down makes her want him even more. Greed, lust . . . that's a darkness, you know."

I didn't want a lecture in religion or ethics. I tried to steer around it.

"She's always traveled with you?" I said.

"Yes and no. When it gets too much she leaves, but she always returns. We're the nearest thing to a family she has, and whether she can be with him or not, she finds herself back here trying again."

Could the girl not just take no for an answer?

"Gabriel told me that none of you had a choice in becoming what you are. And that when there was an opportunity, and for those that sought it, he granted salvation." I pondered. "But how is it that he found Hanora in the first place? How did he find any of you?"

"Drink your tea, love, it's getting cold."

Sipping obediently, I waited for my answer.

"Chance really, coupled with the fact that Gabriel is atoning for something—" He stopped. He didn't want to go any further; I had to push him along.

"Ruadhan, you can tell me. What happened to him?"

"Not really the business of either of us. You asked me if he was involved with Hanora and I've told you he's not. Though why does she concern you so much?" His bushy eyebrows lifted as my cheeks flushed pink.

"Oh, little love, he cares about you, but, well, not in that way."

He leaned over the table to squeeze my hand, like some doting father picking up the pieces of his daughter's latest heartbreak.

"I didn't say he did!" I said, snatching it back.

"You're very, very lovely, but one thing I'm certain of is that he would never enter into a relationship with a mortal. He's done that once before and, from what I understand, it didn't exactly work out."

I wanted to push for more, but sensed Ruadhan wasn't yet done.

"I really shouldn't be talking to you about this. . . ." His eyes meeting mine, he continued, "Ah, Cessie. I don't pretend to know the ins and outs of his life. But I do worry about him." He pawed his stubble thoughtfully.

"This girl, the mortal girl he fell for, what happened with her?"

He cast his eyes to the floor, looking as though he was on the verge of walking away from the conversation.

"I care about him, too, you know," I whispered. "If I could just understand."

"He made a fatal mistake—he fell in love. He's only ever spoken to me once about her, you know. Roaming the Earth, he seeks her out, searching for her soul. You asked how he came to find us. That's how. He was traveling toward supernatural energy. I don't fully understand why he thinks her soul is Earthbound. I told him she must be in Heaven." He shook his head, confused himself.

"So he's atoning for falling in love? That doesn't make sense. Why would he feel guilty about that?"

He paused and somberly answered, "He told me that he killed her."

I nearly spat out my lukewarm tea.

Ruadhan leaped up, knocking over his chair in the process. "I've said too much," he mumbled.

Grabbing his arm, I dared his gaze back to my own. I threw out one last question. "Did he tell you her name?"

Sure now he must be talking about someone else, my whole body began to feel heavy. It seemed no aspect of my life was exempt from conflicting emotion. Whatever Ruadhan's answer, it was a double-edged sword.

It suddenly felt like I was playing Russian roulette. As Ruadhan started to speak, I could almost hear a chamber rolling over. I squeezed my eyes shut and held my breath, waiting to find out if my dreams were about to be shot down.

"Aye, he did." He paused. "Said her name was Lailah."

Ruadhan broke free of me, rushing away. My initial relief from knowing that there hadn't been someone else faded and I was left feeling dumbfounded.

Why did Ruadhan think Gabriel had been the one who killed me? It had been Ethan. It made no sense. But then nothing seemed to make any sense these days.

I remained at the table and forced myself to revisit the memory of my death, of my body falling, of blood trickling past my face.

As unexpected and as instant as a bolt of lightning, I felt Gabriel there with me.

Startled, I tried to make my mind go blank.

You remembered . . .

It was as though the whole world had been swallowed up and all that existed was his voice.

He killed me. Ethan killed me.

Silence.

As if he were a passing breeze, a chill slid in between the cracks of my mind, and I was still.

I'll be with you soon.

And just as quickly as he had arrived in my consciousness, he left.

Returning back to reality, I decided that Ruadhan had to be mistaken. I knew Ethan had killed me; I'd seen it, I'd even relived it. Ruadhan was wrong.

My feet itched underneath me, ready to act. Bolting down to my basement bedroom, I showered as quickly as I could. As I dried my hair and applied a thin layer of makeup, questions rolled over in my mind. I had to get answers. Today. Starting with what happened in that motel room with Hanora.

I brushed past the table that the chess set sat on and I peered down. It was Gabriel's move and I hadn't noticed until now but he was about to put me in check.

It came as no surprise, but I was a tad disappointed that I was failing miserably.

I bet the Lailah that Gabriel had once known was better.

Reaching the dresser, I rifled through the clothes and I was grateful for a moment that Brooke had salvaged some of the nicer pieces. Choosing a white blouse, I tucked it into a turquoise chiffon skirt. Sure enough, Brooke had picked out a matching cardigan, so I bundled it on, also sliding my chalky legs through footless tights and throwing on some ballet flats.

He must be close. If he was able to connect with me it meant he was near, and I felt the urge to look my best for our impending conversation.

As I opened the door to my room, I froze. He was standing in front of me.

My knees wobbled underneath me. Gabriel regarded me with sparkling eyes and a beautiful smile—stretching all the way up to his deep dimples. It was as if his mere presence brought the sun out of hiding, as rays found their way through my window, striping across his face.

He pushed back the loose strands of hair covering my right eye before pulling me in to his chest and holding me as if he hadn't for a million years.

I have missed you so much, Lai.

I clutched his white T-shirt in reply. I was gripping it hard, not sure if it was out of love or anger. Tipping my chin up to face him, he found my lips just as quick. His kiss was gentle, yet powerful.

He determinedly locked his eyes with mine and grasped the back of my head with his palms, placing both his thumbs against my cheekbones. He stared down at me, forcing me to search the glittering windows into his soul.

I lost myself in his eyes, my anxiety and hurt feelings washing away. He trailed his fingertips along my neck, across my shoulders, and down my arms, eventually reaching my hips.

Tugging at my blouse, he slid his hand underneath the soft cotton. Placing his palm to the small of my back, he drew my body in closer. As he pressed me against him, my breathing hitched in response.

I fingered his waistband and rose to the tips of my toes. I needed him.

Gabriel lifted me from the ground and I wrapped my legs around his waist and placed my hands on his chest. His heartbeat was strong and fast. He wasted no time devouring me with his sultry kisses; our lips tangled together as a sense of yearning swelled between us.

His aroma of citrus seemed to intensify as my touch peeled away his layers. And at his core was an incandescent white light that pulsed, refracting off my crystal. A halo formed around us. Together we shined, at the center of our very own fire rainbow.

Our lips separated as he set me down, and I finally came up for air.

"Where did that come from?" I asked, once I found my breath.

His smile changed, and he said, "When I tell you the truth about me, about us, you may not ever want to see me again, let alone touch me."

My body knotted as I felt his worry stretch from his being into mine. "I'm afraid for us," I said. "There are things I haven't told you either."

My face screwed up in apprehension. I couldn't help but feel our happy reunion was on the cusp of being muddied in dirty half truths.

"Let's take a walk," he said.

"What about the Angel you've brought?"

"He can wait. What I have to say to you can't."

He took my hand and led me out the front of the property. We walked hurriedly up the long road to an ancient, abandoned water mill. Gabriel offered me a spot next to him on the trunk of a fallen tree.

The winter's sun was fighting to overcome the layer of white clouds that were gathering around it. The Pyrenees Mountains, with their snowy peaks, were visible in the distance. I marveled at them, gathering my courage. If I didn't tell him now I never would.

"Gabriel."

"Lai."

We spoke at the same second and I grinned nervously at how in sync we were.

"Please, Gabriel, I need to tell you some things before I lose my nerve. . . ."

His eyes caught mine. I could stay happily submerged in their brilliant blue forever, but this time, I resisted the plunge.

Gabriel squeezed my hand reassuringly, as if there was nothing I could say that would affect him. I was sure that that wasn't the case.

"Where to start . . ."

"Try the beginning," he said.

His gentleness made me calmer.

I took a breath, deciding to begin with Ethan. Gabriel knew about him, at least back then, back when we first met—but I needed to fill him in on the recent developments, plus it might be easier if I worked up to the more difficult conversation.

"Okay. So, the night I met Jonah, when Eligio's clan was attacking us, there was a Vampire. I didn't recognize him at first, but he seemed to know me somehow. When we left the house, I had a vision of the Purebloods and the clans, and I watched as that same Vampire left them. I didn't know why. I saw him again at the airport and then he turned up at the market in Mirepoix."

I felt his body stiffen.

"He had an old woman hand me a ring. It had a coat of arms on it and I noticed that it matched some of the markings on my own ring."

I felt for my circle under my blouse. "Touching it caused me to fall into memories of the past. I recognized him then. I'd seen him in other visions, but I never knew who he was to me. Finally, in the last memory, I fell back in. I relived an argument we had in a barn and he grabbed me and I hit the ground. I came out of it just as I was about to die."

I could sense Gabriel's growing trepidation, but I pushed past it.

"When I came to, he was there, standing over me. I suddenly knew his name. Ethan. I guess he was the fiancé you mentioned. I watched him give me my ring." I tapped my chest again where it sat cooling my skin.

"Ethan was not a Vampire when you were betrothed," Gabriel said, his voice low.

"Something must have happened to him after. I don't think he meant to kill me, it was an accident. My memories of him are happy ones."

Gabriel's grip on my hand tightened. "Your parents had arranged for him to marry you," he said. "Ethan was the son of the local squire, and of a higher standing than your own family." He paused. "Your father offered you and, from my understanding, sweetened the deal with this gem, to be placed into a band for you and into their family." He organized his thoughts again. "Ethan was not a bad person. You grew up together, you told me once he was like a brother. Then you met me, and you decided you couldn't marry him. . . ." He trailed off.

"Because I fell in love with you."

He smiled at me, but it was a sad smile.

"He's following me. He's here somewhere and he wants retribution, I don't know why."

"How do you know that?"

"He told me, right before I fell into the ice," I said.

Gabriel snatched his hand from my own and turned my face toward him. "You fell into ice?"

"It's all right, Jonah was there. He pulled me out. I'm fine, honestly. There's more." I didn't want to delve into the details of that particular rescue. I didn't fully understand and I still wasn't ready to face whatever it was that had happened.

"There's a girl. You will think I'm crazy, but she just sort of turns up. I don't know who she is; I never see her face because she's always shrouded in shadow. I see her, but then . . . I don't know, things get hazy, I can't remember. It's like she somehow creates black spots in my memory. She was there the night Frederic attacked me. She killed him, I'm sure she did."

A deep twinge of pain shot through my head, rumbling into a dull ache as I tried to recall.

"It's okay." His voice soothed me and I was able to continue.

"Ruadhan saw her, he said he did, in the Hedgerley house. But he said she was a Pureblood. I don't understand—why would a Pureblood Vampire protect me?"

He didn't offer any answers.

I turned my body toward him and, biting my bottom lip, I said, "Also, I kissed Jonah."

There. I'd said it.

I didn't have much of an explanation. Gabriel's eyes stretched wide, and he took both my hands back in his own.

"I didn't really mean to. We went to this nightclub and there was this guy . . . Jonah just kind of stepped in and helped me out. I was angry with you because I thought you were with Hanora and I don't know, I just . . . It's weird, when I'm with him, I don't entirely feel like myself."

"He's a Vampire. He can influence you in ways you don't know."

He gave me an out, but I had to be honest with him.

"I don't think he'd do that. When we're together, something comes over me and I find myself acting on impulse. It wasn't the first time, or the last, I'm sorry," I rushed, feeling totally ashamed.

Gabriel sat next to me in silence, his hands still covering mine. Finally he squeezed them and said, "Jonah overstepped the mark, not you, Lai. You're in a very vulnerable position and he shouldn't have taken advantage. I trusted him with you."

I met Gabriel's gaze and just as I was about to interject, I stopped as I watched the veins in his neck jut out and a spark of warning suddenly flared in his eyes. "I'll kill him."

He jumped up and I gulped hard, reaching for his arm.

Seeing Gabriel so angry was unfamiliar; he wasn't like that.

"Gabriel, no—" I stuttered, pulling him back toward me.

He met my eyes and immediately softened; taking his time he sat back down. "I'm sorry. It's okay, we'll work it out." He forced a smile, an unsure, upset smile that made me die a little inside.

He was the last person I wanted to hurt. I loved him.

"I'm sorry. That night he'd helped me at the club after, well, drinking from a stripper."

"What?"

"I was upset with Jonah and left, and that's when the guy came after me. . . ." This confession wasn't getting any easier. But I might as well get it all out now.

"I blacked out, and when I came to, the guy was dead."

I tried to connect to Gabriel's mind, but he'd closed it off. I guessed he wanted to deal with my revelations in private.

"Jonah said I killed him, but I couldn't have. I'm not like them. I—I . . ."

Feeling my eyes welling up, ready to spill over, Gabriel pulled me in to him and held me tightly, running his hand in a circular motion over my back.

"I don't know what Jonah's game is," he said. "But I'm sure you didn't kill him, Lai."

I sobbed a little. "Don't be mad; I know you're upset, but Jonah's been really good to me. He's looked out for me and kept me safe."

Gabriel squeezed my hands reassuringly. "I should have been here protecting you. I'm sorry I had to leave." He kissed the top of my forehead and mopped up my tears with his fingertips.

"I need to tell you something extremely important, Lai."

He was deadly serious and as I raised my face up to meet his, I braced myself for the worst. Was he about to tell me that he had been with Hanora after all?

"It's about when we first met—"

A voice cut through our exchange. "Sorry to interrupt this little heart-to-heart." A man appeared next to us, eyeing me with interest.

As he stood a few feet away from me, I felt the strangest sense of déjà vu creep over me. I had never met him before, but I felt like I knew him. And in some strange way, he looked like me. His skin was milky white, and his large eyes were a unique shade of blue that was strangely similar looking to my own. Most important, he seemed uncomfortable in his surroundings. As though he were a fish out of water. He could only be the Angel whom Gabriel had brought back with him.

Gabriel stood up, startled by his sudden and uninvited arrival, and I quickly followed suit.

"Azrael, this is Cessie."

My ears pricked at Gabriel's choice of name for me, and I took it to mean that Azrael hadn't yet earned Gabriel's trust.

"Delighted."

He extended his hand to mine, his eyes narrowing as I reached out politely. As his cool skin stroked my own, I was overwhelmed with the strangest vibration that caused goose bumps to run up my arms.

My mind was filled with an intense light that finally burst into droplets of silver and gold, exploding like an enormous firework.

I yanked my hand away and stumbled, grabbing for something to steady me. Gabriel wrapped his arms around me and we both stared at Azrael, whose expression was unreadable.

He finally nodded and smiled. "Seems I'm your Creator. Or would you prefer Dad?"

I looked to Gabriel, astonished. His expression mirrored mine.

TWENTY-SIX

I PACED ANXIOUSLY AROUND the living room. Eventually Ruad-han interrupted my racing thoughts.

"Sweetheart, sit down. Let me make you something to eat; I haven't seen you touch a bite in two days."

I stopped briefly. He was right; I hadn't eaten since before I had fallen into the stream.

"I don't want to eat, I want to hear what they're saying!"

Azrael had called a council with Gabriel. Alone. I was stuck out here while they discussed me. It was hardly fair.

"I know, love, but patience is a virtue! Let me whip you something up. What would you like?"

I had an idea. "Eggs." I knew we didn't have any.

"I'll check." Ruadhan scrambled around the fridge and the cupboards, scratching his head as he came away empty-handed. "No eggs."

"That's okay, I'll pop out and get some. Jonah said one of the distant neighbors has chickens."

"No! Not by yourself. I'll go fetch some; I can be there and back in a few minutes. Just stay put."

As soon as he sped off, I tiptoed down the wooden stairs and sat on the last step. Gabriel and Azrael were just outside the basement, but their voices were muffled. The chessboard momentarily distracted me, as I saw that Gabriel had now put me in check. Worse still, on closer inspection, I realized that he had actually put me in double check; having brought his bishop diagonally across the board, now both it and the knight—two equal forces—were threatening my king.

I scanned the board and, though I tried hard, the white and the red just seemed to merge; I couldn't see a way to escape.

Great. I wasn't getting any better at this game.

Straining to hear, I crept slowly along the side of the wall, hiding behind the half-open door.

"She was infected. She's not like you or I. You need to understand that." Azrael's voice was calm but assertive.

"There's no darkness in her; you're wrong."

"She was created from light, but she was infected and changed by the most terrible evil and then she was born into this dimension. That makes her more powerful and destructive than any being in the three dimensions," Azrael said.

"I won't accept that. I've seen nothing of her that would suggest it is true!" Gabriel's raised voice made my hairs stand on end.

Then there was silence.

I was trying desperately not to react, holding my breath, but Azrael's revelations caused my heart to thud hard against my chest. The emotions rising inside me must have given me away: Gabriel appeared in the basement.

"You wouldn't make a terribly good spy." He crinkled his forehead and extended his hand to mine, leading me through the doorway.

I kept hold of Gabriel's hand and addressed Azrael. "You know what I am?"

He looked to Gabriel and then back to me. His eyebrows raised, he seemed surprised that I had dared to interrupt their private conversation.

Tilting his head Azrael said, "Yes, Cessie. There is a reason you are different. You were created in the first dimension—our home—as an Angel Descendant, but something happened to you. . . ." He trailed off as Gabriel bore holes through him with his stare.

"It's okay," I said. "Tell me what happened?"

"You were infected by a Pureblood Vampire, when your mother—my Angel Pair—was carrying you. Not just any Pureblood Vampire; his name is Zherneboh. He was the first Pureblood to emerge from the third dimension. Your mother fled and it seems she gave birth to you here in the second."

Gabriel took his hand from mine and wrapped his arm around my waist, as if bracing me for the worst of this wild story.

I shook my head. "But I am . . . I was human. It was only when I died that I woke up and I was different."

"You were born here. In your first death, your mortal, human-self indeed ceased to continue. But you came back immortal, inheriting your true lineage."

"You mean I became an Angel?"

"No. You might have been created in our world, but when the Pureblood infected you, it mutated your DNA. You have your light, but you also have darkness now—"

345

"That's enough!" Gabriel shouted. "Lailah." He caught himself. "Cessie."

"What did you call her?"

Azrael moved closer and Gabriel nudged me backward protectively.

"My name is Lailah," I replied, in the smoothest tone I could muster.

Upon hearing this, Azrael circled the room, finally smiling to himself. "Do you know that Lailah is a name given to an Angel of Freedom and the highest-ranking Angel under an Arch Angel?" Azrael said. "Your mother left you one thing at least. Hope."

Gabriel turned his body in to mine. "Azrael has been wandering this dimension for nearly two hundred years. He doesn't know anything for certain; he's surmising."

I glared at Azrael. "Gabriel's right, you can't know what the effect would be from what that Pureblood did, and you can't know for sure that I am the child you lost."

Azrael pulled his crisp shirt down and neatened his blond hair. It was strange to think that this being—who looked no older than Gabriel or me—was in some bizarre way claiming to be my father.

"You told me that a Second Generation drank from her?" His tone had returned to calm, almost caring.

Gabriel nodded.

"Was it the female you traveled with?" he asked.

"No, his name is Jonah," I answered too quickly.

"Is he here?"

"He's not back yet," I said.

"Well, let us go and wait for him."

346

We lingered uncomfortably upstairs in the living room. Ruadhan set an omelet in front of me, which I played with on my plate.

Gabriel called Jonah from his cell. If Jonah showed up, then perhaps Azrael would show his hand.

Azrael gestured to me and sat next to Gabriel on the sofa, no space between us. "Out of curiosity, Gabriel, what does she look like to you?"

The sun was lowering and, in response to the dwindling light, Azrael flipped on the lamp next to him and gestured again. "I'd say she's got long blond hair, blue eyes, pale skin, average height, slim. You?"

Gabriel turned to me, confused with the question, and shot back to Azrael, "The same, she's always looked the same." His reply was brisk and smooth.

"Ruadhan, is it?" Azrael called over to my Irish protector, who sat at the table with his nose in a book—though I could tell he was only pretending to read it.

"Aye."

"How would you describe her?" he pushed.

Ruadhan drew his neck in a little and eyed me. "Exactly the way you said. She's a sweet little thing, when she's not up to mischief." He grinned at me, which made me feel a little bit better.

"Hanora!" Azrael bellowed.

My body stiffened; I didn't want to see her. The door upstairs creaked and I watched as Hanora delicately descended the stairs until she stood next to Ruadhan.

I couldn't help but notice that underneath the silk headscarf that she had wrapped around her hair and over her ears were burn marks, bubbled and scarred down the porcelain of her neck. Vampires healed quickly; I didn't know what could cause that kind of damage to sit on the skin for a prolonged period of time.

"You?" Azrael asked.

Hanora eyed me with contempt; if looks could kill I would have been dead in an instant. "She's a bit on the short side."

Hanora didn't miss her opportunity to have a dig. I gathered she'd been listening in from the other room.

I turned to Azrael. "Why are you asking them what I look like?"

Before he could answer, the front door slammed and the whole house shook as Jonah catapulted up the stairs, with Brooke behind him.

"Cessie, are you all right?" he fired, assessing the scene.

"She's fine," Gabriel half growled, standing up from the sofa. "This is Azrael. He's an Angel and he's come to help us."

Gabriel took my hand and squeezed it. I stood and saw Hanora flinch from across the room. Wasting no time, Azrael paced up and down the living room, holding everyone's attention.

"You are Second Generation, of course." He spoke in the smoothest of voices, directing his statement at Jonah.

"Too good-looking to be a Pureblood, don't you think?" Jonah spat sarcastically.

"Gabriel tells me that you drank from her. Just the once, was it?"

Jonah shifted uncomfortably, finally nodding. Swaying a little he shuffled Brooke behind his back. I knew by this sly move that he was unsure of where this was leading and his instinct now was to protect Brooke. They could after all be ended by an Angel and they didn't know or trust this particular one.

"Is she appealing to you?"

"I'm sorry?" Jonah said.

"Was she appetizing?" Azrael continued.

I felt Gabriel's body tense.

"What does that have to do with anything?" Jonah replied.

"Don't you find it interesting, given that you are a dark creature that enjoys drinking from dark souls of humans, that you would find her so pleasing, given that she is a light soul?" Azrael glared at Gabriel. "I'm interested to know, from the perspective of a Vampire who has drunk her blood, how you see her?" He looked back at Jonah.

The lines in Jonah's brow deepened as he considered Azrael's bizarre question.

"You have a pair of eyes, don't you?" Azrael pressed, glaring at Jonah with contempt. He clearly wasn't used to conversing with Vampires, and he seemed to be running out of patience, and fast.

Finally, shrugging his shoulders, Jonah smiled at me and said, "Cessie is quite striking. Dark eyes, gray, verging on black . . ." He hesitated before he continued. "Either way they are twice the size they probably should be. Long, loose, jet-black curls that bob in the arch of her back . . . pale, like she's never seen the sun." He watched my jaw drop.

I looked to Gabriel and then to Azrael, puzzled.

"Jonah, stop messing around," I huffed. "Just tell him so we can stop this ridiculous conversation!"

But Jonah's earnest eyes told me that he wasn't joking.

"I don't understand." Hanora spoke first.

"Lailah is not very different from all of you. She's just better at hiding it," Azrael answered calmly.

My eyes shot to Ruadhan, who stood still as a statue as the realization of my name and what that meant dawned on his expression.

Before I had a chance to say anything—do anything—Hanora's ordinarily silky voice, now serrated like a spear, sliced through the air: "If she's like us, you can't possibly feel anything for her!" she yelled at Gabriel. "You've told me, you've always told me that you can't. Or you'd be with me! Wouldn't you?"

Gabriel released my hand and scratched his temple pensively.

Everyone in the room was staring at me. I felt exposed and I wished that I could vanish into the background.

Gabriel's nonresponse made my eyes well up. Without thinking, I made for the sliding door and was in the garden faster than I knew I could run. Panic overwhelmed me. I found myself teetering at the top of the sloping lawn.

The gray beginnings of night were creeping through; they engulfed me. I jumped as a small bat flew past my head. Staring down at the lit-up property, I observed the pandemonium that had ensued; Gabriel was at Hanora's side, grabbing her flapping arms, while Ruadhan circled the room with his head bowed down. The news that I was harboring some Vampire heritage had set Brooke off; she was crying and yelling. Jonah seemed to be trying to calm her, and though they were a full thirty feet away from me, I couldn't miss the multitude of blazing red eyes.

"Sorry. They needed to know." Azrael came up behind me and rested his hand on my shoulder. I edged away from him.

"Where did you come from?" I said.

"Same place you did and in the same manner. Seems you can mask yourself just like we can."

"We?"

"Gabriel and I. How interesting that there's nothing wrong with your Angelic powers in this dimension. Maybe the apple doesn't fall too far from the tree; you are my daughter after all." Azrael's words were monotone, drifting to my consciousness.

I started to shake. "Why—?"

"Lailah, they had to know. You can't stay with them, and I fear if they didn't reject you, you would never have left. You're only prolonging the inevitable." His words were soft, as though he cared about me.

"They wouldn't hurt me."

"Let's consider that, shall we? The boy drank from you. He's connected to you now and he'll never stop trying."

I remembered what Gabriel had told me; I was a drug to him. Now that Brooke knew, she would turn on me. Of course she would.

I began to panic as I thought of the way Jonah had explained my appearance. Worse still, I didn't know if I was freaking out because of what that implied about my soul, or whether it was because Jonah was actually chasing someone else.

Because the girl he described standing in front of him was certainly not me.

"But to be honest," Azrael continued, "it's not them that worry me the most."

He indicated for me to sit on the metal bench next to him. Now I knew that Azrael was my father, I felt compelled to do as I was told, so I nodded and took a seat next to him.

"Do you know how it was that Gabriel first came to find you?"

I shrugged my shoulders.

"He was sent by the Arch Angels to seek you out and to kill you."

Azrael's words startled me and I jerked back. "No, that's not true," I said. "I was killed by Ethan, not Gabriel. All this time, he's only tried to keep me safe. . . ."

The conversation with Ruadhan fresh in my mind caused a spike of doubt to jab me. He had said that Gabriel had confessed to killing the mortal girl he had loved—Lailah—me.

"Gabriel was created and born from light. He cannot kill you by his own hand; but here, on this plane, he has the power to influence others. My guess would be that this Ethan you speak of did not kill you of his own accord."

"No, it was an accident and then I lost Gabriel—"

"He had you killed," Azrael interrupted. "He thought his job was done. But it wasn't, and here you are together once more. The very fact that he has left you in the company of Vampires should convince you. . . ."

I looked into Azrael's faded eyes. They seemed tired.

"I don't believe you," I protested. "Gabriel loves me, I know he does!"

"He does not love you, Lailah, he is simply on duty. If he wasn't, he would be fallen, would he not? He exists here immortal and in full capacity of his powers. We Angels are made in pairs. Gabriel has his own waiting for him in the first dimension. You're keeping him here, away from her. So you must believe me when I tell you that he seeks your end."

I couldn't deny it. Gabriel had told me that he had been created as one half of a shared light. A terrible pain flowed through my chest, making it hard for me to breathe.

"And what about you?" I said. "Did these Arch Angels of yours send you to kill me too?"

I had no reason at all to trust Azrael; I hadn't even known of him until today.

"I returned here to find your mother, my Angel Pair. I have been searching for her for nearly two hundred of this dimension's years, but her light has drifted from my reach."

I don't know why, but I found myself reaching for my necklace and I tugged it above my blouse. Azrael's eyes immediately focused on my gem and, as he reached for it, it began to glow a luminous white.

"That crystal belongs to Aingeal. She left it for you?" he asked, unbelieving.

"I—I don't know. For as long as I can remember, I have always had it," I answered.

"Then I may never find her." Azrael's body seemed to lose its elasticity as he slumped beside me. "All I have left now is you," he said, his voice broken.

We sat together, the icy breeze skimming our cheeks. I looked back to the house. Gabriel was still trying to restrain Hanora, but his face kept searching the garden. Maybe Azrael was right; if Gabriel loved me, why wasn't he with me now? Why was he with her?

"What should I do?" I asked.

Azrael pulled himself upright and turned my body in toward him. His eyes widened as he said, "Jonah sees your features heavily influenced and altered by the venom that Zherneboh spread. But believe me, it is just the tip of your darkness. You are harboring the most deadly of evils inside you." Rocking himself on the bench, he continued. "You've proven you cannot truly be killed in this form and Zherneboh changed you for a reason. A terrible purpose has been bestowed upon you. It is only when you lose yourself to the void that the evil can be truly ended, and Lailah . . ." He paused. "You will, and you must, be ended along with it."

I watched him and considered his severe declaration.

"And even if I knew how, even if I could find this evil you speak of, what if I don't want that? What if I want to live?"

"Light and dark can never coexist; they are two separate forces. One will always overcome the other. If the day ever came that you could finally realize what you are, and if you were somehow able to accept both sides . . . well, if that day were to come, all the dimensions would eventually fall and it would be the end of all things."

"I don't understand."

Even if Azrael was right, even if I was half light and half dark, and even if there were some extreme evil buried beneath my skin, how could I bring about the end of all things?

"You are the only being that can exist in your form across all three dimensions. With or without the evil, in the wrong hands you are the ultimate weapon in a war Zherneboh has been waiting for you to wage."

I closed my eyes and blew out a long breath, as I tried to comprehend everything he was telling me. I didn't believe him. Or maybe I didn't want to believe him. A sudden sense of rebellion hit me as I cleared my mind and I shook off Azrael's grip, propelling myself to my feet.

Facing him, I shouted, "No, no! You're lying! Gabriel did not come here to end my existence! He loves me, I know he does. . . . Everything you are saying is a lie!"

"Then why don't you ask him yourself?"

Azrael inclined his head to the right and I spun around to find

Gabriel a few feet away from me. I took in his citrus scent and smiled; Azrael couldn't be more wrong about him.

Gabriel moved to my side, wide eyed, and said, "We have to go. Just us, we need to leave now! I couldn't stop Hanora; she's told her Gualtiero, they know where you are and Zherneboh is coming."

I looked back to Azrael, who, nodding, encouraged the question from my lips.

"But I saw you with her, how could she have told them?"

"Explanations later. Come, we have to move!"

He grabbed my hand and pulled me after him, but I dug my heels into the grass. He turned back, a puzzled look smacked across his face.

"Did you come here to kill me? When we first met, was that what you were here to do?" I said it. I almost laughed as I did; it was the most ridiculous, ludicrous . . . But he froze and bowed his head to the ground.

"Gabriel?" I asked.

If I had been made of glass, I would have shattered into a thousand pieces.

"Yes." His voice was soft.

The ground beneath me didn't seem to exist anymore. I felt unmoored and truly alone. I always had been.

Lailah, I can explain. . . .

I looked to our fingers entwined together, and as I loosened my grip and allowed my hand to break free, his connection to me fell with it.

I staggered, reeling away from Gabriel and reaching for the metal bench to steady myself.

If Zherneboh were coming, then all of them would meet their ends. Jonah, Brooke, Ruadhan, Hanora, maybe even Gabriel.

Regardless of what Azrael said, I had already cost Gabriel too much. Zherneboh sought *me* out, not them. I had to get far away from here. I had to stand alone.

I was petrified, but I had to save them.

Nodding swiftly to Azrael, in acceptance of his words, I fled into the darkening night.

As I ran, I thought back. I recalled how I had sprinted into the house in Creigiau to recover my crystal; I'd made it past Jonah. I had been stronger than him. And when the Vampires had stormed the house in Hedgerley, I'd saved Jonah by plunging a metal bar through a Vampire's chest. I hadn't known where the strength I had exerted had come from, but it *had* come.

It was becoming almost impossible to deny it anymore. I was not human. I was what Azrael said.

Somewhere inside me, I possessed my own supernatural gifts, and I hoped that they would serve me now, when I needed them the most.

TWENTY-SEVEN

THE SUN HAD SET AS I ground to a halt at the foot of Monts d'Olmes. Ahead of me was forest; behind me, the road was empty and still. It was so quiet, like the calm before a storm.

I hoped Gabriel and the others wouldn't follow; whatever lay ahead was mine alone to face. And though I knew that I was hurtling toward my inevitable end, I felt better knowing that they would continue on. Everyone would.

I looked up at the tree line. The mountain seemed so tall and I had never been much good at climbing. Whether I was light, dark, or both, I should be able to speed up the side.

I closed my eyes and thought of jumping high, and launched myself off the ground.

I didn't travel far, falling to the loose gravel and grazing my hands.

This wasn't going to come easily.

Instead, I willed my feet to move and broke into a sprint, following the winding roadside.

The more I ran, the faster I became. Before I knew it, I was hungrily eating up each corner in no time. Eventually the route came to an end.

A lit-up ski resort nestled in the forest greeted me. Snow was thick on the ground; it surrounded me and I shivered. I had to go on.

I spotted a trail through the trees. I would have to find my way to the mountaintops far away from here, where no one else could possibly be.

As I sourced a route, knee-deep in snow, a sudden sense of dizziness struck me and I reached for my temples, closing my eyes, hoping the sensation would subside.

As I did, a pair of black orbs filled my mind and a dreadful shrill hissing deafened me. I blinked them away, but Zherneboh was close. The taste of a bonfire was on my tongue; he filled my lungs. I had to move faster.

The sky was a sheet of white, despite the nighttime fast approaching.

As I found the entrance to the thick woods, I was briefly reminded that it was a few hours till Christmas Day, and it made me sad. Here I was, willingly entering yet another mythical forest, only this time I was unsure of whether I was the sleeping princess or the deadly monster that lurked within.

It was harder to push through at any speed; the incline was steep, even for whatever supernatural gifts I possessed. I took a moment to shove the sleeves of my cardigan up to my elbows, before determinedly continuing.

Jonah came to my mind and I was sorry that I hadn't had the chance to say my good-byes to him, but it was for the best. I was quite certain that it wasn't just his connection to me through my blood that made him feel something for me, or he surely would have tried to drink me dry by now. Something else had stopped him.

I mulled over my barely formulated plan. I would reach an opening soon enough and wait for Zherneboh there. I needed Ethan to make an appearance for things to go the way I wanted them to. Given I was alone, I was confident he would show. If Azrael was right, and there was some evil deep inside me waiting for an opportunity, then it might peak in Zherneboh's presence and then I could be ended—with Ethan's help.

Zherneboh would have nothing left to chase.

There would be no war.

Ruadhan could go on without me to burden him; Jonah would lose his connection and his pain would evaporate with me; Brooke would have Jonah back; and Gabriel . . . well, Gabriel could go home, back to the light, back to the Angel that awaited his return.

I wouldn't keep him here any longer.

I willed my feet to race faster, ignoring the sharp branches that scratched my face as I whipped past them. I skidded to a stop at a ledge, narrowly avoiding a fall. The mountain dipped down into a large slope, finally breaking into level ground.

At the center of the clearing was a lake, frozen, perhaps fearful of my arrival. But it was beautiful, a deep gray merging into thick white ice at its core. It separated me from the other side and, as I explored the backdrop, I came into full view of St. Barthelemy and Galinat's peaks, which looked over at me.

It must be night now, but at this height the clouds swirling and growing caused the sky to wear a thick white cloak. And I realized that here, right in this very spot, it was neither light nor dark. It was somewhere in between.

This place was me.

Bitterly cold, I trenched through the thick white carpet of snow to the edge of the lake. A large cluster of rocks provided a perch on which to sit and wait. I teetered precariously on the tip of a boulder and scanned my surroundings. No sign of movement.

The lake was hibernating and I glanced down and took in my reflection. The same face I had always known stared back. I wished her well in her journey; I had no idea where she would go. If things went the way I had planned, she would be left caught in this moment, nothing more than an echo trapped in the water.

It was the most fragmented twitch in the air that told me he was standing behind the rocks.

"It's strange, isn't it, that your face is one of the first that I can remember. . . ." I said. "And at the end, it's the last I will ever see."

Brushing myself off and with one final glance at my reflection, I rose to face him.

He stood, only marginally taller than me, his hair still tied back in a loose knot at the nape of his neck, his expression blank. I looked to his clenched fist wrapped around the hilt of a sword, which was sheathed in a holster at his hip. The sword looked older than he was, displaying his family crest at the base of the brass hilt.

"I've come to seek retribution. You owe me your life." Ethan addressed me as though he was reading me a death sentence.

I nodded. "May I ask why I owe you my life when you already took it once?" My tone falsely oozed confidence; in reality, my insides were somersaulting.

I needed to buy some time.

"But I didn't," Ethan said. "Here you stand, and here I am, one of the Devil's brood. Because of you."

My eyes flickered down to where his white knuckles clenched around the top of the sword, ready to release it from its cage.

"What happened to you?" I asked. "I don't understand. When I knew you, when you knew me, you were human. . . ."

I edged backward. I wanted answers and I needed him to be patient.

He didn't reply but stepped closer to me.

I put my hands up defensively and said, "Listen, you can have your revenge, I won't stop you. But first, please let me understand." My voice was cracking, giving me away.

He considered my request before finally answering. "You were going to leave. I watched you meet with him, but you were promised to me. I found you in the barn; you were about to run away with him, I knew it. But, Lailah, I had not meant to harm you."

His eyes grew larger as he struggled to recall the emotion that he had once felt, before he was like this—before he had become dark. "I only wanted to stop you from leaving with that stranger. I wanted to be the one to give you everything—"

I interrupted, "Stranger? You mean Gabriel?"

"I did not know his name. We never met." His expression lost its fleeting softness and twitched instead to irritation.

"What do you mean you never met him? You must have spoken to him the day you found me ready to leave?"

Azrael had said Gabriel had influenced Ethan, but how could he have if they had never even met?

"Lailah, I did not make his acquaintance. When you fell, I thought you were dead. I ran, like a coward no less, into the land. I wasn't expecting to find one of the Devil's own there."

"You mean Eligio?" I asked.

"Yes, my Gualtiero."

Ethan's brow tightened as he struggled on. "By my own hand, I lost the one—the only one—I had ever . . ." He stopped, dwindling. "Loved."

He seemed to struggle to even recall the emotion. "I wanted death to find me and he did. I did not falter when he changed me. A fitting punishment for taking your life, it seemed, was that Eligio should steal mine."

I bowed my head, entirely sorrowful. It was my fault that he had been turned. "I'm so sorry."

The snow began to fall lightly at first, but within moments I found it hard to keep the cold flakes from blinding me.

"You have no comprehension of what it is like, serving a Gualtiero," Ethan continued. "Locked away until he deems it fit to release you to carry out his violent acts, and then . . . the terrible darkness. It takes control. It eats away at you, until there's nothing left. . . . It becomes you." He paused, treading ever nearer. "I live now for death, for their blood—the only satisfying thing left on this godforsaken Earth. Well, at least that was the case until I saw you again."

His lips trembled as he salivated.

I sighed deeply before replying. "You can take my life, but not right this very moment. I must ask you to wait," I interjected swiftly. Now I had to bargain, though I had next to nothing to play with.

"Why would I do that?"

Without hesitation, he glided the sword from its sheath and pointed the tip under my chin, scraping my flesh.

"Because if you kill me now, I will just wake up. You must wait for Zherneboh, the Devil, to come and when he does, then you must strike me here. . . ."

I moved the blade down toward my heart, blood seeping from my neck as I did. I had killed a Vampire by plunging a jagged piece of metal through his heart. I hoped that it would work for me too.

He paused, the cruel steel resting at my chest, and I watched him take in the scent of my blood. "I told Eligio about you the night I first saw you again. He didn't believe me. But something had thrown him back into Hell as he began to come through the rift. Something immensely powerful. And so he had to consult . . . with the Devil."

I nodded, keeping my eyes fixed on his, which were starting to spark.

"I heard them talking; they said you were one of theirs. I thought it impossible. But your blood . . ."

He moved in a little closer, drawing in an overtly long breath. "I shall have my retribution and I shall take away the Devil's creation. Payment for two centuries of servitude that I didn't owe!"

The pain in my forehead hit me quickly; I reached for my temple, a terrible shadow filling my mind. It took all my will to replace it with an image of the land upon which I stood. My thoughts were released just in time for me to feel Ethan's blade jabbing under my collarbone.

A gust of wind blew across the clearing. I let the wave of flakes collect on my eyelashes.

I was out of time.

"I am truly sorry, Ethan."

The blade sliced my skin, making its way as far down as my hip before it left me. It bounced off the rock and fell into the snow. Ethan was falling. My eyes flew open as I stumbled to the lake's edge. I saw that he had been knocked from his feet and wrestled to the snowy ground by Jonah.

They both stopped and flashed their amaranthine orbs as the drops of my fresh blood dripped into the white below me. Ethan rushed toward me, but Jonah was fast, throwing him high in the air and pouncing on him ferociously.

"No, Jonah! Don't hurt him!"

The slash running down my skin stung and I toppled into the shallow gray water. It only cooled my body for a second before the fire relit. The damage was hardly life-threatening, but the slice sizzled through my flesh nonetheless.

"Let me in." Gabriel's voice floated, his soft words parted the fierce wind.

Scrunching my eyes shut and shaking the snow from my lashes, his figure appeared next to me.

"Y-you shouldn't b-be here," I stuttered.

"Where else would I be, but by your side?" Gabriel said, his expression stern.

Feeling the land shaking beneath me, I peered around the rock to witness Jonah and Ethan in the distance, still embroiled in a terrible battle.

"Gabriel, please, help them!" I couldn't bear to be responsible for more loss.

I fell to my palms as I struggled to get to my feet. Gabriel shifted my weight from behind and swept me from the shallow beginnings of the lake, propping me up against the rock's face, my shoes still dipping into the freezing water.

"Then will you let me help you?" he insisted.

"Yes." I didn't have time to argue.

Gabriel hesitated, but then in an instant he was gone from my side.

The wind and snow were brutal now. I scrambled around the rock just in time to see Jonah hit Ethan hard, knocking him into the snow. He was by far the stronger of the two.

"Ethan!" I screamed.

Panting for breath, I desperately tried to clamber past the rock across the deepening snow. A hundred feet away, none of them could hear my cries because of the wind ripping its way through the trees.

Gabriel came into view, taking up position next to Jonah. I watched helplessly as Jonah withdrew a flask from his jacket and soaked Ethan's body in a clear liquid. His foot was on Ethan's neck, pinning him to the snow. Gabriel forced Jonah back, and Jonah placed a cigarette to his lips defiantly. He reached in his pocket for his lighter.

As if in slow motion Ethan, now free from restraint, launched his body from off the ground, bolstering himself behind Jonah. I looked on as Jonah flicked open the metal clasp, and as the end of the cigarette glowed orange with his first puff, he flung the open flame behind his shoulder.

"No!" I screamed.

Ethan's body erupted into flames.

It wasn't a quick end. He circled insanely, falling, as his body melted.

As the flames reached deeper than his flesh and bone, he seemed to explode, becoming nothing more than swirling ash, dispersing in the blizzard.

I crumpled in a ball. Ethan was gone and I was to blame.

"Lai." Gabriel was immediately at my side.

"Why did you come? You sought my end, and I was giving it to you. But instead Ethan's gone and he didn't have to be!" I cried, clutching my aching chest with my hand, blood trickling through my fingers. "I owed him. . . . He was the only one. . . . It's all my fault!" I gasped, bent double, trying to take the deepest of breaths.

Gabriel turned my chin up to meet his eyes. "Breathe, Lailah, calm down."

His pretense of concern for my well-being only filled me with resentment.

I responded by flinging my body toward him, smacking his chest with my fists, but it was hopeless.

Everything seemed so hopeless now.

I sank back into the snow, my hands covering my face. Gabriel sat down beside me. "The Arch Angels sent me to take your life; I don't deny it, and I didn't question why. Not until I met you. I thought you were mortal, Lai, and still I fell in love with you. And so I rejected them. We were going to run and I would have protected you. . . ."

I wrapped my arms around my knees, squeezing them in to my body. "You told Ruadhan that you killed me . . . ?" I whimpered.

"I blamed myself. I took too long. . . ."

"You didn't influence Ethan. . . ." I stuttered, finally looking up to meet his eyes.

"No. I came to take you away, but instead I found you lifeless. I thought they'd discovered my plan and had sent another to claim your soul. I spent a hundred years searching the in-between—a prison—thinking they had hidden your essence there. I nearly lost myself seeking you out; I started to hear your voice echoing in my mind. I returned to Styclar-Plena and they told me that you were alive, that I had to find you again and complete the task they had passed to me. I refused. I didn't believe you were still alive. I was tormented. . . . I hadn't been able to save you. . . ." he rushed on.

"You didn't fall?" I asked. "Even after you rejected them, they let you keep your immorality, along with your abilities?" It seemed illogical.

"I didn't understand why either, not until these last weeks. Then it became clear; I was the only being from our dimension who could find you. That's why they would not grant my request, they wouldn't allow me to fall." Cautiously he stroked my cheek with the back of his hand. "And I am so glad that they didn't."

"Perhaps they thought that when you did find me, you would understand and you would change your mind." My thoughts crept back to Azrael and his revelation that I was harboring some terrible evil inside of me. And that I had the potential to end all the worlds.

"Never." His jaw locked, entirely certain.

Gabriel's eyes found their way to the slice running down my body, and his eyes became wide as he pleaded silently, begging me to let him help.

I didn't have to ask him again—I knew he was telling the truth, and I opened myself to him. As soon as I did I was filled with such love that it sped through every part of me.

"Hate to break this up, but we need to move." Jonah didn't stand too close. I realized my blood, still flowing from my skin, must have been causing him a lot of distress, so I nodded to Gabriel, accepting his assistance.

Gabriel kneeled over me and I arched my body backward, letting my long curls tickle the snow below. Steadying my back with his open palm, I felt the tenderness of his breath spread over my skin.

I didn't close my eyes as the snow cascaded on top of a backdrop of glowing gold and silver, flowing through my skin and spreading through my veins.

It was incredible.

He breathed his energy across the wound, and my skin magically glued back together. The pain was gone in an instant, the burning replaced by a cool tingling sensation that rippled down my skin. Every inch of me absorbed his light and I felt my cheeks glow as the last of his efforts wrapped itself around me.

I pulled my body up to meet his face and I nestled my cheek next to his, threading my fingers through his golden locks, sewing myself back into him.

I was pulled out of the moment when, from over Gabriel's shoulder, I saw a black mark creeping in the distance of the sleeping lake, expanding and growing larger, incongruous in the snowy setting.

Jonah saw it at the same second and shouted, "Gabriel! He's coming!"

TWENTY-EIGHT

GABRIEL PARTED FROM ME and ushered Jonah behind him, racing forward before I had a chance to stop him. Now Jonah was at my side, helping me back to my feet. As Gabriel sped across the snow, drawing an invisible battle line, a harrowing figure, cloaked totally in darkness, flew through the expanding gateway.

It had to be Zherneboh.

The cracking of Jonah's fangs as they broke through his gums caused my body to shudder. With eyes blazing the brightest I had ever seen them, Jonah snatched my wrist, yanking me through the deep snow.

"What are you doing? I won't leave him!" I chucked my body away from Jonah, escaping his grasp. His eyes shot to me, his body rigid and firm. I had never seen him so terrified.

"He will end us. There's no fight here, only a massacre!"

This time he wrapped his firm arms around my waist and hoisted me into the air.

I turned to see that Gabriel had produced a sheet of light, keeping the Pureblood from crossing over to where we were. Jonah started to run. I couldn't see Zherneboh; the silvers and golds twirling and sparkling behind were too bright, his darkness remained pinned to the other side. Gabriel couldn't hold him there forever, and my mind raced as to what would happen to him when he finally let the sheet fall.

I struggled, kicking and flapping my arms. Jonah was picking up speed when a fierce hissing split its way through the quiet, piercing my eardrums.

It was like a siren calling to me.

The sensation of Gabriel's gift receded, giving way to a rising heat in my chest. I felt my eyes begin to burn and I pawed them, feeling the thin skin around my sockets cracking. My nails started to ooze blood. Jonah stopped suddenly. As he did, I broke free, landing with a thud in the snow.

The shrill noise had dissolved the sheet of light and I turned in time to see Gabriel stumble to the ground.

Jonah shouted at me, "You can't help him. Go! Now!" He paused for a split second, regarding me the same way he had when the Hedgerley house was under siege—as though it was the last time he might ever get to do so—and with one last look he sprinted in Gabriel's direction.

I hauled myself up from the snow. The clouds' spilled shapes seemed to part briefly, which allowed me to see Zherneboh clearly in the distance. He was immense and towering, and my eye was drawn away from the swollen scar on his forehead, down to his clenched fist, where long bladed talons sliced their way through his knuckles, prominently pointing in Gabriel's direction as he strode toward him. He was the Pureblood that invaded my visions, and he was going to kill Gabriel, before he claimed what was his: me.

Grappling to my feet, I let out a violent scream and ran—no, flew—over the snow toward him. As I neared, I felt my blood boil as he held Gabriel suspended in the air several feet away from him.

Zherneboh flashed his black orbs toward me, returning my glare. I couldn't move. Gabriel fell to the snow. It was me who was now suspended in midair. I took in his horrific features; his tattooed markings grew up his neck as if displaying themselves for my benefit. His mouth was vile; every one of his teeth pointed and jagged. His lizardlike tongue, split at the end, ran in and out of the cracks.

Lailah, run!

Gabriel's words found my thoughts, but they flickered, dipping in and out, like he was a radio station that was out of my range.

Zherneboh let a roar bellow from his throat; it bounced off the sides of the mountains and I was sure that the forest stood still for him, shuddering.

Suddenly Jonah flung himself onto the creature's back, but Zherneboh no longer seemed to care for distractions, keeping his stare glued to me.

I was helpless to stop Zherneboh's razor claws penetrating and ripping through Jonah's cheek and down his neck. He flung him aside as if he weighed no more than a matchstick, sending him hurtling into a distant cluster of rocks, all the while keeping his eyes locked with mine.

My attention flashed to Gabriel, who lay prone in the snow, manufacturing a ball of light in his palm, concentrating intently. Flashes of lightning struck within the mini typhoon, but as Gabriel sat up to expel the light, Zherneboh opened his mouth and released a thick wave of black smoke. It raged toward Gabriel, dispersing his ball of light and knocking him over. Then it wrapped around his throat, the smoke seeping in between his perfect lips, slowly choking him as it invaded his insides.

The anger inside me bubbled and spilled into the center of my consciousness, and I smashed through the snow.

As I caught my breath, I stared up at the sky; a few inches ahead, she hovered. I covered my ears, but the sound of her fangs breaking into place made my skin crawl.

It was the girl in shadow. She had come.

I tried to reach for her hand, but withdrew as I watched blades shooting from her knuckles and blackened blood smearing her white skin as they burst through. I witnessed something crawling under her skin, running from her wrists up to her elbow. I stayed still, mesmerized by the lines that inked her skin, staining her. The shapes formed, creating the outline of hundreds of quills overlapping one another. I tried to stand and fought to grasp her long, flowing black curls that drifted down just above her hip.

I couldn't reach her; she was already moving toward the Pureblood, whose attention was now firmly placed on her.

I tried to find Gabriel, but it was as though he had blocked me—I couldn't hear him and he couldn't hear me. I watched helplessly as he fought with the smoke, his body glowing as he tried to overcome it.

I shouted for her, but she didn't listen to me as she glided toward Zherneboh. The edge of his top lip rose and he snarled, finally turning.

She stopped about forty feet away from him as he revolved back to the now shrinking black smudge that levitated in the distance. He stretched out his clawed hand in front of him as he grew the gateway.

The smoke began to evaporate as Gabriel's light won the struggle; he coughed and spluttered, but he was okay.

I called to him, but he didn't even look at me. He was desperately scrambling to his feet, falling as he tried to get up.

The air shifted behind me. Azrael had appeared. He was with Ruadhan. My lovely Ruadhan. I tried to shout to him to leave, but the words didn't leave my lips. I couldn't let him be ended. And as the fondness I felt toward Ruadhan filled my consciousness, I remembered Gabriel's light and his love.

I was on my feet. I didn't know who to go to first, and I stood rooted to the spot, my attention swerving to the scene behind me.

Through the battering of the blizzard, I observed Azrael heave Ethan's discarded sword from the ground, tilting his head from side to side as he considered it. He drew a small gold box from his pocket. Whatever was inside glowed as he smothered the tip of the sword with the substance.

I twisted my body back to the girl; though the backdrop was a perfect white, she was still shrouded in shadow. I flew across the snow as she began gliding forward. I lined myself up with her body as I reached her and we stood side by side. I had to know who she was and I had to convince her to help us.

"Please!" I cried.

But she just continued forward as if I didn't exist.

I grabbed for her shoulder, but my hand moved through her as if she were made of air. I stopped as short, sharp memories of her flashed across my mind.

She came to a halt before Zherneboh, whose attention was now embroiled in harnessing the diminishing gateway to the third

373

dimension. I watched him ooze black ink from out of his palms, which floated toward the smudge, cascading into its center. It began enlarging in size. Then the realization of what he was doing hit me. He was going to take her through with him. But why?

Inhaling quickly, I turned to find Gabriel.

As I did, the girl in the shadow reflected my action and turned to meet me.

I froze.

Glowering back at me was me. She wore my face, only she had sharp canines resting slightly over her lower lip and her eyes were enormous black holes, boring into my own.

I bounced backward, in shock, as did she. I moved my hand in the air and she did the same. Confused, a thousand questions ran through my mind. Why was she mirroring me?

As my thoughts whirled, a forceful cracking disturbed the stillness and my attention became transfixed on the sword that struck from behind, fissuring its way through her shoulder blade, piercing straight into her heart. The blade broke through the sternum and punctured the front of her form.

Zherneboh let out a harrowing screech.

I lunged forward to the girl and as I did, she seemed to melt into me. My eyes fixed on the sword that was now perforating my own chest. Shaking, I brought my hands to clutch either side of the blade; it was then that I saw the tattooed markings covering my arms and the loose curls cascading down my face, coal black.

The truth was undeniable. The girl in the shadow wasn't mimicking my face. . . .

She had always been me.

374

There was no other explanation. She was an extreme darkness that had been hiding inside me all this time, patiently waiting to take over.

I jolted forward as an explosion of light soared from behind me. I felt Zherneboh's presence in me disperse as he left this plane; Gabriel had pushed Zherneboh back through to his own dimension, sealing the gateway.

As he faded away, the tattoos running the length of my arms began to shrink, disappearing slowly. The sharp daggers boring through my knuckles began fading away, until my skin was white and clean once more.

She was dying.

I turned around and lifted my face to find Ruadhan, his hand still held in midair where he had gripped the hilt of the sword, and Azrael positioned several feet behind him.

"Cessie?" Ruadhan's voice quaked. "No, love! No!"

He reached to wipe a tear from my cheek, and pulled away, his hand covered in blood. "You said it was a Pureblood!" Ruadhan screamed. "You said she was safe!"

Azrael smirked triumphantly behind him.

I tried to speak. I ran my tongue along the razor points of my teeth and felt them as they became blunt once more. I dropped to my knees.

Gabriel was at my side first, but he flinched, withdrawing from me as he took in the blade lodged through my chest.

"What did you do to her?" Gabriel shouted, turning to Azrael.

Gabriel's words surrounded me, but he wasn't with me; there was no sense of his connection. All that existed now was a void.

"I didn't do anything. You can all see what she was harboring inside her now. You couldn't do your job, so I had to do it for you. Albeit by Ruadhan's hand."

"I didn't know . . ." Ruadhan's voice was empty, his arms hanging low at his sides; he seemed to sway.

"You created her, how could you . . . !" Gabriel stuttered.

"Two hundred years I have wandered this disgusting world searching for her mother. I struck a deal with the Arch Angels—I find Aingeal, I find the Descendant. I find the Descendant, I end her existence. Then we could both return home. I'll settle for my own return, I don't need Aingeal. I will have the light of Styclar-Plena."

He spat on the ground where I perched, numb.

"You think they'll let you return when you are so tainted?" Gabriel said. "You've been corrupted by this world, and now you will fall."

Azrael staggered backward as Gabriel lunged for him. He reached for the back of his neck, and when nothing happened, he seemed to panic.

"How can I save her?" Gabriel yelled as he grabbed him.

"You can't. The demon inside her is already dying. Look, see for yourself," he said, gesturing to me. "The demon strikes when Lailah goes beyond her dark Vampire side. Likely her Pureblood lineage morphs through her skin in extreme situations, or of course when there happens to be a Pureblood in near proximity."

"Azrael—" Gabriel gripped him by the collar urgently.

"When the demon dies, she will just be left with the two sides of her very nature—a hybrid of Angel Descendant and Second Generation Vampire. Zherneboh's venom will still run through her blood, the darkness fighting inside her against the light. The difference now is that she knows they both exist: the light and the dark. She won't be able to hide from it anymore, and in her inability to accept both parts of what she is, she will lose her immortality and that frail human body that she was born into will break and she will be ended. . . ."

I coughed, choking, and Gabriel flashed to my side. Still holding tightly to Azrael, he shouted, "How do you know all this?"

"She was not the first, but she is the last."

Gabriel's attention locked on me, and Azrael took the opportunity to break away. As he fled, Ruadhan made chase.

Consumed in such evil, I couldn't feel my body. Gabriel perched next to me.

"It's okay, Lai. You will be all right."

My head throbbed; images of memories I didn't know I had invaded my mind. Ripping Frederic apart, limb by limb; torturing the Vampires in Hedgerley; and then Bradley's face conjured in front of me. The image repeated on a loop, until I finally focused in, unable to stop, and watched as I grabbed Jonah from behind, tossing him into a tree, rendering him unconscious while I set about tearing Bradley to pieces. Flecks of black curls blurred across my sight; images of feasting on his blood and remains, before finally turning to the wall; and then the memory dissolved.

I felt my body convulse, her evil coursing through every inch of me.

My eyelids fluttered as I began to remember all the dark acts that I had committed and denied as my own, filling the black spots in my mind.

She was weak now, though she clung to me, her shrieks echoing insanely around my head. I had to push her out, but she was strong and fighting for survival, despite the blade in my chest.

I could taste the ash that invaded my lungs, and I clung to the smell. Then the scene around me distorted. Time fractured. I reached behind my shoulder and gripped the hilt of the sword. Using her supernatural strength against her and squeezing my eyes tightly, I wrenched the blade from my chest, flinging it across the snow.

My blood splattered, forming a red carpet against the white.

I drifted backward, resting on the ground beneath me, staring up at the white flakes that were descending and cooling my face.

As I lay in the cold, the blizzard calmed so that it felt as though I was in a glass snow globe. Time tipped the magical lake and forest upside down, leaving the symmetrical shapes to sway delicately across my vision.

The sword skimmed the surface of the icy lake, and finally the castle with its swans fell into its freezing center.

The monster of my fairy tale was slain and time resumed once more.

Gabriel was reaching for me, but he was too late. He couldn't compete with fractured time; it made me so much quicker.

When she left, so too did her anesthesia, rendering me paralyzed with pain.

"No!" Jonah's urgent voice cut through the now still air.

I flicked my eyes open to see Gabriel kneeling over me. A brilliant light balanced gently on the tip of his lips.

"Gabriel, you'll end her!"

"I need to dispel the demon! I can't feel Lailah, I have to save her!" he shot back.

"The demon is gone, look at her, look!" Jonah was shaking Gabriel away from me.

"The marks have left her. You're seeing her the way I do, the part of her that is like me. If you fill her with your light now you might kill her."

Jonah's hand was tugging Gabriel desperately away from me. I watched him fall to his knees. He looked lost.

My body convulsed, now agonized. I clutched my chest as a volcano of pain erupted inside me. Tugging off his jacket, Jonah pressed the leather down forcefully against my chest and I let out a scream as he applied pressure.

"If we let her darkness take over, let her stay like me, maybe . . . if she drinks from me, she might have a chance. . . ."

"You'll eclipse her light." Gabriel's reply was short and hollow.

"Maybe, but she might go on. . . ." Jonah said.

"Like this? There must be another way! If she can find her light, if she can somehow accept both sides of what she is, she will survive this!"

I listened in, unsure of what light he was referring to. With every passing second, the part of me that seemed to know Gabriel only drifted further away.

Reaching for the smallest pocket of air that sat in my lungs, I whimpered. My body was shutting down and my mind fell over itself, bewildered and confused.

"I heard Azrael. He said she would never be able to accept. If you love her, let her go. Please let me try."

I didn't hear Gabriel protest any further and his silhouette disappeared from the corner of my vision, clearly unable to bring himself to watch.

Jonah was staring at me now, bloodied and bruised. Despite my incoherent senses, I tasted his scent as it rode the breeze.

Jonah pierced the skin around his wrist and laid himself on his side next to me. He didn't hesitate to raise his bloodied hand to my lips.

As I stretched my neck toward him, I caught his dark pupils gazing down at me and I was distracted for a moment by them. I paused as they grew bigger, anticipating me. I managed to push my nose toward him, a burning rising in my throat but, as I snatched his wrist and pulled it close, something caused me to stop, going against every fiber in my body.

How do you see light against light?

My hand shook, flinching in trepidation.

It was only as the darkness crept forward that for a few moments in time, the faint crack of a bright, shimmering silver contrasted against the void.

I remembered those words and I battled to recall when I had heard them. They were spoken with such softness. . . .

As my eyes met Jonah's once more, I gasped as, in the black of his pupils, I caught a glimpse of my reflection shining back at me. Lasting for only the briefest of moments, a miracle of silvers glowed back.

It was in his darkness that I found my light.

I remembered the image in the lake. Lailah.

Suddenly his cinnamon scent was not so appealing. I pushed his hand away from me, remembering who I was. I would not be consumed by the darkness; I would not let half of me become trapped forever.

"No." I struggled.

"Lai?" Gabriel tumbled urgently as he spun back to me, rapidly dropping to my body.

I looked from Gabriel to Jonah. I recognized who they both were to me, recalling how each made me feel.

One moment Gabriel's luminous features took up the space in my mind, but no sooner than it had, Jonah's shadowed face appeared, replacing it.

Back and forth the images flipped, so fast that they became nothing more than black and white, until the flashes of light collided with the shadows in my mind and both elements of what I was burst, allowing the black and the white to merge, creating a fantastic gray matter.

It was surreal; for the first time that I could remember, I felt at ease inside my own skin.

But as I reached for Gabriel's hand, he looked back at me, his expression empty. It was then that I conceded that Gabriel wasn't with me. His connection was gone. He couldn't see me anymore.

I was alone.

Azrael had been wrong; he hadn't counted on the strength of Gabriel resonating through my being to be able to lead me home. However, as I touched him, it dawned on me that even in my own acceptance, he would never be able to see past the darkness that was part of me. And I couldn't go on without him.

It was in that realization that I knew my end was inevitable; on that, Azrael had been right. I wouldn't continue to torture either of them.

With my end, I would set them both free.

Without Gabriel's connection and now unable to do anything about it, I embraced the pain that was filling me. Drifting away from my consciousness, I allowed my body to succumb.

"Inevitability," I whispered.

But Gabriel refused, unwilling to let me leave quietly.

Pulling my body up, he hovered desperately over me, glued to my eyes, searching them urgently. I watched his; they seemed to die with me.

There he stayed until finally, as my eyelids began to flutter to their final sleep, the faintest flicker of my extinguishing light entered his violet-blue sapphires.

I caused an asterism; I was the creator of the six-rayed points that now reflected back at me. His stars of Ceylon expanded, verging on the precipice of an explosion into a gigantic supernova.

I knew it then. How had I been so blind?

"I'm your Pair. . . ."

"I know." He smiled, and a tear as clear as crystal fell down his cheek. "I told you to have faith in me. . . ." He trailed off as my body began to relax and my breathing became shallow and faint.

Lailah! Lailah!

There was nothing I could do now. My body was failing me.

He had found me, but this time, he really was too late.

As my wide eyes froze, resting on his, Gabriel's words seeking me in our private place faded. As they drifted away, I heard him one last time.

Like an echo, growing louder as it hit me, he shouted . . .

Command the choice to decide.

EPILOGUE

THE SUN WAS ON THE CUSP OF RISING. A thin layer of white fog swirled over the land, moving gently with the calm breeze. Strangely, it did not entwine itself where she lay. Instead, it floated underneath her resting place, refusing to pass over her.

Jonah sat unmoving, like a loyal servant, on the ground beside my sweet Angel. His eyes only removed themselves from her to scour the vast land surrounding where I had chosen to place her down.

"It's been seven days, she's still not breathing."

I placed my hand on his shoulder. "And you haven't fed for the same amount of time. You need to—"

"No. I won't leave her." His reply was swift and still he refused to remove his focus.

"I'm here. No harm will come to her while I'm with her. You know that. Brooke will be suffering. If not for yourself then for her."

I didn't like how attached he had become. But then, I had realized now that it was not my Angel for whom he longed; it was Cessie. The part of her that was like him.

Begrudgingly he rose to his feet and looked down at her, checking once more for any sign of life. I reached for Jonah's arm to steer him away from my sleeping wonder, but he was unwavering.

"Where'd you think she is?"

"She's right here," I answered firmly.

"If she wakes up—"

"*When* she wakes up," I cut him off.

I didn't like him reaching for her hand, and I fought the urge to stop him from squeezing it. Tolerance was something I had plenty of; I had lived through the meaning of being patient. But the touch of his skin on hers made my insides recoil.

"Jonah." I moved his hand away, tucking her delicate fingers back underneath the white blanket, as if the need to keep her warm was the reason for my action.

"Will she remember us? Do you think she'll remember the things she couldn't before?"

"We'll see. Right now we need to have faith that she will find her way back. That she will fight and not surrender herself to death."

Inside, I clung onto my own hope that she would find a way; there was nothing but emptiness for her otherwise. She would simply fail to exist and then nothing would matter.

"She feels cold. I don't think we should be keeping her out here."

I moved around him and placed the back of my hand on the porcelain skin of her forehead. "It's for the best. Out here she has the day and the night. It might help. Could you stay with her for a minute while I get another blanket?"

"Yes." He nodded obediently at me.

I hadn't left her side since I had carried her from the snowy mountains, bundled in my arms. I would give him a moment alone with her—albeit reluctantly—while I collected some extra warmth. One thing I was certain of was that Jonah would sacrifice himself long before he'd let any harm come to her.

"Then you'll go and feed and take care of Brooke. She needs you. You can come back when you're ready. We'll be here." Hesitantly I took a step backward, but as I turned to leave something stopped me. "Jonah."

"Yes."

"You drank from her, you see her in darkness, but I don't understand . . ."

"What?" Still he didn't take his gaze from her face.

"Your blood fused with hers, the part of her that is like you. . . ." I stuttered as I said the words. "You had every opportunity," I gulped. "You didn't let your thirst take over."

Now he turned to me. "I love her."

I stopped, rooted to the spot. "What? How?"

"I may have seen her in a way you didn't and believed she was like me. But I watched her. Her gentleness, the sweetness of her touch . . . things that her features couldn't mask. I might desire the darkness within her, but I fell in love with the light that I heard in her laughter."

Completely stunned, words escaped me. Although I hadn't known in the beginning, Lailah was made for me. One light split into two, bound together forever.

Despite the deceptions that had been crafted and the things they had done, we had found each other again. And here was a Vampire, a stranger she'd happened to discover by chance. He'd managed to see past what was staring straight back at him. I'd only been able to see one half of what she was. Jonah, on the other hand, had been able to see all of her; and yet, in her last minutes, still she fought for me.

I bowed my head, ashamed of myself.

Returning speedily to the barn, I raced into what had been her bedroom.

I hadn't been in here since I'd held her, and I could taste her citrus scent lingering in the bedsheets where she'd slept. I picked up a pillow and nuzzled my face into its center, breathing her in. She was my home, my everything, the most precious thing I had ever touched, and I had let her down.

I sat heavily at the foot of the bed and considered the life she must have led while I had searched for her. This world, a world she was never meant to have existed in, scarred by the people in it, whom I had failed to protect her from. And now she lay lifeless.

And just as I allowed myself to consider that she might never return, her chess set on the wooden table caught my eye. The rising sun had drifted through the glass window, and the shiny crown of the ivory king reflected the light against the wall. The day was waking, the first morning of the new year.

Standing up cautiously, I drifted over to it.

Lailah's king was out of check.

I scanned the board for any other irregularity; the last time I had been down here I had moved my piece, placing her king in danger. When could she have positioned her piece? Was it before she had fled to the mountains? Had she moved it when she had listened in on my conversation with Azrael? But no, she couldn't have; she was being deadly quiet, perched on the steps. I would have heard if she had walked across the room to the board.

As the day began to dawn, so too did her message, hidden in our game. She was telling me that she was out of danger. She was asking me not to give up on her.

Though it was a fifty-mile distance, I returned to the clearing in the blink of an eye. I found Jonah thrown back, away from the thick stone upon which I had laid her. The air swirled and gathered like a typhoon surrounding her. A black storm, flashing with whites and golds, illuminated the space. The frost that had covered the stone had vanished, as though hiding from the spectacle. A low rumble sounded, and cracks started to form along the ground as the Earth split.

Yanking Jonah back as it began to open up, I shouted, "Lailah!"

The earthquake pulsated beneath my feet, unbalancing everything that surrounded her. As the sun rose, strobes of energizing light cascaded through the storm. Somehow, I could faintly hear the sound of the song Lailah and I had once shared, reverberating and bouncing off the trees that were being blown every which way, holding desperately onto their roots in a bid not to topple over.

I grappled past the tempestuous tornado that was skimming my body, but it flung me back despite my strength, acting as a force field and enveloping the most important being ever to exist.

The dark storm twisted, encouraging a pattern of white mist that sparkled in waves, merging as it crowded over where she lay.

The Earth stood still with it, watching silently, waiting.

And then, in an instant, it was over.

I don't know who was faster, Jonah or I, but as we both arrived at her side I ground to a halt. Her face was unchanged, but her long cascading curls were now a mixture of coal-black with stripes of white-blond searing through. Her lips were no longer an innocent pink but a sharp red, heating her still-white skin. The blanket I had wrapped around her body had swept away and the deep V-neck of the dress Brooke had sacrificed displayed the skin around her heart. No longer was it broken; there simply remained a scar where the blade had pushed through her chest.

She sparkled in the sun's presence, as did the crystal gem that still hung from her neck.

I could hear her. Very gently, I felt her tickle my consciousness. She was returning.

Neither Jonah nor I could take our eyes off her, and, breath held, I opened my mind up as far as I could imagine, begging her to reach out.

Her body remained still, and as I waited, I found myself grinding my nails into my palms.

Her eyelashes fluttered before flipping open in one swift movement, and I immediately locked my eyes onto hers. They were still a sapphire blue, matching my own, but now they were muddied, flecked with tiny dark spots. The black voids of her massive pupils sucked everything in with them, including me.

If I hadn't known any better, I would have thought that every clock, in every world, had stopped ticking as she turned her head gently, bowing her face to the side. She stared straight back at me.

I heard her voice then, gathering the Earth as it moved at an impossible speed toward me.

Gabriel...

Acknowledgments

Thanks to . . .

All of my wonderful family, for your love and support.

Mom—For daring me to dream. You always believed I could do it, but as John Lennon once said, "A dream you dream alone is only a dream. A dream you dream together is reality." Building snowmen with you is by far my favorite pastime!

Dad—For all your love and inspiration. "So shine your light so bright."

1L–whoever you are, wherever you are, we love you!

Gillan—For making *everything* possible. When, one day, this life is over, I will tell them the best thing about it was you. In the meantime, please don't ever stop turning up your collars!

Penny—My second Mum, whose love and devotion to family is unparalleled. You make the world a better place simply by being in it.

Gill & Ken—For taking me to Waterstones when I was twelve, and for opening up your home in Neylis and giving me a spot unlike anywhere else in which to write; for touring me around endlessly in the name of research, and for always keeping my glass full.

All my dearest friends—You know exactly who you are! Some of you read the story early on and offered me encouragement. Some of you listened patiently while I waffled on and didn't complain! Some of you simply spent your time with me over a Pimm's and shared the events of your lives with me. All of you are the family I chose for myself. I raise my tea-flag and salute you.

The Wattpad readers—You put *Lailah* high upon your shoulders and allowed her to be seen through the crowd. You took the story into your hearts, put a stake in your respective Gabriel and Jonah Camp and declared yourselves "Styhards." "Thank you" could never be, and would never be, enough.

All the fantasic team at Wattpad HQ.

Kelly and Angie—Keep telling your wonderful stories, and never, ever give up.

Beth Collett—My personal proofer. The written word quivers in your presence!

Calvin, Sally, Michal, and Amy—Quite simply put: Thank you.

While working through the early hours writing a book can be a solitary task, bringing it to the world is nothing short of some serious teamwork. For this I would like to thank Macmillan/Feiwel and Friends.

Special thanks to Anna Roberto, who discovered *Lailah*. With all my heart, thank you, for finding her.

Jean Feiwel, for welcoming *Lailah* and me into your one-of-a-kind family.

Liz Szabla, truly the most incredible editor I could have hoped to work with. You championed *Lailah*'s story, sacrificed your free time to bring it to bookshelves so soon, and you knew just what to do to shape the story so it is the best it could possibly be. Jean told me that you were the most caring and insightful of editors, and she couldn't have been more right.

Bethany Reis, for doing a fantastic copyedit and making me sleep easier at night.

Angus Killick, for giving *Lailah* your "stamp," and thinking outside the box.

Molly Brouillette and Ksenia Winnicki, my fellow Whovians and corn dog connoisseurs, who enabled me to cross a road trip around America off my bucket list. Oh, and also worked tirelessly to tell the world about *Lailah*. To you I say: Allons-y!

Caitlin Sweeny, for working smart to market *Lailah* digitally, and making it all seem so effortless!

Kathryn Little, for looking after trade marketing, and ensuring *Lailah* reached all the right people.

Rich Deas and his team, for capturing the essence of *Lailah*'s story in one, very beautiful cover image.

Anna Booth, for the gorgeous interior design, and for hitting a home run with the very first swing!

Dave Barrett, who does a fantastic job keeping the wheels moving and the machine well-oiled, and Nicole Moulaison, for being a perfectionist who ensures that everything is nothing short of the very best quality.

Gabby Oravetz in the Contracts department, for looking after this quirky Brit all the way across the Pond!

The Swoon Reads Team—on behalf of every writer out there trying—for innovating, opening up the gates, and giving all those with a story to tell, the best and most swoonworthy place to tell it.

You, holding this book and reading this line right now. Characters only breathe when someone, somewhere, is living their story.

BONUS CONTENT

FOREWORD

BOOK 2 OF THE STYCLAR SAGA

GABRIEL

"Tick. Tock. Tick. Tock. Tock. Tick." The hands of the invisible clock perpetually rolled over and over.

This was nowhere. But time did indeed subsist in this place. That clock was perhaps present to remind nowhere's company of the inescapability of nothingness. A form of torture, to know that time continued to move forward for everything else, and everyone else, in a place where they still existed; while those that had gone lay lost, wrapped in the fabric of the unknown.

Thoughts, only thoughts, here at the center of a room, only there were no walls, no floor, and no ceiling. No longer possessing a physical form, all that was here were my erratic, barely conceived thoughts.

And they considered that this was nature. This was what happened when everything you were just stopped and no other worldly force intervened.

But then, someone had put that clock in here.

Trying to hide from the sound of the "tick, tock," concentrating instead on the faintest smudge of an imprinted memory.

All thoughts were fragmented and stifled, but they struggled on regardless—anything to block out the sound of nonexistence echoing around this dwindling semiconscious state.

A strange image of an object—small and thick, with a jagged edge around its top—flashed from an old memory into thought.

Focusing on *it*, there was no comprehension as to what *it* was.

The anonymous object started to fuzz and blur, but this mind wasn't going to release it so easily. Think of it, and remember it. King. A word. Recognition. King. It had a name.

Now it existed.

The sound of the "tick, tock" filtering back through made it harder to concentrate, and somehow the sound of its malevolent hands was getting louder.

King. King. King. Its name now resounded in time with the strikes. Balancing it, holding the image steady.

Check. A new word forming—check. My king was in check. My king. Me.

That thought only caused further struggle.

Me. I. I wasn't me. I wasn't anything. I didn't exist. There was no I. And then the idea started to dissolve. . . .

Lailah. The word almost whispered into life, repeated again, *Lailah . . .*

A name. Things that didn't exist didn't have a name. But that one belonged to me. I had a name. One I swore I would never forget again.

Lailah.

Strange, at the end of the room, a circle appeared.

The "tick, tock" quickened as it increased in its raucousness. Peering into the glass window I saw it had an image locked inside—someone beautiful sat at the foot of a bed—I knew him. And a chess set sat upon a table.

I concentrated on the king, feeling a spark of light flow through my mind. And as I began to feel something, whatever it was quickly began to recede as the face I was watching dulled with a shadow of sadness.

"No." I heard my voice; it wasn't in my mind. It bounced off the sides of the room that were now forming. "No!" I shouted again. As I did the king moved for me, it moved itself out of check.

Command the choice to decide.

Command the choice to decide.

The words looped themselves in my mind, and I felt a chill below me.

The room had a floor, and I had feet.

"Tick, tock, tick, tock, tick, tock . . ." The clock sped up, booming with every strike, almost deafening my mind into silence once again. And with every turn of the big hand, I felt as though my head was being pounded and smacked against the newly formed wooden walls.

I could see my hands now ahead of me, and as the floor started to fall away and the ceiling began to cave in, I placed my palms against the glass in desperation, watching him.

The glass shattered as the space bounced and rocked from side to side, and his image left along with the shards, shortly to be replaced with a new window, a way back to the world.

Heavy lumps of wood came crashing down around me. I squeezed myself through the gap of the face, staring down into oblivion. I stood straight and teetered on the ledge of its gold pane.

I searched upward and found three perfect spheres floating above me, lined up in a row. One, a luminous white; the second, an amalgam of sapphire blue and emerald green, hung in the middle; and the third was a black ball containing swirling gray clouds, as though a storm was trapped inside.

I cast my gaze back down and to my right, and as the prison broke apart I saw a number, 9. I struggled to retain my balance through the falling debris raining down on me from above. I snapped my attention to the left to see a number, 3, cracking and falling away.

Even with such incoherent thoughts, I realized that I had been locked inside a grandfather clock. I was a nonexistent prisoner of time. But I was beginning to exist once more, so time would have to halt long enough to release me.

My head thumped and throbbed with the clank of the hands as they banged angrily. I kept my balance, but they began twirling at an incredible speed around what remained of the clock face, so fast everything felt like it was spinning.

I had commanded the choice; now I had to decide.

"I want to go home! I want to live!" I shouted at nothing and no one.

The heavy brass pendulum swung as the dial finally slowed and hovered at 12. The casing that had enclosed me broke away as the clock chimed for its last time, sounding the beginning of a new day.

I remembered his face as I closed my eyes, his name forming at the fringes of my consciousness, and I fell from the ledge of my prison.

The hands of the clock stopped ticking.

Every clock, in every world, stopped. Just for me.

ONE

THEY SAY THAT DEATH IS a part of life. And that the only thing in life that is truly certain is death. I guess "they" had never met me.

I gasped for air, and was relieved to feel it filling my lungs, circulating some form of life back through my sleeping body. I wasn't sure if it was my dulled senses causing everything around me to feel as though it was moving frame by frame at a snail's pace, for, as I watched him, he didn't move; he merely stared at me with the most remarkable, utterly unreadable expression.

Rays of sunlight shone through the trees, creating shadowed stripes across his face, but nothing could dull those sapphire eyes as they gleamed back at me.

Everything, including him, was utterly serene.

I released a steady breath as I felt the frost of this new day begin to tingle on my lips. It was as though I was blowing a bubble through a magical sphere, as the image of him and the snowy landscape behind him seemed to stretch. Gently, as I exhaled, it expanded. He and the whole scenery around him became caught in my bubble.

I was literally holding the whole world, in anticipation of my first full breath.

It was beautiful. He was beautiful. And I was home.

But as I watched him inside it, standing rooted to the spot, a dark swirling cloud seemed to appear from nowhere. Then, as it dispersed, his full form came into focus, and his mesmerizing midnight orbs blemished the beauty of the snowy scene. And even though it had occurred to me, while I basked in the light radiating from *those* eyes, that nothing would ever be able to remove me from them, unexpectedly they no longer held my attention.

Instead, his black orbs pulled me in, sucking and destroying the light and peace I had felt. And before I knew what was happening, my gaze became imprisoned by them.

Panicking, I inhaled sharply, and the bubble I had created came rocketing back toward me, shrinking as it did. A strange new scent rode the breeze hard, rushing all around me, until finally it caught me straight in the back of the throat. From zero to a thousand, the whole world slapped me in the face as the bubble burst.

Without warning, peace erupted into chaos, everything becoming audible all at once, booming into my hearing. The sound of a bird chirping miles away stabbed my eardrums; the distant noise of the wind hitting tree trunks felt like tidal waves smacking me underneath them. And that step he took toward me—the sound of his shoe pushing the snow down underfoot—almost caused my eardrums to rupture as it crunched with his weight.

I sat bolt upright, cracking my neck toward the origin of the overwhelming scent. Finding the owner, I regarded the shadowed stranger daring to look back at me, daring to approach me. But my attention was drawn away from his eye, to his elbow, where the smallest trace of blood was smeared against his pale skin, and where I witnessed the final moments of a wound healing.

A strange sensation flooded me, as my teeth fractured and my top lip quivered. My skin seemed to crawl with an intensifying hotness, rising from inside me somewhere. I didn't decide to get up; I didn't elect what happened next. It was as though my body was free from the restraints of my mind, as my legs found their way to the ground. Letting out a low moan, my body attempted to stretch, but it wasn't fully awake yet and I stumbled down to the snowy blanket beneath me. I clawed my way to my feet, getting ever closer to that scent, as my body propelled itself in the stranger's direction. I came to an abrupt stop as strong arms wrapped themselves around my waist, turning me away from him, but I struggled against them.

The coolness of his breath skimmed my earlobe as he said, "Lailah, no."

This caused me to pause, and my red-hot skin began to simmer against him. My gums ached as my new fangs receded, and my body felt weak, causing me to collapse, but he held me tightly and eased me to the ground, enfolding his arms and legs around me from behind, cradling me in a protective embrace.

"You need to go." He spoke hurriedly over his shoulder. His protective voice cut through the jumbled noise invading my hearing.

"But . . ."

His footsteps moved closer from behind me, and I growled, my fingernails grinding into the earth beneath the snow in response.

"Go. Now," my protector repeated.

I noted briefly his hesitation, before the wind whipped as he sped away through the clearing.

My ears throbbed. Throwing my hands up, I covered them and, rocking myself back and forth, I let a scream escape my lungs.

"Shhhh, it's all right, I'm here, shhhhh. . . ." he whispered, cupping his hands over my own.

It was then I felt the trickle of liquid seep between our entwined fingers, and I knew my eardrums were bleeding.

As the sun rose higher in the sky, the glow of twinkling stars seemed to move around me, and I recognized the sight; I had seen them before. Dropping my hands to my knees, I was surprised to see that the flashes of diamonds were exuding from my skin as well as his. His light seemed to wrap itself around mine and I felt a sudden explosion of energy. As the diamonds from his skin and my own merged together, I felt his connection to me rekindle.

He held me there for what felt like an eternity, and I closed my eyes, allowing the sun's rays to sink into my new skin. Finally, the noises dulled into a low hum, but I didn't feel right; I felt dizzy.

Rising to my feet, his arms around my waist, he helped me up, and I hesitated, stumbling a little, as I broke away from him. I sensed him follow me, but I held my hand in the air, signaling for him to stay back. I stood, precariously balancing my weight, barefoot in the snow. Holding myself calmly, I breathed in and out, forming a rhythm, taking my time. He waited patiently.

"I may not remember you, but I never forgot you," I whispered. "One shared light, split into two . . ."

Memories, thoughts, feelings all began appearing, as if I was staring into a kaleidoscope. I watched, engrossed, as each new shape formed, becoming more prominent than the last as they moved into focus.

"Styclar-Plena. The third dimension. Earth. Home—choice. I had a choice. . . ."

But with every turn of the cog, the blur that filled the space in between the luminous charms brought with it a different type of memory: a scar, reimprinting itself, damaging me again. Michael's demise, Ethan's end, Frederic, Bradley . . . She was gone; the girl in shadow was ended. I had died, but I was back. He led me home, his face, the thought of him, and the thought of me.

And when finally the kaleidoscope was only repeating its pattern, and I knew once again without having to count the number of edges to each shape, I stopped.

Bowing my head, allowing the length of my bangs to shield my eyes, I turned slowly toward him. Peeking, I observed his dimples dip at the sides of his cheeks as he seemed to frown. His pupils expanded, anxious of what I might say.

"Gabriel." I allowed a small smile to creep across my lips before I said, "My Gabriel. You waited for me."

The knots in his body seemed to loosen a little as he murmured, "I knew to wait for you this time."

Stepping cautiously toward me, he tilted my chin up with his index finger and cleared my vision with his free hand before cupping my cheek in his palm. He looked me square, exploring these new eyes. But the very fact that no sooner had he met them with his own than he looked away didn't go unnoticed.

I had fought my way back, and yet with just one silent glance in the wrong direction, it screamed that there was another great chasm forming between the two of us. I didn't know it yet, but it wasn't the appearance of these new eyes that had caused Gabriel to look away. It was, instead, the fleeting thought of what now lay behind them.

I sighed heavily and began to pace through the clearing, oozing a false sense of confidence, as though I knew what I was doing, I knew where I was going, when really I knew nothing. But I was afraid that the longer I stood here, the greater the unspoken divide between us would become.

He raced to my side and took my hand with his own. "Do you remember everything?" he asked tentatively.

"I remember . . . I remember the last six years. I remember the memories and the dreams I have had for the same time. I can't recall anything before. And I know the things she did. The girl in shadow." I gulped. "Me."

"She was an extreme darkness, Lai; she's gone now. You accepted both sides of yourself before your heart stopped. It's probably why you haven't forgotten."

As we moved through the snow underfoot, the trees' bare branches seemed to bow, as though they were tucking themselves away. They seemed to pity me.

"I'm different. Again, I'm different." I sighed and let my hand drift away from Gabriel's.

"No. It's just now, for the first time in your existence, you know where you come from. You know what you were born out of and into. You're you. What gifts you have, how they work on this plane, is something we have to work out, but we will work it out together."

I wasn't sure how right he was about that. My body didn't feel normal. I didn't feel human anymore. I had been born into human skin, having been birthed here on Earth. And when I had died at seventeen nearly two centuries ago, I had woken up inheriting my immortal lineage. Now, after everything that had happened, I was very aware of the fact that this body of mine was not the same as it once was.

"I smelled blood, and fangs cracked through my gums, Gabriel." I paused to allow the weight of that fact to sink beneath Gabriel's sea-of-glass exterior. He barely noticed. I didn't even cause a ripple. "I'm light and dark; I know it to be true now. And I don't even really know what that means for me yet. But Azrael said I could exist and keep my form in any of the three dimensions. So they will come for me. They will all come for me."

He stopped dead in his tracks; at last something I had said had caused some sort of reaction. "Yes, they will. Once they know you are alive, and they will find out. They will seek you and they won't stop until they have you. So, we run. We cut all ties and we leave together, and we hide. You have been through enough. It ends here." Gabriel's jaw locked and his eyes widened with conviction.

He shocked me. No longer softening the blow for my benefit, he seemed to have hardened. Either that or he was taking my choices away from me, perhaps for my own good. I wasn't sure.

We hadn't walked for long when a château fort came into view. It stood alone, with a brewing fog clouding at its base.

I looked at Gabriel with raised eyebrows. "Seriously, this is where you've been staying?"

Gabriel seemed to have more money than sense, and I made a mental note to ask him where his wealth came from.

"It's very small. I couldn't take you back to the barn, Han—" He stopped.

The very suggestion of her name made my toes curl instantly. Sadly I hadn't forgotten her. In fact, there were a fair few things concerning that Vampire that I would have gladly left behind.

"It wasn't safe," he finished.

Standing now only meters away from the entrance, I rocked back on the heels of my feet dubiously. Gabriel halted and reached for my hand. As he slipped his fingers between mine, I knew he could sense my unease.

I didn't know how long I had been trapped between life and death, but he never seemed to change. His broad shoulders and strong arms made me feel safe. As long as I allowed him to wrap me within them, I felt untouchable. He was an unbreakable wall, protecting me, and I knew he'd meet his end long before he'd let anyone tear it down and pry me from him again. And God, he was gorgeous.

"I love you, Lailah."

Gabriel surprised me, and I looked to him with wide eyes.

"I. Love. You," he repeated firmly.

This was the first time he had ever actually used those three words like that. He had always been so cryptic and indirect. Though I guess now I understood why.

"I should have said it sooner. I didn't think I had to, because I felt it. I have always felt it and so I thought you knew it. Every day we have been together, I *should* have said it."

Right now, I had no inclination to debate the specifics of the love he was proclaiming for someone whose eyes he had struggled to meet only half an hour ago, or even what that meant for us now. So instead, I smiled, though I was sure that the sadness curved with the edge of my lips was obvious enough for him to read. Having faced the end—the real end—and come through the other side, I was suddenly so tired. I was done with the complications of Pureblood Vampires, Arch Angels, and being a pawn in a battle between the two. I wanted it all to stop. I wanted my happy ending.

So I tightened my grip around his hand and said, "I love you.

I'll do what you say; I will go wherever you want to take me, for as long as you will have me."

It was true. I'd woken from my cocoon a Hedylidae, not a Morpho butterfly like him. But if he felt for me even a fraction of what I felt for him, I would flap my confused wings as hard as I could and follow him to the ends of any and every world, without question.

I immediately felt a sense of angst swelling within him. As he tilted his head, his blond curls fell slightly into his vision, stopping me from being able to read the message his eyes were writing.

Finally he said, "Really?"

"Really," I said. I had no idea why he seemed so surprised.

Gabriel let go of my hand and began rolling his fingertips in circles within his palms. "What about Jonah?" His tone dipped.

I scratched the tops of my arms pensively before I replied, "Sorry—who?"